D1474273

¡Limekiller!

NOVELS

Joyleg (with Ward Moore)
Mutiny in Space
Masters of the Maze
Rork!
The Enemy of My Enemy
Rogue Dragon
The Kar-Chee Reign
Clash of Star-Kings
The Island Under the Earth
The Phoenix and the Mirror
Peregrine: Primus
Ursus of Ultima Thule
Peregrine: Secundus
Vergil in Averno
Marco Polo and the Sleeping Beauty (with Grania Davis)
The Boss in the Wall, A Treatise on the House Devil (with Grania Davis)

NOVELS WRITTEN AS ELLERY QUEEN

And on the Eighth Day
The Fourth Side of the Triangle

COLLECTIONS & CHAPBOOKS

Crimes & Chaos
Or All the Seas with Oysters
What Strange Stars and Skies
Strange Seas and Shores
The Enquiries of Dr. Eszterhazy
Polly Charms, The Sleeping Woman
The Redward Edward Papers
The Best of Avram Davidson
Avram Davidson: Collected Fantasies
And Don't Forget the One Red Rose
The Adventures of Dr. Eszterhazy
Adventures in Unhistory: Conjectures on the Factual Foundations of Several Ancient Legends
The Avram Davidson Treasury: A Tribute Collection
The Investigations of Avram Davidson
Avram Davidson: The Last Wizard with A Letter of Explanation
The Beach at Rosarito. Being a Selection from the AdVentures in AutoBiography
El Vilvoy de las Islas
Everybody Has Somebody in Heaven: Essential Jewish Tales of the Spirit
The Beasts of the Elysian Fields by Conrad Amber
The Other Nineteenth Century: A Story Collection by Avram Davidson

¡LIMEKILLER!

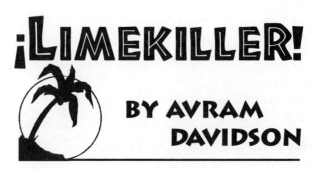

BY AVRAM DAVIDSON

EDITED BY GRANIA DAVIS
AND HENRY WESSELLS

INTRODUCTIONS BY
LUCIUS SHEPARD & PETER S. BEAGLE

OLD EARTH BOOKS
BALTIMORE, MARYLAND

¡Limekiller!

ACKNOWLEDGEMENTS
"Bloody Man" (*Fantastic Magazine*, August 1976).
"Manatee Gal, Ain't You Coming Out Tonight" (*The Magazine of Fantasy & Science Fiction*, April 1977).
"A Good Night's Sleep" (*The Magazine of Fantasy & Science Fiction*, August 1978).
"There Beneath the Silky-Trees and Whelmed in Deeper Gulphs Than Me" (*Other Worlds 2*, edited by Roy Torgeson. New York: Zebra, 1980).
"Limekiller at Large" (*Asimov's*, June 1990).
"A Far Countrie" (*Asimov's*, November 1993).
"Along the Lower Moho (The Iguana Church)" (*The New York Review of Science Fiction*, June 2000).

PUBLISHER'S ACKNOWLEDGEMENTS
The publisher would like to thank Peter S. Beagle.
The editors would like to thank The Avram Davidson Society.

Published by:
Old Earth Books
Post Office Box 19951
Baltimore, MD 21211-0951
www.oldearthbooks.com

Book design by Robert T. Garcia
Garcia Publishing Services
Post Office Box 1059
Woodstock, Illinois 60098
www.garciapublishingservices.com

10 9 8 7 6 5 4 3 2 1

ISBN: 1-882968-26-3

PRINTED IN THE UNITED STATES OF AMERICA
By Thomson-Shore
Dexter, Michigan

CONTENTS

For
Faustino Zuniga, J.P.
Alan E. Nourse, M.D.
Kathleen Redman
"among the great company of the dead, who increase around us
as we grow older." (Ommaney, *The Shoals of Capricorn*)
and, among the great company of the living,
Ethan Davidson
H. Austin Miller
Burton Moore

Portrait courtesy of Grania Davis and The Avram Davidson Society.

THE ADVENTURES OF JACK LIMEKILLER IN A FAR COUNTRIE

THE LATE, GREAT Avram Davidson (1923-1993) lived enough for many lifetimes and wrote enough for many lifetimes. During the 1960's, he lived and wrote in the former colony of British Honduras. In his unpublished travel account *Dragons in the Trees,* he described it as "a place that you can put your arms around."

British Honduras became the Central American nation of Belize, famed for its Mayan ruins, beautiful coral reefs, and friendly ecotourism. Avram's experiences in that timeless tropical land became a series of magical realist tales, recounting the amazing adventures of young Jack Limekiller in the somewhat-more-than-colony of British Hidalgo.

The Limekiller series drew an enthusiastic following, and three of the six stories were nominated for Nebula or World Fantasy Awards. Avram Davidson completed the story cycle shortly before he passed on in 1993. He was planning a Limekiller collection, and the notes and dedications were discovered among his papers. The collection wasn't published during his lifetime, but the wonderful tales of the Bloody Man and the Manatee Gal live on in one fantastic volume, thanks to Old Earth Books.

–Grania Davis

INTRODUCTION
BY LUCIUS SHEPARD

I BELIEVE JACK Limekiller may have been the man whom Avram Davidson wanted to be; though it might be more accurate to say that Limekiller was the man Avram hoped that he, in essence, was: a gentleman of sorts with – like Avram – an insatiable curiosity, a quick, old-worldish mind, and a quirky, pungent view of life, but a bit more swashbuckling, armed with less of a temper, and perhaps standing a few inches taller than his authorial original. I think that Avram was happy when he wrote these stories, and I'm quite certain he was happy when he accumulated the experiences that inform them. They are, of course, rife with his offbeat erudition and playful use of language and voice, but in much of Avram's work, that playfulness is underscored by a gloomy, embittered cast of mind. In the stories you're about to read, those qualities are not so much in evidence. There is darkness in them, to be sure, but it's lent a joyfully exotic gloss that reflects Avram's love for the tropic in which they are set: British Honduras; called by him, British Hidalgo; now called Belize.

I've had the good fortune to live in that country, where Avram also lived for a time, and although I may not have walked in the exact places where he walked, although I can't absolutely guarantee that, say, a certain one of his fictional towns is, in fact, the real town of Orange Walk, I've gone down similar roads in similar towns, and have seen sights and heard musics that resonate with those he saw and heard. It was a beautiful place, British Honduras, an old colonial state, and yet lacking to a large degree the impotent rancor that typically pervades colonies. Avram says of it, ". . . more than a colony but not yet a country, and often left off maps because its name seems larger than itself." There was about its people (and what a various people they were, in heritage African, East Indian, Anglo, Spanish, Middle Eastern, Arawak, Caribe, etc., etc.) a sweet spiciness of character and a lucidity of soul that a casual observer might have characterized as "innocence," but was, in truth, nothing of the sort. Villains of every stamp have abounded in Belize during every era, and the earliest of them soon learned how to exploit those who had crossed the ocean to exploit them. The people of British Honduras were not innocent, then, but were infected by the vivid personality of the land that bred them, stained with its macaw and parrot colors, imbued with a gravitas by the power of the sea that hemmed them in against the savage modernity of Guatemala and sanguinary Mexico. Their violence, too, was of the land, steeped in a piratical tradition (many of the citizens of the country could trace their ancestry back to Kidd and Lafitte and divers lesser men who sailed the waters of the Caribbean beneath a black flag), and though to say other than that violence is violence, no matter its tradition, would be implausibly romantic, I will assert that in the main their violence lacked the mad dispassion of contemporary atrocity. Slaughter for them was a family thing, an occupation to which they were born.

Unfortunately, the country that inspired the Limekiller stories no longer exists. The colony has become a full-status nation and in its nationhood has fallen prey to the great afflictions of the past century. Its fabulous creatures, manatees and tapir and jaguars and such, are dwindling toward extinction, and the mahogany forests, mentioned as depleted in the text, have now been decimated. AIDS is everywhere. Street crime is endemic. Belize City, formerly the capitol, is a sewer crawling with drug dealers. No longer can you take a night stroll without experiencing anxiety in Orange Walk or Buttermilk Cay. And where there is no crime, no drugs, no filth and disease, there is a plague of Americans. Much of Belize has been sectioned off into tourist-friendly enclaves, environments in which some aspect of the land has been preserved, albeit in a cultivated fashion, dappled with bars and hotels whose ambiance – fishing nets and floats, lots of Ye Oldes, pirate chic, etc. – has been designed to conjure (yet serves merely to parody) the quaintness of colonial days. Thus, the ragged, blustery, charming spirit of the land has been deracinated and, rather than the pungent accents and eighteenth century idioms that pepper the speech of the indigents, now you are more liable to hear flattened Midwestern vowels and Tennessee drawls. One of the only places where you still can find the country that – once – was a place well worth a visit, lies here within these pages, as witnessed by the fictive eyes of Jack Limekiller and recorded by the peerless unorthodoxy of Avram Davidson's talent and vision.

For the term of our acquaintance, spanning his last thirteen years, Avram posed the image of a diminutive, acerbic grand-fatherly man with an untidy gray beard. On the surface, he was a crusty fellow. He did not suffer fools gladly and was frequently impatient with and demanding of his friends. Like all truly committed writers, artists who live through their work, he dis-played a mixture of arrogance and insecurity toward his stories (how else can one feel about something upon which one labors to distraction?), but although his arrogance was often visible, he rarely put his insecurity on public exhibition. He told jokes whose involute form and Classical references more often than not puzzled those who heard them, and he was given to quoting passages from Virgil in the Latin whenever exasperated. In many regards, he was a man of unbending principle. For instance, being a Jew, he would never sell his books to German publishers, even when he was having serious money troubles. In his personal relationships, principle would sometimes gave way to childishness. He could be vastly self-pitying and was often verbally abusive to those whom he believed had slighted him. Doubtless all these characteristics were integral to his person, yet he was a man whose mental life was vastly separate in tone from the face he presented to the world. And beneath that surface, still vital inside his (by the time I met him) infirm body, resided a soul unalloyed in its questing nature and relatively undamaged by his service as an infantryman in World War II, by divorce, financial difficulties, poor health, by the thousand disappointments and shocks that attend all but the quickest of lives. I could never clearly gauge the shape or colors of that soul, but I imagine it as a colorful mist swirling within a glass globe that is itself held by an ornate bronze claw, rather like an object that might advance some narrative function in one of Avram's fantasy stories concerning Vergil, a spiritual artifact of unknown antiquity and unfathomable purpose, having a value that the world would someday recognize and understand and celebrate more fully than ever it did when it was housed in the flesh.

That soul was, quintessentially, the soul of a recluse. I usually picture Avram alone in a darkish room made claustrophobic by tumbled books and stacks of yellowed newspapers and magazines, old tins stuffed with whatnots, and a track winding through them that allowed access to other, equally cluttered rooms. The dank basement apartment in Bremerton, Washington, where he spent the final years of his life, was devoid of natural light and devoid, also, of any bright color, of television, of all but the most basic modernities. Like a wizard's cell, it stood in relation to Avram's person as did his body to the soul that hobbled about inside its own teetering house. He lived, you see, mostly far from Bremerton, amid mostly unreal kingdoms of his own device, one of which – British Hidalgo – was slightly less unreal than the rest and added a crucial touch of the material to the lively next-to-nothingness contained in that glass globe. But for all the limitations of his physical existence during his later years, Avram traveled widely, as he did for all his years, through the borderless countries of his brain and brought us back his stories for souvenirs.

I first met Avram some twenty years ago at the Clarion Workshop at Michigan State University, where he was a teacher for one week and I was a student. Avram was ill and taking various medications, thus not at his best. The teaching of writing is an elusive process; indeed, there are those who claim it can't be taught. During his time at the workshop, Avram – by virtue of his illness – did little to disprove this. That said, if he had not taught at Clarion, I doubt I would have become a writer. He validated me in a way I needed, treating me less as a student than a colleague, encouraging me to challenge myself, to explore and not exploit my gift. Yet in his encouragement there was ever a cautionary note. Once while we were going over a manuscript of mine, he said, "This is very good." Then, giving me a deadpan look, he added, "Are you sure you want to be a writer? You'd make more money as a podiatrist." He was a walking life lesson relating to the potential hardships of a writer's life. One day at lunch, we (the students) were gathered at table in the cafeteria when Avram approached, cane hooked over an arm, carrying a tray laden with four entrees, two salads, several desserts, innumerable rolls. We gaped at him, wondering first how this smallish man was planning to consume so much food, and, secondly, wondering why he would attempt such a monumental consumption. He took a seat, hung his cane on the edge of the table, unloaded the tray, arranged his utensils, taking an inordinately long time to accomplish this. Finally, he looked at us and pointed to the banquet in front of him. "Why all this?" he said. "Next week, it's back to soupbones."

After Clarion, I didn't see Avram for several years, though we carried on a correspondence; but when I moved to Seattle, I took the ferry across the Sound to visit him with some regularity. During those visits, I would help him with errands. He was by then limited to a walker, incapable of leaving the apartment without assistance, and he would often call me and ask me to come visit, and when I did, I would find myself pushing him about Bremerton in a wheel-chair, obedient as a horse to his demands, helping him with the groceries, bill-paying, library returns, and that sort of thing. I was being used, of course, and there were times when I became impatient with him for taking advantage of the relationship. But it gradually dawned on me that this is what friends did – they used one another – and that I was using Avram every bit as much as he used me, though my usage of him was less labor intensive: as mentor, touchstone, resource. On occasion, he, too, would become impatient. Once, when I was beginning to write my own Central American stories, I wrote him a letter expressing some insecurity as to whether people would think that I was encroaching on his liter-ary turf. A few days later, I got back a post card that read: "That's right, Shepard. I've staked claim to the entire Caribbean littoral. It's mine, all mine. Keep your grubby hands off." I was so confounded by this burst of acerbity, it took me a goodly while to understand that he was telling me I was an idiot for assuming that any writer could dispossess another of the opportunity to examine a certain region or historical moment. At any rate, our friendship passed, as most friendships do, through phases of intimacy and neglect, waxed minimal, became exuberant, grew intensely divisive and reached grudging accord, and then, one morning shortly after I learned he was failing, I picked up the phone and was informed that he had died . . . a death, I believe, that warranted much more of a salute than it received.

It's customary at this pass, in most introductions, to list through the included stories and give a brief preview of each, saying that "Bloody Man," for instance, is a ghost story concerning, among other subjects, pirates. But that would be misleading and more than a little shallow as an approach to Avram's work in general or the specific. For one thing, given the ghostly status of the country where they take place, all the Limekiller tales are, by virtue of that alone, ghost stories, regardless whether a literal supernatural-type ghost can be perceived flitting about in them. For another thing, these are not like other stories in the least, and you cannot so easily sum them up. If you haven't read Avram Davidson before, you are about to enter uncharted territory as regards the art of the narrative. Certainly you will be able to find, should you care to look closely, traditional narrative mechanisms buried among Avram's sentences – foreshadowings, structural elements, and so on. Yet you don't feel them moving you along as you do in more traditionally narrated stories. No grinding noises such as are made by primitive machines. No great grandiose tidal sweep of, yee-haw!, Writing. No stampede of eloquence. No institutional overlay of Bauhaus Existential. No Stylemaster style. Reading Avram, and in particular, reading the Limekiller stories, you are simply dropped into the exceptionally active mind of the narrator and twitched along from thought to thought, something like the way a sun-dazzle will appear to be shifted from point to point on the surface of water slopping against the pitch-coated pilings of a pier in Avram's (and Limekiller's) own Point Pleasaunce. The mechanics of the story become obscured and you are made dizzy, dazed, much like Limekiller himself might feel, walking, (shall we imagine?), in the strong sun, slightly trashed by a hangover, trying to figure out some minor money hassle, distracted by this slash of color, that burst of song, or . . . Well, perhaps a sample would be instructive:

> "Night . . . and not the plenilune, either. You can bet your boots, Limekiller has no boots, he has, though, a shovel! Limekiller feels that if he eats another pannikin of rice and beans or of the thin chowder called fish-*tea* that he . . . that he . . . . What he is after, he is after turtle eggs, so significant a source of insult in the rich, *rich* Chinese culture, largely represented in British Hidalgo by the canny and philoprogenitive merchant Aurelio Aung and about 327 of his descendants. Better be exceedingly careful in talking about turtles to the Aung. More better say as little as possible about eggs at all to any of them. To ask, even to ask, 'Don Aurelio, do you think it's going to rain?' would bring conversation to a sudden and deathly still halt. As for that sole man ever to have placed his hand on the ancient and naked head of old Aurelio Aung (for what reason, knows only God!), death did not exactly come on swift wings, but it is

certain that Aurelio Aung III felled him with a kick he had learned before kung fu became well-known in the regions of the dark west and that Aurelio Aung Jr. had assisted III to propel the man down a flight of stairs at the bottom of which a throng or tong of unnumbered Aung were waiting to and did kick him with many sharp kicks of their sharp-pointed shoes (they being fashionable, and Old Aung had imported them and sold them in considerable numbers), before P.C. Oscar Spencer C. Featherstonehaugh Smith, then on duty, had finished strolling over quite leisurely . . ."

This, the opening of "Limekiller at Large," inundates you with atmospheric fact, with a tumbling-downstairs rhythm to accompany the single tumbling-downstairs event detailed, and submerges you in the mind of the narrator, né Limekiller, without saying a thing about him, other than he is hunting turtle eggs with a shovel. But as you are twitched and shifted, like a sun dazzle, across the light chop of Avram's prose, you come to know so many things about Jack Limekiller and about the many things he knows, it feels that you are not reading a story, but listening in on his self-conversation, that little talk we're always having with ourselves, that flippy voiceover that captions all our experiences, this being an especially clever and artful specimen, yet every note authentic. And so when you reach the end of the story, though you have endured, witnessed, felt what Limekiller himself endured, witnessed, felt, though you have sensed the incidence of character development, conflict, denouement, etc., it seems less a story than a passage of time that had a story in it, along with innumerable other flashes and dazzles that related to the story in obliquely enchanting and curiously illuminating ways. That last, I suppose, is as good a definition as any of an Avram Davidson story.

So . . .

Having experienced one such enthralling passage of time with embedded story, the obvious next step would be to proceed on to another, just like Jack Limekiller would and did. Here, in this little book, you'll be able to do that five more times and will likely expect to continue passaging thereafter . . .

Unfortunately, only six Limekiller passages exist.

Or, as Avram might have said, six are all there is and six is all there are.

These are they, and they are, in my view, whatever anyone else may tell you, regardless of whether a book entitled The Best Of Avram Davidson rests on a thousand and one shelves, the best of Avram Davidson, his most evocative, most generously spirited, and most Avramesque work. Despite his previously mentioned response to my letter, I think Avram did stake claim to a place and time that no other writer should touch. That place and time resides here in this little book, complete with dialects, recipes, shanties, magic, duppies, pirates, drunkards, tapirs, manatees, pretty girls, a hero or two, and, of course, ghosts. Open its covers and a mist will boil forth, swirling, many-colored, to surround you – a mist rife with a myriad distinct voices, bursts of idiosyncratic speech, fragments of all-but-forgotten lore, a strange druggy perfume compounded of the smells of shandygaff, jacaranda, brine, palm oil, gasoline fumes, creosote, orange groves, and ought else. These stories are far more than the relics of a great fantasist, a great writer, a man whom I knew and venerated and – when he wasn't pissing me off – loved.

These stories are his soul.

JACK LIMEKILLER
BY PETER S. BEAGLE

LIMEKILLER? CHRIST, OF course I knew Jack Limekiller – used to come in here all the time. Canadian, right? Canadian. Skinny kid, drank Montejo Dark mostly. Looked older than he was, or anyway you had that feeling about him. Lord God, Jack Limekiller. I haven't heard that name in . . . Christ, who remembers? Limekiller. Damn.

He bought a boat. That was it – Limekiller bought some kind of a small boat. Quit his job, picked up his check, shot it all on a boat, with a bit left over to throw a party in here for his friends, the night before he took off. I remember, I couldn't keep from asking him, "Limekiller, what the hell you want with a boat? You know how to sail?"

"A little," he says. Then he grins at me. "No, not really. But figure I can learn."

"Oh right," I says. "No problem. Where you planning to study at, Captain Limekiller, sir?"

"The Caribbean," Limekiller says, rolling it out. "Pirate country. Buried treasure country. Duppy country." He told me what duppies are, and I've been trying to forget ever since. "I'm going to plop my boat down in the St. Lawrence, point her south and just keep going until I bump into something. There's a place called British Hidalgo that sounds about as far from Canada as a Saskatchewan boy can get. Maybe that's what I'll bump into, British Hidalgo."

So I says, "Well, good luck, captain," and we drank to it. I says "Don't forget to write. I got a nephew that collects stamps."

Weird thing is, he didn't forget. I still get a postcard anyway sometimes. Really pretty stamps, too, with birds and fruit and stuff on them. Old Jack Limekiller. Damn. Tell him Pete says hello.

¡Limekiller!

BLOODY MAN

"**Y**ES, MR. LIMEKILLER," said old Archbishop Le Beau. Having acknowledged Jack's self-introduction with politeness, he now returned to his task of scaling fish. Some were still on the block and some were in the basket and some were in the pot. A time there was (and a place) when archbishops moved before a train of state. But not this archbishop, in this time, in this place – to wit, Point Pleasaunce, in the sub-tropical colony of British Hidalgo.

"They tell me . . ." Limekiller hesitated, briefly. Was it *My Lord? Your Lordship? Or was it . . . it was, wasn't it . . . Your Grace?*

Some saints levitate. Some are telepathic. It was widely said and widely believed that William Constance Christian Le Beau was a saint. "Just 'Archbishop' will do, Mr. Limekiller," the old man said, without looking up. *Scrip . . . scrop . . . scrip. . . .* Jack found himself looking covertly around. Perhaps for loaves.

"Ah . . . thank you, sir . . . Archbishop . . . they tell me that I might be able to pick up a charter for my boat. Moving building supplies, I understand. Down to Curasow Cove? For a bungalow you want built?"

Flop went the fish into the basket.

"Something of the sort, Mr. Limekiller. The bungalow is not for me, you know. I already have a bungalow. It is for my brother Poona."

Jack blinked a bit at this, to him, Bomba-the-Jungle-Boy note. But it was soon cleared up. The retired Anglican Bishop of Poona, in India, had reached an age when he found English winters increasingly difficult. The Mediterranean, where retired British bishops had once been as thick as alewives, had for some long time been in the process of becoming too expensive for anyone who did not happen to own a fleet of oil-tankers . . . which, somehow, very few retired bishops did. And so this one had – perhaps after fasting, meditation, and prayer, perhaps on the spur of the moment – written to his ecclesiastical associate, the Most Reverend W.C.C. Le Beau, Archbishop emeritus (or whatever) of the Province of Central America and Darien – smallest Province in the Anglican Church – asking for advice.

"And I advised him to consider Curasow Cove. The climate is salubrious, the breeze seldom fails, the water is deep enough to – well, well, I don't wish to sound like a land agent. Furthermore, English in one form or another is the language of the land. To be sure, Poona speaks Hindi and Gujerathi and a few others of the sort: precious lot of good that would do him in Sicily or Spain." *Scrip . . . scrop . . . flop!*

It was desired to enable the retired Bishop to move into his new home before very long. ("Just let him get a roof over his head and a floor beneath his feet, and that will give him the chance to see if it serves him well enough for his taste. If it does, he can have his furniture, his Indian things and all the rest of it sent over. If not, well 'The world is wondrous large, leagues and leagues from marge to marge.'") Ordinarily, there were enough boats, Lord knows, and enough boatmen, at Point Pleasaunce, that lovely and aptly named little peninsula, to have moved material enough for several bungalows at a time.

But the present season was not an ordinary one.

Every serviceable vessel from the Point, as well as most of those available from other parts of the colony – those not already committed to the seasonal fisheries or to the movement of sand or fruit: and, in fact, so many, even, of those, that both commodities were soon likely to be in short supply – were busy plying between King Town and Plum Tree Creek. There was no road to speak of into the Plum Tree Creek country, one was in the building, but the Canadian-American corporation setting up the turpentine and resin plant at the headwaters of the creek, which thrust so deep into the piney woods that it might better perhaps have been called Pine Tree Creek – the corporation was of no mind to wait. Hence, a constant line of boats, some pure sail, some pure motor, some sail and auxiliary engine, moved along the coast carrying machinery, gasoline, fuel oil, timber, cement, metal-ware, food: and, empty, moved back up the coast for more.

As a non-National, Limekiller stood no chance of a crack at this lucrative commerce as long as any National-owned vessel was available. However, as a citizen of a Commonwealth country – to wit, Canada – he did stand some chance of a permit to take a charter for this other and infinitely smaller project. The greater the interest the archbishop might take in his doing so, the greater his chances of getting it. And well the archbishop knew it.

The kitchen, like every other country kitchen in the Out-Districts (which was any and every district save that of King Town, Urban), consisted of a wall in the yard behind the house in good weather, and underneath the house, in bad. Every house not a trash house stood on high legs to catch the breeze and baffle . . . or, anyway . . . slow down . . . the entry of the less desirable fauna. The archbishop scarcely had to stoop to peer into the cook-pot as he added to the fish some tinned milk, sliced vegetables, country herbs and peppers; though certainly he had once been tall. Whilst it was cooking, the old man without further word retired to the tiny chapel, its doors wide open, where he knelt before the altar. Limekiller did not join him, but others did: old (the very old), lame (the very lame), some partly, some altogether blind, and a few quite small children who, Limekiller thought, may have been orphans. There were an even dozen of them, besides the old priest himself. They were still there when Limekiller returned from a long walk.

With no more word than at the beginning, the old man got up, and, followed by his congregation, made ready to eat the supper: a gesture sufficed to invite the newcomer.

Afterward he wrote out and handed over a paper.

The Permanent Under-secretary

Honorable:
    Pray help Mr. John Limekiller help me to help the Lord Bishop.

                                    Yrs in Christ,
                                    William C.A. Darien

"I trust that may do it," said Archbishop Le Beau.

Jack thought it certainly would may. British Hidalgo was, and its people believed it was, and announced on every occasion that it was *"a Christian country."* Limekiller rather thought the brief document would easily serve as neck-verse, should he commit manslaughter upon ten Turkish merchants.

But though the letter moved the Permanent Under-secretary to initial and stamp it with no more delay than it took him to do those two things and to murmur, "Certainly . . . Certainly . . ." – lining up the supplies was another thing entirely.

Joe Jefferson, at the woodyard, said, "Well, Jock, as you come in the name of the Chorch, I won't lahf in your face. Ahl I can do is to tell you, Impossible. We have twenty men in the bush now, cutting stick for us as fahst as can be cut. Even if you'd take it green, Jock, even if you'd take it *green* – no, mon, Jock. Me waiting list –"

"Pine Tree Creek?"

"Pine Tree Creek."

And Velasquez, in his dusty warehouse at the wharf's edge, did no more than shrug, shake his head, point. Where, usually, sacks of cement were piled almost to the ceiling, now only a scant score or so sat on the floor. "And they going out in the marning," he said.

"Pine Tree Creek, I suppose."

A deep nod. No more.

And Witherington, the White Jamaican at the hardware house, "I couldn't give you a nail, b'y, fah me own cahfin! *No* corrugated iron! *No* pipe! *No* screw! Pine Tree Creek project wipe me clean, me b'y! I am waiting now for goods to come in from Kingston. And as soon as the ship comes in, you know where the goods going to go?"

"Let me guess, Mr. Witherington. Pine Tree Creek?"

Witherington's answer was to throw up both arms and to cry, "Hallelujah!"

There hadn't been such shortages in King Town since the War; on the other hand, there hadn't been such prosperity since Prohibition had been repealed in the United States, bringing rum-running to an end.

However, puissant and powerful though Hector Manufacturing Company of Pittsburgh, Pa., and Sudbury, Ontario, was, there was evidently a thing or two which it didn't know. Its compradors, flying back and forth between three countries, had assumed that the leading suppliers in a capital city, even a colonial capital city, even of a small colony, would be well-stocked with supply. Perhaps at one time this had been true. Perhaps even fifty years ago, when some of the ancient English and Scottish families had still been in business, it might have been true. But, one by one, the Depression had closed their doors. One by one they had closed up their old houses on the Foreshore, and vanished away. The declining trade in precious tropical woods – mahogany, rosewood, cedar – had shrunken the colonial purse. Levantine merchants (commonly called "Turks") had come in, and Chinese, too; Baymen had set up in business; and so had more than one or two with (to employ the American expression) "Spanish surnames." The old order changeth – right? And, so, suddenly, did the old order of the weather.

In the whole of the nineteenth century, only two hurricanes had struck British Hidalgo. In the past thirty years, it had been struck by five. And after one's stock had been washed away once . . . twice . . . three times . . . one feels a certain hesitancy in building it up again.

It might, indeed, it certainly would have been possible to have set up warehouses in the Out-District capital of St. Frances of the Mountains, thirty miles from the coast: and to have filled orders from there in less than a day. But no one did that. No one at all did that. Perhaps the idea of the cost of shipping goods sixty miles did not appeal. Perhaps. . . . Ah, well. What was done, instead, was to keep on hand as small a stock as possible. And if an order for more than one had in stock was received, one of course took the order . . . took an advance against the full payment for the order . . . and then one ordered the balance of the order. . . . From Jamaica, perhaps. From New Orleans. From Puerto Cortes, "in republican waters." Even from London.

And when the "next few days" or "the next week or so" arrived, and no supply, what then? Well, for one thing, the customer could wait, he could bloody well wait, returning day after day to hear whatever imaginative account the local supplier chose to supply him with –

"Beeg strike in Leevah*pool*, sah."

"Ahl de American ship tronsfer to *Veet* Nom, sah."

"We cable Jahmaicah, sah. We waiting reply, sah."

"Sah-*mill* break *down*, sah. Sending to Nicaragua fah new sah, sah."

– not seldom the customer simply returned to wherever he had come from, never to come back – never, to his sorrow, having heard or assimilated the saying which even Cervantes had known: *He who would carry the wealth of the Indies back with him, must carry the wealth of the Indies out with him.*

And, in such cases, the goods ordered eventually arriving, there they were, making such a brave display as to assure the next customer that all was well.

The next customer, in this case, being the Hector Manufacturing Company of Pittsburgh, Pa., and Sudbury, Ont..

Hector had made agreements with every supplier in King Town, and had ignored every supplier in the rest of the country. Hector was being supplied, it was still being supplied, one large cargo ship could have carried off everything in every warehouse in King Town down to Pine Tree Creek. However, no large cargo ship could get closer to King Town than two miles off-shore, whence cargo was lightered in – transferred, that is, to motor-barge. And it was thus impossible for any large or even moderate-sized cargo ship to engage in the coastal trade. So Hector's cargo came down little by little, but it came in such a steady procession that Hector had not realized what was coming next.

To whit, and for quite a while: nothing.

In the meanwhile, that was exactly what Jack Limekiller was able to aquire in King Town.

Nothing.

He came up with the notion that he might at any rate try and see if things might be any better in Port Caroline. He even had the very get-up-and-go notion that he would actually telephone Port Caroline. That is to say, Port Caroline not being a person, it could not itself be telephoned: but he would phone some of the leading merchants in that other Out-District capital.

Very little research sufficed to advise him that none of them had a telephone. Not one. Not a single one. Supposedly, if any of the leading businessmen in Port Caroline required to phone someone of an equal status in, say, King Town, he simply walked down the street to the Telephone Office, in an out-building adjacent to the Post Office, and phoned from there. Cheaper to buy milk than to keep a cow, eh, Jack?

Well, there *was* the Royal Telegraphy. Her Majesty's Government did not exactly go to much effort to advertise the fact that there was, but Limekiller had somehow found the fact out. The service was located in two bare rooms upstairs off an alley near the old Rice Mill Wharf, where an elderly gentleman wrote down in-coming messages in a truly beautiful Spencerian hand . . . or maybe it was Copperplate . . . or Chancery . . . or Volapük. What the Hell. It was beautiful. It was, in fact, so beautiful that it seemed cavalier to complain that the elderly gentleman was exceedingly deaf, and that, perhaps in consequence, his messages did not always make the most perfect sense.

Gambling that the same conditions did not obtain at the Royal Telegraphy Office in Port Caroline, Limekiller sent off several wires, advising the Carolinian entrepreneurs what he wanted to buy, and that he was coming in person to buy it.

"How soon will these go off?" he asked the aged telegrapher.

"Yes, that is what I heard myself, sir. They say the estate is settle, sir. After ahl these years." And he shook his head and he smiled a gentle smile of wonder.

Limekiller smiled back. What the Hell. What the Hell. What the *Hell.* He waved a goodbye and went downstairs. "The estate," that was, of course, the Estate of Gerald Phillip Washburne, reputedly a millionaire in dollars, pounds, *pesos, lempira, quetzales,* and who knows what: the estate had been in litigation for decades, and, as regularly as the changes of the moon, it was reported settled. The case was like something out of Dickens . . . and so, for that matter, was the Royal Telegraphy Office.

Downstairs, suddenly, it all seemed futile. He leaned against the side of the building. Why not just say, The Hell With It: and go meekly back home and try for a nice, safe, low-paid, pensionable job with the Hudson's Bay Company? He would only have to counterfeit a Scotch accent, and that suddenly seemed so much simpler than all this. This early evening breeze sprang up and blew a piece of the local newspaper against his legs. He reached down to detach it, picked it up, automatically glanced at it. *WANTED* [an advertisement read] *One watch dog that gets vexed easily and barks and bites.*

"*I* might apply for that job," he said, to himself. Then he burst out laughing.

What the Hell?

The waters around Port Caroline were on the shallow side – in Baytalk, the dialect of the Bayfolk – "shoally." A pier jutted out into deeper water about two miles from town, and here the packet-boats made their stops: the *Hidalgo* twice a week, the *Miskitian* once a week, and the *Bayan* according to Captain Cumberbatch's mind, pocket, or bowels. ("De sahlt wahtah bind me up, b'y," he had observed to Jack.) Most of the Port's own vessels preferred to put in at the mouth of Caroline Creek itself, which ran right through the middle of town. As there had been a bar building at the mouth of the creek for almost half a century, these vessels tended to be very shallow-draft vessels, indeed: even so, getting them across the bar was often a matter of tide, wind, and many willing bodies to heave and haul. It may not have been efficient. But it was companionable.

Limekiller had made the personal acquaintance of a rock just far enough from the pier to be free from mooring fees, and, with some degree of diligence, dropped his anchor at the proper angle to it. He didn't bother with the skiff, and was wading ashore, his shirt up under his armpits and his trousers draped around his shoulders, when a voice cried, "Have you no shame, sir: wearing nothing but that . . . that tobacco pouch! – in the presence of Her Majesty's proconsul?"

Jack knew that voice, called in its direction: "Unless an indictment for *lèse majesté* is involved, Her Majesty's proconsul can either wait till I'm ashore, or look somewhere else. Sir," he added.

"Haw Haw!" was the answer of H.M. proconsul, videlicet the Royal Governor, Sir Joshua Cummings. The day had passed, perhaps fortunately, when colonial governors were appointed from the ranks of old generals who with lance and sabre had struck terror (or perhaps joy) into the hearts of contumacious Hill Tribesmen on distant Asian frontiers: Sir Joshua had been a sailor. No man-of-war larger than a gunboat, probably, could nowadays enter the shallow and coral-studded waters of the Inner Bay – but the Bayfolk, and, for that matter, the other Nationals of the Colony – had no interest in how well or how ill their governor might have manoeuvered a destroyer: they observed with great interest, however, how their governor managed sloop or schooner (or even skiff, dingy, or launch): their conclusion was, "Not bod, mon, you know. Not bod ah-tahl." Stout, white-bearded, jovial, in his ceremonial white uniform, his white helmet with white plumes, Sir Joshua made a fine appearance at such occasions as the opening of the Legislative Council or the Court Sessions or the observance of the Sovereign's birthday. The Bayfolk enjoyed seeing him at that. Nevertheless it was likely that they appreciated seeing him even more in his sea-faded khakies, at the tiller of his sailing-launch for the opening of the annual regatta – in which, of course, he did not compete.

Still, the Bayfolk, who numbered eighty percent of the people of the Colony, and who were for the most part Black, had mixed feelings about it all. On the one hand, they would have really preferred a governor who was Black; on the other hand, they had a feeling that a governor who was Black was not really a governor at all. And sooner or later these feelings would have to be resolved. But not just yet. Time, as we are incessantly reminded, does not stand still. But in the Colony of British Hidalgo it was still standing as near to still as anywhere.

"There. Now that you are decent once more, allow me to offer you a drop . . . lift, I believe they call it in North America. *Thought* I recognized your boat. Thought I'd just wait a bit for the pleasure of your company." H.E. the Governor was in what the Bayfolk called "De R'yal Jeep;" actually, it was a small Land Rover which flew a small Union Jack in place of a license plate. "*And* what brings you down to this friendly little port named after Old Snuffy? Eh? Oh. Didn't know Queen Caroline took snuff? Course she did. Up to her *ears* in the stuff, silly old scow. Or was that Queen Charlotte? *I* can't keep them straight. Eh?"

Jack knew that last *eh?* was not a reference to the queens of the House of Hanover, but a friendly reminder that a question had been asked and not answered. "I'm trying to locate building supplies for a bungalow for the Bishop of Simla. . . . I think."

Sir Joshua, who had been driving on the left, now shifted to the right. On the back roads, one drove where the fewest pot-holes were. "Oh yes. Simla? No, no. Poona. Bishops, bishops, bishops, eh, Mr. Limekiller? There's the regular bishop, the regular Anglican Bishop of Hidalgo; then there's the RC Bishop of King Town; then of course there is dear old Archbishop Le Beau, *quite* a compliment for him to have picked *us* to settle amongst. And now this one. Thought I'd try it on our regular bishop, 'What do you think of all these incoming episcopies?' I asked. Thought I'd goad him into some expression of jealousy, then I'd taunt him with a lack of, oh, well, *some*thing, you know. All he said was, 'The more the merrier.' There you are, never *can* trust these parsons. . . . . Damnable stretch of road, remind me to make a note of it, drop a hint to the Ministry."

Coconut walks lined the land side of the road. Sluggish and frothy waves slopped lazily along the beach. Overhead, though not very much overhead, brown pelicans languidly flopped through the heavy air. "And you, Sir Joshua? Are you out here investigating reports that someone has been poaching the Queen's Deer?"

An animal far too large for a pig and far too small for a cow ambled out of the bush, narrowly avoided making a deodand of the Royal Jeep, ambled back. The chief function of the tapir, that odd, *odd*, animal, seemed to be to cause just exactly such hazards on the back roads. Jack was sure that he had heard Sir Joshua utter the words, "Bloody man," at just the second the "mountain-cow" made its unsought epiphany. But he thought it best not to repeat the question. Perhaps the phrase was directed towards himself. Perhaps he had Presumed. Sir Joshua was a kindly older gentleman, Sir Joshua was being amiable in giving him a ride: Sir Joshua was, after all, he *was* the Royal Governor, and so –

"The damndest things, Jack, bring me out to the damndest places. It isn't all cutting ribbons for new bridges and signing pardons, you know. Here I am, supposed to be trying my best to phase myself *out*, you know . . . and then, again and again, Government tries to phase me *in*. However. Mum's the word – Wish it *were* the Queen's Deer!"

If he had any small thoughts that perhaps arriving in the Royal Jeep might give a certain cachet, a position of advantage to his business here in town, the sight of every place of business closed for lunch-cum-siesta put an end to them. He thanked Sir Joshua, and left him to his reception at the local District Commissioner's or Police Superintendent's office – they were side by side in the one building. The next building was the Post Office: of course it, too, was closed. Much to his surprise, however, the door of the Telegraphy Office adjacent opened, and in the doorway appeared Mr. Horatio Estaban, the (local) Royal Telegrapher. "Mr. Limekiller, sir!"

"Hello, Mr. Estaban."

"Mr. Limekiller, sir, as I am just now going home to take my luncheon. As I suppose you are heading for down-town. If you would oblige us by distributing these, if you wouldn't mind, sir," and he held out a number of envelopes.

"No, I wouldn't mind," Limekiller said, scanning the addresses, all of which were familiar to him. "But aren't they all closed now?"

Mr. Estaban, already headed in the direction of his luncheon, said, over his shoulder, "They must open by and by, sir. – At your own leisure and convenience, Mr. Limekiller. Thank you so."

The reason why the names and addresses on the telegram envelopes were all familiar to him was that they were all of the local suppliers to whom he had the day before sent telegrams.

And, in fact, as he very justly suspected, the envelopes contained the very telegrams which he had sent.

Shop after shop presented closed doors to him as he walked along the shore road beneath the jacaranda trees which had covered the sand with their purple blossoms. True: the establishment of Abdullah Ah Ko was open, that is, its door was open, but Abdullah Ah Ko himself was fast asleep in a chair set just far enough back out of the sun so that no one could enter without climbing right over him: and, anyway, industrious and estimable person that Abdullah Ah Ko was, his stock, ranging from black tobacco-leaf to plastic raincoats, contained nothing of any use in the way of building supplies.

One place of trade and commerce was open, wide open, anyway as wide open as its swinging doors allowed of: and that was The Fisherman Wharf, LICENSED TO SELL, etc., etc. Proprietor, and even now behind the bar of The Fisherman Wharf, was the justly-famous Lemuel Piggott, sole perpetuator of the grand tradition of the shandygaff. He acknowledged Jack's entrance with a nod – the current volume of sound inside The Warf made this the most sensible method of communication – and reached down a tall, clean glass. From one cooler he got out a glistening black bottle of Tennant's Milk Stout, from another he extracted a glistening green bottle of Excelsior Ginger Stout; he opened first one, then the other: then, with infinite dexterity, he poured them both simultaneously, one from each hand, into the one glass.

By this time Jack had bellied up to the bar. Piggott waited until the new customer had become the better by several gills of the lovely mixture before asking the traditional, "Hoew de day, mon?"

Limekiller had scarcely time to make the traditional reply of, "Bless God," when the man at his right, addressing either nobody or everybody, continued – evidently – a discourse interupted by the last arrival's arrival.

"An' one day, *me* see some-teeng, mon, *me* see some-teeng hawreed. Me di *see* eet, mon. Me di *see* di bloody mon –"

"Hush up you mout'," said Piggott.

But the other, a much older fellow, did not hear, perhaps, or did not care, perhaps. "Me di see di blood-dee mon. Me di see he, ah

White-MON, ahl cot een pieces ahn ahl blood-dee. Wahn, two, t'ree, de pieces ahv heem dey ahl come to*ged*dah. De mon stahn op befah me, mon. He stahn ahp befah me. Ahl bot wahn piece, mon. He no hahv wahn piece een he side, mon. He side *gape*, mon, gape w'open. Eet *bleed*, mon. Eet BLEED!"

And now other faces than the proprietor's were turned to the narrator. "Hush up you *mout*, mon!" other voices said, gruff.

Brown man, glass of brown rum in his brown hand. Sweat on his face. Voice rising. "Ahn so me di *know*, mon. Me di know *who* eet ees, mon. Eet ees de blood-dee *Cop*-tain. Eet ees Cop-tain *Blood!*"

Brown man spun around by another Brown man. Brown fist shaken in brown face. "Me say, 'Hush you mout', mon!' Ah else, me gweyn mahsh eet shut fah you – you hyeah?" And a shove which spins the other almost off his balance, careening against the bar. But not spilling the drink. First man saying nothing. Shaking. Sweating.

Limekiller had seen the D.T.s before. Thank God, he had never had them yet. And did not plan to.

He suddenly became aware of a scientific fact: that no one who confined himself to shandygaff could possibly get the D.T.s. Calcium in the milk stout and essential oils in the ginger stout would prevent it. Probably prevent scurvy, too, as well as whitlows, felons, proud flesh, catarrh, apoplexy, cachexy, and many another ailment of the eighteenth century.

Which seemed to be the century, at the latest, which he was now living in. Captain Blood, hey? Whoopee.

It was not yet time for the Port Caroline commercial establishment to resume its not-quite-incessant labors. It was time, therefore, for another shandygaff.

The place at his side was now taken up by someone else. Well, the bar was long, the bar was said to be made of rosewood and mahogany: and, if so, it must date from days when Port Caroline enjoyed more activity than Port Caroline did today and had done these forty (at least) years: before the Panama Disease destroyed the bananas and the banana trade. Before cutting without replanting had destroyed the timber trade. Before the building up of the sand bar at the mouth of the Caroline Creek put an end to the carrying-trade with the whole of the Great Central Valley. Before –

Ah well. Port Caroline Town was after all only one of the many places, all over the world, of which it could be said that it had a great future behind it.

Somebody was next to him at the bar. He felt, Limekiller felt, that the someone next to him at the bar was wanting to talk to him. He would have checked his new bar-neighbor out in the mirror, except that he was a facing a well-laid design several feet long by several feet tall of bottles, climbing the wedding-cake-like carven shelves. So, he could either snob it out by not turning to look, or he could risk the chance that the man next to him either did not really want to talk to him, or was maybe wanting to talk unpleasant talk to him: though this, to be sure, seldom happened: But the fact was: some people simply did not want to be looked at.

The matter was almost at once resolved. "Scuse me, sah, you doesn't mind I ox you ah question?"

It was now permissible to turn and look. The same fisherman who had spin-dizzied the other fisherman. Not, however, seeming inclined to repeat it with Jack. "Fire away, friend," said J.

"What you t'ink, sah, ahv de Ahrah*wock*?"

A few years earlier, this question asked him in North America, Jack would have at once said, "The Arawack are extinct." And, as far as North America is concerned, the Arawack *are* extinct. In Central America, however, not necessarily. Limekiller said, perhaps cautiously, but, certainly, truthfully, "Well, they have never bothered me . . ."

This was perhaps not what the man meant. The Fisherman Wharf, Jack recollected, was not, after all, an Arawack bar, it was a Bayman bar. The Arawack for the most part lived farther south, in a string of tiny coastal hamlets, many of which, oddly enough, had Scotch names: Aberdeen, Inverclyde, Mull, and others.

The fisherman said, "Mon, what I mean to ox, dey Block like we, nah true, sah? Nah true, dey Block like we? Some of dem, dey blocker than some of we. Why dey no like ahd eet dey Block like we? Suppose, sah, you say to dem, 'What, you no Block? You not Nee-*gro*?' You not know, sah, what dey ahnswer? 'No sotch teeng,' dey say. 'Notteeng like dot. We Eendian,' dey gweyn tell you. Dey not want fi speak Bay*tahk*. Dey w'only want fi speak dey w'own lahnguage, sah, which dey not want teach noo-*bod*-dy. Ahnd wot de troot, sah? De troot ees, dey mustee."

Jack didn't know the word, his face showed it.

The fisherman, seeing that, explained. "'Mustee,' sah, what we cahl mustee, eet means, meex. Wheech ees to say, dey ahv meex race. Yes sah. Block men from Africa, lahng, lahng time w'ago, dey meexing wit' de w'old Ahrawock Eendian een de West Eedies, sah.

Dey loosing de African lahnguage, sah. Becahs, sah, dese w'old-time Africa men, sah, coming from many deeferent tribe, sah, no common tongue, sah: and meengling weet de Ahrawock Eendian, dey adop de Ahrawock tongue. De Eendian become Block, de Block becoming Eendian. Ahftah while, sah, mi-*grat*-ing from de West Eendies. Settling *here*, sah."

Still cautious, Limekiller said, "Yes, I believe you are correct." A curious people, the Black Arawack. A mystery people, sure enough, with their black skins and their Indian faces and their archaic and (save of course to themselves) their unknown language. Mysterious, but certainly harmless. Harmless, certainly – but different. Harmlessly different, but – still – *different.*

"Yes, sah," the fisherman said. "Dey settle here, Enn Breeteesh Heedalgo. But sah. *We settle here forst . . .*"

It had been a fairly faint and fairly forlorn hope which had brought Jack down to Port Caroline. As far as imported goods were concerned, merchants and suppliers there did not order from abroad: they ordered from King Town. There did not seem to be any more stock in their warehouses than in the capital (and only) city: however. None of them had ever studied Business Administration at Harvard. Their ways of administering business would have flunked not only any test administered in North America, they would probably have failed any Mexican examination as well. But their ways were their own ways and they knew their own country . . . knew, certainly, their own local District and their district's ways.

Wilbur Velasquez, Hardware and Ironmonger, does not depose, but says: Yes, Jock, I does hahv dot amoent ahv roofing metal [corrugated iron]. Yes, Jock, I weel sell eet to de bee-shup, sortainly. Noew, Jock, de w'only problem: Hoew we go-een get eet doewn from Mt. Maria?

Ascander Haddad, Dealer in Ground Victuals, Citrus Fruits, Cement: Well, Mr. Limekiller, as it is for the church, very well, Mr. Limekiller. I have three sack of cement, store at my farm at Mile 23. I have another sack in the shed at my other house at Bendy Creek. Suppose you can find some way of bringing them down, you can have them at same price.

Gladstone Lionel Piggott, Lumber Contractor and Dealer in Wood, Timber, and Planks: Me b'y, I be delighted to help you. Motta ahv foct, ahlthough I do not hahv your requirement directly at hond, not here in Port, I hahv a pile ahv season timber exoctly cot fah your need. Some five year ago I dismontle sah*mill* doewn aht Bamboo P'int, but timber still pile ahp, ahnd nicely season by noew, you see.

It all made sense, it made, all of it, excellent sense. Wilbur Velasquez had moved the corrugated iron to Mt. Maria because, at the time he had moved it, people were roofing houses at Mt. Maria. The cultivators there were cultivators in a small way, they were of a thrifty disposition, they straightened nails as long as there were bent nails to straighten; and they bought sheets of corrugated iron as they had money to spare to buy them. One by one. Sheet by sheet. It would not have paid Wilbur to have moved the material sheet by sheet from Port Caroline, so he had moved it en masse, and erected a *ramada* to cover it. Since that time, however, there had been a decline in the price of bananas, and, as a result, no one now at Mt. Maria was buying corrugated iron. And, as Wilbur did not know who would want it next, or where, or how much – being (as he more than once point out) neither a prophet nor a prophet's son – he had simply . . . and sensibly . . . left it where it was.

Ascander Haddad had cement in sack at his two properties because he sometimes required cement at his two properties. Moreover, his neighbors, did *they* require cement, and from time to time they did, would certainly find it more convenient to buy it by the bucket right there at Mile 23 or at Bendy Creek, rather than come down to Port for it. It was not news to Ascander that no fresh supply was coming soon from King Town, but that was no reason why he should have moved such supply as he had from right where it was.

And Gladdy Piggott, cousin to Lemuel, like every small lumberman in the colony, followed the age-old practice of moving the saw-mill – or, exactly, its machinery – from cut-over site to un-cut-over site, every few years or so. His present machinery was standing idle back at St. Austin's Range, because, for one, he had not felt like bidding for the most recently offered Government contract; and, for another, because most of his sawyers had moved on to Pine Tree Creek, formerly Plum Tree Creek. And, as for the cut timber left over at the old mill at Bamboo Point, why, that was safe enough there, it was even getting seasoned there. It was like money in the bank, there.

Paint, now. There was some paint of the sort wanted, in Port Caroline. Not enough. There was enough to make enough, though, at the Forestry Station in Warree Bush – where, no one knew why, more had arrived than had been ordered, last year: and had of course stayed there ever since. Why not? It was perfectly safe there. If someone were to require it . . . someday . . . well . . .

And so on. And so on.

Stepping out into the pre-dawn was like stepping into a clean, cool pool. Already, at that hour, people were about . . . grave, silent, polite . . . the baker setting the fires, the fisherman already returning with their small catch. The sun climbed, very tentatively, to the edge of the horizon. For a moment, it hesitated. Then, all at once, two things happened. The national radio system, which had gone off the air at ten the night before, suddenly awoke into Sound. Radios were either dead silent or at full-shout. In one instant, every radio in Port Caroline, and in the greater Port Caroline Area, roared into life. And at the same moment, the sun, suddenly aware that there was nothing to oppose it, shot up from the sea and smote the land with a blast of heat.

Trucks began to roar and rattle along the rutted roads, past the bending coconut palms, past the golden-plum trees whose fruit was never suffered to become ripe, lest the worms get at it, crushing under their wheels the violet flowers of the jacarandas. But these were either Government trucks or else the trucks of the Citrus Company: it made no difference to them what supplies Jack Limekiller wanted. And as to the privately-owned trucks, well . . .

"Well, sah. Mile 23? Well, sah. Me nevah go pahss Mile Ten, sah. Pahss dot p'int, sah, not ee-nahf business warrant de treep, de time, de gahs, sah."

Ascander Haddad, who had the two or three sacks of cement at his house there, made the trip daily. But he made it in the smallest motor vehicle in all of British Hidalgo: and he made it with his widowed sister, who acted as his secretary-treasurer, and who was the largest woman in all of British Hidalgo. There was not even room for a bag of corn-starch, let alone sacks of cement.

Mount Maria? People lived at Mt. Maria, they were not recluses, not hermits, they came to Port, didn't they? They trans-ported things back, didn't they? Yes. Yes, they did. And they did it according to a twice-monthly schedule involving the Mt. Maria Bethlehem Church and the Mt. Maria Bethlehem Church Vehicle (it surely rated a capital letter, being always referred to as "De

Vehicle"). However, attend: Firstly, the twice-monthly trip of The Vehicle had just occurred. Secondly, the or The Vehicle had gone back to St. Frances of the Mountain for its annual overhaul.

There were rumors of mules, of ox-carts, or of horse-drawn drays. People assured Limekiller that they had seen them. But, then, people assured Limekiller that they had seen Jesus, too.

And so, speaking of *which* –

Or, rather . . . Whom.

The Anglican Church in Port Caroline, a fortress – for the most part – of old-time Methodism, was very, very small, and very, very white. Father Nollekens, on the other hand, though also very, very small, was very, very black. He was not a native of the colony, he had been born in Barbados, and educated at Coddrington College, that ancient (and, incidentally, also Anglican) foundation there.

"Why, yes, Mr. Limekiller. I had word from His Grace that you might be around. You are having difficulties in gathering the building supplies for His Lordship's bungalow." These were not questions, they were statements. "Now suppose that you give me a list of the places which you will need to visit. And we will inform you." Father Nollekens did not say of what they would inform him

"Well, thank you, Father. Let's see, I will be . . . I will be . . ."

Father Nollekens waves his small hand. "Oh, do not concern yourself, sir. We will find you."

Jack waited until he was outside before he shrugged.

He was moodily loading up on the fish-tea and country peppers at the My Dream Restaurant, Mr. and Mrs. Jones, Proprietors, when a heavy-set man whom he recognized as Peter Bennetson, the trucker, approached, and said, "You muss eat fahster, Mr. Limekiller, as we do has quite a journey to mehk."

Jack blinked. "I thought you don't go beyond Mile Ten."

"Well, sah, tell de trut', seldom does I do so. But when Fahder Nollekens mehk requess, muss obey." Bennetson smiled. Limekiller left a tiny tip, paid for his meal, followed Peter out the door. The truck was enormous, it was not the same one at all which the man had been driving the last time. Had Jack underestimated the powers of the Church of England? "You're an Anglican, then –?"

Bennetson was polite, but he was firm. He was a Catholic, a Roman Catholic. But he was also a member of the local Lodge of the Wise Men of Wales: not only was Rev. Fr. Nollekens also one, but he was also one of the Grand Chaplains of the *Grand* Lodge of the Wise Men of Wales, an organization not previously known to Jack – and perhaps equally unknown to Wales. "Yes, sah. When ah bruddah ahsk, ahl we uddah bruddah muss obey."

It took the whole day, but they got it all, every last bit of it . . . even the seasoned timber from Bamboo Point, which was connected to the known world only by what was termed, on the official map, a "Truck Pass" – a term not having anything to do with motor vehicles at all, as many a foreigner had learned the hard way – a truck pass, in Hidalgo, was a trail passable by ox-drawn wagons, of which one or two were rumored to survive, still, in the remoter regions. In the five years since this trail had last been used by anything larger than an iguana, it had been considerably overgrown . . . and, in Hidalgo, overgrowth grew over very, very rapidly. But it all yielded. Sometimes, more easily than others. Fortunately there were three of them; somewhere along the way, on or about Mile 20, they had picked up what would in North America be called a hitchhiker: here, there was not a name: one simply "hailed" a passing vehicle with a wig-wag motion, the car (or truck) either stopped or didn't; and it was customary for the hailer to ask, at the conclusion, "How much I have for you?" It was customary for the driver to tell him. Limekiller never learned the young man's name – he thought of him as Mile 20 – but the young man was a not-so-easy-rider and evidently thought the labor he helped put in was worth the free trip . . . to say nothing of the time . . . but perhaps, without this lift ("or drop") he might have stood back at the milepost all the long, hot day.

The sun was declining behind the green mountain, if not the green sea, when they made their last trip through Port Caroline on route to the pier. Limekiller suggested that they stop at The Fisherman Wharf for a cool drink. No protests were received. Inside the bar-room, its massive arches made in a style of masonry no longer practiced locally (and perhaps nowhere else), a polite degree of polite interest was shown in their day's work and its purpose.

"Eendiahn *bee*-shup going lo-cate een Curasow Cove."

"Very good teeng, mon. Very good teeng."

"Me weesh he ahlready dere *noew!*"

This sentiment, innocuous to Limekiller, seemed freighted with more meaning than was universally welcome; and the man who announced it was several times invited to hush his mouth: and did so.

"Say, that reminds me," Limekiller said, looking up. Many eyes looked at him, waiting politely to hear what he had been reminded of. "I'll need a crew. Say, two men? To help me? There's no pier down there. Help me unload, and so on." There was a slow silence. "Anybody interested?"

Suddenly, no one was looking at him. Much interest was for some reason developed in looking at the large picture of the Queen, whose Royal simper Jack had long found insufferable – until visits into republican waters and their ports, and exposure to the prominently display photographs of, instead, sundry scowling generals with fat chests covered by medals, had gradually made Her Majesty, simper and all, look very, very good and innocent in contrast. "Two good men? Usual wages, and all found?"

No takers. Many men closely examining the labels on the bottles behind the bar as though they had never seen them before. To be sure there was much of interest to label-fanciers, particularly rum bottle label fanciers: but . . . still . . .

Jack turned to the man at his right. "How about you?"

"Well sah. I like to oblige you. But I muss go to Walker Caye for fetch coconut." The man to Jack's left would equally have liked to oblige him, but had to honor a standing agreement to go dive for crayfish. A number of the bar's patrons simply did not hear the question, and, in fact, a number of them simply left the bar. Peter Bennetson tugged at Jack's sleeve. "Best we be getting on, noew, Jock."

Jack, well aware of the smell of rotten apples, agreed, but he could not resist pausing to ask the tallest man present, as he passed him, "What about *you?*"

This time there was neither politeness nor excuse. The tall man glared at him, growled, "You teenk I om *cra-zy?*" And he turned his back, deliberately, with a toss of his head, and an ugly mutter.

Back in the truck, bumpetty-*bump*-bump along the shore road, Jack asked the trucker, "Now, what was all that about?"

"'Deed, sah, I doesn't know. I suspec' ahl de men tired frahm lahng day work. Tomorrow you weel doubtless find some crew."

Limekiller turned to the silent young man beside him in the cab of the truck. Mile 20 was still gamely earning his way. "Well, how about *you,* then?"

The lad's voice was low, but it was in no way indistinct.

"*No,* sah!"

Skippy the Cat, the first mate of the *Saccharissa,* announced over the water between boat and dock that several Barbary corsairs had tried to take the sloop for a prize, but had been repelled with immense loss of life.

Limekiller, also tired from the long day's work, slept later than usual. As always, before leaving from the day, he set out food and water for Skippy, a semi-domestic white short-hair, who had lost most of his tail in an encounter with forces unknown, before first meeting Jack. Who, on departing, cautioned him as always, "Keep the ship, now." And the first mate answered, as always, that there was powder and shot a-plenty in the lockers.

This time there was no Royal Jeep waiting at the shore end of the pier, so Limekiller, re-assuming the most of his clothing which he had shucked for the splashing walk ashore, simply picked up his feet and walked. It was barely two miles to the center of Port Caroline Town, a point which he, somewhat arbitrarily, designated as the corner on which The Fisherman Wharf was located. The coconut walks ("walks," here, meaning groves) ended rather abruptly where the shore road became a path across an immense field in which a long-ago cleric had pastured his horses: it was still called The Padre's Paddock, but was now used for football, baseball, and cricket. Usually swarms of boys were engaged at play, but this morning: not one. The point where the shore road emerged again as a singularity was marked by a small obelisk topped by an even smaller bust of Queen Victoria.

"Mornin, Ma'am," Jack said, tossing off a sketchy salute. "I am pleased every time I see you, that no one has drawn a moustache on you." And, indeed, no one had: but along the left flank of the obelisk someone had scrawled a pair of intwined hearts and the legend *Dendry Love Betty.* "We are very slightly amused," said Queen Victoria.

Would she have been amused to have seen the crowd in front of Government Buildings near the center of town? Probably only in the archiac meaning of the word, as "amazed." Certainly, Jack was amazed. There may have been only a hundred, or a few more, men in the crowd, but for Port Caroline, and on a weekday which was not a holiday, it was an immense throng. Sure enough, the Land Rover of Governor Sir Joshua was there, and, as Jack, standing only slightly on his toes, peered over the heads of those in the street, he caught a glimpse of Sir Joshua. He was with Mr. Simeon Edwards, the soft-spoken Black man who was Superintendent of the Central Police District: both were talking to what was perhaps a delegation of the men outside.

"What's up, friend," Jack asked a man on the outskirts of the crowd.

"Mon, de Ahra*wock* di tekh ahp we feesh-eeng *groend!* Ahn we no gweyn *stond* fah eeet!"

This statement was confirmed and extended by others. Black Arawak fishing-vessels, moving up from the southern waters of the colony, had occupied the traditional in-shore fishing-grounds of the Port Caroline Bayfolk: and it was to protest this violation of ancient custom that the Caroline fishermen were gathered here before the habitation of authority, to wit, Government Buildings. Another peep inside showed the broad face and shoulders of the District Commissioner. D.C. Esequiel Bosco was a man of the utmost integrity. He was also a member of the Black Arawak people.

Limekiller thought it discreet at this point to ask no more questions, but several of the Baymen around him thought it in no way indiscreet to supply him with at least some answers to questions unasked. And these, collectively, were approximately thus:

"Suppose dey [the Black Arawak] stay doewn Sote. Suppose we Bayfolk stay ahp Nart. Dees only lee' beet country, but beeg enough fah bote ahv we. Beeg enough fah bote ahv we, eef we each stays in we w'own place. Even de Bay hahv feesh enough fah feed bote ahv we. But w'only juss enough. Noew, what de arrangement? De arrangement, sah, de w'old custom fah hondred year aht leas', we Bay*folk*, us feesh Nart ahv Pelican P'int, sah, ahn de Ahra*wock*, dey feesh Sote ahv Pelican P'int. Ahn de bess place fah cotch feesh fah we, eet ees hahfway between Pelican P'int narteast t'ards de Scotchmon Cayes. Een fact, eet ees so good een yield feesh, we cahl eet De Garden, sah. We torms eet De Garden Groend.

"– Now, sah. Suppose we sees wahn Ahara*wock* hahv he boat dere. We not say nut-teeng. Suppose we sees two Ahrah*wock* hahv dey boat dere. May-be we grumble lee' beet. But sah. But sah. Consider. Consider. De whole Ahrahwock *fleet*, sah, ahs you might say, ees feesh-eeng dere. Feesh-eeng een oe-ah groend. Well sah. Dey dere forst, we fine dem dere dees marneeng when we arrive. Dey stay dere. What we do, we no cotch nah-teeng becahs dey ahlready cotch eet ahl? Hoew we feed we pickney, sah? Hoew we fine meelk? Bread? Rice ahn bean? Sah, ahl-ways ah struggle, sah: but de Laard provide feesh fah we –"

And, indeed, the waters of the Inner Bay did not exactly teem. "Give us this day our daily fish" would have been a reasonable form of prayer: each day there was just so much fish at any given spot. And when that just so much was gone, there wasn't anymore. Not that day.

"Ahn hoew we pay we rent, sah?"

As Limekiller had no answer, he ought to have done no more than shake his head, sympathetically. But he did not think of this. And, entirely without thinking, entirely automatically, he said, "Well. . . ."

It just happened that one of those twenty-minutes-after-the-hour, angel-is-flying-overhead, sort of pauses, occurred just then. And so his "*Well . . .*", delivered in an ordinary tone of voice, sounded forth in a manner more declarative. It reached the ears, even, of those inside the front office, who looked up and out. At which, those outside, seized by what Mackay has somewhat prolixly called Extra-ordinary Popular Delusions and the Madness of Crowds, decided, for one, that though Limekiller was outside, he ought to be inside — and, two, that although he was not a Bayman (not, indeed, a professional fisherman, not even a National of the Colony), he was certainly a boatman: and perhaps also made aware that he was, certainly, White, and, perhaps, since White men were few in Port Caroline and there was no Poor White class there at all —

"Go een, Mr. Limekiller, go een, do, sah, do!"

"Tell, dem, Jock, go een ahn tell dem, mon!"

Exactly what he was to tell them was not specified, but they began to push him forward, they pushed him all the way to the very verge of the office, where he did catch hold of the wall-corner — to the Governor, whose face at the moment was not indicative of any great degree of welcome, he said, protestingly, "Sorry, Sir, I have really no idea what this —"

To which Sir Joshua, in voice between grunting and growling, replied, "Well, for God's sake, boy, don't keep on tottering there, like a virgin at a whorehouse door: *Get in!*"

Limekiller released his hold, and was propelled inside of the gates of authority. The crowd sent up a cheer. They had at any rate accomplished *some*thing.

Sir Joshua sighed. He had been sighing at intervals. "You ask why, if the Arawak are occupying the northern, or, anyway, the north-central fishing-grounds, why don't the Baymen simply go and occupy the southern fishery? Well, they say it's too far . . . they say it isn't theirs . . . that it's inconvenient . . . that they are not familiar with it. . . .

"And all of this is true, you know. Mind you, they are not under oath. They are telling the truth, but they're not telling the whole truth . . ." Sir Joshua, however, showed no immediate disposition to tell the whole truth, either, and let that aspect of it drop.

Superintendent Edwards asked, softly, "This . . . this old agreement, which the people speak of, now —"

"Well," said Sir Joshua, "yes, I do believe that there was some sort of agreement about a division of the coastal waters as far as fishing was concerned. Some sort of treaty, you might call it. I believe my father mentioned it to me, once. He was born here, you know. As to the documents, the records, well. Documents just don't have a way of lasting long in this country's climate. It is just the opposite of Egypt, you know — Copies of the records? Why, they would be in London, I suppose. *If* they survived the War. I have cabled an enquiry, but you must remember that this is part of what was once a vast Empire and the accumulation of records was also vast. Why, even if they'd begun with microfilm and electronic computers and all of that the day they'd been invented, it would still take a hundred years — at least — to get it all, er, ah, mm, arranged . . . that way. I say the documents must be in London, a figure of speech, they might as likely be in an otherwise empty old coal-mine in Wales or a semi-disused guildhall in the Midlands or an unoccupied castle in the Hebrides . . . confound it! in an *occupied* castle in the Hebrides! Superintendent, you have no *idea* what went on over there during the Evacuations. We may never get it all back together again. . . ."

The very clear thought came to Jack that a more immediate problem was getting it all back together right then and there. Unless it was like Humpty-Dumpty. There was an obvious question and he addressed it to the obvious person.

"But why, District Commissioner, *are* the Arawak moving their fishing north . . . and, well, perhaps a better way of putting it would be — Why have they stopped fishing in their old waters in the south?"

Mr. Bosco looked at him with those indescribable, yet unmistakable Arawak eyes. At first he only said, "*Ahhh*. . . ." And then he said, "It is because they are afraid of the Jack O'Lantern."

Limekiller knew at once that he must not laugh, but the effort not to laugh showed. D.C. Bosco said, without resentment, but without embarrassment, "You North Americans, Mr. Limekiller, you think that because you give this name to a carven pumpkin with a candle inside of it, that this is all it means. I do assure you, quite solemnly, that it is not so. Down here in these waters and on these coasts, sir, Jack O'Lantern is taken as serious as Jack Ketch."

Limekiller's mind ran away with sudden, odd, grisly notions. Jack Ketch was the hangman's name . . . or nick-name . . . *neck*-name? Jack O'Lantern, Jack O'Lantern, I know you of old / You've robbed my poor pockets / Of silver and gold / . . . No, that was Jack O'Diamonds. He did now, though, he knew that he did know. And so he did. Up from the middle-depths of his mind, bending a bit, perhaps, on the way up − "That's the lantern of the ship that isn't there, isn't it? I mean, you see lights and you expect the ship, but no ship comes? I mean, oh, it's St. Elmo's fire, or something . . . isn't it . . . the Will o' the Whisp?

"You mean, D.C., that the Arawak are as afraid of an optical illusion as though −"

No sooner had he said it than he was aware that even St. Elmo's Fire was no optical illusion; he remembered Byron's ". . . marshes' meteor-lamp, . . . creeping onward, through the damp. . . ." He was prepared for reproof. He was not prepared for what he heard next.

"The Arawak do not − That is, you see, Mr. Limekiller: Jack O'Lantern, this is the Bayfolks' name for it. The Arawak do not in their own speech call it that."

Limekiller gave his head a faint shake. "They don't. The *don't*? Oh. Well, uh, what do they call it, then? If not Jack O'Lantern?"

"Call it, Jacques Hol*land*er, Mr. Limekiller."

Mr. Limekiller stared. Something seemed to hit him, hard, on the inside of his head Jack O'Lantern. Jacques Hol*land*er. Jack *Hol*lander. "Oh my God!" he said. "So that's it. *The Flying Dutchman* . . . !"

But, after all, that was *not* it.

Not by any means.

Emerging from Government Buildings, Limekiller told the men outside − truthfully − that the Government had cabled London about the matter. They were not naive enough to believe that this would mean an immediate end to their immediate problem. But . . . still . . . the fact that London had been cabled. . . . *Lon-don* . . . that showed that at any rate the matter was being regarded as important. "Something must be done," an ex-King had once said. Well . . . something had been done. Not very much, maybe. But something.

Not enough, however, to make anyone any the more willing to consider shipping south with Jack Limekiller.

Still, when he got back to pier and boat, he found that the entire cargo had been laden aboard.

He had not expected that, and, on reflection, he considered that it was maybe more than he had any right to expect, at that.

Limekiller was certainly not afraid of any Flying Dutchman or Jack O'Lantern, no. But he had his own fears. He did not advertise them, but he knew what he had. Limekiller was an acrophobe. He was, in common speech, afraid of heights. He would not, he could not, have climbed to the top of his own mast to save himself from being hanged from it. So he could, now, well understand how men who were afraid of neither gunfire nor hurricane could all but (in old John Aubrey's blunt phrase) beshit their breeches at the thought of facing this spectre of the sea.

"Me go near *he?*" the last one asked had said. – And no need, anymore, to say how "*he*" was. "*Whattt?* ME go near HE? No, mon, no. No bloody fear me go near he. What me fear, mon, me bloody fear he go near *me!*"

Limekiller understood.

And, also, he understood that, somehow, somehow, he was going to have to undertake the task of bringing his cargo down and, somehow, getting it ashore, all by his lone.

All that he knew about Curasow Cove, really, was that the curasow was a large bird which roosted in trees and was regarded as good hunting. The shore showed on the map as dry, and not "drowned," land; and the water was free from coral-heads. The map did not show how deep the Cove was; of course, the deeper it was near shore, the easier his task would be. The map was fairly new, it was far from perfect, but it was the only completely new map of the colony and its waters that there was. Witness that it was new: no seemingly solid mass was shown off the north-east shore

and labelled *Anne of Denmark Island.* What showed there instead
was the mass of shoals and shallows and mangrove "bluffs" (i.e.
bogs) and here and there an islet: which was what really *was* there:
as Limekiller well knew, having been there himself. But every
other map, without one single exception which he knew of, showed
the same fictitious and seemingly-solid *Anne of Denmark Island.*
Perhaps there had really at one time been such an island of that size
and shape, it might have been broken up . . . half-drowned . . .
eaten away . . . by hurricanes. This had happened to more than
one cove.

As to when the original map, or chart, from which all the others
(except this newest one) had copied . . . or been copied from
copies of copies . . . as to when *that* one had been made, or made
by whom: Limekiller had no idea. Captain Cook, maybe.

He had a good enough wind to take him out. Port Caroline was
soon enough merely a white blur with red spots marking its roofs.
He passed Bamboo Creek and The Nose and Warree Bight; past
Warree Bight he had to put in closer to shore to avoid coral-heads.
The beach was the highway down around here, with paths – not
visible from his distance – leading back to the numerous "planta-
tions" in the bush. Anyone expecting anything resembling anything
from *Gone with the Wind* – white columns and all that – in the way
of a plantation, well. . . . Hereabouts the word retained its simple
and original meaning: it was a place where things were planted.

In other words, a farm.

Almost without exception the farms were small, from an acre to
three. None of them would have ever been plowed. It was the hut
and hoe culture, as it had obtained among the American Indians,
as it had obtained among the West Africans. Moving down the
coast by wind and current, Limekiller could see the ever-present
procession along the beach: mostly women in bright dresses, walking stately and proud: a stance which may have had something to
do with social personality, but which certainly had much to do with
their carrying almost everything balanced upon their heads. Babies,
no: babies were carried on the hip. Everything else went by head:
bundles of yams, sticks of firewood, a basket of fruit – even an axe.

All this was as expected, what was not as expected was the
incoming mist. Mists were not unknown but mists were not common. The last one Jack had seen had been, exactly, on the Night
before Christmas. It was not night now and it was nowhere near
Christmas. Be all of which as it may, love laughs at locksmiths and

the weather often laughs at the weatherman, and there was a mist on the waters and coming towards him from the south; that is, just then, against both the wind and the current – of course, there could be a different wind and current down there . . . however far away "down there" was . . . in which case he wanted to know about it. Being a one-man crew, he had no log to toss astern for reckoning his speed, he did that by guess and by God.

So, now, he turned his face shorewards to get a better guess as to how fast he might be going: the shore was bare of a single human figure. Where, a moment ago – surely, only a moment ago? – there had been twenty to forty figures strolling on the strand, now his eyes saw not a single one. Not one, not even one. It was as though they had been been swallowed up by the sand. Which was of course impossible. It was of course possible that they had all been bound for one destination, some local equivalent, perhaps, of a barn-raising or a husking-bee . . . maybe one of the jollifications locally called "funs" . . . and had all turned up one and the same path. Possible.

If so, however, he had been day-dreaming and had lost track of time. He returned his attentions to the mist.

And the mists parted, in part, and he saw the man in the long-boat.

The man in the longboat was bent over, Limekiller could not see his face, only the arch of his back under his white shirt. He might have been searching for something at the bottom, or doing something else – somehow, his position suggested strain – could the man be sick? According to ancient and local maritime custom, Limekiller ought to have had a conch-shell next to his free hand, ought, also, to have had a distinctive conch-call all his own . . . ought to have known what call to sound upon this oldest of sea-horns to signify, Are you in trouble? – or, simply, Get the Hell out of my way! As, however, he had no conch and the whole custom was almost in complete abeyance, he merely shouted, *"Longboat ahoy!"*

It worked. The man looked up. The two vessels were getting closer now. He could see now that the man was not wearing a white shirt. The man was not wearing any shirt at all, the man's face and throat were reddened, tanned, by sun and wind, but his body was the white of a White man who does not usually go shirtless. The man in the longboat started to raise one hand – the other seemed, although Limekiller could not be sure, seemed to be pressed to his side – they were not close enough for Jack to be sure of that, or sure of another notion he had, that the man had no clothes on at all – Hell, yes! – the fellow *was* sick! – Sick or injured . . . *what* a look of pain and agony upon that face!

"Hold on, hold on! I'll throw you a line! I'll –"

He was not sure what else he was about to offer. He saw the man raise his other hand, streaming with blood – The mists closed in as though a curtain had been pulled across. Jack swung the tiller sharply. Surely to God he would not want to run down a boat with a wounded man in her! The man might not be able to swim, and even though one was always being assured that sharks were seldom to be seen in close to shore around here, still. . . . He did not run the boat down. He did not see anything of it. He called into the mist for the fellow to give him a hail so he could put about for him – There was no answer. The mists showed nothing, then the mist was all around him, and, oh, God! What piercing cold!

It could only have been a matter of seconds. He had sailed through the mists. He was shivering, shivering, trembling, under the hot sun. Never mind any of that, had to find that fellow, find his boat. He put his helm around. . . .

There was no mist.

There was no boat.

Curasow Cove *was* deep. It was not the Mindanao Deep, to be sure. It was deep enough for the *Saccharissa* to come right up to shore. In fact, Limekiller was able to moor her to a palm tree. He was in several ways grateful for this; for one thing, he had not relished the notion that he might have to do Robinson Crusoe stunts and float elements of the cargo ashore. The timber, for example. To say nothing of many, many trips of the skiff for to fetch the non-floatable items: nails, paint, corrugated iron, and such. Fortunately, Curasow Cove was deep enough so that he didn't even get his feet wet, unloading. It was so deep, Limekiller mused, bethinking himself not to trip with the anchor-chain round either ankle, it was deep enough for Full Fathom Five's father to be lying there, now, his bones turned to coral and his eyes to pearls.

The curve made in the shore by the water was paralleled, a bit back, by another curve made in the bush by absence of bush. Either a difference in the soil, or some recent "cleaning" of the land, or what . . . like the tonsure of a Celtic monk, the ground curved gently back against the trees . . . not far away . . . never far away, trees, in those latitudes . . . a sort of lawn, covered with heart-shaped green leaves containing, measure for measure inside, a red-heart-shaped design. These were locally called Bleeding Heart, and they looked mighty dignified and worthy of a bishop to wait him with.

There was deep water, so. A bit back in the bush was a stream, so: it trickled into the Bay – not much of a stream, but betokening a spring. The King Town Municipal Water Service did not after all extend its pipelines down this far; neither did the distilled-water man and his *garrafones* interest the Nationals. So the bishop was in luck in a few several ways. Limekiller got his back into his work and imagined the place as it would look, with standard coconut palms along the shore, just for fancy (as well as for nuts) . . . a bit back, perhaps behind the bungalow, would be dwarf cocounts: more convenient for a man of retired years, who could scarcely be expected to shinny up a tree whenever he wanted some fruit.

Jack had piled quite a bit of cargo well above high water-mark, and was sweating heartily. He thought of how nicely a cold beer would go down about now, and happily it was that he remembered having let one down upon a string into the deep, deep waters of the Cove: the surface was warmed by the sun, but the depths. . . .

He took hold of the string and, suddenly, he was on his knees, in a shaking spasm of chill which racked his whole body.

"Why, Mr. Limekiller," the medical officer had said, some while back, when he was asked, "yes, I can prescribe you an anti-malarial drug, but I advise against it. You see, malaria has been almost stamped out here, and, even if you should get it, we can fix you up in a few days – whereas, should you get bad reactions or side-effects from the medicine itself, it might take *months.* . . ."

So here he was, miles and miles from any human being, and it had to be here and now that he suddenly came down with it.

He was on his knees, head bent, and he was looking down into the greeny depths of the cove, a few feet away. Something was down there, something manlike and white. Something which slow, now, began to rise towards the surface, slowly turning as it did so. It was the body of the man in the mist, the man in the longboat: he *had* fallen overboard, he *had* drowned, and his body had drifted ashore . . . here . . .

The drowned face turned his way and looked at him – or appeared to – and the drowned face. . . . But wait, but wait! Do

the faces of men who have drowned change expression before
one's very eyes? Do drowned bodies clutch one side with one
hand? Do the faces of drowned men suddenly change as though
their mouths were open and screaming, down way below the
water? And, most horrid of all: do drowned men bleed . . . ?

By and by somebody hailed him. He had been half-sitting, half-
lying against the pile of planks. "Mr. Limekiller! I di recognize you
boat, sah. Teenk me come ashore, ahsk hoew de day – Eh, Mr.
Jock. . . . You sick, mon? Sick?"

"Think I just had an attack of malaria," Jack mumbled. The chill
was gone, the fever hadn't come. He just felt very, very bad. Who
was this, now, with the familiar voice. He peered out of his half-
closed eyes.

"Eh, Jock, me gweyn fetch you some-teeng *good*! Bide a bit!" As
though there were anywhere for Limekiller to stray off to! In a
minute the man was back. Harlow the Hunter, that was who he
was. In his hand he had a bottle with a bunch of. . . . "Ah! right,
noew, Jock, dis naught but *rum* with country yerba steep een eet.
Suppose you tehk some. Ah lee' swallow. Eh?"

Whatever kind of country herb the twigs were, they had given
a bitter taste to the rum: but that was okay. Anything was okay. He
wasn't alone now. He took a sip. He took another sip. He put the
bottle down, and thanked the man for it.

Harlow looked in his eyes. "Very odd, Jock. You wyes not yellow ah-*tahl*! Cahn't be malaria. No sah. Muss be some-teeng else."

Limekiller felt he could let the diagnosis wait. "What are you
doing down around here, Harlow? I thought all the Baymen south
of King Town were ferrying stuff to Pine Tree Creek . . . or else
holed up in Port Caroline."

Horlow looked puzzled. "Mon, I no care for keep no ferry
schedule. Hahv wahn lee' caye oet in de Welshmahn C'yes, I juss
be oet dere husking coconut, mehbe wahn week, mon. Ahnd what
you mean, 'hole up in Port Caroline'? What you mean, mon?"

Jack took another dram of the infusion. "I mean, oh, *you* know.
God. The Jack O'Lantern. The, the Flying Dutchman –" But
Harlow at once shook his head, vigorously. Negatively. The Colony
of British Hidalgo was small. And its population was small. It was,
nevertheless, a place with diversity: the little room of infinite riches,
in a way. Even its folklore was not of one piece of fabric.

"What you mean, Flying Dutchmon, mon? What you mean, Jock, Flying *Dutch*-mon? Ees no such teeng, Jock. No, mon, e's no such teeng. Eet ees ah *Eng*-leesh-mon! Eet ees Coptain *Blood*, mon! Ahn he ahl-ways hahv een he's hahnd ah mahp, mon. Ah chart, mon. Becahs he seeking someteeng, mon, Jock. But what he seek, mon, he cahn *nev*-ah fine! He seeking sal*va*tion, mon. He glahry in hees chart, mon. But what say de Laard? De Laard say, 'Lef heem who weel glahry, lef heem glahry een dees: Dot I am de Laard who mehk Heaven ahn Ort, mon.'"

There was, of course, no drowned body in the Cove.
Nor anywhere else to be seen.

As long as Harlow had no idea of Jack's particular reason for talking about it, he talked about it a lot, all the while insisting that Limekiller sit still while he himself stacked and stashed. "Ah, Jock, me nevah hear of no Coptain Blood who steal de King jewels frahm London Tow-ah, like you say. Ahn ahs fah de cinema, mon, dot feelm, weet Errol *Fleen*! Why, dey hahv de fox ahl *rahng*, mon. Ahl *rahng*! Why, me di lahf aht de feelm!"

A faint scent of something sweet came on the breeze. Spice-seed, perhaps. Limekiller felt a good deal better already. "What were the facts, then, Harlow?"

"Why, de fox, Jock: Foct *ees*, de bloody cop-tain he di sail under a corse, true, fah true. He corsed, ahl right. You know dot? Ahl right. But you no di know *why* God corse heem, *why* de Laard God fi corse heem. Fi why? Becahs, mon, he lef dem heeden teenk he *God*, mon. Dem heeden sovvage, dey di teenk *he* God, mon: ahn he *lef* dem teenk so. Dis wah de nature ahv hees seen, mon. De Laard say – nah true, Jock? Nah true? – 'Dow sholt hahv no oddah God befah ME,' mon. So he DOM, mon. De Cop-tain Blood, de Bloody Mon, de DOM, mahn, teel ahl etornity. Een de lahs day, he weel fine forgeevness. He *weel* fine morcy . . . not teel den. Not teel den. Teel den, Jock, he *muss* sail de Seven Sea, mon, wid he side ahl tarn w'open, wid he side ahl bleed-*deeng*, Becahs he deny hees Laard, mon, ond so he muss bare de same *wound*, mon, becahs –"

Limekiller said, remembering, "But the Captain's wound was a larger one than that. It's larger than the wound of a spear-thrust."

Harlow had two planks on his shoulders. He stood absolutely still for a moment. Then he said, "Hoew you know dees, Jock, mon?"

Jack said, "Because I've seen him. Once, yesterday, at sea. And once, today . . . Right here. I mean. . . ." He pointed towards the shore, "right there. . . ."

Harlow set down his planks. Slowly. Slowly. By accident or by design, the shadows took the form of a cross. And then he did something which seemed to Limekiller, then and thenafter, to be — considering — a very brave thing.

He sat down next to Limekiller, and he put his arm around him.

Very well. They had been mistaken, up there at Port Caroline. It was not the Jack O'Lantern, who sailed at night. It was instead Bloody Man, Captain Blood, who sailed by day. Who sailed by day, appearing from time to time, often in his longboat, sometimes walking the sand, sometimes merely standing at the water's edge: but always, always, with his hand pressed to his side and his face a face of pain and agony. Always, that is, except when he took his hand away. And showed his bloody, gaping wound.

If these visitations, these apparitions, followed anything resembling a regular schedule, then Harlow the Hunter did not know of it. He did know, however . . . or, anyway, he had anyway heard it said, that at any given season of his re-appearance, he showed up, first, in the south . . . and then, slowly headed north . . .

First, in the south. This would explain both why the Black Arawak had so suddenly, and so unlike them, abandoned their traditional fishing-grounds in the south: and headed north. And why the Baymen would not, why they really, *really*, would not, consider shifting themselves to the southern fishery. "Slowly heading north. . . ." Well, one such show, and the north-central fishing-grounds were going to be emptied, too. For sure.

How long had this all been going on? Harlow had no dates, as such. But he had at least something like a date. The Bloody Captain, Bloody Man, Captain Blood, had been appearing since about the time, he said, "When we di fight de 'Painiard oet by St. Saviour C'ye."

For hundreds of years the Great Barrier Reef had served to protect this obscure corner of Central America from the otherwise all-conquering Spaniards. In theory, at least, by logic, certainly, the

Spaniards must have realized that something, Something must lie
the other side of the great Reef . . . something other than "Chaos
and the void." But, with so much else to concern them, savage and
perhaps not-so-savage empires teeming with gold, hills of almost
solid silver, shires and shires of well-tended arable land: why
should they have concerned themselves over-much with the question of, Something lost beyond the reef . . . ?

Besides. The English knew the only channels *through* the reef.

And the Spaniards didn't.

But, of course, they had tried to find it.

They got as far as St. Saviour's Caye, once. In those days, St.
Saviour's Caye was co-capital with King Town. There had been a
battle there. Or, there had not. National historians were divided on
the point. Legend, however, legend said that there had been a
battle there. And the date assigned to this battle, legendary or
otherwise, was sometime in the 1790s.

There was nothing, or almost nothing, nowadays, on St.
Saviour's Caye. Time and the sea and the savage winds had torn at
it. It had once been a green and lovely isle, with stately houses, with
taverns, a church, a graveyard. . . . Now it was perhaps a third of
its former size. Sand dunes covered it. Heaps of ruined coral lay
decomposing, stinking. Here and there a piece of a long-dead tree
lay, roots up. Sometimes the rare antiquarian might discover a slab
of marble, carven long ago in London, with a funerary inscription
on it. And that was it. That was all. That was St. Saviour's Caye.

If, however, Bloody Man had headed there before. . . .

"Well," Limekiller said. "It is the Church which sent me here –"

"Yes, mon. Yes, Jock."

"And so I am going to lay the whole matter right in the arms, or
the lap, maybe, of the Church. Right, Harlow?"

"Well, sah. . . ."

"What do you think?"

Harlow was small and Black and thin and strong as wire-rope.
He nodded his head, slowly, slowly. "No bet-tah place, me teenk,
b'y. Een fock, me b'y: No oddah place. . . ."

The Archbishop said: "It has been one of my sorrows that I've
not found the way of being of more service to the Arawak people,
Mr. Limekiller. To be sure, they are not quick to give their
confidence, as a rule, to outsiders. Perhaps one shouldn't wonder,

considering their history. Still . . . Still . . . Perhaps it is because I am not White enough. Or, again, perhaps it is because I am not Black enough. It is the pity of history that such things should matter."

Archbishop Le Beau was, in fact, what the Bayfolk called "clear," meaning in terms already beginning to sound archaic in North America, a light Coloured person. He was, in fact, almost exactly the color of an old papyrus.

And he said: "Well, Mr. Limekiller, you are not the first to tell me this story. But you are the first to tell it me in the present tense and in regard to so near a point in time and space. We do have a duty. In regard, of course, to the people of this coast who are so stricken with fear. . . . And also . . . and not, I believe, not less, to this poor, wretched wanderer. I must go out there. Even a few years ago, even five years ago, I should have gone out alone. I cannot do so now, I must have help. Would you be afraid to go with me? To help this wraith, and to give him the rest which he has been so long seeking? I am not. But then, of course, sir, I am old. I am very, very old. . . ."

For a moment, during which no one else said one word, the aged priest seemed deep in meditation. Then he said, "There have always been those who clearly believed that any souls which have fallen from Grace – as this one's clearly has – are irremediably damned, and that 'their worm dieth not, and their fire is not quenched. . . .' But I am not one of those. Others say, that such a soul is, becomes, more or less automatically the captive of the Fallen Ones, about whom perhaps the least said, the better; for they are not likely to submit to having Grace restored to him. They may fight, you know, my sons. They might fight back, for they have had him in bondage a long, long time: they might fight back. And as to what weapons they may use . . . who dares consider?"

He made a gesture. Somewhat, he straightened his age-bent body. Then he looked up and around.

Jack was not happy at the notion. Not at all, not at all. And neither was Father Nollekens, whom they had found at Point Pleasaunce when they arrived. Least of all was Harlow happy. But it was Harlow who spoke first.

"May-be, Your Grace, we tehk alaang wan rifle?"

"'Not by might and not by valor, but by My Spirit, saith the Lord of Hosts.' Besides, of what use? You would surely not suggest anything like a silver bullet? This is not an enemy, this is a soul in torment." Harlow said no more.

The archbishop continued. "I am a Christian man, and so I do gird myself in the armor of Christ." He held out his hand to a small, black case. "There are the sacraments. I never go very far without them. It is my viaticum, my victuals for the journey. One never can know when, or even how, it may be needed."

Limekiller said suddenly, "You think it will protect you – us! Maybe it will –"

The old man looked at him with something which was not entirely approval and which was certainly less than reproach. "Another citation from Scripture, sir. 'Let not him who putteth on his armor boast as him who taketh of it off.'"

There was in all this a certain Something which Limekiller did not understand. But Father Nollekens did, or thought he did.

"But, sir," he said, leaning forward, "But Your Grace, there is no provision for this!"

"Well, then the Lord will provide."

"But, yes, but Your Grace: it has no precedent."

"Neither had the Resurrection."

The small Black priest clearly felt he was not winning, but he tried once more. "Ah, but Your Grace – Have you no fear of the discipline of the Church?"

The archbishop looked at him, and stroked his white, white beard. "My dear boy – Forgive me. My dear Father. . . . When one is eighty years old and a retired archbishop in a Church which never had an Inquisition and which has no pope, one may answer your question very easily: No."

He gave the same answer to the next question, which was Jack Limekiller's. "Do you think, Archbishop, that he . . . that it . . . that the person we're talking about . . . may be heading for St. Saviour's Caye?"

"Certainly his destination of desire is the Holy Saviour, but not, I think, that Caye. No."

The night breeze blew through the windows of the small house, which, blessedly, were screened. The Bayfolk commonly had the habit of turning up their gasoline lamps to full power, thus producing a great amount of both light and heat, and then closing the solid wooden shutters of their un-screened windows in order to keep out the "flies" which the light attracted; as for the heat of the lamps, well, that made the nights no hotter than the days. Screens cost money, true: and when they had the money to buy the screens, they didn't. They had other things on their priority lists. The room was simply furnished, and, which pleased Jack also, nothing in it was made of plastic.

"Where, then, do you think he's bound for?"

The saintly old man said, softly. "Where would a dead man be bound for, in these waters? Why, sir, for Dead Man's Caye."

Jack broke the silence, and it seemed his own silence, it seemed the others were satisfied enough by that answer. "But . . . Archbishop . . . isn't Dead Man's Caye a myth?" They shook their heads at this, all three. "It's *not*? I always thought. . . ." To be sure, he had given no systematic thought at all for it. He had heard the words, had thought them figurative. Did a drunken fisherman insist on setting off a state of drunkenness, be sure someone would say, perhaps with a sigh, perhaps with a scorn, "Mon, he gweyn no-*place* but Dead Mon *C'ye!*"

And, although he was aware enough that he had slipped out of the allegedly logical time-stream of the post-mid-twentieth century and into some odd and un-timebound area where other laws, at least, obtained, still . . . he clutched for some semblance of familiar things. He said, almost like a child who says, But you *promis*ed – He said: "But it's not on the *chart!*" And he spread his hand over the map as it lay spread out on the table.

The old archbishop nodded, faintly sighed. "No. You are correct. It is not on that chart. Not on that new chart. On old ones, yes. Dead Man's Caye doesn't break the surface any longer, even. It was smashed by the Great Storm – the hurricane, we would call it – of 1910. I well remember – but that is neither here nor there. No. The new chart, no. The *old* charts, now. . . ." He reached his parchmenty hand to the rack of scrolls, more and more reproducing the note of a time and place even more antique than the Caribbean. He might have been the last Librarian at Alexandria, taking up a map made by the hand of Claudius Ptolaemeius himself. Archbishop Le Beau spread it out so that it was roughly approximate to the new one. "Look here," he said, pointing.

And yet his "here" was not where Limekiller's eyes at once settled. Without willing it or even witting it, his eyes at once went to the largest off-shore piece of land on the old map (and it was *old*): sure enough. *Anne of Denmark Island.* This, then, may well have been *the* map, the original map, the master printed map, that is, from which all other maps down to this most recent-printed one, had copied. And his eyes flitted from the outlines, familiar enough to him, of the once-solid island named for the once-solid queen of James I . . . flitted to the corners of the margins of the chart. He knew that he ought to be looking where the archbishop was pointing, and so he did look there – but not before he had looked elsewhere: several fingers of the old man's other hand, holding the chart down to keep it from rolling back up, obscured some of the words Limekiller was looking for. But not all of them. Uncovered were the letters spelling, *k, Lt., R.N.* Very well, enough for now, some Lt. Black, or whatever, had made the old map, and had made it for the Royal Navy. *Now* –

Sure enough. A mere speckle of land. But it had its name. And its name was *Dead Man's Caye.*

"It is there we shall be going, in the morning, my sons."

Limekiller felt, anyway, some feeling of relief. "Might as well wait for daylight, I suppose," he said.

The old man's sunken eyes opened wider, looked at him. "It is not daylight that we are waiting for," he said, "Night or day, it is all the same. We are waiting for His Excellency. For the Governor."

Not less than three times did waterspouts, those smaller cyclones of the sea, appear: and the third time there were three of them, evidently on a convergence course which would inevitably reach the vessel with a violence it could not hope to survive. "Steady at the helm," the archbishop said. "If we flee, they will pursue." The helm stayed more or less steady. Nearer and nearer came the waterspouts, like great gray-green twisting sea-serpents dancing on the surface of the sea.

"Elements of God, be not elementals of unrighteousness," the old voice said (voice so feeble, and yet so strong); "unholy trinity deceived by Satan, I bid you three times in the Name of the God Who is One: Begone! Begone! Begone!" There was a sound like the simultaneous crashing of a thousand great waves. The sea heaved and swelled, the boat was drenched, the boat veered, shivered, tilted.

The boat righted itself. When Limekiller had wiped his eyes almost dry, dry enough to look around, the waterspouts were gone. But a small stand of tall mangrove trees, perhaps the only trees in

all creation which can grow up out of the salt, salt sea — this stand
of them was gone. Where it, they, had been, to starboard, the wrack
and wreckage of them floated on the torpid waves.

Something moved and muttered in the small hold. Something
scrabbled, gobbled in a voice clotted by something thicker than
phlegm. Perhaps, Limekiller thought, feeling his bowels both twist
and — almost — loosen — it was not in the hold at all, but —

There was a coral shoal clearly visible, a few feet down, to port.
"Port the helm!" a voice screamed, all but in his ear. He had never
moved so swiftly in his life, he fell forward and down upon the
wheel, the cutlass slashed the air where his head had been. The
man screamed again and raised the cutlass again, the man was
filthy, vile, face distorted with no normal rage, face framed in
tangled beard, and, in the tangles, things that smoked — The man
was gone. It was *not* "Bloody Man." The shoal slipped astern and
behind.

"Teach," said Sir Joshua, in a voice fainter than Jack had ever
heard his voice. "It *was* Teach. Goddamn him . . . that is . . . ahh
. . . Oh. Hm. Ah, well. . . ." His voice died away. The air stank of
sulfur. And of worse.

But the clean breezes of the Bay soon swept all that away — a
matter for which Limekiller was giving thanks — when he heard
Harlow give a cry without words, saw his arm sweep outwards. Jack
looked, saw an enormous shark, had not realized a shark could be
so huge, had not believed such a shark would ever pass inside the
reef: the shark was moving, and moving faster than he would have
allowed for any shark to move: in a moment it would, must, surely
strike them: and then —

"Ah, Satan, cease thy follies!" the archbishop said, almost impatiently. "Canst *thou* hope to enthrall leviathan, and draw him on
with a snare?"

Surely the shark swerved. Certainly the shark missed them. A
moment or so later, looking back, Limekiller though he saw a fin
break the surface, heading out to sea again. But perhaps it was only
a porpoise. Or a piece of flotsam.

Or nothing at all.

"It's a good thing the Colony is already autonomous," Sir
Joshua said, wiping his red face with a red bandana — *not* part of his
official accoutrements. "They don't really need me very much at

all. Not, mind you," he added, stuffing the kerchief away and at once wiping his face on his forearm; "not, mind you, that I particularly want them to realize it in any particular hurry . . . ah, well."

Dead Man's Caye lay dead beneath them. The water was clear, the mass of sand and coral could be clearly seen. If Limekiller had stepped over the side and stood with both feet upon the surface of the sunken caye, his head would still be above the water.

They had been there quite some time. They had encountered nothing untoward since arriving – in fact, they had encountered nothing there at all, except a huge manta, locally called "sting-ray," which, following the sun and avoiding the shadows of the clouds, flapped lazily away from them –

And it was hot.

And there was no cold beer along, this time, either.

In part to make conversation, in part only thinking aloud, Limekiller said, "I was looking at His Grace's old chart last night, and –"

Sir Joshua at once fell in with the subject. "Yes, indeed: man was a natural mapmaker. Man was a natural explorer, too. Some say, you know, that he was naturally proud, that is, over-proud. I suppose one would call it *hubris*. Oh, I don't mean that he was a bloody Captain *Bligh*, though, mind you, Bligh has had a bad press, you know, a damned bad press . . . However. . . . Beside the point. Yes. Polk's men adored him." Jack thought to himself, '*Polk*,' hey. Not '*Black*.' As for the rest, Jack hadn't a thought at all. "But there was that one fatal incident. That one fatal show of weakness. *We* might not consider it such, but such it was. You recollect Kipling's story of the man who would be"

Sir Joshua's voice simply had ceased. There was no diminuendo. No one would have been still listening, anyway. No one would have been looking at him, either. Everyone had suddenly, in one and the same instant, become aware of two things. One was sudden mist and cold.

The other was the head of a man protruding from the water just abaft the stern. The man's body could be seen, wavering in the water, white and pliant. The man's face and throat were between sun-reddened and sun-tanned. Once again Limekiller felt that deadly chill, but this time he did not fall into trembling. He was able to look the man's face straight on. Chill though the air was to him, beads of sweat appeared on the face, and flowed downward, and fresh droplets took their place.

Sir Joshua's crimson countenance had gone a very faint pink.

And now the aged archbishop was there, and he had his vestments on, or, at any rate, he had some of them on. He knelt and spoke, as simply as though he were speaking to a familiar congregant in a familiar setting. He had, in fact, been speaking for a few seconds. ". . . if you have received Christian Baptism and if you desire to receive the Sacrament of Holy Communion according to the usage of the Church of England, indicate this desire by bowing your head."

The head bowed slowly down until the chin touched the water.

"Almighty, everlasting God," the archbishop went on, "Maker of mankind, who dost correct those whom Thou dost love, and chastise every one who Thou dost receive; we beseech you to have mercy upon this Thy servant visited with Thine hand . . ."

Limekiller could no more have recollected every word or gesture than he could those in a dream. They went on. They went on.

"My son, despise not thou the chastening of the Lord, nor faint when thou are rebuked of him. For whom the Lord loveth, He chasteneth; and scourgeth every son whom he receiveth. . . .

"Do you declare yourself to be truly repentent . . . ?"

Again, and again slowly, the head, face a mask of pain, of agony, the head bowed itself to the brim of the sea.

The archbishop began to recite the Lord's Prayer, and, one by one, all those aboard joined their voices to his. Then they fell again silent, only the old man's voice continuing.

"While we have time, let us do good unto all men; and especially unto them that are of the household of faith . . ."

Not a breath disturbed the surface of the sea.

"Ye who do truly and earnestly repent you of your sins. . . .

"Draw near with faith, and take this Holy Sacrament to your comfort. . . ."

". . . our manifold sins and wickedness, which we, from time to time, most grievously have committed, By thought, word, and deed, Against Thy Divine Majesty, provoking most justly Thy wrath and indignation . . . We do most earnestly repent, And are most heartily sorry for these our misdoings; the remembrance of them is grievous unto us; the burden of them is intolerable."

Limekiller could no longer look upon the face, and indeed, it had seemed, before he looked away from it, that the face could no longer look at them: it had closed its eyes.

"Almighty God. . . . Have mercy upon you; pardon and deliver you from all your sins. . . ."

The old priest had opened his black bag some time before, had arrayed its contents upon a cloth upon a board. He needed hardly pause at this point. "Take and eat this in remembrance. . . . Drink this in remembrance that Christ's Blood was shed for thee . . . forgive us our trespasses . . . deliver us from evil . . . grant that those things which we have faithfully asked accordingly to Thy will may effectually be obtained, to the relief of our necessity, and to the setting forth of Thy glory; through Jesus Christ Our Lord.

"*Amen.* . . ."

When Limekiller next looked, the water was empty. Almost a full fathom beneath the surface, the sandy bosom of Dead Man's Caye lay open to his gaze. He saw . . . he thought that he saw . . . the prints of human feet. Even as he gazed, the water slowly moved, sand slowly trickled along and down and into; in another moment, all was as before.

As long, long before.

First, they went to tell the Arawak that they could leave the northern waters. Next they went to tell the Baymen that they could once again go south. And to both they told that Captain Blood, the Bloody Captain, Bloody Man, would never sail his longboat ever along these coasts and shores. Were they believed? They were believed. As Harlow the Hunter put it, "'By de mouds of two weetnesses shahl ah teeng be estoblish.'" And such a two witnesses as an archbishop and a royal governor are not to be held lightly in their testifying to such a matter as that one.

The old high priest remained in the stern all the voyage back, praying, presumably, or meditating. Sir Joshua was at the helm, and Jack Limekiller was next to him. "What are you going to tell them in King Town?" he asked. "What report will you make to London?"

"Presumptuous boy," Sir Joshua said, without malice. "Why – I shan't tell them a *thing*, in King Town. They won't even ask. In fact, they are no doubt simply delighted to have had me available in this crisis. Whom would they have sent, instead? The Minister for Social Development? The Under-secretary for Public Health? – As for London, I can't tell *you* a thing, my boy, 'twouldn't be constitutional, you know. Suffice it to say: No trouble from London. In fact, no trouble *in* London. What would you think? A question asked in the House of Commons? Tchah. Put it out of your mind."

Far, far ahead, the Mountains of the Morning lifted their hazy peaks against the early evening sky. Faint, faint, yet much, much nearer, the low-lying coast began to come into focus. "Gladly," Jack said. "So . . . well. . . . Oh, yes. I want to ask you. What *about* Kipling's story, *The Man Who Would Be King* . . .?"

"Ah, yes. Well. Well, I didn't mean that our poor man would have been king. I mean that Daniel whatever his name was, Daniel Dravit, was it? Kipling's character. Where was I. Mmm. Yes. Back there in Kaffiristan. White Kaffirs of the Hindu Kush. Fact, you know, not fiction. Well, the story was fiction itself. What I mean is: fellow in the story, Daniel, allowed the heathen, the kaffirs, to think he was a god, you know. Didn't in so many words say so. Let them think so. And when the wench bit him and drew his blood, why that was bloody well *that*. Well, similar thing with poor Cook. The Hawaiians thought that *he* was a god, one of their native gods. Name of Lono. Symbol of Lono was white cloth on a pole. They had no sails, you know, Hawaiian chaps, I mean. When they saw Cook's ships coming in, poles crowded with white cloth sails, why – obvious conclusion – Lono. And Cook let them think so. He went along with it. Let himself be worshipped, accepted offerings, the whole thing – Then there was all that trouble at the shore, forget just why, and some native chap hit him with a spear, twasn't a fatal thrust, no. The blow itself wasn't fatal. But he groaned. *Cook groaned!*"

Sir Joshua took a hand from the wheel, put it to his side, made realistic noises. "– What? A god groan? A god feel *pain*? Native fellows were *fur*ious! They'd been *done*, you see, and suddenly they knew it. Pranged the poor fellow, cut him down, and –"

Limekiller had been listening with a mixture of fascination and confusion. Now he had to stop the narrative and get a firmer grip and grasp on it. "Excuse me, Sir Joshua –"

"– ah – Mmm – Yes, my boy. What?"

"What is the connection?"

Sir Joshua considered this. Evidently it confused *him*. "Connection with *what*, Jack?"

"I mean . . . what is the connection between Captain Cook and . . . well, with *any*thing? Anything at all? That was in Hawaii. And we –"

At a sudden hail from Sir Joshua, Harlow came and took the helm. Sir Joshua, taking Limekiller by the arm, led him back and sat him down. "Now, my boy," he began. He seemed to be struggling with a slight show of temper. Then control won. "Now, my boy, it is exactly Captain Cook who . . . well *confound* it, boy!" Control lost. "Who in blazes do you think this so-called Bloody Man, this alleged Captain Blood *is*?" In a lower voice, he said, "Was. . . ."

There was a rather long silence. Then Limekiller said, "Do you mean it is supposed to have been Captain Cook? *The* Captain –"

Sir Joshua shook his head, sadly. Then he asked Limekiller what he meant by "supposed to have been"? Had not Limekiller *seen* the whole thing? Hadn't Limekiller described the gaping wound in the man's side? Had he or had he not?

"Yes, yes! But . . . as I told Harlow, when he – well, in another connection: the wound which I saw was far too large for a spear-thrust. You yourself just said the spear-thrust wasn't fatal. He was killed, Cook, you said, he was killed when they cut him down."

"Ah, yes," Sir Joshua said, somberly. "They cut him down all right. *And then they cut him up!*"

And then it all came back to Limekiller. "Polk," there was no "Polk," that was only his ear, catching at a name he was not expecting to hear, and catching instead a name which hadn't even been uttered. Captain Cook. Oh yes. Of course. Yes, they *had* cut him up. They had cut him all the way up. They had cut him into pieces. And they had sent each piece to one of the district chiefs. Of course, they had brought them back, by and by. Very soon, in fact. For one thing, there were, after all, the heavy guns of His Majesty's ships. And, for another – But the for another didn't matter. They had brought back the pieces of Captain Cook.

That is, they had brought back all but one of the pieces of the body of Captain Cook.

The Hawaiians had been cannibal, then . . . at any rate, upon occasion.

"And that one piece?"

Sir Joshua sighed heavily. Again, he wiped his face. "It was a piece of his right side," he said.

The offices of National Archivist and National Librarian co-existed in the person of Mr. Frances Bustamente. "Here is the very

book, Mr. Limekiller," he said. "And, as to the chart, I have sent
down for it, it should be up here, presently. – Hm, well, that is very
curious."

Limekiller had the heavy old book in his hand. He wanted to
sit down at table and chair and look into it. But Mr. Bustamente's
courtesy required an equal courtesy in return. "What is very
curious, sir?"

"Well, evidently, going by the Acquisition Numbers, we must
have acquired both chart and book at the same time. And they are
both prefixed with AD, that means, the Admiralty, you know. I am
afraid that the Admiralty in London has never given us anything
. . . anything that *I* know of . . . but it did sometimes happen that
the commanding officers of different vessels of the Royal Navy
would sometimes contribute things to the old Colonial Government
. . . in the old days . . . things they had perhaps no further use for.
. . . And we always recorded this to the extent of putting AD for
Admiralty before the Acquisition Numbers. – Well, I shall leave
you to your book, now."

The book was no lightweight, and would have taken more time
than Limekiller could spend in the cool and dim chamber to read;
it did not circulate. *A History of the Hidalgo Plantation and Woodcutters'
Settlements / In the Bay of Hidalgo / In Central America / From the
Earliest Times / With Many Anecdotes and Illustrations* [*etc., etc.*] *by the
Rt. Honourable Sir. L. Dawson Pritchard / Sometime Colonial
Magistrate.* For a marvel, the book was indexed.

Yes, Cook had been here. Cook had not been here long, but –
Evidently he had loved this hidden coast (as it then was). Had loved
it so much that as he sailed away the last time in life he had been
heard to say, "I'll be back. I'll be back. I shall be back. Living or
dead, I shall be back. By God, I shall." And old Esquire Northrup,
waiting to go ashore with the pilot, and who had dined so well at
the farewell that he was probably half-seas over, said, "Well, Cook,
and as I am one of His Majesty's Commissioners for Oaths, shall I
record this one of yours?" – "'*Yes sir, yes sir,' exclaimed Lt. Cook, as
he then was. And, according to local tradition, it was so done. This same
Esquire Northrup, on a later occasion, died attempting to win a wager as
to who in the Settlement could consume the greatest quantity of turtle-soup
in the space of one hour's time.*"

Mr. Bustamente was back. "And here is the chart, Mr.
Limekiller." Thoughtfully, he rolled it out. It was not, or course, the
old archbishop's chart, but it was its twin. Here was the whole coast

of British Hidalgo, its reefs and isles and cayes, its bights and bays. And, there in the corner, where the archbishop's hand had rested, concealingly, there – sure enough – engraved: the words, *Jas. Cook, Lt., R.N.*

"It is certainly very old, Mr. Bustamente said. "I would not attempt to clean it, it is so old. Clean it? – why, these drops and splotches, sir, you see, here and there. Don't know what they are . . . Why! Do you know, Mr. Limekiller! – I believe that they may be blood!"

After . . . how long? A hundred and eighty years? . . . who could say. However, Limekiller said, "Yes, sir, you may be right." It was chilly, in here. He had found out all that he wanted. He got up to thank Mr. Bustamente, and to leave. The archivist accepted the thanks, walked his guest to the door. "I wonder whose blood it could *be*?" he wondered, aloud, "Eh, Mr. Limekiller? Whose do you suppose?"

Limekiller backed off. "I have no idea," he murmured. Limekiller lied.

THERE BENEATH THE SILKY-TREE AND WHELMED IN DEEPER GULPHS THAN ME

BUT TO GO back a bit.
Here is Limekiller with his sun-stained hair and beard, shaggy as a sheep-dog though of course much taller. Limekiller and his boat and beard are now all registered and denizened in a small port on a tropic sea, capital of some place more than a colony but not yet a country, and often left off maps because its name seems larger than itself. If you cannot get there, that is not our fault. Others have.

Peter Pygore owned what Miss Abercrombie, the attorney and estate agent, referred to (before she gave it up) as "a very desirable residence and property," on the West Shore of the Belinda River; though he usually preferred to indulge his desires by residing elsewhere. His house, though, with its towering turrets of 19th century Tropical Gothic, its cupolas and balconies, its yards full of flowering trees, was among the first things to catch the eyes of newly-arrived and house-seeking foreigners.

"Hey!" the foreigners would exclaim. Or, "Oh, look!" And, "Who does that be*long* to?"

"Belahng to Colonel Py*gore*," a National of the country would reply. "But he not reside dere noew. Residing noew at Ho-tel Pel-i-*cahn*."

The foreigners' eyes, dazzled by the sun on the waters of the First (or Belinda) River as it disembogued into the Bay of Hidalgo, and totally captivated by the cool look of the spacious house in its surrounding greenery, would immediately be less weary and more alert. "Do you think it's for rent?"

And the National would ponder and consider, then allow a smile to lighten his face. "We go timely to see heem. I ox heem fah you." In King Town, the capital, Nationals are aware that foreigners have their own odd ways with pronouns, and might not understand such perfectly ordinary usage as, "Us go," or "Me ox."

"We old *friend,* Colonel Py*gore* ahn me. We *good* friend. Good teeng you ox me. Yes sah ahn yes mahm."

The sun was now less strong, the streets less dusty, the possibility of shelter less remote. The foreigners felt now that, after all, their decision to come to British Hidalgo – so remote, so all but unknown, so (accordingly) confused with the Spanish-speaking Republic of Hidalgo – had after all been a right and good one. With tourists so few, surely here, *here,* they would after all find what they were looking for: decent housing at a decent price in a decent climate among decent people. And the National who was guiding them out of friendship alone and to keep them from falling into the hands of the rare but unscrupulous type of people who would not appreciate their friendship, – the National, catching the foreigners' increased cheerfulness, would instantly grow more cheerful himself, and point out landmarks such as the Anglican and Roman Catholic and Turkish Orthodox cathedrals; and places where very good beer and very bad ladies were available . . . sometimes he would omit this last information if there were foreign females present; but not often, as he would have noticed how often this seemed to interest them as much as it did foreign men: though he wondered why . . . "But not noew. Becahs too orly."

And so they would pass through the streets without sidewalks, go by the main market, cross the Swing Bridge, observe the Post Office and the Fire House with its three vintage engines and its two fairly modern ones (the ones which actually answered the alarms) and such indispensable places as the shop and warehouse of Georgoglu who sold rum and Gonsales who sold coconuts and Flemington the plantains prince. And in between each building a flash of the sparkle of the water of the First (or Belinda) River, the sails of the cayes boats as the sails moved up or down the masts but seldom staying in place and full of the wind, as Belinda Harbor (or King Town Port) was right on the Bay. And old men offered for sale parched peanuts and old women hawked fried fish or "conks flitters" and small pickneys begged for one dime: the National would politely decline the offers ("Going just noew to Pelican Bar, Grahndy –") and speak sternly to the beggingboys – "Why you no shame?" – the last word, sounding like "sheahhm," producing, oddly, echoes of the Carolinas, or Ireland. And at least every other person would greet the National and be greeted by him and more people would smile at the foreigners than wouldn't and no one at all would scowl, thus showing the desired absence of any hatred towards foreigners or other pale people.

"You seem to have many friends."

"Oh yes mahm ahn sah. I no vex me heart weet hate no wahn."

"Very good philosophy."

And so they would come at last to the Hotel Pelican, an unusual four stories high with verandahs on all four sides of it, a large yard with children playing on the defeated grass and often an odd animal penned in a corner (an anteater or a tapir calf or a peccary, it might be), and, to one side, a two-story building joined to the hotel by an arcade: the words PELICAN BAR on a signboard. And here they would turn, through the dust of the dry season or the mud of the wet ("In this country," Peter Pygore sometimes said, though often he didn't say anything, "the science of drainage has not only not been perfected, it hasn't even been suspected."), and enter the one room dim and cool, with its eternal aroma of beer and rum and limes and country yerba. Always, always, always: here the newly-arrived foreigners would turn in with whatever National they had found to help them. Sometimes it was one National and sometimes it was another.

But it really did not matter which one. Although Colonel Peter Pygore never would even rent his house, the National got at least a drink and a dollar or two for his pains and troubles, and the foreigners anyway had as good an introduction to Old British Hidalgo as they were ever likely to get: unless they had applied directly to one of the official offices, and this, somehow, few of them managed to do.

Limekiller's introduction to the country had been similar, if not the same (in fact, it *was not* the same). For one thing, although he had noticed, and how could he have helped noticing? the Pygore Place, standing out as it did somewhat like Queen Victoria in a muumuu, or Queen Liliuokilani in hoopskirts – a contradiction there, of course, for although Queen Liliuokilani *had* worn, at least sometime, a hoopskirt, it is as sure as anything can be sure that Queen Victoria had never worn a muumuu: would she have been amused? not at all likely – Limekiller had been fairly content with noticing and observing it from the outside. He not only did not think of buying, he did not even think of renting, it. He thought of buying a boat, and while the story of how he came, finally, to buy one, may be told, it will not be told here.

Or, at any rate, not here and now.

And, for another thing, he had been younger than the other foreigners whose fairly typical introductions we have had described. And, also, he had been then alone.

So, then, there was Limekiller. Alone. With a boat. And, wondering, as wonder we must all, at least sometimes, what next?

Legally, a license was needed for any vessel to carry any number of passengers anywhere at all for any purpose at all within the waters of the colony; but this law had not always been enforced. In fact, Jack Limekiller had a very good idea that, like so many laws, it had never been meant to be enforced, it had been meant to be enforceable. To be sure, old Royal Governor Sir Samuel Stoniecroft had been very intent on enforcing it and had done his best to do so. But his reasons, whatever they may have been, had gone with him, first into retirement, and then into the grave; and, if they had not, they had gone into some musty muniments room in the basement of Somerset house or the Old Bailey or somewhere of the sort: and might be there yet, misfiled behind a mouldering file of indictments for, say, high treason by having had carnal knowledge of the favorite of the Prince of Wales during the War of the Roses. Only one licensee from the days of Governor Stoniecroft still survived, and that was old Captain Peter Kent: and he had lost his document during Hurrican Hephsibah, or perhaps it was Celina, he was not sure, and it did not bother him. No one would ever ask for it.

Thus it was: Nationals were never vexed to show evidence of a license. Very, *very* offensive foreigners might even find themselves suddenly deported for not having had one. Other kinds of foreigners, well, it all depended. And Jack Limekiller felt he could have slept more soundly if he could ever figure out a pattern as to what it all depended on. But he well knew that aliens in Hidalgo might well go mad trying to find patterns in a country which did not really feel the need of them.

Fairly early in his stay there, fairly fresh from Canada and wanting to do things "right," as right was understood in Canada, he had spent several days going from office to office in search of enlightenment which he did not find. At first he was purely puzzled: how could government officials not know the laws of their own government? Then, later, he suspected that he was being, given the old runaround. Later than that, much later, he decided that it was nothing of the sort. No one could give him an opinion on the matter because at the time no one *had* any opinion on the matter. Almost every employee of Government was a National, and hence a boat-man by birth: and they all knew about not rocking boats. "A license, Mr. Limekiller? To carry passengers, Mr. Limekiller? Well, Mr. Limekiller . . . you see, sir . . ."

Here came a pause. "The issuance of such licenses, you see, sir, is not the function of this office." And this may very well have been the truth of God: it may have been that whichever office whose function it was or had been, had been abolished or expired. Does not many and many a *North* American city have ordinances for-bidding peddling without a license and carefully refrain from providing a means of issuing such licenses? Who is that man or woman who has never − in *North* America − felt himself on the verge of madness after the tenth or twentieth repetition of, "That is not my department"? − how lucky they are.

And then one day, after Jack had given up and was wondering what to do next − sell his boat, maybe, and give up − *not* sell his boat but sail her away, avoiding or hoping to avoid the graveyard shoals of the waters in the next republic south − or try sailing her *north* to sell, maybe sailing in between the hurricanes and wonder-ing if they could really be more trouble than he had been cautioned (*warned*) the United States Coast Guard might be − over a friendly drink at a friendly bar, he had fallen into conversation with a friendly National. (Not the one first described.) The conversation had lasted a while and covered many subjects, including . . . suddenly . . . the sale of lands forfeited for unpaid taxes.

"Thou shalt not covet thy neighbor's land," muttered Jack.

"Ah, but Mr. Limekiller. Government is not really very cov-etous in this colony − this country," the man corrected himself. Old ways, including old ways of speech, might die hard: but dying they certainly were. The man was in his late 30s, ruddy-brown in color,

Caucasian in features. "Taxes may remain for three years unpaid before Government even sends a notice. After at least three notices are sent by post, Government waits a year before publishing a notice in the official *Gazette*. After three such notices have been *gaz*etted, the property is placed upon the list of properties to be sold. In fact, you see, Mr. Limekiller, it usually takes ten years before land is offered for sale because of unpaid taxes.

"And after ten years, Mr. Limekiller, one may safely assume that the owner is dead, or unfindable, or indifferent; and that the same is true of his heirs . . . if any. Now, you see," he unfolded a copy of the *Gazette*, about the length and width of a news magazine, though not as thick; "here is the current list of tax forfeitures to be offered for sale next month." Jack could scarcely have cared less, but politeness obliged him to look at the list. It took up an entire page.

"'*Five thousand acres located at Gumbo Tree, Benbow District*,'" Jack read aloud. "'*Owner, The Floridana Tropical Agriculture Company. Arrears, $5,550* . . . ' Say, that comes hardly more than $1.00 an acre. Odd."

The man smiled. "Not very odd, considering that, for one thing, most of the land is under water, the rest is pure mangrove bluff, there is no access by dry land, scarcely any even by shallow-draught boat, and that the Floridana Tropical Agriculture Company is no longer in existence. It had a short career. A very short career."

"Land-scam, eh?"

"It may be so."

How familiar Jack was to become, eventually, with those words.

And the list continued down to the bottom of the page, where nestled numbers of small properties of odd sizes involving measurements in roods and perches, and on which odd sums of money were owed. "I don't know what I'd want with land that nobody else wants," Limekiller said. What did Limekiller look like? He was not taller than most men in a country where most men were tall. His hair, which had once been light-blond, had grown light-brown, had begun to turn dark-brown, was now, under the inexhaustible suns of the Spanish Main, beginning to turn dark-blond in streaks and – but enough of Limekiller's hair (and beard), which was rather long. His face was broad and so was his nose. His eyebrows thick, his eyes sometimes seemed blue or green or something darker than either, sometimes (seemingly) depending on the color of the Carib Sea: which is, however, never wine-dark; sometimes they were also bloodshot and often this was the result of saltwater or of lack of sleep and sometimes, of too much National rum, and even – though not very often – the result of a native herb locally called "weed" when it was not called "ganja" . . . and this was rather interesting because some of the older Nationals sometimes called a certain kind of banana "ganja," and both plants, after all, are members of the hemp family . . . His family name indicated descent from at least one man who once burned limestone in a kiln or kill, presumably in England; sometimes he said that his mother's family were Ukrainian, sometimes he said Scotch, and sometimes he said they were Kalmuk Tartars who entered Canada by way of Bering Straits on dogsled during a particularly frozen winter: perhaps he was not serious in saying this.

"What would I want with land nobody else wants?" he asks. "I have enough troubles without it."

His nameless companion says, "Ah, but some of these small parcels of land are so cheap, Mr. Limekiller! You could plant them in mango or coconut. Eventually, you might re-sell them, perhaps." A tray materializes on the table, trough Jack recalls ordering nothing more since the initial round.

"Re-sell? I'd have to show it, wouldn't I? And I can't even get a license to carry passengers –" He looks rather moodily into his glass, raises it in thanks, drains it.

"Ah, but Mr. Limekiller. *Gov*ernment would not require you to have a license to carry people to whom you were showing your own land for possible sale, you know."

There seems something more in this statement than in the glass. He considers it. "Government *wouldn't*?"

"No, no. *Cer*tainly not."

Jack considers this for a long time and then ha says, "Oh."

"It has been a pleasure speaking to you, Mr. Limekiller. I hope," the man adds in the charming phrase of his nation after a first meeting, "I hope we'll be no more strangers."

"Hoew you like Mr. Lof*ting*?" the barkeeper asked Jack, some small while later.

"Who?"

"Honorable Mr. Lorenzo Lof*ting*, Permanent Under-secretary to Government."

"Well, I'll tell you, Ferdinand," Jack said; "I was advised, when I first came here, to sign the Visitors' Book at Government House.

But . . . somehow . . . either I didn't have a clean shirt, or my trousers were torn, or, or something. So I never did. And so I never get invited to occasions where I'd be meeting people like that."

Ferdinand stared at him. "What you mean, Jock? You just spend close to wahn hahf hour tahkeeng to heem. You no cahl dees 'meet-teeng?'"

It was Jack's turn to stare, then. "You mean . . . that nice fellow who – you mean *he* –"

"Yes mon."

Again Limekiller considered for a long time. And, again, said, ". . . Oh."

It might have come as a surprise to Dostoievsky, who wrote in the near-slums of St. Petersburg, or even to Tolstoy, writing on the noble estate where he had been born, that a writer is supposed to have to move and write somewhere else . . . in order to do good writing. On the other hand, Vergil might have dug it. He wrote about Mantua, Carthage, and the Tiber: but he wrote about them in Naples. However, Vergil was an exile, not an expatriate. Other images haunt our thoughts, floating like phosgenes before our eyes. The Stevensons in Samoa. Hemingway in Paris. Oscar and Bosie, sipping sticky liqueurs in a villa near Florence. (It *wasn't* near Florence? Okay, it *wasn't* near Florence.) Paul Bowles in Tangiers, Ian Fleming in Jamaica, Maugham on the Riviera, Wouk in the Virgin Islands: some of these images of course haunt us less than others.

Perhaps all of this anyway merely echoes what men of boats have been doing since before there were men of books. "*Happy he who, like Ulysses, has made a good voyage.*" The man spent a generation trying to get from one part of Greece to another, and we call this a good voyage? Clearly, rapid transit was not what was had in mind, nor was he the first war veteran in no hurry to see the folks back home. Nowadays Penelope would have acted differently, unshipped her loom and had it stowed aboard the pentacoster, or whatever, before Ulysses could have made the morning tide . . . What? Not in the Mediterranean – that "tideless, dolorous midland sea" – Well . . . Whatever . . .

Fifty years ago if a married man had the urge to go down to the seas once more (or, likelier, for the first time) he had to tell his wife that he was going down to the corner for a bag of rolls; then he would run like Hell. Today, he has only to dream aloud in order for his wife to say, "Yes! *Let's*!" Amelia Bloomer, Lucy Stone, Carrie Chapman Catt, did you envision all that lies in this apostrophe-*s*? "What we would like," she says . . . or maybe he . . . "We heard that we can get a boat built cheaply down here," he says . . . or perhaps she. "We thought, maybe, a little bit of land on the coast or on a river or on one of the cayes," they say. They ask: "What do you think, Mr. Limekiller?"

"*We've heard that you have some land for sale, Mr. Limekiller.*"

"*They say you know all about the boat situation here, John.*"

"*Could we see it, do you suppose, Jack?*"

Now, Limekiller does not really want to sell his two acres up at Spanish Point, in the country's farthest north; nor his three acres on the Warree River in the country's farthest south; nor his half-acre out at Rum Bogue Caye, nor his equally-small properties along the coast at, respectively, Jack of Nails (north-central) and Flower Bight (south-central) – not unless he should get some irresistible sort of prices for them . . . for any one of them . . . all of which he bought for less than a good second-hand van would have cost him. After all, these lands represent his legal *raison d'être* for taking people up and down and around about and in-between. At, of course, a reasonable charge. It was Government's way of giving him permission to make a living without actually having giving it to him.

Given its choice, Government would probably have preferred for foreigners to have sent money in a plain sealed envelope, and stayed back home and not bothered it. Failing that, it would have been satisfied if visiting foreigners had been satisfied with the services which Nationals had to offer, however minimal: foreigners, somehow, tended not to be satisfied with that. Nationals, unless it was during certain fishing seasons, wanted to come back home every night: foreigners usually wanted to keep on going. In short, the emerging nation of British Hidalgo was slowly, very slowly, beginning to emerge into grappling with tourism. There was a gap . . . a very, very large gap . . . Limekiller, *to an extent*, was capable of filling part of it. He was not a better man because he was foreign. It was perhaps unfair that, being foreign, he could take care of other foreigners in ways that Nationals could not . . . as yet. Very well. For as long as "as yet" might last, Limekiller was given a semi-free hand. Maybe one could learn by looking, listening, observing. Maybe some of it would rub off.

Anyway, although it might be a shame that he was making money which a National ought by rights be making, at least he was spending all of it, well, *nation*ally. Better that he be on hand to take visitors where and how they wished be taken than that the visitors should depart a day after they arrived. To be sure there were other foreigners engaged in tourist-taking-care-of, some of them not even (as was Limekiller) citizens of a Commonwealth country; mostly they were from the States, mostly they operated newish and slick and fast, fast motorized boats; they took middle-aged to elderly, and always obviously prosperous, fishermen of the sport sort on gilded tours. This was all easy for local understanding.

"Beatniks" were also easy for Government to understand (in the Republics, this class was still termed *existensialisto*), or, anyway, Government thought so. When they had first appeared, long-haired and oddly-dressed, they were assumed to be a sort of White Rastafarians; it was now accepted that this definition was in general too broad, as it was now accepted that not every White man with long hair or beard was a "Beatnik." But what was it then, about "Beatniks," which made Government unhappy? Well, for one, they spent no money, or anyway very little. They were given to bathing nude: dis*gust*ing! They did not obey the unwritten but perfectly well known local codes about where one smoked weed and where not. And they lived lazy. Bad examples. So Government did not want "Beatniks." This was also easy for National understanding.

Less easy by far was the intermittent appearance of foreigners who were not rich-looking, yet not "Beatniks" either. Lack of communication, we are often told, is the curse of our time. But Limekiller did no longer feel his time accursed.

Limekiller: an afternoon at the Hotel Pelican. Bathsheba and he were sleeping together, that is, they had already made love and Bathsheba and he had fallen asleep, only she was still sleeping, her smooth tan body as calm as a child's next to him; he had awakened. Every room still had the ceiling fixtures for the old, slow fans; in most of them however there was no longer any fan: there was here, though, and he had paid extra for the room on account of it. Jack watched the fan go humming around and around and listened in complete idleness and utterly complete satisfaction to the slow hum of voices outside . . . somewhat away . . .

He did not have to go to the third floor verandah to look down; he knew what he would see, as he knew what he was hearing. On the second floor verandah several young women looked out and watched the slow passage of people up and down the street, watched the children (some of them theirs) either in the yard or right there on the verandah playing and tumbling or sleeping or also sitting and watching; while they, the young women, talked easily as they finished up between them a huge platter (someone was, or had very recently been, both prosperous and generous) of food: rice and beans with chunks of vigorous native beef, chopped hard-cooked eggs, salad and fried plantains . . . and, to Limekiller and others from the frozen north, incredibly hot (but only pleasurably so to the young women) country peppers with onions and sugar and salt and lime. They ate neatly, delicately licking off their fingers after each mouthful.

". . . jumble . . ." someone had said . . . the first words Limekiller clearly heard on awakening. And someone else had said, rather more quickly than the regular tempo of their speech and conversation, "*No tahk aboet eet!*" So they didn't talk about it; whatever "it" was.

There was a long, quiet, dreamy moment, during which Jack almost dropped off to sleep again, but didn't, and almost moved to place himself, spoon-fashion, against Bathsheba's back . . . but didn't . . . And after that long, quiet, dreamy moment, broken only by the sounds of the mule-carts down below, passing from the Post Office to Corn Meal Wharf where the green-tagged mail sacks would be laden aboard the *Egret* packet-boat, *clup clup, creakcreak, rattle, clup,* one of the young women renewed the conversation.

Limekiller, knowing her voice, knew that she would be already dressed for the day by now, in a tight frock which showed bosom and belly and buttocks. She said, "I nevah tehk no mahn fah money, no not me. Eef I like heem I go weet heem, eef he want geeve me money, sometime I let heem geeve. But I nevah tehk no fuh*king* mahn fah money, no not me. I hyear gyel say, Why you no tehk ah mahn fah fifteen dollah ah night? Suppose I tehk ah mahn fah fifteen dollah ah night ahn right away he mehk me ah beh-*bee*? What good fifteen dollah? What good fifteen dollah fah wahn night? No, gyel. Eef I no *like* ah mahn. I *no* tehk heem . . ."

A long moment passed. In the bar beside the yard, men's voices grew loud, and women hooted with laughter. They were beginning early in the bar beside the yard.

But on the second floor verandah: not yet.

"Henrietta, she gweyn to surgeon, surgeon he give she lee peels, so no hahve pickney, no hahve behby. You *hear*?"

They heard. They had plenty to say, having heard. Limekiller wondered why Bathsheba would neither go nor let him go to surgeon nor pharmacist for little pills or any other contraceptives; he had suggested; she had refused; the subject closed. But the subject of Henrietta was, on the second floor verandah, not yet closed.

Henrietta, she hahve wahn abortion when she strain she-self. – "Abortion," here, in the old sense of miscarriage. Henrietta, she hahve wahn pickney die young ahn bory in Baby Heaven (the Infants' Burying-ground), wahn she do away with ("abortion" in the modern, or North American, sense), ahn t'ree living child she hahve, bock home, by Bullet *Creek.* "Henrietta, she says *E-nough.*" (Jack was inclined to feel that Henrietta had a point. But –)

But Minerva, she of the tight frock, was not so inclined. "I ahm ah Cot-o-leek, ahn dat ees ah *seen*," she said, emphatically.

Another woman (Ernestine? Ernestine.) declared that she was not a Catholic although had been bap*tize* one; nevertheless neither did she hold with taking little pills not to have baby. "It is ahgainst *Na*ture," she said. "If you make mellow, you suppose make child," she said. "God want it so. Nah true?"

"Fah true, fah true, Ernestine!"

"I say, leff it to Nature. God want it so."

"Fah true. – Here come Jeremy."

Jeremy, the limber, light young man ("clear," in the local language) who acted as assistant manager and courier to, in, and around about the Hotel Pelican, came up the stairs with the five bottles of Fanta, dancing to the music of the jukebox in the bar. "No fahget leff me de pints, now: *mind*," he cautioned them. The deposits on the bottles (and in British Hidalgo, all bottles were "pints" regardless of measure) were his commission. Jeremy, not that it mattered, had a long chin.

And, somehow, from hearing (and, thus, seeing) this every-day peaceful vista (can one *hear* a vista?), Jack's mind and eyes oh so softly and without transition slipped along the Northern highway and its few but striking signs: *Bless God Farm . . . Grine Meat for Sale . . . Tresposser Will Be Prosecuted . . . Banns Read In This Church . . . Cashew Wine for Sale . . . Trespassers Will be Persecuted . . . Colonial Immigration Ordinance, 1955 and Subsequently Amended (Section 4) This entitles JOHN LUTWIDGE LIMEKILLER holder of Canadian*

Passport No. 684,660 issued at Toronto on 7th Feb. 196 – to enter British Hidalgo and to remain therein subject to his/her

they *could* have asked JLL to have dropped his drawers at the border and so decided if it was his *or* her, but no

compliance with the provisions of subsection (6) of section 4 of the Colonial Immigration Ordinance, 1955 as Provided that Thou shalt not practice cozenage or guile nor deal with the Devil

Limekiller knew that he had fallen off back asleep; and, on hearing the words:

". . . jungle . . ." knew that he had awakened again, and that, to prove that the whole imagery had come full circle and that time was timeless, he would at once and once again hear the words, "*No tahk aboet eet!*" – and he did.

And next he heard, "Some of dese womans, dey using dey bodies, you does know what I means?" and, well, if one didn't know what she meant, here, *here* at the Hotel Pelican, second biggest house of assignation (in effect: whorehouse: but not exclusively, though) in King Town, where in the hell would one know? – But one of the familiar voices swept this aside with another question: "Why Minerva no want we tahk aboet *jungle?*" – only, only, he being more awake this time than asleep, it sounded more as though the word were *jumble* . . . if one wished to be more precisely phonetic (and what in the hell was all this bullshit about phonetics when he was lying well-spent, half asleep, in a whorehouse?): ". . . *jumble* . . ."

. . . and one voice: "Becahse she fright. – What? *You* no fright from *jungle?*" Ans.: "*Whattt?* In King *Toewn?* No, gyel, me no fright *here.*"

His total reply to all this was the simple, *Eh?*

He must have said it out loud. "*Eh?*"

Because at this, Bathsheba awakened, rolled over, applied her hand to That One Talent Which Is Death To Hide, and, as it wasn't really hidden at the moment, anyway, John Lutwidge Limekiller instantly forgot all about any goddam conversation elsewhere, no matter how near, whatsoever.

On whatsoever subject.

Usually such intervals were, anyway, after the second time, followed by Togetherness in the form of a shower, followed by a long interval of patient impatience or impatient patience on his own part, the whilst she applied various unguents and lotions and sprays and as he was disallowed . . . perhaps by some colonial Ordinance to him unknowe . . . from all the secrets of *usually* . . . ointment of rosewater, for all he knew to the contrary; after which they slowly made their way, via the Pelican Bar – the one beside the yard – to any of two or three restaurants: not this time, kid, however.

Not being invariably at his keenest and sharpest at such moments, he did but repeat the all-purpose, "*Eh?*"

To which the lovely Bathsheba replied, "Because I *say*, is 'Eh.' I have some things to do, I have to see my auntie, and my other auntie, and my sister, the one who lives with," he had given up either trying to figure out why, when she wished to, she could and would slip from Baytalk into Standard (if slightly, and beautifully, accented) English, or the numerifications of her enormous family: "So please, Jack, let me have $20, and I will meet you downstairs at the stroke of ten."

He let her have $20.

He wished she would not have to go.

He realized and acknowledged that she would, anybody, everybody, would, sometimes, often, seldom, now and then, late or early, have to go.

And, anyway.

So.

That left six or seven hours.

First stop: the Pelican Bar. (Beside the yard.)

He was greeted by a loudly voice which he could have done without; "Pussy is like beer, you don't buy it, you just rent it: *right*, Jack?"

"Pour Mr. Duncan his pleasure," was Jack's answer, perhaps a trifle evasive, perhaps not; in British Hidalgo there had evolved a more perfect union of fornication, freedom, and the old time religion than is usually encountered in English-speaking nations. "And let me have a double glass of the inwariable, me dear."

"Ah, Limekiller," said a voice out of the shadow corner. Professor Brolly, Jack knew the voice; no one knew what the real name was: a younger, chunky Neville Chamberlain in khaki shorts and an Albert Schweitzer set of moustaches. "Pro*fessor*," said Limekiller, politely, towards the shadow. "Pray ask," to the barkeep, "the Professor to allow me . . ." By the sounds of things, things were sounding up pretty soundly in the bar; and he would not be or have been the only one to be spending in a rush, or whatever – Dory Duncan: no one needed Dory Duncan, Jack didn't, loudmouth and so forth: but no need to make him an enemy; was he worth it? – no.

"We were just discussing, Limekiller," said the voice from the shadow corner, without even seeing him one would know the professor was leaning on his umbrella; "thought you might be interested, seeing you come in, just discussing –" A burst of noise from another part of the wood, or anyway, of the bar, interrupted – ". . . *jumble* . . ." Professor Brolly: hadn't Professor Brolly just said that? Limekiller thought: *What?* was this some sort of Moebius strip? was this like one of those weed-trips when everything occurred again and again, time ceasing to have significance, when what one had just said one recognized as having been said before . . . before . . . again . . . again . . . Surely Professor Brolly *had* said, "*jumble*" . . . , perhaps "*jungle*"?

But before he could turn and deal with this mystical business, the bartender had placed a glass on the bar; Jack hoisted it, tipped it to the wind's, well, not *twelve* quarters, say three . . . say *three*? Fine. Three. The bartender had repeated, *a double glass of the inwariable*, with amusement, though not hilarity; he thought that John L. Limekiller was merely pretending to imitate a White Creole, whose inversions of the letters *V* and *W* were perennial, invariable, and infinite sources of amusement. To others. There. Down there. In the all-but-lost-little Colony of British Hidalgo, down here on the boggy barm of what someone – would anyone here *ever* forgive him for it? *no*: had once, and in *print*, called The Spanish Minor . . . it wasn't even that *fun*ny – ah well . . .

And then, even as he turned, with intent to enter the shadow corner where Professor Brolly was, to pursue the matter of this odd sequence of syllables which had, seemingly, begun to pursue him (John Limekiller, not Professor Brolly), throughout this semi-immediate area and scene – just then a burst of noise louder even than usual even here, where the monastic virtue of silence was appreciated no more than that of celibacy, struck his eardrums, and swiveled him around to the other side of the bar; no, there was no face on the bar-room floor, there was –

There was and there followed one of the most extra-ordinary occasions and scenes which Limekiller had ever witnessed. Even to begin with (dead, like Marley? *by* no means) the action at the semi-far table had, God knows, elements of the grotesque perhaps enough to last a lifetime longer than Marley's – the little man with the enormous head and hands, Congo-black of skin and Mayan-large of nose, standing treat for a small mob of men and women (these last, those good-time ladies of the place who were not still peacefully discussing this-and-that, Henrietta or whatever, back up on the second story verandah): "sporting girls," in the local idiom . . . Roaring, the "lee man" was, now, with laughter, now slapping his huge hands on the table and now pointing to one and another at his table and screaming words incomprehensible to Jack; quickly, quickly, like some well-rehearsed and oft-performed set piece, men would reach across the shout of words and the spread of table to shake his huge hand and women would bend down and kiss his huge and balding head (screaming, themselves with laughter; shrieking high-pitched jest) or − the women − tickle him under the arms or grab towards his nipples or his crotch: gestures he would at once or as soon as he could, try to reciprocate; all the while rounds of drink were being set down *slop-slop* and dirty glasses removed − this play alone Jack would surely long remember − but this was not *it* . . .

Even while (via the bar-mirror) half he looked away out of politeness (". . . *a gentleman does not* stare, *John* . . .") and half he looked on out of fascination, out of the corner of his eye he saw (thinking: what *next*? what is *this*?) out of the corner of his eye someone crawling out of the background to hide behind, a low partition; a man it was, mouth on one side wryly drawn down, eye a-wink, and then pull from one pocket what Limekiller first thought were chicken-feet: it was plain, from the nudges and the winks and suddenly-smugly blank faces that others, too, saw this − and then someone with a look of assumed astonishment which would not (so Jack thought) have deceived a child, held up a hand for silence.

This was a while in coming; the lee mahn noticed nothing, and continued to shout; only now was Jack able to hear him somewhat clearly. ". . . up, drink up, you ahl me guest . . . bock from bush now . . . glod be bock . . . anyway . . . no fright in bush, some *people* fright in bush, fright fi bobboon, fright fi tiger, fright fi wild hog, fright fi jungle, I doesn't fright but anyway *glod* be bock from bush . . . see ahl me friend . . ." Gradually his voice wound down as he became aware of the silence; he looked around, half-puzzled, half-quizzical. People, meanwhile at and crowded about his table, were looking questioningly at each other; shrugged or frowned as though in concentration; one of the women asked, "What I hear? What − ?" The very little man with the very large head now quite paused in his frenzy of jollification and his large mouth opened and showed his large teeth –

– then the man on the floor, hidden behind the partition (Limekiller, his long height lengthened by his seat on the high bar stool could see in the bar's mirror what the little man, the lee mahn, could not) the man lying down slowly scraped and clicked the claws of the bird-feet on the floor: and again. And gave a sort of bird-squawk, which –

The effect was instant, almost unimaginable, and, to Limekiller, absolutely terrifying: but not to Limekiller alone –

The very little man screamed as though in the most intense pain. He pushed at the table so as to draw his chair back and he struggled to get up. But his chair was wedged in and did not move, and (Jack could see) others surreptitiously pushed back down and against the table so that *it* could not move. For a second more, as the lee mahn pushed and wrestled (and screamed: and screamed) the table stayed in place, as though some part of some insane *séance*. Then it shot up on one side as the very little man flung it up, it shot up on one side and bottles, glasses, everything on it, shot off it, crashing to the floor – the very lee mahn climbed up on his chair, women now screaming too, climbed to the windowsill, from the windowsill he leaped to an empty chair and from there to an empty table and from that table clambered in a frenzy onto the bar –

– place in an uproar, many people almost hysterical with laughter, shouting and holding their sides, heads thrown back and chests and bosoms heaving –

– bartender shouting and pointing the very little man, the lee mahn, *off, off, off!* . . . and he trying desperately either to run down the length of the bar or try jump down on the other side of it: but someone holding on to his coat-tails and preventing this, and the terrified lunging forward all unaware of what was holding him back and the tiny feet slipping on the slick-wet bar –

Jack had been looking at all this in the mirror behind the bar and of half a mind to intervene and yet more than half paralyzed with astonishment, ignorant of what could it all *mean*, and . . . even . . . by reason, perhaps, of his being a foreigner, perhaps by reason of . . . – Jack, looking in the mirror behind the bar saw something green and yellow and blue and red come peering and peeping up behind the low partition halfway back the bar-room: saw, at this moment, the very little man seem to go absolutely insane, great drops of sweat literally flying from frenzied face as he whipped it from side to side seeking escape, only escape: and then the mass of feather-colors came soaring through the air and the very little man crouched and piddled like a crouching dog and screamed and flung his arms over his head and hooted: there was no other word for it: *hooted* his terror. The bartender produced from nowhere a cricket-bat and brought it down with force. *Once. Twice.* A *third* time.

And all the while the pandaemonium of mad laughter went on.

And then it stopped.

As though waiting.

And in a very tiny voice the very tiny man with the very large hands and head asked, words a-tremble, "You keel eet, mon?"

And then it be*gan* again.

Slowly, slowly, the very little man uncovered his huge head and peered, oh so slowly and oh slow frightenedly, from under one upflung arm. Shuddered. And shuddered. And shuddered. There on the bar was the shattered body of a parrot. It had been killed, all right. That is . . . well . . . anyway, it was dead. It had been, evidently, dead a while, and the sawdust with which it had been stuffed was scattered all around.

The feet, of course, were not there.

The very little man's very large eyes blinked. His very large mouth opened. Closed. Opened. He swiveled round on the bar. Faced the silent crowd (*now* silent). Pointed a trembling finger at large. Said: "*Ha.* You try fi fool me. *Ha.* You w'only try fi fool me. *Ha.* But me no fool. Me w'only *play* —" And at this he started to stand up, slipped in his own urine, and came down with an immense soggy-slapping pratfall. The place at once erupted again with laughter loud as battle. And the very little man put his very large hands up across his very large face and began to weep, noisily, as a child might weep: a cry of purest sorrow, devoid alike of petulance or rage.

At once the mood of the mob changed. Where, a moment ago, he had fallen (slap) and sat alone, the lee mahn was now surrounded. Men clapped him on the back. Women kissed him. People shook both his hands, still wet with his own tears. And now loud murmurs arose, and angry looks and glances were cast. "*Who do dis t'ing? Which place he be? Mehk I* see *him. I w'only rip his reins out!* Who go fi play dis trick on poor lee Willy Weekins? Bobboon's bostard! Get-of-a-whore! Mehk I see which side he be!*" — But the scoundrel had fled.

Now arose the only White woman in the place, she was a *large* White woman, not fat: *large*: a well-known and well-respected prostitute, with a face as richly colored (and as lineless) as that of an immense wax doll; she took from her vast purse now a vast lace handkerchief. In a voice indicating a touch of, only, well-bred concern, she said, "My. You've spilled your beer." And began, in a most genteel manner, gently to dab and to mop. – And then, when Limekiller (now, and only now he noticed: on his feet) expected the place to burst out yet again in laughter: there was not a sound.

Until, after a second, only, "lee Willy Weekins" himself broke the silence. "Yes! Yes! (T'ank you, mah'm. T'ank you kindly.) I di spill me beer. Ha-*ha*! Ha-*ha*! Well, plenty more beer! Bar*ten*der! Hi, I say *you*: bar*keep*! Leff us hahve some beer! Who want beer? Rum? Whiskey-soda? *Drinks*! I ahm Willy Wiggins, holding Government Lease Number 523 fi cut rose*wood* at Wild Hog Eddy – *ho*!" He clapped his huge hands as though summoning a host of servitors. "– ond I di sell ahl me cut stick ot highest price to Tropical Hardwood, *L.T.D.*, ond so noew I want fi buy drink fi *ahl me friend* – no*body* else money *good* today! Drinks ahl-*roend*! Drinks –"

Limekiller was outside. He *had* wanted another drink, but he didn't want one now. Not of this round, not the next nor next.

At the door the poor were waiting; well, *one* of the poor was waiting: one of the Town's official, i.e. tolerated, beggars; very ancient of days. You had to *be* very ancient of days to qualify for the free bed-and-breakfast at the Christian Army Hostel for Elderly Men; but the funds for the Christian Army Hostel's dole did not extend beyond bed-and-breakfast; automatically, Limekiller gave him a coin; was politely thanked. And the old, old man, who had evidently been looking in, said to Limekiller, in a tone of wonder, "Dat lee mahn, you know, sah, he fright w'only fi parrot."

Yes (thought Limekiller), he certainly was "fright for parrots" *Why*? Who could say why. Some men were afraid of heights. Or depths. Some were terrified of spiders. Or the dark. Some feared capital, and some feared labor. Some were afraid there was a God and some were afraid there wasn't. The fright of one was of life and the fright of the other one was of death. *Some people fright in bush, fright fi bobboon, fi tiger, fi wild hog, fi jungle . . .*

Wee Willy Wiggins was only fright for parrots.

It was less than a figure of speech to say that, until the stroke of ten, Limekiller was at loose ends, for Limekiller's ends were never as loose as some people's. Perhaps he might want solitude and quiet, if so, he did not loaf listlessly, he went where he knew he could find it. Some went to find it in one of the local cathedrals (small as King Town was, it had no less than three of these; of course, they were small, too), but, although Limekiller was not a scoffer, thinking there more to the lines *Mock on, mock on, Voltaire, Rousseau / Mock on, mock on, tis all in vain: / You throw the sand into the wind / And the wind but blows it back again* . . . or however it went . . . than mere rhyme: still Limekiller did not usually go to a cathedral if he wanted solitude or quiet . . . or, as was usual, both: he went to the National Library. This was, he sometimes amused himself (rather easily, perhaps) by thinking that this was a Constitutional Library, just as the Monarchy was a Constitutional Monarchy. Nationals in general liked the idea of having both, but liked neither much to bother with, nor much be bothered by, either. So there was never any chance of crowd or noise at the National Library. He spent some while there, now browsing, now reading: mostly in old books about the country (there were few new ones).

He spent some time, after that, resuming the Great Bronze Nails Quest; the Quest for the Numinous Nails, one might call it; again, one might *not*. He thought it would be a good thing to have some bronze nails handy for his boat: *Bronze does not rust.* And the more the local hardware shop keepers shook their heads and announced, in a variety of accents, that There Was Nothing Like That, the more he persisted in seeking That.

But, today, as every day: *no* bronze nails.

Oh well.

He caught the late afternoon opening of the Swing Bridge, which opened twice a day without toll charged of boats too high to pass under; for those willing to pay toll, the Captains – they were all officially Captains; the titles had been granted in lieu of a rise in pay – were willing to bend to their capstan as times a day as might *be*. But it did not open often for such spend thrift passage. Idly he looked about the small crowd which always gathered whenever the Swing Bridge swung, he noticed how the Black Baywomen tied their kerchiefs back at the nape of the neck, while the Black Arawack women folded theirs over the ears and fastened them (kerchiefs, not ears) beneath the chin – older women, that is: Young of either, no. No kerchiefs need apply; plastic curlers in public: yes; kerchiefs: no. He could not imagine Bathsheba in one, for instance, although at least the older of the two aunties she'd found it essential to be calling on right now almost surely would be wearing one. Bathsheba –

Someone very near at hand just then said to someone else, "Look me crosses! Look me troubles!" . . . this last brought to Jack's mind how, his first day in the country, tarrying a while in some shade in Lime Walk Town, seeing one after another the freight-and-passenger trucks booming down the Northern Highway with proud and lofty titles painted on their sides (for they had names, like stage-coaches and railroad trains): *The Nation Builder*, *The Great Central American*, *Royal Oak*, *Pride of Hidalgo*, and so on: there, lurching slowly and oh so painfully in their dust: a four-wheeled handcart with unmatched sides and wobbly wheels, laboriously pushed by hand (and arms, back, and legs): on its side in straggling letters its name, *God Sees Me Sorrow* . . . Bathsheba –

Finally, the Tropical Hardwood (Ltd.) tug and its line of logs-mahogany, these, chained with chains – had passed up river; the bridge captains had bent to their capstans, an act greeted with cries of caution and protest from the few, the one or two, high-masted vessels yet to pass . . . but this was mere ritual play; all boats were suffered to pass before the bridgemen set actually to work and the bridge swung slowly around once again, connected both shores, and made King Town one again . . . and the crowds from both sides began to pass across; their conversations uninterrupted:

"Gi'e me a borrow of t'ree shillin, nah so, mon?"

"*Whatt?* Me gi'e you nutting like dot, mon!"

"Well, juss you wait, mon. Every fot foewel have she w'own Sunday."

"Dot woman? Tahk, tahk, tahk; me t'ink she eat pahrot head!"

"She w'own head w'only *emp*-ty, gyel. Like jumble bahlroom."

Some of the talk was clear enough to Jack. Sooner or later the proudest poultry wound up "biled," baked, fried or roasted. By every principle of sympathetic magic, eating a parrot's head *should* make one talkative (Parrot: Wee Willy Wiggins: Jack shuddered). But what was a jumble ballroom and why a simile for emptiness? – At once: a hint:

"No tahk aboet jumble [*jungle?*]; eet mehk me blood crahl!"

"*Whatt*, gyel? You t'ink you een *bush*?"

Reaching the other side of the Swing Bridge, halting for a moment to consider which way he himself should now swing, it came to his mind that there had seemed today to have been a number of times when someone had wanted to talk, when someone

else had demurred, with a *No tahk aboet it!* And, in each case, the
implication that despite . . . whatever it was . . . one was safe enough
here in King Town. – *Town*, from the days when it was the Colony's
only settlement, nowadays it was the Colony's only city: and had its
own *Lord Mayor*: same as London, although elected not by Liveried
Companies but by the Municipal Council: did the local Lord
Mayor, Limekiller wondered, give banquets of turtle soup, calipash
and calipee, like his brother of London? Turtles enough there were,
around here, for sure; he'd passed the Central Main Market earlier
and seen a full half-dozen lying on their backs and languidly now
and then waving their flippers: though, that *Buy me* was the signal's
intended meaning might be doubted. Up ahead: Mrs. and Dr.
Duckerson; at once Limekiller turned aside.

There was to be sure nothing really malevolent about Mrs. and
Dr. Duckerson: why then had he instamatically turned aside (and,
as a result, found himself in Spyglass Alley, a thoroughfare – if that
were not too broad a word – wherein he had seldom been and had
no good present purpose for being)? Here's why: *Dr.* Duckerson
was a semi-retired chiropractor from some roaring North American
metorpolis such as it might be Lincoln, Nebraska, or Medicine Hat,
Manitoba . . . *was* Medicine Hat and its putative plumed war-
bonnet *in* Manitoba? and, for that matter, was Lincoln in *Nebraska*?
wouldn't Illinois be a likelier –

"Too many torpical suns have beat upon your brain,
Limekiller," he told himself. "What is now requisite is something of
a cooling nature;" at that moment . . . do you understand? . . . *at
that exact moment!* . . . a swinging door swung open, and a voice said,
calmly, "Ah, Limekiller." And the swinging door swung shut again.

Not, however, before J.L.L. had marked its location. Over the
door hung a sign; was it a rebus? consisting of the single painted
word *THE*, followed by a telescope (or, yes yes, a *spyglass*) aimed
directly at an Object, despite the Object's being so near at hand
that, really, no optical instrument was needful to identify it as a
"pint," that is, a bottle: one which was not, presumably, intended to
contain ketchup. Or Fanta. Limekiller applied the slightest of
pressure and the doors flung open, disclosing, as First Disclosure, a
most comely young woman; a *'Panyar'*, that is to say, a Spaniard;
that is to say, with a greater degree of genotypical accuracy, a
Mestiza: "pure" Spaniards in British Hidalgo there were none: and
for that matter, probably, none in *Spain*, either; "Ah, my dear," he
said, companionably.

Her reply was somewhat less companionable: "Don't you, 'Ah, my dear' *me*," she said.

"But why not."

"Bathsheba tear my eyes out, '*why not.*'

Her companion said, "You see, my dear Mr. John, you have already been as it were branded with your lovely lady's brand;" and he laughed. And then he said, "Join us, do, sir." *He*, evidently, was taking no occasion for either offense or defense from John's simple – and it had been meant as no more than that – greeting. Neither was he, immediately, identifiable in what, after the glare of even the middle-late-afternoon sun, seemed to be what others have described as an Impenetrable Gloom. And as to why *this* should be so, when the comely young woman should at once have been obvious *as* a comely young woman, well, let us suppose that she had been sitting in a better light.

So Limekiller, having already resisted the temptation to pull his shirt high enough, and his trousers low enough, to disclose an absolutely unbranded hip . . . had had sense enough to resist a gesture which would have provoked only male laughter and female Oh Go Away Closer screams in the Pelican Bar, where such disclosures were, if not common, at least not terribly uncommon: particularly on the part of members of the Right Royal Regiment; Limekiller said, "Thank you; I will, if I may."

The bar was small, clean, and quiet; he had been there once before; why had he not come again? Before trying to think why, he turned to the barkeep, who had himself turned into a waiter and was even now waiting for the order, and declared for "A chaparita of –" he hesitated naming his poison and it was now named for him. ("Of Governor Morgan," said the new-found host, specifying the by-far-the-best local rum.) "Thank you, sir," said Jack. "– and an entire lime," said Jack, "plus the tallest glass in the house, and all the ice not needed to keep the snapper fresh." This harmless play, with its implication that The Spyglass was a fishing-boat without a "wet-well," was received with good humor on the part of the waiter, the young woman whose Christian name certainly ended in -*ita*, her companion, coming more and more clearly into focus by the moment: and even from the shadow corner was now heard a chuckle with which Limekiller felt familiar: one thing at a time, however.

Just then, thank God, and not before time, either, the penny dropped. He pretended it had already done so. "Well,

Superintendent," he said, (he hoped) smoothly. "Nice to be in your company in some capacity other than that of a malefactor – not that *that* wasn't as nice as it could possibly have been, I hasten to add."

Clement Edward Alfred Cumberbatch, one of H.M.'s Superintendents of Police, waved his long brown hand. "A mere detail, Mr. Limekiller. Only a formality. Dismiss it from your mind forever. – Besides: I am off duty now."

Limekiller was swiftly recruiting his health from the tallest, iciest, lime-iest, rum-iest glass in the house when a voice from the shadow corner said, "*I* am off duty now, too. But then, as you all know, I am always off duty."

Miss -*ita* greeted this with a sound something like, "*Tchuh!*", a sound much used by the women of British Hidalgo; but the Superintendent swept it and its implications away. "On the contrary. Professor, in my opinion you are always *on* duty, because you are always adding to our stock of knowledge."

"Professor!" Limekiller exclaimed. "How did you get here so soon? I swear I never saw you by the Swing Bridge –" Instantly he said this, something insistently desired to remind him that he had seen someone else by the Swing Bridge, even less expectedly; but no time was allowed for reflection, introspection, or, possibly even –

"Never use the Bridge," the Professor said; this was not an advice to others, it was a statement of personal preference. "I left right after you did, but I went down Shipwright Lane and hailed the ferry."

"The, uh, *ferry?*"

Limekiller had not known there was a ferry, either by way of Shipwright Lane or anywhere else in King Town; in the Out-Districts: *yes*: a few several of them, some larger than others but all of them winched across the rivers by very hard labor; and all highly visible. "*What* ferry?"

The dark bar-parlor was becoming clearer now; there on the walls were the Inevitable Powers, side by side . . . sider by sider on the local walls than they usually ever were in real life: The Queen's Own Majesty, in a long gown decorated with some sort of Order, and what Limekiller (having seen it, even, a million times in Canada, let alone British Hidalgo) thought of as The Royal Simper . . . this, on the Queen, not her gown . . . and, wearing a short-sleeved shirt open at the neck, and a cheerful grin, the Honorable Llewellyn Gonzaga MacBride, the Queen's Chief Minister: here-abouts. The Spyglass's walls were even more loyal than most: there

was also a fairly new photograph of Sir Joshua Cummings, the Royal
Governor, looking tickled pink in his official bicorn hat with dodo
feathers or whatever the hell they were — and if *that* were not
enough, there was even an old, old, very old photograph of *De W'old
King*, several kings or so ago, wearing an admiral's uniform, a beard,
and a look of such glassy-eyed rectitude and flexible stupidity as
made Limekiller's heart swell with loyalty to the House of Windsor
and all its works . . . but perhaps this was only the rum . . .

"Grandy *Smith* ferry," said Miss -*ita*, barely able to conceal her
scorn at the ignorance of Bathsheba's bondsman.

Limekiller still looking blank, it was explained to him that there
was a Mrs. Widow Smith, who held, by grandfather (or perhaps
great-grandfather) clause and/or other immemorial usage dating
from such time when the memory of man runneth not to the
contrary (in King Town, say, around 1936), the right to row of pole
passengers across the First (or, Belinda) River in a small boat, from
Shipwright Lane on one side to Humble's Wharf on the other; and
to exact for this service the immense fare of five cents: "One simply
stands as near the shore as possible without sinking into the ooze,
and shouts and wigwags; after a while she trots out of her cottage
and waves her apron, and at this point a young girl, aged about
twelve, appears in the boat and takes one across. Mrs. Smith has
innumerable descendants, all of whom seem to be young girls aged
about twelve . . . *Strong* ones. — Sad scene back there at the Pelican,
eh Limekiller?"

"'*Sad?*'" Limekiller.

"*Tchuh!*" — Miss -*ita*.

"What was that?" — Superintendent Cumberbatch. Informed
that *that* was "tormenting little Will Wiggins again," the
Superintendent gave a sigh, and shook his head. "Bad scene, eh,
Mr. Limekiller?"

"'*Bad?*' I think it was absolutely the worst scene I have ever
witnessed. Worse, in fact, than the one which brought me before
you . . . *that* time."

That time. Early on in his stay in the country, Jack, merely
relaxing on a bench in what was officially named Queen Adelaide
Triangle, but seldom called anything but Jack-ass Junction since
donkey-carts had once gathered there to ply for hire (allegedly they
had been banned because Lady Stoniecroft, the long-ago
Governor's wife, had suffered extreme shock at the sight of seeing
one or more of the animals in that state of extreme good health for

which the jack-ass is famous . . . or *was*, when the jack-ass was more numerous, and, hence, more often seen, flaccid, retracted, or Otherwise) – merely relaxing on a bench, shared by someone of whom he had noticed nothing more than a tendency towards narcolepsy; Jack had been frightened almost to the point of falling *off* the bench when the bench's fellow-passenger had suddenly jerked awake and simultaneously began (a) to utter hideous screams, and (b) to fall upon Limekiller with blows and kicks too uncoördinated not to be easily resisted; they had both been almost immediately trotted off to "gaol" by a pair of police constables: hence Jack's first interview with the Superintendent.

"Of course Mr. Limekiller was released at once . . . '*Almost* at once . . . ?' . . . well, it might be so, my dear Mr. John; it took a bit of time to draw up the Report; you don't mind, I'm sure . . . As for the other chap, poor chap, we simply tidied him up and put him on the *Great Westerner* truck with instructions to the driver not to let him off before Gangalong Grove, where his proper home was, he had people there to take care of him . . . *odd* affliction, is it not so, Professor, suffering from nightmares in the day-time?"

Professor Brolly (Jack, sipping rum and lime and melted ice-water, had a sudden vision of the Professor seated in the tiny wherry and being ferried across with his umbrella carefully opened and covering his head; imperturbably his own master in whatever craft) said, "The ephialtes may attack at noon as well as midnight." He brushed his bushy moustachioes up with a single finger, right-side, left-side.

Miss -*ita* looked as though she were wanting very much to say, "*Tchuh!*" once more, but she did not say; Cumberbatch said, "*The* . . . ?" and paused, polite, expectant.

"The ephialtes. Perhaps you may know them as the epialtes."

Clinkle-clinkle. – the ice in Jack's glass. He refreshed it from the chaparita; squeezed in some more lime: keep away the dreaded scurvy; *whose* discovery? Captain Cook's, maybe. Was said to have sailed these waters as a younger man. If so, in either case, had either experience helped him at the end? Ha.

"No," said the Superintendent, without pretense that the word was on the tip of his tongue. "I believe not. Tell me."

"I shall," Professor Brolly said. "Greek word. Word*s*. Literally? '*On-leapers*.' Cognate with our English word, *elves*. Nothing playful about the ephialtes, though. The incubus, the demon who sits on one's chest. Causes nightmares, fevers, chills and–"

"*No tahk aboet eet!*" – Miss -*ita* suddenly found more words to say than, "*Tchuh!*" And electric sparks went on and off inside Limekiller's head.

"Time for my tiffin," said Professor Brolly, very calmly. His comment not desired? *Very* well, then: it had never been made. He gathered his solid body and arose. "Nice to have met you all agayn. *Day*: Superintendent. Miss Muñoz. Limekiller." He bowed slightly, tucked the bumbershoot under his arm, and departed. Miss Muñoz was meeting nobody's eyes; her expression was something more than merely sulky, now. Superintendent Cumberbatch's eyes, however, met Limekiller's. Their lack of expression was extremely expressive. Whatever had now to be worked out between C.E.A. Cumberbatch and Miss -*ita* Muñoz, the presence of a third party would not assist. Cumberbatch was off duty? Limekiller had best get *on* duty.

*Ro*sita! *That* was it! Not that it much mattered; if he, J. Lutwidge Limekiller, owner and master of the boat *Saccharissa*, now standing in King Town harbor with all her apparel etc etc, – if he bore the visible brand of Bathsheba (was he quite sure he *liked* that? Bathsheba was very *nice*, to be sure, and this and that and the other thing, and particularly one certain Other Thing; and, she being both very desirable and very desired, it was as though her favored man wore, himself, something like an Order . . . *still* . . .), then, certainly, Rosita Muñoz, he now had been for some while realizing, bore that of Clement Edward Alfred Cumberbatch, one of H.M.'s Superintendents of Police . . . on duty or *off*: a good thing to know. And to remember.

Jack's thanks, his polite farewells, his hopes of meeting them both in the near future, were received with impeccable amicable politeness by the gentleman. The lady made some small soft movement and some small soft sound. Not particularly joyous ones.

But at any rate she did not say, "*Tchuh!*"

The Fort Benbow Hotel was very much like the Empress Hotel in Victoria, in that it served afternoon tea; otherwise it was not much like the Empress Hotel in Victoria. Jack had not really been much of an afternoon tea addict, and the current CO of the Tea Ceremony in the Fort Benbow knew even less about it than *he*: horrid brew. Still. One must show the flag; in he went, mingled, sat, had tea: listened. Sooner or later, someone would say it. All the *its* which, seemingly, somehow had to be said, in the posh Fort Benbow.

And sooner or later, someone *did* say it: that This country was The End of the Line. And someone else said, again, Be that as it may This country was small enough to put your arms around and Love. And, so, inevitably, someone said, But that it was *odd*, though, what had happened to the Old Kingdom Chipchaks (again).

And, since hardly anyone who had lived here any length of time wanted *very* much to go through all of this all over again . . . and over and over and over . . . someone who *had* to be new here had asked, *What* had happened to the old Kingdom Chipchaks? Limekiller at this point eyed the door. "*Ah*," came the swift answer to the question, "*That is what's so odd*!"

The Chipchak Indians had developed a very high level of culture in what was now British Hidalgo. *Quite* large buildings. Temples, and . . . ah . . . *temples*. Very large temples. Ruins scarcely touched by archeologists, you know. And then, for some reason still a mystery, the whole Chipchak nation had simply picked up and *moved*. En masse. Hundreds of miles. Into what was now the Republic of Saragosa. And had there rebuilt their entire civilization . . . ("And their temples?") *And* their *temples*; quite. And, as the "*New* Kingdom" Chipchaks, had re-flourished, until conquered by the Hutecs, who had in turn been conquered by the Spaniards. And no one had any idea *why*!

Why the Chipchaks had moved, that is.

"My word."

"Well, for gosh sakes."

Pause. Limekiller, and nor he alone, eyed the door again. But the door was too far, the crowd was too thick, and, besides, a possible charter to go sailing off to see some nice Old Kingdom Chipchak ruins (*The* most damnably dull-looking ruins ever ruined, and quite over canopied with undergrowth and overgrowth a lot more troublesome than if with luscious woodbine, sweet musk-roses, or with eglantine) . . . was, well, a possible charter. And, so, not to be spat upon.

Even a charter de facto, if not de jure; *possible conversation*, "Now, Mr. Limekiller, we here in Government do not wish to make things difficult for you, but we have our laws as any nation has and so we must investigate possible violations thereof; is it true that from Wednesday last to Monday this, you were carrying a party of tourists on excursion, and without having a proper license for same, sir?" – "Well, Chief Supervisor, no, not really, I was merely showing some visiting businessmen some land I own down at Wherever, with a view to their possibly buying it; for which as I am sure you know, Chief Supervisor, no license is required." "Oh. Ah. I see. Yes. Quite so. The Ordinance . . . The Statute . . . We are so very understaffed here at Government, Mr. Limekiller that sometimes oversights . . . Oh no, thank *you*, Mr. Limekiller!"

Two reasons for not waiting till meeting Bathsheba at the stroke of ten in order to eat. *First.* It was absolutely certain she would say, "I ate at my auntie." *Second.* It was absolutely certain that Jack was hungry *now*. A paradox: that, whilst Bayfolk home-cooking is as good a style of home-cooking to be found anywhere and better than manywhere, Bayfolk home-cooking almost never reaches the cook-rooms of Bayfolk restaurants. Crab soup with crab spawn? Venison with crabboo-fruit? Turtle stew? Cowtail braised and made with broth? Coconut bread? Mango jelly? And more and more and – Yum *Yum.* But.

But, somehow, Limekiller did not know why, it was almost never that one found any such thing in any King Town restaurant, the home of the Fry Chicken, the Hom Somwich, and the Tin Soup. *Why?* Odd.

There was also, yes indeed, "Spanish" food, very little like Mexican food (equally very little like Spanish food sans quotes), but certainly a change from Tin Soup (it came in *tins*, is why), Hom Somwich, and Fry Chicken: but Spanish Town was perhaps just a bit further than he cared just now to walk; the Grand Shanghai was what destiny seemed to have in store for Limekiller tonight; and, as he entered its doors, he at once perceived what else destiny (*karma*, he felt now he had to call it) had in store for him tonight, viz. Mrs. and Dr. Duckerson: "Why, you jist sut right down and have your dunner wuth us, Mr. Limekuller," said Mrs. Duckerson: she was short. But she was sturdy.

Down he sat.

"Doctor and me we saw *the* most puttiful case taday," said she. "Man was I mean to tell you jist all cruppled up; soon's he heard who Doctor was, well of course he wanned a git a nad*just*munt; but Doctor he hadda uxplain a him that he is not *lye*-sinced to practice down here; oh how he dud plead and carry on. Have the chucken chow mein, Muster Limekuller."

*Doct*or Duckerson paused with a forkful of what was, presumably the chicken chow mein, although very often even The Third Eye could not disclose the mysteries of what one ate at the Grand Shanghai regardless of what one had ordered. "Subluxation of your third vertebrar," said Doctor Duckerson. "*I* say that subluxations of your third vertebrar cause more of your so-called civilized ills and ailments than any single subluxation of any of your other vertebrar; now –"

"Eatcher dunner, Daddy," said Mrs. Duckerson, who had perhaps heard more about your third vertebra and its subluxations back in Cowpat, Kansas, or Buffalo Bleep, B.C., than had been required by marriage ceremony.

Doctor's question, slightly filtered through his forkful or Good Enough For Round Eyes, seemed to say something like Now what about our little trip Mr. Limeskinner; but he was for the moment over-ruled. "Lettum eat hus dunner, Daddy," said Mrs. Duckerson.

One of the reasons why Limekiller had been avoiding close and frequent contact with Mrs. and Dr. Duckerson was the matter of what she (echoed through Doctor's/Daddy's shredded yard-fowl and whatever Mesoamerican substitutes for Chinese vegetables was most recently found most economical by the management of the Grand Shanghai) had been referring to on and off as "Our luttle trup" – the destination of our luttle trup was Limekiller's little piece of land at Flower Bight. And he hadn't been wanting to make it.

Not since he had made the close acquaintance of Bathsheba. Anyway.

On the one hand, Jack would have wished to prolong his meal in hopes that perhaps the Duckersons might tire of waiting and so depart without his having to make any statement positive or negative. And on the one hand, the nature of his meal was not such as to encourage him to prolong it at all. Although not precisely a *feinshmecker*, or gourmet – a tour of duty out of the Royal Canadian Naval base at Esquimault had cured him of any tendency towards finickly eating, as what tour of duty out of what naval base wouldn't? – he was not invariably averse to complaining about some dish particularly deficient in edibility: wherever. But tonight's waiter on-duty at the Grand Shanghai bore upon his very scrutable countenance such a look of deepest melancholy, reflective perhaps of a time there was e'er China's woes began (say, about the 3rd century before the Christian Era) that Limekiller's heart, not the very hardest article at all times, smote and prevented him.

So, by and by, and after the final cup of tea (the nature of which might well have caused riots and/or wall posters in either China), he shoved away his dinnerware and faced The Question.

"Now what about our luttle trup, Mr. Limekuller?"

"Momma nye been lookin forward to it oh ever since we heard aboutcher piece a propitty fer sale down there, Mr. Limeskinner."

"'Flower Bight,' now I think that's ever such a nice lul name, whut *kine* da flowers would they be, Mr. Limekuller."

Jack indicated vaguely they'd be all kinds of flowers such as one finds in these parts ("In season, of course," he added); he did not feel up to explaining that the Bight was supposedly named for one Flowers, perhaps originally *Flores*, perhaps not, who had either hanged someone for piracy there long long ago, or had been hanged by someone there for the same crime, or even perhaps both, though probably not simultaneously: then again, considering the Hidalgoan Method of Historical Construction, Flowers (or Flores: names had a way of changing here as they crossed the Spanish River in either direction) had merely perhaps complained of being charged sixpence more for a bag of nails than he considered right, *Mahn be no better nor a pirate!* the complaint may have gone; what time he or someone next to he in a dram shop or punch house at that moment may have echoed, *Mahn should be honed, dom pirate!* and someone else, hearing or likelier half-hearing may have lurched away home, via a longish sea-voyage and replied at its end to *What News?* with *Flowers, he hong one pirate*, or even, for by that time all details would have become mazy and muzzy, *One pirate, he hong Flowers* . . . there were enough men named Flowers to go around; and by the time the story had been told either way and not even very often, it would have become fact. *If I tell you three times, it is true*, was a basic principle of the Hidalgoan Method of Historical Construction. – And, very often, *If I tell* me *three times* . . . or maybe only one or two times would have done. It often did; and not only in Hidalgo.

"Momma nye we been looking fra nice place to build us a place to spend the real cold months –" Jack knew those months and winters.

"*Oh* them cold wunters, they wull kull us if we don't git away and put a locum in charge from anyway December through March –" And Doctor added, gloomily, Not that finding a good locums was a very easy thing nowadays. (Particularly, Jack thought, one who was fully aware of everything involved by your subluxations of your third vertebrar: suddenly he could stand no more of it.)

"Folks, I have some particular business to attend to in a half an hour or so, and after that it will be too late to get in touch with you. Can I talk to you again in the morning? The, ah," he hastily took a quick peek into his private life, "*later* morning?

Doctor gave a sort of affirmative confirmatory grunt and Mrs. Doctor looked at him with birdy-bright eyes; Jack suddenly had a sort of satori that neither one of them was as ding-dong dumb as he had taken for granted: they might, in fact, know all about him and . . . there being very few secrets in British Hidalgo . . . Bathsheba . . . they might, satori succeeding satori, even be able to figure it out for themselves: even the Mrs. and Doctor Duckersons of this world have by now learned about *That*; for all *he* knew, they might even be just as *good* at it; furthermore Jack, with a rush and a flush and a flash back to the days when he stealthily examined the palms of his hands, plus a flash and a rush to a future he did not much anticipate, but *still*, had a fairly clear scene of some wheat farmer and/or timber-topper confiding an Intimate Problem to Doctor and being informed, "Your subluxation of your third verte-brar is a particular source of common difficulties in your sectial activities; take yer shirt off and git up on that table . . ."

"Why of course, Mr. Limekuller," said Mrs. Doctor: "We retire on the dot of mudnight and we do not retire un*tull* the dot of mudnight. You kin call us tull then, or, like you say, later on in the morning. We are stopping at the Ruvver View Hotel, any time."

Jack, hasting along with long strides towards the Pelican, observed that the clock on one of the cathedrals stood at ten to ten; he would just make it; there was luckily no chance of the Swing Bridge doing any Swinging at *this* hour: not even Governor Sir Joshua Cummings, were he suddenly to decide on a moonlight cruise, would be able to bring the bridge captains back to the capstan at this hour, and would either have to unstep his mast or forget about it: common sense suddenly told him that the Governor's boat must be moored by Government House, down-river from the Bridge, anyway. Anyway, what was his hurry? Either Bathsheba would be late, and full of explanations involving her aunties, or, if on time, she would, if *he* were late, instantly involve herself in some conversation with, well, *any*one: and wait for him.

His hurry was, he told himself, that he was very much in like with Bathsheba, and wanted simply very much to be with her again. And, *You lying, horny, son of a bitch, he answered himself*. . .

Coming from the side lanes to the main streets he entered a stream of human traffic perhaps even thicker than in the heat of the day; *was* that Bathsheba's back he saw ahead there, two blocks away? He would give her a hail, and – She moved from the dimlight into the full glare of a streetlight: certainly it was Bathsheba he had seen ahead of him at least twice that afternoon, at the Swing Bridge and – walking next to her, and on the inside, as though having never heard that a gentleman walks on the outside, was certainly no gentleman: it was his back, too, which Jack had seen . . . vaguely he felt he knew *whose*, but he was after all not immensely familiar with every back in town:

He quickened (as they used to say) his steps:

But, they two evidently having turned into any one of several lanes, find them he could not.

Perhaps he had been mistaken.

He stepped into the yard and was halfway across when the bell of another cathedral began to ring. It had not yet told its full tale of ten when he had scanned every female face in the bars Bathsheba was not there.

Lots of other people there, though. Many more than usual. Ha. Of course. All the not-every-night-regular faces were White tonight. Which meant that whichever battalions of the Right Royal Regiment had been off on manoeuvres in the Bush were now returned. *Whooppee!* He would grab Bathsheba and they would go somewhere else and have a drink or so, before – Well, he would if he could find her. He ordered a-then-and-there-drink and stood with his back to the bar and as near to the door as he could, upon an impulse so sudden he hardly realized what he was doing, he left the bar and was circumnavigating the block; he would find her and escort her back, thus preventing any of the Right Royal from intercepting and offering her some frightful insult, which she, unsophisticated daughter-child of this tropical Eden, might not instantly recognize as such: it was not only a damned odd-shaped block, it was a damned *long* block: coming back in the door of the Pelican Bar and not even giving a look to see was his drink still there, *there*, not *there*, but there, in the middle of the bar-room floor (the partition having been removed in his absence), amidst the other dancers (music by juke-box) was either Herb or Hughy or Alfy or Dicky – there were not a great number of given names in this particular mob of Licentious Soldiery (something missing from that quotation? let it wait) – dancing not precisely cheek-to-cheek, he was snugly pressed up against the fore-front of and was clutching both of Bathsheba's buttocks in his very large hands . . .

She swum right around and, seeing Limekiller there, made some sound he could not hear, he only saw her mouth moving . . . for a moment . . . then she had disengaged herself from Dicky (Hughy – Alfy – Herb) and hot-tailed it (*le mot juste*, murmured a bitter little voice in Limekiller's suddenly hot ears) either to the ladies' room or the back door – they lay along the same passageway –

And her soldier (and anyone less-aunty-like could not have been imagined: but sure it was him she had been with ever since leaving Jack earlier that day . . . *not*, however, before collecting the twenty dollars National Currency), having first turned and gaped after her, now turned, gaping still; and, seeing Limekiller, stood facing him with his legs slightly apart and his hands at his sides: they were not yet formed into fists, but – And on his face a look mingled of sheepishness, truculence, and –

Brutal. Was the missing word. *Whose?* A Brutal and Licentious Soldiery: who gave a good dribbly-shit *whose*?

Moved by some sudden, secret, and unseemly thought, and knowing all the while that the thought was not at all a nice one; but *moved*; Limekiller turned on his heel and left the bar, walking very rapidly. Once inside the hotel he restrained himself from galloping up the stairs, there was the room, here was the key, the door opened, the light switched on, there was the still-rumpled bed and he was sure there had been no pillow lying in the middle of it when he had left the room and he buffetted it to one side –

Someone, and someone male, had left his signature upon the sheet.

And the ink was still wet.

The soldier did not seem to have moved in the meanwhile.

Limekiller thrust his hand deep into his right-hand pocket. Hughy (Alfy? Dicky? Herb?) flinched very slightly and prepared to assume a stance. Limekiller tossed something through the air; the soldier flinched again, ducked only slightly, but did catch it – give him that – and, forgetful for the moment of a possible sudden onslaught, glanced at it.

It was a huge oval of ornately embossed and engraved leather, one of the few surviving from the Pelican's better days, and attached to it was the comparatively small key.

Lance-corporal Throstlethwaite or Thimblepate or whatever his name was, simply went on standing there, holding it. Not no *fooking knife.* Not *no fooking grenade.* He was, for the moment, more puzzled than fight-prone.

"You can use the same towel, too," Limekiller said.

Turned and left.

In the street, darkness alternating with lamp-glare, he told himself, Well, what about it? She was your whore, you were her john. Business is business, no banns were read, she's got a perfect right to . . . No, not in the bed he paid for; she hasn't got–

Then he stopped and clapped one hand to his head. But what was the woman's reason, not for what she did, but for how she *did* it? Why had she told him to, meet him there "at the stroke of ten," when she intended to appear there with another man at the same stroke? It beat the be-jesus out of him to figure that out; but, as is usual in such times, after considering his heart and his pride, next he considered his purse: *Fifteen dollah fah one night,* fiddlesticks: Twice the same amount per diem would not have covered it all (and fifteen dollars a week was a tolerable local wage for harder work than that), beginning with . . . beginning with . . . well, never mind what it had begun with, the affair had contained no sordid matter of wages-and-hours disputes: consider the gold earrings he had bought, innocently without considering whether they were for pierced ears or not; they were, hers weren't, she snatched them out of his palm with cries of, "Oh, for them, for *them,* I *will* have my ears pierced!" – whatever had been pierced in this *petite affaire* had not been Bathsheba's ears.

What *had* she done with them? Sold them? Traded then for some other jewelry? Or, like what's her name in the Bible, traded them like the mandrakes for another man? He would never know now, and, had he asked her earlier, likely not even then . . . "Dese women here," someone had said, moodily, and in no joyful mood either, "even when got nutting to gain by tell lie, tell lie anyway, juss fah keep in proctice, mon." – and his friend nodded a nod of sad experience, adding, "Ahn why dey wear dem tight frock even when so *hot,* mon? To mehk ah mahn w'only *luss,* mon; *why.*"

Well, lust, love, or lunacy, it was all new and hot and hurtful, and hateful, whore or no whore: it all hurt; only that one puzzle remained: *why* had she made such a precise date? in order to present him with his successor? to make the case quite plain? to prevent boring discussion? to increase her self-esteem by having two men (at least two . . . and who knew how big the brawl might have grown?) publicly fighting over her?

It might have been any of these, it might have been all of these, it suddenly occurred to Limekiller that neither Bathsheba nor any of her lady friends had ever really shown the slightest actual interest in keeping appointments by clocks, or in other quanta of time, and also it suddenly occurred to him that the switch-over could not have been for purely professional reasons, for lance-corporals in the British Army earned barely enough for buy beef, let alone for pickles, too: therefore her reason might well have been none of these: her lovely little head had very little in it, lovely or otherwise; her arrival with her soldier in the Pelican Bar at nearly the stroke of ten (and ten would be about the lance-corporal's quota, Limekiller thought, bitter, jealous) was, then, purely a coincidence and she had simply forgotten not only all about her appointment with Limekiller but all about Limekiller himself –

– and this, the likeliest of reasons, hurt more, far more than all the others, "'*Love me little, not for long,' is the burden of my song . . .*"

Where the hell *was* he . . . *now*?

The display of well-worn Japanese lanterns told him soon: alongside of the River View Hotel; in he went, it was not yet eleven, let alone mudnight: there sat Mrs. and Dr. Duckerson, looking comfy and content and sipping at straws in tall glasses jammed with ice and fruit and something (maybe) not approved by the Palmer College of Chiropractic. They greeted him with placid chirps.

"Ready to start tomorrow morning, early?" he fired his starboard gun.

Doctor considered, Mrs. Doctor had perhaps already considered. "*Well,* Muster Limekuller, I am *so* glad that chore other business is all taken care of and that we kin finely git started on our luttle trup, but now what *I* think, I think that tomorrow morning, early, is jist a luttle *too soon,* what do you think, Daddy?"

"Think so, too," thought Daddy. Added that he would Tell Him What: "Split the difference. Commence the charter as of when the sun is at high meridian tamorra (nuther words: *noon*) and leave day *after* tamorra, early. Give *us* time to get ready, give *you* time to get ready. *Kay?*"

"And meanwhile sut down and join us in one of these putcheresque native drinks," invited Mrs.

But Jack was in no mood for such liquid even if slightly alcoholic fruit salads, which no native would willingly have drunk, anyway. He had become more rational very rapidly, made polite rational thanks and polite rational excuses, accepted the revised rational time-table. And left.

The Bucket of Blood held at least equal dishonors as Worst Dive in Town, the Poor Man Port had its own vigorous advocates, the Bucket of Blood was nearer. It was reached via a boggy yard; "If me customer gweyn *fahl,* time he leave," said Bitty Billy Blood, the licensee, "I want he fahl *sahft,* live come bock ah nudder day." "Stone dead hath no fellow," was Our Mr. Limekiller's comment. "Fah true, Johnny," was the reply.

Usually The Bucket was lit by a gruesomely ghastly bluery-greenery-flickery fluorescenty tube, much admired by locals. Tonight, however, this damnable engine, to Jack's expressible relief, had already flickered its last deathlight flicker, had joined Stone Dead, and, the tube having no fellow, The Bucket was lit by and only by three small thin candles. It looked, smelled, and sounded just like the middle of the 18th century – ex*act*ly, felt J.L.L., the right century for his present mood:

"A curse upon the Spanish Dons," he announced, just to firm the matter. "God save the King Across the Water," he added. "'The woman's a whore, and there's an end on't,'" he quoted. "A chaparita of your incomparable cattle piss, Billy Blood," he ordered; "and spare the ice as not being natural and the water as conducive to fluxes and phlegms; goddamn bitch whore tramp trull trolloppe drab *slut,*" he shut his mouth and opened it again only to allow the passage of the trash rum; it resisted slightly.

"Mon," said Bitty Bill, raking the shillings, "soun' to me, you hahve mah*co*by tonight."

"Any mahn hahve woman, hahve mah*co*by," said a bystander . . . by-*drink*er, rather; and evidently an experienced lay-analyst. Mah*co*by: rich, evocative, poignant Bayfolk word: untranslatable to Standard English save by many, *many* words: *hell* with that.

"Any cure for it?" asked Limekiller, with a slight gasp: The Bucket's rum was *rough*, and Bitty Billy Blood did not even dilute it to the full measure by law allowed.

"*Yes*," said Bitty Bill, firmly. "Drink shitty canal wahtah."

Limekiller pondered this alleged remedy and all its implications for a moment or so.

Then he went back to the rum.

Jumble beans.

Now, had either the United Church of Canada or the Continuing Presbyterian Church thereof been in charge of Jack's constitution (repatriated or otherwise), he would and should have awakened with all the full horrors of hangover, but – and although the words *drunkenness and fornication* did mumble faintly in his ears – he merely felt faintly faint and queasy as the rosy-fingered dawn poked him in both eyes. So much for his ears and eyes; his *mouth*? God's Wownds. His *nose*? His nose reminded him that he was moored off Corn Meal Wharf and that on Corn Meal Wharf Grandy Janedy always had a pot (a cauldron, rather) of cow-foot soup for sale to early-bird boatmen. He was somewhat draggy, getting to her stall, but once there no words were necessary. He didn't even need to point, just gave over a shilling, helped himself to a battered bowl and spoon, she dipped him a dipper of the gluey but *oh*-so-savory and nourishing pottage, he sat down on the curb, clattered a moment with the spoon, then simply lifted the bowl, and drank . . . and drank . . . with occasional pauses to chew the solids . . . which by now were fairly soft and merely semi-solids anyway . . . *and drank* . . .

Immediately he felt better. After a second bowl he felt fairly fine. Grandy Janedy, understanding All, had allowed him his silence. For a while. He no longer needing it, "I see you does have you jumble beans," said the oldest practicing alchemist in King Town.

"Beg pardon, Grandy Janedy?"

"You jumble beans . . . Dot is good." She had made a gesture before turning to another customer. Limekiller looked where she had pointed. On his left wrist was a, well, a sort of bracelet of strong thread on which were threaded a number of black-and-red colored berries. He would not have thought of them as *beans*, but, what the hell. *Funny* thing to wake up with: much to be preferred, however, to a tattoo and a case of clap. In between each "bean" was a knot, and, seaman though he thought himself to be, these knots he did not recognize. Well . . . *Oh* –

Yes. He had "shouted" a drink of rum for an old Baywoman, in The Bucket, last night, and he retained some morsel of memory of her placing the bracelet round his wrist. What it meant, *God* only knew, maybe they had plighted their troth; at this hour of the day and after those hours of the night, if Brandy Janedy's only comment was, *good*, well, so be it and be it so: instantly he forgot all about it, and, handing back bowl and spoon and adding his thanks, he considered the tasks the day held for him.

The voyage, or Luttle Trup, as he by now half-thought of it himself, could not last less than one long day, and *could* last as long as two. Or three. Fresh or even cooked meat could last as long as the ice, and the ice, in the styrofoam cooler, would last . . . well . . . not very long. Fish he might catch, he might not, the Duckersons might like the way he cooked it, they might not, Mrs. Duckerson might wish to cook it herself, she might not. *So*: canned goods (*tinned*, here), and in sufficient quantity, was a must. Rice and beans and the coconut oil to cook them with *would* they eat them/it? He had found that adding annatto, the native . . . was it pimiento? . . . added not only an exotic taste but also a reddish-orange color; otherwise, "rice-ahn-bean" did tend to look lustreless; Jack himself was not an annatto fan especially, but business was business. *Fruit*: yes! fresh fruit. Bananas for snacks, plantains to cook, breadfruit chiefly so that they could say they'd eaten breadfruit, maybe find some good oranges *and* if lucky something both unusual and tasty enough to bother taking. Star-apple, mawmee-apple, if in season –

Had he thought, when contemplating with joy the prospect of restoring his newly-acquired (but oh by no means new) boat from its draggle-tailed and half-tipsy state, that in becoming a boatman he would become a caterer, too? *No*, he had *not* –

– What might be in season, though, might not necessarily be on sale in the Central, or Main, Market (or any other King Town market, for that matter). It had, early-on, seemed to him that the local economy had holes in it, large and gaping holes in the matter not so much of production (it had those, too) but of distribution; and he had the flashing thought that somehow he might help fill those holes; he was awhile in finding out that this amounted to hoping to fill the holes in a piece of lace: the holes were part of the pattern.

Time for a drink.

By the rarest coincidence, there was the Democracy Club, aptly-named, and wide open for trade: *tlot-tlot*: in he went; "Hello, John," said a familiar voice in familiar tones. In what war in which regiment Pygore had served as Colonel, Limekiller did not know, anymore than he knew why Pygore was as Pygore was: *unless.*

"Hello, Peter, Have a drink."

"Thank you. I have a drink." And almost always did have. His tired eyes surveyed Limekiller. Blinked once. Said, "Not afraid to stand beneath the ceiba tree, I see." Limekiller followed this not.

"Why? Something crap on my head?" Raised one hand to test, gingerly. Caught sight of the black-and-red berries on his left wrist: he hadn't noticed that some fibre smooth but oddly-spun was wrapped around the more common cotton thread. *Ceiba.* So that was it: the so-called silky-tree or silk-cotton tree or wild-cotton tree or kapock – or was it pollack-tree? Damned tree had too damned many *names*; "devil-tree," that was another one. It was a damned big tree, too. And there was nothing nasty on his head. He had misunderstood. Oblique Peter Pygore . . .

Limekiller signalled a drink. Asked, "Why should you call these, 'jumble beans'?"

"I shouldn't, I should call them 'jungle-beads,'" Pygore said. Or had he said something else? People had heard.

People looked; well, *some* people looked; someone said, "You go jungle side, make sense wear jungle bead."

Someone else said, "*Me* not gweyn jungle side," with an air of emphasis and determination.

Someone else, yet, said, "Suppose jungle come *you* side? Maybe you sorry you *not* wear jungle bead, nah true?"

But the first someone else did not respond with "fah true," or anything like it. What he responded with – and a look of scorn and distaste at Jack's funny wristlet – was the odd comment (and it had, somehow, the sound of a quote): "'Who do good fi jungle, is dem jungle does fright.'"

Now there were sounds of disagreement around the tables. "Mon, wear jungle beans not '*do good fi jungle.*'" "No, mon, '*do good fi jungle,*' mean —"

But Jack was not to hear what it meant, for at that moment, a voice — and, again, a *woman* said, in a low tone of deep intensity — said: *again*: those words which he had heard . . . and heard and heard . . . recently, namely, "*No tahk aboet eet!*"

He had been totally puzzled by almost all the conversation following the original comment on the wristlet; now was moved beyond puzzlement into both irritation and a rather unusual display of temper; he brought his glass down, *slam*, on the bar. He said, "Damn it, damn it! What the hell *are* all these jungle things which people keep saying, 'Don't talk about it'?"

Deep silence.

And a very tall, very imposing, very *black* Black man, who had not turned before, although right next to Jack, turned now, and said, "Well, Mr. Limekiller, sir, if many people or even *any* people ask not to talk about a certain subject, whatever subject, is it not perhaps the better part tact, sir, *not* to —"

"*Not* to talk about it; very well, sir: rebuke taken, silence is golden, pray pardon, ladies and gentlemen," and, while polite murmurs indicative that he had perhaps apologized more than the offense required were still being murmured, Jack, carried on by momentum, said, "— but I don't even understand why all of a sudden people seemed to have started calling it *jungle* when ever since I've been here everybody I would swear calls it *bush*?"

Some of those who had become so suddenly so deeply silent now continued so; some sounds of scoffing, some of snorting, were heard. A tentative laugh, soon ceased. Odd looks at Limekiller. And Col. Peter Pygore, who had first spoken, said, "Oh, John L., you are sometimes too much," and gave his head a weary shake. And added, "Verger, *you* tell him. Whisper it in his shell-like little ear."

"I could *hit* you, you know, Pygore."

Peter Pygore, gaunt and grey, stopped being a cynic, became a stoic. "Limekiller, it does not lie within my power to prevent you."

The very tall, very imposing, very *black* Black man, now said, "I suggest, Mr. Limekiller, that we move our glahsses . . . with Col. Pygore's leave? . . . to Col. Pygore's table;" this was done, and so, of course brawling had become impossible; the rest of the room, like the rest of the world, carried on with its own affairs as busy as before: politics, horse-races, infant baptism, new linoleum, prices, prices, costs, costs, my turn to buy, your turn to drink: The Man of Mien now did indeed say, if not in an exact whisper, then in a voice low but clear, into Jack's ear, "The word in question, Mr. Limekiller, is not *jungle*. It is *jumby*." And added, Jack not having moved, his mind not having yet assimilated the correction, "Of course, as a Christian, sir, and after all, I *am* verger at St. Alfred;" St. Alfred was *the* Anglican Church, after of course the Cathedral; "so I can give no credence to such superstition. I merely define the terms . . ."

Jack now remembered him, and recollected his name. "Mr. Ethelred, you will have to define the terms more clearly," he said. *Jumby* beads? *Jumby* side? – "side" in, the local sense of place or direction? – Do *good* for *jumby*? "Because I still don't –"

Peter Pygore now said, and Limekiller could sense the effort he made to sound neither weary, scornful, nor patronizing, "'*Jumby*,' John, is what in some other Caribbean places is called '*Duppy*.'"

Limekiller said, "Oh." He had heard of that; that is, he had read about it. Back in Canada. One did not *hear* the word there, it was not a household word, exactly, like *bath* or *chesterfield*. "It's a spook . . . sort of . . . you might say . . ."

"You might," said Peter Pygore.

"You might," said Verger Edward Ethelred. Added, "But I am an Anglican, and I do not believe in such things."

"But what the funk does it *mean*, really?" Limekiller had, as it were en route, slipped the *n* into the word as a sop to Mr. Ethelred's possible Anglican susceptibilities. "I mean –"

Pygore looked at him with tired, grey sunken eyes; eyes not made for such seas as these hereabouts. "It is *said*," he gave the verb passive a gentle emphasis, "that *duppy* derives from 'doppelgänger,' I believe . . ."

Another well-remembered voice; "Believe that, you'll believe anything." A finger swept up a bushy light-brown moustachio. A figure sat down.

"The matter immediately ceases to be mythological," said Peter Pygore, immediately becoming slightly less weary-and-fain-would-lie-doon; "and becomes grammatical."

"Hello, Professor," said Limekiller. A professorial nod to him, to the verger, the umbrella was set in the corner; perhaps – it was trotted along, wet *or* dry – perhap, was Jack's sudden enlivening thought, perhaps it contained a sword!

"'The thing contained within the thing,' or whatever the accepted gibberish is," Peter said. "I had better rephrase it. *Thus*: 'I believe that it is said that the word "*duppy*" derives from the word "doppel-gänger ". . .' *Now* what do you say?"

"I say I will accept it, put that way. But only," Professor Brolly cautioned, "put *that* way."

"How do *you* derive it, then?" – Peter Pygore

"*Oh*," the professor leaned back his chair against the wall, "I really do not de*rive* it. I believe . . . *I* believe . . . that it is almost certainly either an African or Amerindian word. And I would merely wish to point out the almost inevitable sequence and progression of the words *duppy* . . . *jumby* . . . *zomby* . . ."

Pygore at once leaned forward, his face at once alive. "I. Had. *Never. Thought.* Of *that.*"

It was Professor Brolly's turn to crow, and he took it. "I daresay *not*," he said, equitably. "But *I* had." It was a fairly mild crow.

Someone, the words and music of the immensely popular (*God* knows why) song *Move Up Now, Jamaica* (after all, this was not Jamaica and local enthusiasm for Jamaicans moving up, or, at any rate, across, into the Colony of British Hidalgo, was nil) blaring from a corner, now complained that the sound from the jukebox was "W'only sahft" – it was loud enough for Limekiller, who, pressed, would have declared his belief that it was loud enough for Moses . . . Peter, Paul, Silas . . . take your pick . . . and, certainly, loud enough for *him*. "Me pay me shilling," the protest went on, "so why me no hear me music bet-tah?"

The proprietor demanded to be told what he could do. "I ask Electric Williams," he said, "but he say he hahve to go fix light-*switches*, Government Hoess. So what I can *do*?"

The lover of loud music expressed his indifference if everyone in Government House went stone-*blind* before or after nightfall; but he had gone too far. "*Whattt*? Governor not refuse de R'yal Consent, new tox on *rum*? Close you moet, mon!" Sir Joshua Cummings had not indeed precisely refused the Royal Assent to the proposed new tax on rum; he had merely said (in writing) that "past experience had shown that when such excise tax was increased beyond a certain level, the major effect was a prolifera-tion of illicitly distilled spirits, with a loss rather than an increase of revenue to Government;" and had added his hope that the Legislature would see fit to take this aspect of the matter into consideration; it had. For the time being.

The faded blue walls would not jump tonight.

Or would jump less.

Jump . . . the verb struck faint signals in Limekiller's mind. But –

"– but, Haiti being a *Roman* country," Mr. Ethelred Edwards continued something Limekiller had missed; "there is inevitable more superstition, I hope I May use the word without offense to anyone present –" he paused . . . briefly . . . but either there were no highly active members of Catholic Action at the table, or else Mr. Ethelred was simply too, well, *big*; he went on: "But as for such belief that a sorcerer, or, as I believe the Haitian word is, *houngan*," for an Anglican, Mr. Ethelred's accent was anyway remarkably good; "can raise a corpse from a grave-site consecrated to Christian burial and make himself master of such corpse and use him or her for a slave, and a very economical one because requiring no food: *No* sir! There is *no* such belief or tradition or superstition in this colony at-*tahl!*"

Pygore was weary again. "Good," was his only, very faint, and perhaps only very faintly un-totally-convinced word on the subject.

Limekiller was just a while thoughtful. Then he asked, "Well, since there is no such superstition here, why are there, well, similar ones?"

Mr. Edwards said, "Well, you know, Mr. Limekiller, that this colony is not and it never was a sugar plantation colony – oh, we've had some such, and we have some such now, as a matter of fact: but not much. Not many. Ours has been a country with an economy based on forestry. And this has made . . . makes . . . an immense difference. I don't wish to go into the economic difference it makes, I will leave that to the learned gentlemen from the United Kingdom and the United States. But you *see*, Mr. Limekiller . . . One cuts the sugar cane regularly. And when it has been cut, the land is *bare*. Well, to be sure, the ratoons are still there, the roots, as it were. But, and this is my point, in a cut-over sugar field, there is no place for anything to hide. And, or rather should I say, but? – in a forest there is *every* place to hide. Because we never cut our forests bare the way you have done in North America. We cut the mahogany, but for each mahogany tree cut there are a hundred other trees left standing. Rosewood: same thing. Logwood: same thing. Cedar: same thing. Even more commonplace wood such as pine, 'emery, Santa Maria, sericoty: we cut selectively."

"Wise of you –"

"Oh, it is not wisdom, it is – but again: beside the point. And what is the point?" Outside an automobile went by, very very noisily. Verger Edwards inclined his head. "*That* is the point. Have you not noticed how the people here walk all over the roads and streets despite the automobiles? As if there *were* no automobiles? So different from either the United States or the United Kingdom? It is not because the people here are stupid, Mr. Limekiller –"

"I never said they *were.*"

"I know you never . . . But the reason is, you see, Mr. Limekiller, that, until very recently, there *were* no automobiles here! A fact, a *fact,* Mr. Limekiller! Do you know, sir, that when I was a boy – when *I* was a boy, there were only two motor vehicles in the entire colony? *No: three.* One was a truck, down in the Southern District, it had been shipped in from one of the Republics, and we never saw it here, because there were *no roads,* then, Mr. Limekiller! But *here,* here in King Town, there were only two automobiles. Only two! And one belonged to the Royal Governor! When I was a boy . . . and I am not yet forty years old, sir, not yet forty years old! In one generation we have moved . . . moved? we have jumped, leaped, been dragged, as it were, into the automobile age. There are now one thousand motor vehicles in this country, sir. One *thousand!*"

He paused to let this sink in. Jack felt it sinking. Then Verger Edwards went on, "We moved by boat, when, indeed, we did not move by foot or by horse or by mule. I can remember making a trip to visit my maternal uncle up in St. Michael's of the Mountains, it was during the War, and it took two weeks to get there . . . by boat, by boat! . . . coming back, it took but one week, we had the current behind us . . .

"Go down the coast from north to south or come up the coast from south to north, do you see any coastal highway with endless lines of cars? No. We have no coastal highway; we still have three incorporated townships, sir, with which there is no communication by road whatsoever . . . and only one of them even has an air*strip.* People move by water here, still, still, in this oh whatever is the year of the reign of our sovereign lady the Queen? Doesn't matter.

"If I had to sum up in one word the thing which distinguished our small settlements here from settlements of the same size in North America or England or Scotland, the word I should choose, should have to choose, is *isolation.* And this means that not alone the bodies of the People there, or their houses, were isolated – *sir:* their *minds* were often isolated: And, God knows how very often how isolated their *lives* were. We now have a radio system. *That helps.* We have books, magazines, newspapers . . . we have visitors, tourists, capitalists . . . But I feel almost less than a patriot if I have to explain to you, no, I can*not* explain to you, so I simply declare to you: in some places we are still living in the nineteenth century."

"Yes, I –"

"No, Mr. Limekiller, you *don't*: In some places we are still living in the *eighteenth* century:"

"Well –"

"There is no 'Well' about it! Mr. Limekiller, in some places, *we are still living in the* seventeenth *century* . . . ! Sounds which no one in your world has heard in living memory except perhaps in the farthest wilderness, almost everyone here has heard. The panther's scream: (The 'lion,' we call it here.) The wild hogs in their hundreds, like a flight of aëroplanes, they sound! Everything that moves, walks, or crawls or . . . or whatever . . . in *your* forests have been recognized and classified a thousand over. Even the creatures which are extinct, in *your* country, you know what they were, and you have their skins and bones in your museums: *But not here.* There are still things alive and quick in the remoter parts of our own nation, and if they do not seem remote upon the map, try to reach them, try to reach them by way of a path too narrow for a mule or along a stream which has to be portaged every quarter of a miles you will realize very soon how remote; there are things living there which have not only never been classified, they have scarcely ever been *seen!*

". . . sometimes their tracks have been seen . . . sometimes their dead and decomposed bodies have been seen . . . sometimes: *not* . . .

"– and so far I am speaking to you only of simple animals and reptiles and so on so forth: but there are other aspects of life than that . . . down here! Not five years ago – not five *years* ago, Mr. Limekiller, we had a report of a dying man in one of the back places in one of the Out-Districts, there was no Anglican priest there just then, so Father Swift went to bring the Sacrament and I went with him: it took us almost a week to get there and the man was already dead, he had been bitten, Mr. Limekiller, and he had been mauled, Mr. Limekiller, and things worse than that had been done to him, Mr. Limekiller: we could give him Christian burial, but we could not identify the nature of the teeth which bit him nor the claws which mauled him, and when we were shown the tracks of whatever it was which had done these things to him, we photographed them: and the photographs are still in one of the public offices: and they have never been identified: and even *this*, Mr. Limekiller, is merely, oh, do I dare say *merely*? – physical. And as for that which is perhaps not physical in any way we recognize in this our twentieth century of Christian knowledge . . .

"I tell you, Mr. Limekiller: where one lives, still, in the seventeenth century, seventeenth century things still happen . . ."

In how many different centuries *did* this small country live? – and in, nevertheless, one and the same time? Bigger than Rhode Island, the USA's smallest State? Bigger than Prince Edward Island, Canada's smallest Province? *Yes* . . . but, then, what *wasn't*? "No bigger than New Jersey," it was said; and, "No bigger than Wales . . ." Even Wales had its witches and New Jersey, its Jersey Devil, though . . .

But . . . something else had been said. And Bathsheba had said it. They had been on their way to a small stall kept by some old grandy-woman or other, who sold otherwise-almost-obsolete sweets: *Roppadura*, a form of the ancient brown-sugar-loaf, but moister, smaller, and more, well, lopsided, as it were: and, anyway, via the hands of Grandy Whatso– or Whosoever, flavored with ginger; she also sold *catabrú*, a kind of archaic coconut candy – for Bathsheba had not only of a swift sudden developed a sweet tooth, she had developed one for the sweets of her childhood: Fry and Nestlé and Hershey, go away: some other day, but not today . . .

He and Bathsheba, then, had been threading their way through a maze of lanes where, seemingly, she knew everyone – and there happened also to be passing by, on the other side (like the Levite in the parable?) a man as thin as a stick; small and spare and of a reddish complexion, yet not ruddy: a White Creole? Maybe – she hid her face in her hand as they passed him, this man; he did not look at them; *God* knows that she did not look at *him*; what his name was Limekiller could not recollect, only that, as he wondered *why* she behaved thus, it came to his mind that –

– the man had passed on past the likelihood of hearing –

"He's an *óbeah*-man, isn't he?" asked Jack, just then.

She made no answer. She trembled. Only so very, very slowly did she lower her protecting hand. *My God, she is* afraid *of him* – no: *she is ter*rified *of him*! the thought came. *What*? Bath*she*ba? How calm and how sure she seemed in re all other things; how – suddenly – yet he had now to admit – there had been other and earlier hints –

how utterly terrified of the uncanny and the supposedly diabolical
. . . her very color had turned from its birth-right tan to something
leaden and liverish . . .

His heart wrenched for her; he tried a religious approach;
surely *that* would work: "Surely you don't believe that a loving God
would give such dreadful powers to any human being?" he asked,
he thought, persuasively. Expecting that at once she would become
restored; but –

"I *do*! I *do*! – in a passion of conviction she had cried the words
in a low and wavering voice; and again she hid her face in her
hand; and she trembled. "Don't talk about it," she said.

Limekiller – did he love her? He often made love to her; therefore, say what you will, in a way he *did* love her – Limekiller sought
swift and deep for some verse, scriptural or even merely literary, for
instant quotation and comfort: woe that he had been raised in the
mere afterglow of the once-fierce fires of the Churches of England
and of Scotland; and could think of nothing, not one word more,
than this:

*The rude mind with difficulty associates the ideas of power and
benignity . . .*

– and what was *that* from? from *Silas Marner*, poor dear horse-
faced "George Eliot," Mary Anne something-or-other-who-gave-a-
spit: utterly useless, now, as, seemingly, utterly true. Insofar as any
comfort to Bathsheba was concerned. *My greatgrandFather was Black
and my grandMother was an Indian woman and my grandFather was an
Englishman and if God had wanted me be born* White *I would have been
born* White: *I am Bayfolk*. . . Well: every man hath his own madness;
every woman as well; and one need not be Bayfolk to be afraid of
and not comforted by the evidence of things not seen . . .

Though some – *some?* – *many* – claimed to *have* seen them . . .

Some Yankee had said to him, quite without hostility, laxly and
idly even, "Canada is kind of nice but it, somehow, oh, it lacks
sparkle;" and *he* had said, instantly, "It's not flashy, if that's what
you mean. . . ." And yet he knew it was in search of either flash or
sparkle that he had left Canada (whose own 20th century, despite
Sir Wilfred Laurier, had never yet come, was yet to come: never).
And whenever, doom here, say on some day of boiling heat or
torrents of rain, he felt in any way homesick, he obliged himself to
remember Canada at its own dimmest coldest starchiest dullest; the

Monday smell of Sunday's heavy greasy dinner in or on Prince
Edward's island; the old red brick farmhouse in the outlands of
Kingston, Ontario, with the hundred year-old scrapbook of church
news for light reading, and the unlovely chemical toilet ("Yes," said
Cousin Alix with great satisfaction, "it is so nice having it, and
indoors, too."); Sunday in Sudbury; the sullen even surly faces of
every all who would answer no question not couched in French, or
anyway *Joual,* simply turning away without even a denial of having
any English. Canada too had heat and rain; Canada had snow as
well . . . and snow . . . and snow . . . and snow . . . and . . .

It was safe enough sailing there, inside (and well inside) the
Great Reef; like sailing in a giant bath; if coral was high enough to
spring the boat, the boat would not much sink.

The Duckersons had brought along a pair of binoculars, they
had not brought along two, but Jack by now realized well that,
however *other* the couple might seem to him, they were nevertheless fairly solid and trustworthy and although he might not have
cared, *had* he awakened with a case of clap, to trust its cure to
Doctor's adjustments of your subluxation of your third or any other
vertebrar: *still*: they did not *drop* things. So he had taken out his
much-be-loved and leather-bound spyglass. And lent it to them.
While he tended the tiller, they allowed their vision, much magni-
fied, to pick and play along the white and distant strand and the
green walls of woods behind them . . . and, perhaps, for he did not
attempt to calculate the angles of their viewing, perhaps also and
now and then the Mountains of the Morning . . . these last
obviously named by people who had lived on the other side of the
said mountains: the Japanese after all had not themselves in Japan
named their nation The Land of the Rising Sun: if you live in Japan,
the sun rises from the Pacific.

"What's that, Daddy, over there by those two trees?" Mrs. now
enquired.

Somewhat marvelously, her husband knew exactly which two
trees she meant, and at once; "It's a man," he said, "no it's not no
man."

"*I* thought ut was a man, well, ut's gone, now."

Jack suggested it might have been a babboon; adding that,
locally, this meant a howler-monkey. "But *I* thought *they* were noc-
toreal, John," she said. John was so impressed by this combination

of *nocturnal* and *arboreal,* so well worthy of Lewis Carroll, that he did not at once reply. Then he did (noting, also, that she had evidently, for all her to-him-funny speechways, done some homework on the local scene; and why not? showed good sense: *She* was not one of the tourists who asked, innocently, "How about we take a gander at the French and Dutch colonies whiles we're down here?" and who had to be reminded that this was British *Hidalgo,* not British *Guiana,* and that, hence, there *were* no "French and Dutch colonies," not for leagues and leagues . . . Sometimes the penny dropped at once; sometimes the maps had to be shown; sometimes people were very disappointed, *God* knows why . . .).

"There aren't any regular settlements along this part of the coast, Mrs. – Ella. But even when there aren't, here or elsewhere, that doesn't mean that nobody is ever *around* – hey, see that sting-ray?"

It lazed along right under the surface, it would not come and rub its back against the boat, neither did it display any alarm; maybe when you're a sting-ray, you don't *have* to; Question, Where does a 3,000-lb. gorilla sit, Answer, Anywhere it wants to (Second Joe Miller, XI, 6-7). The Duckersons conjointly exclaimed Well they *Nev*er! and of course they never, not in Cow Pat, Kansas, or Moose Mammaries, Manitoba; that was what they were paying for, wasn't it? – to see things they had never seen before?

"Well usn't that unteresting!" she took her last long look at the sting-ray, now lazily tarrying behind; turned back, binoculars in hands. "And what do they do, then, these people who might be over on the shore there, if there's no regular settlements?"

Sometimes (he explained) they might be hunting game – he had to add *game*: the word "hunting," alone, meant scouting out for mahogany trees – sometimes they actually might *be* scouting out for mahogany trees . . . although in a different way . . . "Sometimes the mahogany logs break loose from the rafts or tugs. And they drift . . . they drift pretty far, sometimes. And the logging companies, well, anyway the main one, Tropical Hardwoods, they have their own boats, hm, probably only one boat I guess, which goes nosing up and down the coast looking for lost logs. And if someone else finds a log before the Company finds it, it's usually not too hard to cut the Company's mark off it. Then, well, maybe they sell the whole stick on the black market, you might call it, or maybe they cut it up and sell the planks or the parts, and maybe even, sometimes, they make stuff out of it. And sell *that.*"

The Duckersons nodded, neither slyly amused nor shocked. "I guess then if that was one of them, why, no, he wouldn't be very interested to stick around in plain sight where we could see him. *I* wouldn't even know how to make no report, but I guess Take No Chances might be the propriate motto."

Rum Bogue Caye, a Limekiller property, had not delayed them for long en route, though Ella had said it was lovely. Its golden sands were really tan, what there were of them, to wit: not much. It had a few coconut palms and a few hog-plums trees. Rum Bogue Caye *was* lovely; Ella was right. And when Ella said, simply, "Too *bad* one of those storms would sweep right across ut," why, Ella was right about that, too.

Flower Bight had hills behind it, and from the hills, low hills though they were, gushed a number of springs, and formed Flower Creek; it was short and not navigable for far, but, small as Jack's land was, it included both a piece of coast and a piece of creek: and he navigated it just far enough. A bird he had not learned the name of sang a soft, sweet, mournful song: briefly: was still. Here was the broad-leafed "wild banana," and the wild papaya, with ant-riddled leaves: a grey-silver monkey with a black pate, dignified and rabbinical, made an appearance long enough for the visitors to observe and enjoy it: there, among the leaves.

"This piece of propitty has no buildings on it, I believe you said, John —" by and by, trees, monkeys, birds, or not —

For he, having tired anyway of both Limeskinner and Limekuller, had begged them to call him *John*; even at the price of having in turn to call them *Ella* and *Ed.* In his own mind they of course remained *Mrs.* and *Doctor.* "No," he said, now; "not even a john . . . have to go a ways into the bush for that, better to use the boat's head, though." He always said this little spiel, some people being shy about the things that all people had to do not merely every day but, if healthy, several times a day. He did not add, *Safer.* He merely handed out the gum boots, and broke off a stick for each of them.

"Well, now, remember, Mommy, few you *have* to pick any flowers: *snakes.*" Mommy said she wasn't likely to forget, but she put on her boots and took her stick, like a good one. Limekiller did not tell them that the chances of being fatally bitten by a snake here were very much less than being fatally struck by a car in their or any other home town: better they be over- than under-cautious.

Sometimes he really had to over-do this, particularly with some of the people called hippies, whose religious principles evidently forbade their wearing shoes, let alone boots, save under such duress.

"– No, no buildings here. There *was* a ramada –"

"A lean-to, is that?"

"Not quite: just a roof held up by four poles, keeps off the sun and, sometimes, the rain. – but it fell down. I'll have to put it up again . . . sometime . . ."

Sometime, yes. Were he near any settlement, however small, he could have put it up in a couple of hours, on the old, the good old, barn-bee principle. Supply the materials, the tools, the rum, and *up* it would go! But . . . this far away . . . away from even a hamlet or a habited hut . . . he'd have to bring people here. And, so pay them. Of course he could do it himself, nothing to it, ahahahah. – *Some*time.

"Wellll . . ." Doctor, a.k.a. Ed, stretched his limbs, surveyed the scene, surveyed the soil. Finding this last covered with a blanket of bushery, he said, "Say, isn't thatcher coleus plant growing all around?"

"Yes. Local name: Bleeding-heart." Waited for them to say, How picturesque. To say, Those plants would cost plenty, back home. They said both. Next, Doctor poked and delved with his stick. "*Hm.* Seems like your nice, rich soil here would grow lots of real good corn and," here he paused, adding, "and stuff."

Mrs. Doctor's agricultural vocabulary was not perhaps as rich as your soil, but it was richer than his; *stuff,* she quickly expanded into yams, sweet potatoes, cabbages, coffee, rice, sugar cane, sutrus-fruits, beans, *vetch*table pears; yes: she had done some home-work. He nodded, she pounced. "Well, why *don't* they, then?" she asked. He tried to explain the colony's (very well, the Emerging Nation's, then) lack of a really strong farming background. "For one thing, this was always a timber economy –"

"– and the Spaniards they were always coming and raiding the coast; yes. But, John, that was a long *time* ago. Why don't they farm more, *now*? How come thee poor Government always has to import food . . . when they could grow it here, right here?"

A scented breeze blew down upon them, a breeze from scented Lebanon? well, not really. But scented all the same. Limekiller, seeing their noses wrinkle, said, "Bay. I mean, the kind that bay rum is made from."

Another pounce. "Yes, and they import that, too. Why don't they *make* it here."

Time to be firm. "Well, Mrs. – Ella – because they don't know *how*."

They could *learn*, couldn't they? Yes . . . in theory . . . they could learn . . . what they would live on while they were learning, was of course something else. They could fish, yes. Hunt, yes. There was wild fruit and "other edible plants," yes. "Those who aren't used to the bush, though, Ella, well, somehow, they just don't take even to living in it. Down here . . ."

Doctor Ed now spoke, and what he said was somewhat surprising. From Doctor Ed, that is. Perhaps he had heard something. "Some of them are afraid of living in the country – the bush, as they call it – is that it, John?" Limekiller must have nodded, or perhaps only his face showed it. "Well, what are they afraid *of*? Snakes? Animals?"

John Limekiller suddenly felt no reason to beat around the bush. "The White Creoles are afraid of spirits," he said. "In other words, not the bottled kind. Spooks. *They* call them 'spirits.'"

Ella said, promptly, "Dumpies and jubbies, the Colored Folks call them, isn't that right, John? What? 'Duppies and jumbies?' My mistake!" She gave a sudden, honest laugh, not at the fears of the White Creoles or the Colored Folks: at her own mistake. Jack suddenly liked her a lot more.

"Well, the idear of your National Development being held up by what *I* hafta call 'superstition' . . . well . . ." Further words evidently failed Ed. He shook his head.

How it was Mrs., Ella's, turn to surprise Jack. "Call it by any name you like," she said; "*my* great-grandmother McRae, she came right off the boat from Scotland, and, do *you* know what, John? *She had the second sight!*" Dr. Ed grunted. It was not one of your large, loud, belligerent grunts; but it was audible; it did not disturb her. "'Oh, I can see the spuruts of the living,' is what she used to say; what she really meant of course was the *dead*; not that they were *al*ways dead, of course, just that she put it that way so's not to scare people; and, as Daddy knows very perfectly well, Granny McRae, she was *never approved wrong!* – So don't you talk to me about 'super-stution,' young man," Ella wound up; and closed her mouth in a firm, straight line.

Limekiller was saved from having to defend himself from the charge; "Never knew the good lady myself," said Daddy; "now, what is your asking price for this lovely piece of land, now, John? It is lovely, I don't deny that, not trying to beatchew down, told m'wife I wouldn't, 'No, that's not your way, and isn't my way either,' she said. Eh?"

Limekiller: "Well . . ."

"Might as well ask, before we go into some *in*-depth explorations, they call it; course, can't be expected to sign-seal-deliver right here and now: *still.*"

One thousand dollars an acre was Limekiller's price, not his "asking price," his *price.* Nor would he care to sell less than the whole piece, although of course the buyer could do that himself, if he wished. (And, of course, if he wished to do that too much, he-the-buyer might soon find himself being asked if he had an estate broker's license, or was registered as a land agent under the Act of 20th Victoria, cap. VI, or the other way round: or *stuff.*)

Doctor Ed Duckerson nodded slowly, gravely, thoughtfully. It was not a totally outrageous price, he did not say that he would Think It Over, though of course he would not only think, he would talk it over . . . out loud . . . with, eventually, someone besides his wife. As why *not*? Inevitable as well as reasonable. Inevitably, if one hell of a lot less reasonably, *some*one to whom he would mention it would guffaw, express incredulity, question Limekiller's being more than a mere rogue or scaped tom o'bedlam, wind up saying, "Doctor, I can get you five thousand acres . . . now mark and mind what I say, Doctor . . . five *thousand* acres . . . at *fifty cents an acre* . . . local currency . . . !"

And, unless *this* one were a mere rogue: he *could*!

Sooner or later, Dr. Ed, being no simon-pure fool, would find out that the five thousand acres were either all under water, or mostly mud-and-mangrove, unreachable by road, not on anything like a real river or creek navigable by any reasonable vessel . . . But the sound of LAND AT 50¢ PER ACRE would remain in his mind like a taste in his mouth. And poison the taste of *Land At $1,000 an Acre.*

Daddy was really not going to buy.

Johnny was not really wanting to sell.

Daddy would have had a real nice trip at a real cheap price.

Limekiller would have delayed pellagra, the patron, and the gaol, for another month or two.

But the talk between them went on. And on. And on. Climate. Politics. Prices. Costs. The whole Caribbean Scene. And on. And

Doctor Ed said, "Well, now, a country the size of Jamaica, now Ella and I were, hey, Ella? Say, Ella? Mommy? Now, shucks. Where's she got to?"

"Oh Christ I could kick myself. I hope she isn't lost!"

The bird sang sorrowfully in the vine-clasped trees.

Something made a sudden tiny sound; something flashed . . . another flash . . . another tiny sound . . . something landed, exquisitely . . . perfectly . . . in a cupped leaf he barely had to stoop to reach . . . it must have fallen and struck a few other leaves on its way down: down from *where*? For a second more he stayed his hand, looked up. The bird was darting down, saw his face, darted away again, did neither wait nor pause. Something flashed in its beak: had it somehow eluded him, and – no.

In the hollow of the leaf was still . . . whatever it had been a moment ago.

It was so tiny, so fragile-looking, his fingers seemed enormous as he shook it into his palm rather than try picking it up and loosing it: once on the forest floor he might never find it: what *was* it? A golden ring. A ring so tiny that it must have been made for the finger of, not alone a child, a small child. Either that: or it was faërie gold: and perhaps it *was*!

Perhaps, also, and this was likelier and perhaps at least as marvelous, it was of Amerindian workmanship. Not modern Amerindian; those descendants of the Chipchaks who had returned, after an absence of a thousand years to this land abandoned by their ancestors, they did not work in gold, they bought their gold already-wrought from jewelers – non-national Spanish, moved also here from elsewhere – or from Turks – no matter . . . Ancient American Indian. Old Kingdom . . . or maybe even earlier than that. He gave one tiny moment more of thought to the tiny child whose tiny brown finger had worn the ring, oh, God, heartbreakingly long centuries before . . . He looked up.

The bird was gone, what kind of bird he could not even say: amid the stuff which legends are made on he forced himself to the stuff of known facts: jackdaws were noted for stealing glittery things; crows often did, and no doubt not they alone: somewhere, somewhere, somewhere nearly by, it seemed, the bird had found the ring: *no*: had found *two*, at least two rings: one had dropped; one it still had. Begrudge not.

He grudged not . . . but what did it *mean?*

It meant that not a thousand miles away, probably not even a mile away, there was perhaps an Indian ruin, and, likelier than a mere *perhaps*, a cache of Indian treasure: his heart gave a leap, that was and his mind knew it was, a cliché but his heart *did* leap: And all the while the words repeated themselves in his mind from legal documents he himself had signed and seen been stamped, *All Indian ruins and mines of gold or silver and/or precious stones remain the Property of Her Majesty the Queen, Her Heirs and Assignees* . . . and words which he had not seen himself on any documents but knew to be part of the law of the land, and not of this one small land alone but of how many larger lands across how many distant waters, *Oceans divide us, and the wild waste of seas*: never mind: the old ancient British common law and Crown unite us: in this case particularly the Law of Treasure Trove, from French *trouvé*, Found . . .

He had not yet found Ella: *that* was what he should be thinking of: and only that.

The ring however small and tiny and ancient of days, years, centuries, cycles if not of Cathay than of The Indies and The Lands Beyond, the ring in all legal probability belonged to The Crown, as though The Crown had not jewels enough already, would Her Majesty *et* God bless her *cetera*, begrudge *him*, who had not even grudged the bird the other ring, grudge *him*, John L Limekiller, *this?* – precious little *she* had to do with the ring, anymore than had her grandfather in the comically notorious Canadian case of the ex-Militia member who having neglected to turn in his entire uniform found himself facing the charge of *stealing one pair of woolen trousers the property of his Majesty King George V* . . .

Limekiller at the moment could not stop to figure out the legal wrongs or rights of the matter, that could wait, what could not wait, no not for anything, was the probability that *Buried Treasure* likely lay so near to hand . . .

. . . and foot . . .

The thick ground covering lay behind him, he was for the most part beneath the shelter of the high bush "sticks," trees, "the sticks" which had given their odd old name even in North America to areas less wild than this: something else flashed: not gold: the small red deer the Bayfolk called "antelope;" and if bison were "buffalo," why not? There was a trail, narrow perhaps too wide a word for it, but wide enough for the antelope, and the other deer called simply *deer*, for the wild hogs in their (sometimes) sounders of hundreds, for the panthers called lions and the jaguars called tigers; many names had at first seemed turned around and strange to him –

A vast tree stood in his way: a ceiba or silky-tree: immense: the trail became two trails and branched around it, Limekiller, pausing only to consider if it mattered which branch he took, nevertheless paused. Something moved. There was no beautiful birdsong now. Now and then something gave an ugly croak. Maybe a frog. Maybe not. Something moved. Another flash.

There was a break in the bush, a thinning of the foliage as well as the trees, and he could see it now, plainly; it was a yellowhead parrot, and, as local lore said that the yellowhead parrot was the aptest to learn speech, Limekiller might not have been surprised when the bird began to speak. If *speak* was indeed the word. It had been just doing bird things, preening and grooming and contemplating. Humboldt, a hundred and fifty years earlier, had told the terrible story of encountering up the Amazon a parrot kept by an Indian tribe; booty from a raid on another Indian tribe. All those latter Indians had been wiped out (no, the Old World did not invent genocide; it merely invented Writing, and wrote its crimes down); the parrot Humboldt told of could and did speak. *But no one could understand what it spoke* . . . the language of the defeated Indians had been confined to that one small tribe, there in its own green heart of darkness, and that tribe and its culture and its traditions were extinct . . . and only some few phrases of its lost language survived . . . and survived on the grey tongue of a single bird . . .

But surely this was no human speech which turned Limekiller's heated skin so cold, so suddenly. The voice, if "voice" it was, was like that of no living thing which Limekiller had ever heard . . . or ever heard of . . . it was a mutter, and a nightmare mutter at that.

And, as he knew that parrots have no nightmares, and that this bird was wide awake, he could only realize that the bird was and had to be imitating some living, speaking thing . . . *thing?*

Which might not even be very far off, either . . .

It was not far off at all.

It was here, in another moment only, it was *there*: on the trail; *there*: the trail's other, farther branch.

Farther.

Thank God.

For this time there had been no flash: he simply saw it. It had not been there, it could not have been there, it could not be there *now*, as he melted against the side of the vast tree, no such thing could be, there was no such thing; he lay still asleep somewhere and if he only could force himself to, in a second he would be awake; he could not force himself to: it was the jumby. The jumby paused. It moved on a moment more; again it paused. He now heard it sniff. And mutter. His legs melted too, now, fortunately quite slowly, and so now, besides the silky-tree, there was a shrub between him and it. *It*, with its head reminiscent of the Things in one of Goya's mad-time paintings: *had* Goya gone mad? Had Goya seen . . . *it* . . . ?

Limekiller saw the head move, even as he shuddered at the sound of that sniff . . . and of the frightful mutter which the parrot had mimicked . . ."indescribable?" by no means – one would not wish it described too well. The jumby muttered and the jumby sniffed. What had it *smelled?* – what was it *trying* to smell? And the sudden sullen thought that it might be trying to smell *him* . . . his own body . . . arm-pits, rump-crack, crotch, and all his eternally odorous human body howevermuch washed . . . did *him* (John Limekiller was his body's name) no good at all.

The head, so human if bestial, so bestial if human, so . . . something else as well . . . the head moved. The nostrils, if that was what they were, sank into the sunken snout . . . if that is what it was . . . or *nose* . . . had it been like that, *so*, or anything like *so*, in life . . . or was it the sunken snout of decay, of death, of . . .

If it were not smelling for him, for what was it smelling? it *had* been smelling for him. Could it smell him, then, he, himself, himself alone? or his sweat, his glands, microdrops of his urine and traces remnant of his stool? could it even, now, and was it even now trying to, smell Bathsheba on him as well? the tobacco he sometimes smoked and that other herb he sometimes smoked? the Indians said the beasts of venery could smell not only tobacco but that other venery; hence perhaps why they burned copal-gum before beginning to spoor . . . no copal here, too late for that, too late for any and for all – *could* it smell Bathsheba on him as well? *Iniquity, transgression, and sin* . . . Bathsheba's boughten perfume, God knows how cheap, but use it she would . . . smell *her* body . . . on *his?* and was he here and now to pay by the wrath of some god or some facet or the one One God, for any act of unhallowed copulation which had left its traces though at the latest two days old, or three, *One God in Three*, traces left upon and onto him like as letters of and in fire: could it smell his sperm? his rum? his –

Limekiller smelled *it* now, and, ah God that was something, how it smelled! But even as he crouched and tried to contain every

single one of his body's contents, he relished (of a sudden) the faint
– it was faint, but it was . . . *oh!* – notice of the jumby's stench . . .
more now, he relished it than the, if only in memory, so-called
perfume, perfume unbought in bottles, of a woman's flesh . . . not
invariably such a sweet perfume (was *his*? his own fierce flesh,
though since, yes, washed) and not always a purchased perfume; oh
– he relished this horrid, however-faint, odor more than the
sweetest scent he had ever smelled: for he knew that if he could
smell the jumby, then the faint breeze came from the other side of
the jumby: hence the jumby could not smell *him* . . .

Was he then or had he ever been a Roman Catholic he might
have risk or not then crossed himself. Crouching in the alien bush
he regretted every single regret he had ever had about Canada,
would have buried himself forever in the freezy winter mantle of
Our Lady of the Snows . . . and ah God how he would have given
anything . . . *any*thing? . . . almost anything . . . his testicles? . . . one
testicle: at least . . . to be back there now, at its worst . . . what was
its worst compared to here and now and *this*? He would face up to,
and with penitence or joy, every life lost that day upon the Plains
of Abraham: to be back there, *there* . . . and not here . . . *here* . . .

The jumby's bestial head moved slightly toward Limekiller's
direction, he felt his left hand jerk slightly, saw some faint rictus (as
he crouched behind the immense silky-tree) move that horrid blas-
phemy of a face, saw that face turn away with a jerk of its own . . .

The jumby moved slowly along the trail with that gait or walk
not like that of anyone or anything which Limekiller had ever
seen. It did not lurch, though almost; and neither did it shamble,
and yet – Flow? no, of course not that smoothly – Odd the way its
hands held halfway up the body and slowly moving up and down
and away – It moved slowly along the trail and now and then he
could see its legs and the mud-caked hairs on the immense muscles of them; were its eyes deep-sunken and dim, were they glazed
or was that a trick of the light or had they a translucent membrane,
or –

It had been moving.

It was not moving now.

Something was moving.

Something else.

Limekiller heard it before he saw it, an odd and, dragging
sound, but . . . somehow . . . not one all that unnatural . . . and he
smelled it, too, before he saw it, and it had a stench of rot on and

above its mere animal rankness: yet, stinking though this was, it was (*this*) no such utterly alien stench as the jumby's: *What?*

It was a hog, a wild hog, he thought a young boar-hog, he could not say just then which of the two kinds, warry or peccary, it was; it had been badly torn about the hindquarters, perhaps by one of the great cats, perhaps by one of its own kind, and its wounds had festered: a marvel it was still alive, it stumbled and gave a squeal of pain; and whilst Limekiller had observed all this, in a second or two, not more, that same while the other creature had sunk down and crouched and now it leaped and the wounded swine gave a long and prolonged shriek like that of a very large rat when the right rough kind of cat or dog has it by the neck or throat: this ended so suddenly that he realized it had ended even while it still echoed. *The ephialtes . . . 'on-leapers' . . . incubus . . . demon . . . nightmares, fevers, chills . . .*

Still Limekiller crouched; flies settled in his sweat, ants made trek-tracks up his legs; he would stay and not move, never move, whilst the jumby growled and rottled and tore at its prey: the jumby did not do this.

Once, once only, it wrung its head half to one side – thus he saw the dead hog, torn, dangling from the dreadful jaws – some faint notion in his mind that some faint notice was in the jumby's mind . . . of something behind and aside from it: some dim adumbration of which had caused the hideous head to turn: but which was either not important enough or perhaps somehow unpleasant enough . . . the jumby's head turned again, with a sudden drip-spray of blood; the inhuman-human head slightly bowed beneath the weight of its kill . . . and even a young wild boar-hog being no lightweight: only slightly bowed . . . turned back and away and after a while it-the-jumby had failed from sight.

Still Limekiller stayed there, *there*, behind and beside the great silky-tree, *like the shadow of a great rock in a dry land*. Presently he bethought him that the jumby, as it had not eaten its kill then and there, was certainly taking it elsewhere: sundry scenes suggested them in his mind: the jumby hanging the hog-lych in a tree to (as it were) ripen: the jumby lodging or burying it in a cave for the same purpose: the jumby . . . ah, most horrible scene of all! the jumby carrying its kill away to feed its young! . . . if it *had* young . . . and, if so, and however so, and whatever so or not so: the jumby had *gone*

and was not about to come again quite soon.

* * *

He had given thought to his choices: rise and flee as quickly as might be, and risk the sound of his flight reaching the small and malformed and more than merely animal-like ears of the abomination: take one's time and make haste as slowly as possible, and as silently, and risk that, against all logic (*logic!* what had *logic* to do with what he had just seen?), the thing might yet return and leap upon him from behind . . .

Later, when, despite all efforts (I won't think about it. I *won't* think about it. I won't *think* about it), he thought about it, he was not able to recall which had been his supposed chosen thought: perhaps neither; perhaps, in turn, both. He did remember thinking about something else – perhaps it was not after all, *else* –

Had poor Wee Willie Wiggins also, *firstly*, heard a parrot imitating those same nightmare sounds, allowing for bird-distortion; and, *secondly*, had he, cursed-by-birth and cursed-from-birth, Wee Willy Wiggins, heard/seen the jumby? . . . or perhaps the other way round? The order mattered not a bit: in either case, if so, was it any wonder that the lee mahn was *fright for parrot?*

No. No wonder. Not one bit.

Also he, John Limekiller, later remembered remembering something else as well . . .

. . . odd *affliction, is it not so, Professor, suffering from nightmares in the day-time?* . . . and, *The ephialtes may attack at noon as well as midnight . . . Greek word . . . Literally?* "*On-leapers*" . . . *the demon . . . causes nightmares . . .*

And he, Jack Limekiller, had asked himself, incredulous at this ancient confusion between cause and effect, "*Causes?*"

And Rosita had said, and now he knew *why* Rosita had said . . . why Bathsheba, and oh Lord how many others had said, whenever some hint of it came up: *No tahk aboet eet!*

No. He would never talk about it. He would . . . if only he would . . . if only he could . . . he could . . .

Suddenly he was out of there. Out of the bush. In the clearing. There was his boat, safely moored. There his guests, safe aboard. Both of them.

They did not at first see him. They simply sat there calmly, and calmly talking to each other; now and then pointing with calm unhurried gestures, to something afar off: the mountain range's nearest reach, perhaps. The faint white line of the Great Reef, perhaps. The lay of the land up or down the coast . . . perhaps . . .

So, if there was any real meaning to the advice *Pull yourself together*, he was able to take advantage of it. He seemed to feel that he *was*, literally, pulling himself together. First he pulled his shirt down . . . it had ridden up his belly and buck. Second, he pulled his underpants and trousers up; *they* had slid down, down. Then he pulled his bones and tendons and ligaments and, most of all, his thoughts and mind, *those* he pulled together, too. Then he went on.

"Well, John! We were al*most* worried about you, but I said, *Nooo* . . . John's a nalmost native woodsman, so, no need ta worry bout *him!*"

And, "John, oh, I feel so a-*shame*d: I got jist *so* unturrested in some of those *flowers?* And, well . . ."

The best and the worst of it was, they had *not* worried!

He could bring himself, at first, to say nothing. And, though they both babbled on cheerfully until he was aboard, once he was aboard: then they noticed. "Why, now, John, you don't look a-*tall* well!" "Umm. No. You don't look one bit *well*, John. Why, what –

Nothing like a good, simple truth in due season. "Touch of the fever," he mumbled, coming to a slow halt, sinking down to rest. "Chills . . ."

Doctor Ed, was, after all (licensed to practice down here or not), after all, *Doctor* Ed. "Well, we'll take care of *that*," he said, suddenly brisk, professional, and having the situation well in hand. For a moment, Limekiller, (echoing his ears the words of Professor Brolly: . . . *The incubus . . . causes nightmares, fevers, chills, and . . .*), thought that Doctor Ed was about to give him an adjustment of the subluxation of your third vertebrar; he did not know if he could either stand it, lie down for it, or resist it: nothing, of the sort: from somewhere, perhaps his small carry-all, perhaps his left ear, Dr. Duckerson produced tablets and capsules (chiropractic science has made marvelous strides, and can now polish you off, pharmaceuti-cally, almost as well as establishmentarian medical science; only of course, neither one does that, always) – water – a cup or glass –

And the magic words, "Just take these, and you'll be all right." *Magic* words.

By and by, Limekiller was all right.

For the most part. From time to time, though, on the way back – and they had not tarried long, no longer than it took him to raise anchor and sails – he did feel himself shaken by a spasm. *Spasms.* And, compared to what he had already felt and seen, what were mere spasms? Trifles. Trifles light as air. Ella urged him to put on a

jacket. Ella had a small, a very small, but large enough, flask of Very
Good Brandy. Ed (*Doctor* Ed) regretted aloud that it was impractical
for John to leave the helm and lie down for a very thorough
adjustment; Ed did, however, do various things to Jack's back as he
stayed crouching, over at the helm. Did they, could they, help?
Could they *hurt*?

> *Life is mostly froth and bubble;*
> *Two things stand like stone:*
> *Kindness in another's trouble,*
> *Courage in your own.*

"I'm fine, now," he said. And said it over till they began to
believe him. The ring.

What do with, about, the ring? Ring made at least a thousand
years ago by the Old Kingdom Indians, perhaps, before they'd fled
. . . *And now he knew* why *they had fled*! . . . maybe . . .

. . . only maybe not . . .

He could turn it over to Government, Honest John;
Government, unaccustomed to such alien honesty, might be appre-
ciative; faced with a hillock of paper-work, Government might not.
He could give it to his girl . . . *no.* He no longer had a girl. Woman.
Wife. Free-mate. Boiling the near-past down like the stinking tripes
of a whale in a try-pot, he hadn't any longer even a whore. He
could give it to Mrs. Ella. Who deserved it, if only for the brandy.
That, alas and however (here he took in two reefs of the mainsail,
observed the nimbus of the setting sun behind the Mountains of the
Morning), would involve him in probably infinite conversation, as
the last woman able to accept a gift without many words . . . well,
when *did* she die?

He could keep it, concealed, so very tiny it was, as long as he
remained down here. But that might be forever. And each time he
came across it, he would Remember. *No.*

He would slip it into the poor-box of whichever church he first
encountered; tempted though he was by the thought of laying it
upon the high altar. He would simply drop it in. No one would
know. The church would, likely, probably, what else? sell it. And
some old man or woman might be enabled to fulfill the ancient,
willful (but how natural words) words, *Nay, but we would eat flesh*
. . . He gave one last and terrified shudder at the echo of these last
two words, and the memories evoked.

But no one else noticed.

He brought the Duckersons to the very front of their hotel; no boats might long linger there, *there* being no lawful mooring: but no one would care if he tarried a few minutes . . . an hour . . . They were pleased. They were very pleased. Nothing like that had ever happened to them before, and likely never would (in Cow Pat, Kansas? in Buffalo Bong, Alberta?) likely, again. John had to come in with them. They didn't remember *when* they'd had a nicer trip, John. Wouldn't John like a *drink?* Wouldn't John like to take a nice hot, well, *warm,* or even *cold,* shower, in their hotel soot? Wouldn't John like to have dunner with them?

Maybe the River View Hotel would never have made Duncan Hines or the Michelin three-star list: but it very certainly beat The New Shanghai, and/or any palace of Fry Chicken/Tin Soup/Hom Somwich delights.

They, then, he had not asked for anything in advance, paid him. In nice, crisp, countersigned Travellers Cheques. *How* pleased Mr. Ogilvy, of the Grand Dominion Bank, would be when Limekiller deposited them next day: wiping out his, Limekiller's, overdraft. And almost at once, being of or rather as one flesh, their heads began to nod. Made excuses. Assured him again what a lovely trip they'd had (*they*). Said they would surely give a lot of thought to his offer. Which they would. But they wouldn't buy. He would keep on taking visitors down there, but . . . No. He would *not.* Not *there.* And neither could he sell. Not now, that he knew.

Government might have it back again. Unless, in the meanwhile he would sell it, cheap, to his worst enemy. Whoever *that* might be. Not even to him. Her. Forget it.

The Duckersons had made their last farewells. What, then, next? By all sense, Limekiller should have been more than merely tired. He should have been wiped out. He should either go back to his boat, or – he had money now! – taken a hotel room; if not here, then, well, somewhere. But he was not tired. He did not desire to sleep. Was he afraid he might dream? He was by this time out on the street. The usual late night throngs passed up and down, haling each other, and, by now, him, too. His mind was trying to think of nothing.

He was in the Spyglass again. So was Professor Brolly. So was Colonel Pygore. Little seemed changed. Pygore was speaking. Brolly was listening. Limekiller was drinking.

"And I came upon something when I was in West Africa once," Pygore said . . . murmured, rather. "Well . . ." a ghost of a smile care over his ghost of a face; "came upon *many* things there . . . very damned glad some of them never came upon *me*," with his ghost of a chuckle.

"Oh, drop the other *shoe*, Pygore!"

"Yes. Well. An old Government order." Suddenly becoming crisp in his delivery, as though quoting something: "'*Pilgrimages into the District of So-and-So for the purpose of worshipping the fetish Zumbi, whether in the form of a tree, a juju-image, or an animal, is hereby forbidden under Schedule Such-and-such-a number, of,*' well, whatever date, '*is hereby and until further notice-forbidden, because of the loss of lives resultant therefrom . . .* '"

A silence. Something stirred in Limekiller's rum-numbed mind, and he pressed it still and quiet.

"'The *fetish* Zumbi,'" repeated the Professor. "Never heard of it as a *fetish* . . . or an *animal* . . . and as for a tree, well, they say it hates the silky-tree. Hates and fears it. No one knows *why*. Anymore than one knows why it hates those berry beads. Perhaps they each – tree, beads – have a scent or odor it can't stand . . . – But I never dreamed of it as a fetish or an animal –"

Pygore rubbed his tired grey eyes, formed, seemingly, to see (or seer?) on cooler, greyer seas than these. *And I beneath a rougher Sea, / And whelmed in deeper Gulphs than he* . . . Said, "There are more things in West Africa, Brolly – and, for that matter, closer or farther than there – than are dreamed of . . ."

Now it was the professor who murmured. "Zumbi," he said. "Zomby. Duppy . . . and . . . There *is* a connection. *Has* to be."

"All Hobson-Jobson, Brolly," Pygore said. "One hears a word, or words, which one doesn't know, one assimilates it to a word or words one *does*. So: *can* the natives in India be chanting *Hassan! Hussein!* . . . ? No. What they're chanting is, obviously, *Hobson! Jobson!* And, as we're talking Hobson-Jobson, let us talk about 'duppy' –"

Now it was Limekiller who spoke. Somewhat to his own surprise. Though not much. *Wanted*, somehow, *much*, to say: *Don't* talk about it. Prevented himself. Said, instead: "Barkeep: my round."

"– if you won't accept 'doppelgänger' –"

"I won't."

"– what about *dumby* – with the *b* not silent?"

"Why should the *b* not be silent?"

Limekiller, silent, drank. And drank.

"Suppose one were attempting to pronounce the word and one's native language was not English?"

Brolly said, "Suppose . . . is what you mean . . . the *b* was not silent, but the dum*by was?*"

Not so damned silent, echoed . . . *ech*oed? shrieked . . . in Limekiller's inner ears . . .

"Zumbi, zomby. Mumbo-jumbo? Hobson-Jobson? Zumbi, jumby . . ." *Don't talk about it!* "Well. Let us make up another etymology. What about jumby, from *jamby,* from French *jambé,* from French *jambe,* leg. That is, the adjective would mean leggèd. Seem to recall . . . *Morte Darthur?* One with strong legs?"

A pause, but a brief one. "Not jumby: *Jumpy!* Because it jumps! It does jump! Oh God how it jumps!" *On-leaper,* midnight or midday; Limekiller's leg twitched, his hand convulsed — his face —

"If, John Limekiller," said "Pygore, in his tired, tired voice, "you must also jump, perhaps you could manage to spill your rum into my glass and not onto my sleeve . . ." He at that moment looked up from his sleeve, their eyes met, and Pygore's expression of mildest and almost bored concern turned (and very suddenly and very completely) into one of . . . something else.

Very lightly, very briefly, Pygore placed his hand on Limekiller's shoulder.

Limekiller said nothing.

Pygore said nothing.

Pygore knew.

MANATEE GAL WON'T YOU COME OUT TONIGHT

THE CUPID CLUB was the only waterhole on the Port Cockatoo waterfront. To be sure, there were two or three liquor booths back in the part where the tiny town ebbed away into the bush. But they were closed for siesta, certainly. And they sold nothing but watered rum and warm soft-drinks and loose cigarettes. Also, they were away from the breezes off the Bay which kept away the flies. In British Hidalgo gnats were flies, mosquitoes were flies, sand-flies – worst of all – were flies – *flies* were also flies: and if anyone were inclined to question this nomenclature, there was the unquestionable fact that mosquito itself was merely Spanish for little fly.

It was not really cool in the Cupid Club (Alfonso Key, prop., LICENSED TO SELL WINE, SPIRITS, BEER, ALE, CYDER AND PERRY). But it was certainly less hot than outside. Outside the sun burned the Bay, turning it into molten sparkles. Limekiller's boat stood at mooring, by very slightly raising his head he could see her, and every so often he did raise it. There wasn't much aboard to tempt thieves, and there weren't many thieves in Port Cockatoo, anyway. On the other hand, what was aboard the *Saccharissa* he could not very well spare; and it only took one thief, after all. So every now and then he did raise his head and make sure that no small boat was out by his own. No skiff or dory.

Probably the only thief in town was taking his own siesta.

"Nutmeg P'int," said Alfonso Key. "You been to Nutmeg P'int?"

"Been there."

Every place needs another place to make light fun of. In King Town, the old colonial capital, it was Port Cockatoo. Limekiller wondered what it was they made fun of, down at Nutmeg Point.

"What brings it into your mind, Alfonso?" he asked, taking his eyes from the boat. All clear. Briefly he met his own face in the mirror. Wasn't much of a face, in his own opinion. Someone had once called him "Young Count Tolstoy." Wasn't much point in shaving, anyway.

Key shrugged. "Sometimes somebody goes down there, goes up the river, along the old bush *trails*, buys carn. About now, you know, mon, carn bring good price, up in King *Town*."

Limekiller knew that. He often did think about that. He could quote the prices Brad Welcome paid for corn: white, corn, yellow corn, cracked and ground. "I know," he said. "In King Town they have a lot of money and only a little corn. Along Nutmeg River they have a lot of corn and only a little money. Someone who brings down money from the Town can buy corn along the Nutmeg. Too bad I didn't think of that before I left."

Key allowed himself a small sigh. He knew that it wasn't any lack of thought, and that Limekiller had had no money before he left, or, likely, he wouldn't have left. "May-be they trust you down along the Nutmeg. They trust old Bob Blaine. Year after year he go up the Nutmeg, he go up and down the bush trail, he buy carn on credit, bring it bock up to King Town."

Off in the shadow at the other end of the barroom someone began to sing, softly.

W'ol' Bob Blaine, he done gone.
W'ol' Bob Blaine, he done gone.
Ahl, ahl me money gone –
Gone, to Spahnish Hidalgo. . . .

In King Town, Old Bob Blaine had sold the corn, season after season. Old Bob Blaine had bought salt, he had bought shotgun shells, canned milk, white flour, cotton cloth from the Turkish merchants. Fish hooks, sweet candy, rubber boots, kerosene, lamp *chim*ney. Old Bob Blaine had returned and paid for corn in kind – not, to be sure, immediately after selling the corn. Things did not move that swiftly even today, in British Hidalgo, and certainly had not Back When. Old Bob Blaine returned with the merchandise on his next buying trip. It was more convenient, he did not have to make so many trips up and down the mangrove coast. By and by it must almost have seemed that he was paying in advance, when he came, buying corn down along the Nutmeg River, the boundary between the Colony of British Hidalgo and the country which the Colony still called Spanish Hidalgo, though it had not been Spain's for a century and a half.

"Yes mon," Alfonso Key agreed. "Only, that one last time, he *not* come bock. They say he buy one marine engine yard, down in Republican waters."

"I heard," Limekiller said, "that he bought a garage down there."

The soft voice from the back of the bar said, "No, mon. Twas a coconut walk he bought. Yes, mon."

Jack wondered why people, foreign people, usually, sometimes complained that it was difficult to get information in British Hidalgo. In his experience, information was the easiest thing in the world, there – all the information you wanted. In fact, sometimes you could get more than you wanted. Sometimes, of course, it was contradictory. Sometimes it was outright wrong. But that, of course, was another matter.

"Anybody else ever take up the trade down there?" Even if the information, the answer, if there was an answer, even if it were negative, what difference would it make?

"No," said Key. "No-body. May-be you try, eh, Jock? May-be they trust you."

There was no reason why the small cultivators, slashing their small cornfields by main force out of the almighty bush and, then burning the slash and then planting, corn in the, ashes, so to speak – maybe they would trust him, even though there was no reason *why* they should trust him. Still. . . . Who knows. . . . They might. They just might. Well . . . some of them just might. For a moment a brief hope rose in his mind.

"Naaa. . . . I haven't even got any crocus sacks." There wasn't much point in any of it after all. Not if he'd have to tote the corn wrapped up in his shirt. The jute sacks were fifty cents apiece in local currency; they were as good as money, sometimes even better than money.

Key, who had been watching rather unsleepingly as these thoughts were passing through Jack's mind, slowly sank back in his chair. "Ah," he said, very softly. "You haven't got any crocus sock."

"Een de w'ol' days," the voice from the back said, "every good 'oman, she di know which bush yerb good fah wyes, fah kid-ney, which bush yerb good fah heart, which bush yerb good fah fever. But ahl of dem good w'ol' 'omen, noew, dey dead, you see. Yes mon. Ahl poss ahway. Nobody know bush medicine nowadays. Only *bush-doc-tor*. And dey very few, sah, very few."

"What you say, Coptain Cudgel, you not bush *doc*-tor you w'own self? Nah true, Captain?"

Slowly, almost reluctantly, the old man answered. "Well sah. Me know few teeng. Fah true. Me know few teeng. Not like in w'ol' days. In w'ol' days, me dive fah conch. Yes mon. Fetch up plan-ty conch. De sahlt wah-tah hort me wyes, take bush-yerb fah cure dem. But nomah. No, mon. Me no dive no mah. Ahl de time, me wyes hort, stay out of strahng sun noew. . . . Yes mon . . ."

Limekiller yawned, politely, behind his hand. To make conversation, he repeated something he had heard. "They say some of the old time people used to get herbs down at Cape Mandee."

Alfonso Key flashed him a look. The old man said, a different note suddenly in his voice, different from the melancholy one of a moment before, "Mon-ah-tee. Mon-ah-tee is hahf-mon, you know, sah. Fah true. Yes sah, mon-ah-tee is hahf-mon. Which reason de lah w'only allow you to tehk one mon-ah-tee a year."

Covertly, Jack felt his beer. Sure enough, it was warm. Key said, "Yes, but who even bother nowadays? The leather is so tough you can't even sole a boot with it. And you dasn't bring the meat up to the Central Market in King *Town*, you *know*."

The last thing on Limekiller's mind was to apply for a license to shoot manatee, even if the limit were one a week. "How come?" he asked. "How come you're not?" King Town. King Town was the reason that he was down in Port Cockatoo. There was no money to be made here, now. But there was none to be lost here, either. His creditors were all in King Town, though if they wanted to, they could reach him even down here. But it would hardly be worth anyone's while to fee a lawyer to come down and feed him during the court session. Mainly, though, it was a matter of, Out of sight, somewhat out of mind. And, anyway – who knows? The Micawber Principle was weaker down here than up in the capital. But still and all: something might turn up.

"Because, they say it is because manatee have teats like a woman."

"One time, you know, one time dere is a mahn who mehk mellow wit ah mon-ah-tee, yes sah. And hahv pickney by mon-ah-tee."

It did seem that the old man had begun to say something more, but someone else said, "*Ha-ha-ha!*" And the same someone else next said, in a sharp, all-but-demanding voice, "Shoe *shine?* Shoe *shine?*"

"I don't have those kind of shoes," Limekiller told the boy.

"Suede *brush?* Suede *brush?*"

Still no business being forthcoming, the bootblack withdrew, muttering.

Softly, the owner of the Cupid Club murmured, "That is one bod bobboon."

Limekiller waited, then he said, "I'd like to hear more about that, Captain Cudgel. . . ."

But the story of the man who "made mellow" with a manatee and fathered a child upon her would have to wait, it seemed, upon another occasion. Old Captain Cudgel had departed, via the back door. Jack decided to do the same, via the front.

The sun, having vexed the Atlantic coast most of the morning and afternoon, was now on its equal way towards the Pacific. The Bay of Hidalgo stretched away on all sides, out to the faint white line which marked the barrier reef, the great coral wall which had for so long safeguarded this small, almost forgotten nation for the British Crown and the Protestant Religion. To the south, faint and high and blue against the lighter blue of the sky, however faint, darker: Pico Guapo, in the Republic of Hidalgo. Faint, also, though recurrent, was Limekiller's thought that he might, just might, try his luck down there. His papers were in order. Port Cockatoo was a Port of Entry and of Exit. The wind was free.

But from day to day, from one hot day to another hot day, he kept putting the decision off.

He nodded politely to the District Commissioner and the District Medical Officer and was nodded to, politely, in return. A way down the front street strolled white-haired Mr. Stuart, who had come out here in The Year Thirty-Nine, to help the war effort, and had been here ever since: too far for nodding. Coming from the market shed where she had been buying the latest eggs and ground-victuals was good Miss Gwen; if she saw him she would insist on giving him his supper at her boarding-house on credit: her suppers (her breakfasts and lunches as well) were just fine. But he had debts enough already. So, with a sigh, and a fond recollection of her fried fish, her country-style chicken, and her candied breadfruit, he sidled down the little lane, and he avoided Miss Gwen.

One side of the lane was the one-story white-painted wooden building with the sign DENDRY WASHBURN, LICENCED TO SELL DRUGS AND POISONS, the other side of the lane was the one-story white-painted wooden building where Captain Cumberbatch kept shop. The lane itself was paved with the crushed decomposed coral called pipeshank – and, indeed, the stuff did look like so much busted-up clay pipe stems. At the end of the lane was a small wharf and a flight of steps, at the bottom of the steps was his skiff.

He poled out to his boat, where he was greeted by his first mate, Skippy, an off-white cat with no tail. Skippy was very neat, and always used the ashes of the caboose: and if Jack didn't remember to sweep them *out* of the caboose as soon as they had cooled, and off to one side, why, that was his own carelessness, and no fault of Skippy's.

"All clear?" he asked the small tiger, as it rubbed against his leg. The small tiger growled something which might have been "Portuguese man o' war off the starboard bow at three bells," or "Musketmen to the futtock-shrouds," or perhaps only, "Where in the Hell have *you* been, all day, you creep?"

"Tell you what, Skip," as he tied the skiff, untied the *Saccharissa*, and, taking up the boat's pole, leaned against her in a yo-heave-ho manner; "let's us bugger off from this teeming tropical metropolis and go timely down the coast . . . say, to off Crocodile Creek, lovely name, proof there really is no Chamber of Commerce in these parts . . . then take the dawn tide and drop a line or two for some grunts or jacks or who knows what . . . sawfish, maybe . . . maybe . . . *some-*thing to go with the rice-and-beans tomorrow. . . . Corn what we catch but can't eat," he grunted, leaned, hastily released his weight and grabbed the pole up from the sucking bottom, dropped it on deck, and made swift shift to raise sail; *slap/slap/* . . . and then he took the tiller. "And *thennn.* . . . Oh, shite and onions, I don't know. Out to the Welshman's Cayes, maybe."

"Harebrained idea if ever I heard one," the first mate growled, trying to take Jack by the left great-toe. "Why don't you cut your hair and shave that beard and get a job and get drunk, like any decent, civilized son of a bitch would do?"

The white buildings and red roofs and tall palms wavering along the front street, the small boats riding and reflecting, the green mass of the bush behind: all contributed to give Port Cockatoo and environs the look and feel of a South Sea Island. Or, looked at from the viewpoint of another culture, the District Medical Officer (who was due for a retirement which he would not spend in his natal country), said that Port Cockatoo was *"gemütlich."* It was certainly a quiet and a gentle and undemanding sort of place.

But, somehow, it did not seem the totally ideal place for a man not yet thirty, with debts, with energy, with uncertainties, and with a thirty-foot boat.

A bright star slowly detached itself from the darkening land and swam up and up and then stopped and swayed a bit. This was the immense kerosene lamp which was nightly swung to the top of the great flagpole in the Police yard: it could be seen, the local Baymen assured Limekiller, as far out as Serpent Caye. . . . Serpent Caye, the impression was, lay hard upon the very verge of the known and habitable earth, beyond which the River Ocean probably poured its stream into The Abyss.

Taking the hint, Limekiller took his own kerosene lamp, by no means immense, lit it, and set it firmly between two chocks of wood. Technically, there should have been two lamps and of different colors. But the local vessels seldom showed any lights at all. "He see me forst, he blow he conch-*shell*; me see *he* forst, me blow *my* conch-shell." And if neither saw the other. "Well, we suppose to meet each othah . . ." And if they didn't? Well, there was Divine Providence – hardly any lives were lost from such misadventures: unless, of course, someone was drunk. *Very* drunk.

The dimlight lingered and lingered to the west, and then the stars started to come out. It was time, Limekiller thought, to stop for the night.

He was eating his rice and beans and looking at the chart when he heard a voice nearby saying, "Sheep a-high!"

Startled, but by no means alarmed, he called out, "Come aboard!"

What came aboard first was a basket, then a man. A man of no great singularity of appearance, save that he was lacking one eye. "Me name," said the man, "is John Samuel, barn in dis very Colony, me friend, and hence ah subject of de Qveen, God bless hah." Not alone by his color, but by his speech – which, with its odd reversals of *W* and *V*, sounded like Sam Weller's – Mr. Samuel was evidently a White Creole, a member of a class never very large, and steadily dwindling away: sometimes by way of absorption into the non-White majority, sometimes by way of emigration, and sometimes just by way of Death the Leveler. "I tehks de libahty of bringing you some of de forst fruits of de sile," said John S.

"Say, mighty thoughtful of you, Mr. Samuel, care for some rice and beans? – My name's Jack Limekiller."

"– to veet, sour*sop*, bread*fruit*, oh-*ronge*, coco*nut* – vhat I care for, Mr. Limekiller, is some *rum*. *Rum* is vhat I has come to beg of you. De hond of mon, sah, has yet to perfect any medicine de superior of *rum*."

Jack groped in the cubbyhold. "What about all those bush medicines down at Cape Mandee?" he asked, grunting. There was supposed to be a small bottle, a *chaparita*, as they called it. "Where – Oh. It must be. . . . No. Then it must be. . . ."

Mr. Samuel rubbed the grey bristles on his strong jaw. "I does gront you, sah, de wertue of de country yerba. But you must steep de *yerba* en de *rum*, sah. Yes mon."

Jack's fingers finally found the bottle and his one glass and his one cup and poured. Mr. Samuel said nothing until he had downed his, and then gave a sigh of satisfaction. Jack, who had found a mawmee-apple in the basket of fruit, nodded as he peeled it. The flesh was tawny; and reminded him of wintergreen.

After a moment, he decided that he didn't want to finish his rum, and, with a questioning look, passed it over to his guest. It was pleasant there on the open deck, the breeze faint but sufficient, and comparatively few flies of any sort had cared to make the voyage from shore. The boat swayed gently, there was no surf to speak of, the waves of the Atlantic having spent themselves, miles out, upon the reef; and only a few loose items of gear knocked softly as the vessel rose and fell upon the soft bosom of the inner bay.

"Vell sah," said Mr. Samuel, with a slight smack of his lips, "I veesh to acknowledge your generosity. I ahsked you to vahk veet me wan mile, and you vahk veet me twain." Something splashed in the water, and he looked out, sharply.

"Shark?"

"No, mon. Too far een-shore." His eyes gazed out where there was nothing to be seen.

"Porpoise, maybe. Turtle. Or a sting-ray. . . ."

After a moment, Samuel said, "Suppose to be ah tortle." He turned back and gave Limekiller a long, steady look.

Moved by some sudden devil, Limekiller said, "I hope, Mr. Samuel, that you are not about to tell me about some Indian caves or ruins, full of gold, back in the bush, which you are willing to go shares on with me and all I have to do is put up the money — because, you see, Mr. Samuel, I haven't got any money." And added, "Besides, they tell me it's illegal and that all those things belong to the Queen.

Solemnly, Samuel said, "God save de Qveen." Then his eyes somehow seemed to become wider, and his mouth as well, and a sound like hissing steam escaped him, and he sat on the coaming and shook with almost-silent laugher. Then he said, "I sees dot you hahs been ahproached ahlready. No sah. No such teeng. My proposition eenclude only two quality: Expedition. Discretion." And he proceeded to explain that what he meant was that Jack should, at regular intervals, bring him supplies in small quantities and that he would advance the money for this and pay a small amount for the service. Delivery was to be made at night. And nothing was to be said about it, back at Port Cockatoo, or anywhere else.

Evidently Jack Limekiller wasn't the only one who had creditors.

"Anything else, Mr. Samuel?"

Samuel gave a deep sigh. "Ah, mon, I vould like to sogjest dat you breeng me out ah voman . . . but best no. Best not . . . not yet. . . . Oh, mon, I om so lustful, ahlone out here, eef you tie ah rottlesnake down fah me I veel freeg eet!"

"Well, Mr. Samuel, the fact is, I will not tie a rattlesnake down for you, or up for you, for any purpose at all. However, I will keep my eyes open for a board with a knot-hole in it."

Samuel guffawed. Then he got up, his machete slap-flapping against his side, and, with a few more words, clambered down into his dory — no plank-boat, in these waters, but a dug-out — and began to paddle. Bayman, bushman, the machete was almost an article of clothing, though there was nothing to chop out here on the gentle waters of the bay. There was a splash, out there in the darkness, and a cry — Samuel's voice —

"Are you all right out there?" Limekiller called.

"Yes mon. . . ." faintly. "Fine. . . . bloddy Oxville tortle. . . ."

Limekiller fell easily asleep. Presently he dreamed of seeing a large Hawksbill turtle languidly pursuing John Samuel, who languidly evaded the pursuit. Later, he awoke, knowing that he knew what had awakened him, but for the moment unable to name it. The awakeners soon enough identified themselves. Manatees. Sea-cows. The most harmless creatures God ever made. He drowsed off again, but again and again he lightly awoke and always he could hear them sighing and sounding.

Early up, he dropped his line, made a small fire in the sheet-iron caboose set in its box of sand, and put on the pot of rice and beans to cook in coconut oil. The head and tail of the first fish went into a second pot, the top of the double boiler, to make fish-tea, as the chowder was called; when they were done, he gave them to Skippy. He fried the fillets with sliced breadfruit, which had as near no taste of its own as made no matter, but was a great extender of tastes. The second fish he cut and corned – that is, he spread coarse salt on it: there was nothing else to do to preserve it in this hot climate, without ice, and where the art of smoking fish was not known. And more than those two he did not bother to take, he had no license for commercial fishing, could not sell a catch in the market, and the "sport" of taking fish he could neither eat nor sell, and would have to throw back, was a pleasure which eluded his understanding.

It promised to be a hot day and it kept its promise, and he told himself, as he often did on hot, hot days, that it beat shoveling snow in Toronto.

He observed a vacant mooring towards the south of town, recollected that it always had been vacant, and so, for no better reason than that, he tied up to it. Half of the remainder of his catch came ashore with him. This was too far south for any plank houses or tin roofs. Port Cockatoo at both ends straggled out into "trash houses," as they were called – sides of wild cane allowing the cooling breezes to pass, and largely keeping out the brute sun; roofs of thatch, usually of the bay or cohune palm. The people were poorer here than elsewhere in this town where no one at all by North American standards was rich, but "trash" had no reference to that: *Loppings, twigs, and leaves of trees, bruised sugar cane, corn husks, etc.*, his dictionary explained.

An old, old woman in the ankle-length skirts and the kerchief of her generation stood in the doorway of her little house and looked, first at him, then at his catch. And kept on looking at it. All the coastal people of Hidalgo were fascinated by fish: rice and beans was the staple dish, but fish was the roast beef, the steak, the chicken, of this small, small country which had never been rich and was now – with the growing depletion of its mahogany and rosewood – even poorer than ever. Moved, not so much by conscious consideration of this as by a sudden impulse, he held up his hand and what it was holding. "Care for some corned fish, Grandy?" Automatically, she reached out her tiny, dark hand, all twisted and withered, and took it. Her lips moved. She looked from the fish to him and from him to the fish; asked, doubtfully, "How much I have for you?" – meaning, how much did she owe him.

"Your prayers," he said, equally on impulse.

Her head flew up and she looked at him full in the face, then. "T'ank you, Buckra," she said. "And I weel do so. I weel pray for you." And she went back into her trash house.

Up the dusty, palm-lined path a ways, just before it branched into the cemetery road and the front street, he encountered Mr. Stuart – white-haired, learned, benevolent, deaf, and vague – and wearing what was surely the very last sola topee in everyday use in the Western Hemisphere (and perhaps, what with one thing and another, in the Eastern, as well).

"Did you hear the babboons last night?" asked Mr. Stuart.

Jack knew that "babboons," hereabouts, were howler-monkeys. Even their daytime noises, a hollow and repetitive *Rrrr-Rrrr-Rrrr*, sounded uncanny enough; as for their night-time wailings –

"I was anchored offshore, down the coast, last night," he explained. "All I heard were the manatees."

Mr. Stuart looked at him with grey eyes, smoothed his long moustache. "Ah, *those* poor chaps," he said. "They've slipped back down the scale . . . much *too* far down, I expect, for any quick return. Tried to help them, you know. Tried the Herodotus method. Carthaginians. Mute trade, you know. Set out some bright red cloth, put trade-goods on, went away. Returned. Things were knocked about, as though animals had been at them. *Some* of the items were gone, though. But nothing left in return. Too bad; oh yes, too bad . . ." His voice died away into a low moan, and he shook his ancient head. In another moment, before Jack could say anything, or even think of anything to say, Mr. Stuart had flashed him a smile of pure friendliness, and was gone. A bunch of flowers was in one hand, and the path he took was the cemetery road. He had gone to visit one of "the great company of the dead, which increase around us as we grow older."

From this mute offering, laid also upon the earth, nothing would be expected in return. There are those whom we do not see and whom we do not desire that they should ever show themselves at all.

The shop of Captain Cumberbatch was open. The rules as to what stores or offices were open and closed at which times were exactly the opposite of the laws of the Medes and the Persians. The time to go shopping was when one saw the shop open. Any shop. They opened, closed, opened, closed. . . . And as to why stores with a staff of only one closed so often, why, they closed not only to allow the proprietor to siesta, they also closed to allow him to eat. It was no part of the national culture for Ma to send Pa's "tea" for Pa to eat behind the counter: Pa came home. Period. And as for establishments with a staff of more than one, why could the staff not have taken turns? Answer: De baas, of whatsoever race, creed, or color, might trust an employee with his life, but he would never trust his employee with his cash or stock, never, never, never.

Captain Cumberbatch had for many years puffed up and down the coast in his tiny packet-and-passenger boat, bringing cargo merchandise for the shopkeepers of Port Caroline, Port Cockatoo, and – very, very semi-occasionally – anywhere else as chartered. But some years ago he had swallowed the anchor and set up business as shopkeeper in Port Cockatoo. And one day an epiphany of sorts had occurred: Captain Cumberbatch had asked himself why he should bring cargo for others to sell and/or why he should pay others to bring cargo for he himself to sell. Why should he not bring his own cargo and sell it himself?

The scheme was brilliant as it was unprecedented. And indeed it had but one discernible flaw: whilst Captain Cumberbatch was at sea, he could not tend shop to sell what he had shipped. And while he was tending his shop he could not put to sea to replenish stock. And, tossing ceaselessly from the one horn of this dilemma to the other, he often thought resentfully of the difficulties of competing with such peoples as the Chinas, Turks, and 'Paniards, who – most unfairly – were able to trust the members of their own families to mind the store.

Be all this as it may, the shop of Captain Cumberbatch was at this very moment open, and the captain himself was leaning upon his counter and smoking a pipe.

"Marneen, Jock. Hoew de day?"

"Bless God."

"Forever and ever, ehhh-men."

A certain amount of tinned corned-beef and corned-beef hash, of white sugar (it was nearer grey), of bread (it was dead white, as unsuitable an item of diet as could be designed for the country and the country would have rioted at the thought of being asked to eat dark), salt, lamp-oil, tea, tinned milk, cheese, were packed and passed across the worn counter; a certain amount of national currency made the same trip in reverse.

As for the prime purchaser of the items, Limekiller said nothing. That was part of the Discretion.

Outside again, he scanned the somnolent street for any signs that anyone might have – somehow – arrived in town who might want to charter a boat for . . . well, for anything. Short of smuggling, there was scarcely a purpose for which he would have not chartered the *Saccharissa*. It was not that he had an invincible repugnance to the midnight trade, there might well be places and times where he would have considered it. But Government, in British Hidalgo (here, as elsewhere in what was left of the Empire, the definite article was conspicuously absent: "Government will do this," they said – or, often as not, "Government will not do this") had not vexed him in any way and he saw no reason to vex it. And, furthermore, he had heard many reports of the accommodations at the Queen's Hotel, as the King Town "gaol" was called: and they were uniformly unfavorable.

But the front street was looking the same as ever, and, exemplifying, as ever, the observation of The Preacher, that there was no new thing under the sun. So, with only the smallest of sighs, he had started for the Cupid Club, when the clop-clop of hooves made him look up. Coming along the street was the horse-drawn equivalent of a pickup truck. The back was open, and contained a few well-filled crocus sacks and some sawn timber; the front was roofed, but open at the sides; and for passengers it had a white-haired woman and a middle-aged man. It drew to a stop.

"Well, young man. And who are *you*?" the woman asked. Some elements of the soft local accent overlaid her speech, but underneath was something else, something equally soft, but different. Her "Man" was not *mon*, it was *mayun*, and her "you" was more like *yieww*.

He took off his hat. "Jack Limekiller is my name, ma'am."

"Put it right back on, Mr. Limekiller. I do appreciate the gesture, but it has already been gestured, now. Draft-dodger, are you?"

That was a common guess. Any North American who didn't fit into an old and familiar category – tourist sport fisherman, sport huntsman, missionary, businessman was assumed to be either a draft dodger or a trafficker in weed . . . or maybe both. "No, ma'am I've served my time, and, anyway, I'm a Canadian, and we don't have a draft."

"Well," she said, "doesn't matter even if you are, I don't *cay-uh*. Now, sir, I am Amelia Lebedee. And this is my nephew, Tom McFee." Tom smiled a faint and abstract smile, shook hands. He was sun-dark and had a slim moustache and he wore a felt hat which had perhaps been crisper than it was now. Jack had not seen many men like Tom McFee in Canada, but he had seen many men like Tom McFee in the United States. Tom McFee sold crab in Baltimore. Tom McFee managed the smaller cotton gin in a two-gin town in Alabama. Tom McFee was foreman at the shrimp-packing plant in one of the Florida Parishes in Louisiana. And Tom McFee was railroad freight agent in whatever dusty town in Texas it was that advertised itself as "Blue Vetch Seed Capital of the World."

"We are carrying you off to Shiloh for lunch," said Amelia, and a handsome old woman she was, and sat up straight at the reins. "So you just climb up in. Tom will carry you back later, when he goes for some more of this wood. Land! You'd think it was *teak*, they cut it so slow. Instead of pine."

Limekiller had no notion who or what or where Shiloh was, although it clearly could not be very far, and he could think of no reason why he should not go there. So in he climbed.

"Yes," said Amelia Lebedee, "the war wiped us out completely. So we came down here and we planted sugar, yes, we planted sugar and we made sugar for, oh, most eighty years. But we didn't move with the times, and so that's all over with now. – We plant most anything *but* sugar nowadays. And when we see a new and a civilized face, we plant them down at the table." By this time the wagon was out of town. The bush to either side of the road looked like just bush-type bush to Jack. But to Mrs. Lebedee each acre had an identity of its own. "That was the Cullen's place," she'd say. And, "The Robinson's lived there. Beautiful horses, they had. Nobody has horses anymore, just us. Yonder used to be the Simmonses. Part of the house is still standing, but, land! – you cain't see it from the road anymore. They've gone back. Most everybody has gone back, who hasn't died off. . . ." For a while she said nothing. The road gradually grew narrower, and all three of them began thoughtfully to slap at "flies."

A bridge now appeared and they rattled across it, a dark-green stream rushing below. There was a glimpse of an old grey house in the archaic, universal-tropical style, and then the bush closed in again. "And *they*-uh," Miss Amelia gestured, backwards, "is Texas. Oh, what a fine place that was, in its day! Nobody lives there, now. Old Captain Rutherford, the original settler, he was with Hood. *Gen*eral Hood, I mean."

It all flashed on Jack at once, and it all came clear, and he wondered that it had not been clear from the beginning. They were now – passing through the site of the old Confederate colony. There had been such in Venezuela, in Colombia, even in Brazil; for all he knew, there might still be. But this one here in Hidalgo, it had not been wiped out in a year or two, like the Mormon colonies in Mexico – there had been no Revolution here, no gringo-hating Villistas – it had just ebbed away. Tiny little old B.H., "a country," as someone (who?) had said, "which you can put your arms around," had put its arms around the Rebel refugees . . . its thin, green arms . . . and it had let them clear the bush and build their houses . . . and it had waited . . . and waited . . . and, as, one by one, the Southern American families had "died out" or "gone back," why, as easy as easy, the bush had slipped back. And, for the present, it seemed like it was going to stay back. It had, after all, closed in so mysteriously left, and that was a thousand years ago. What was a hundred years, to the bush?

The house at Shiloh was small and neat and trim and freshly painted, and one end of the veranda was undergoing repairs. There had been no nonsense, down here, of reproducing any of the ten thousand imitations of Mount Vernon. A neatly-mowed lawn surrounded the house; in a moment, as the wagon made its last circuit, Jack saw that the lawnmowers were a small herd of cattle. A line of cedars accompanied the road, and Miss Amelia pointed to a gap in the line. "That tree that was there," she said, calmly, "was the one that fell on my husband and on John Samuel. It had been obviously weakened in the hurricane, you know, and they went over to see how badly – that was a mistake. John Samuel lost his left eye and my husband lost his life."

Discretion. . . . Would it be indiscreet to ask – ? He asked.

"How long ago was this, Miss Amelia?" All respectable women down here were "Miss," followed by the first name, regardless of marital state.

"It was ten years ago, come September," she said. "Let's go in out of the sun, now, and Tom will take care of the horse."

In out of the sun was cool and neat and, though shady, the living room-dining room was as bright as fresh paint and flowered wall-paper – the only wall-paper he had seen in the colony – could make it. There were flowers in vases, too, fresh flowers, not the widely-popular plastic ones. Somehow the Bayfolk did not make much of flowers.

For lunch there was heart-of-palm, something not often had, for a palm had to die to provide it, and palms were not idly cut down: there was the vegetable pear, or chayote, here called cho-cho; venison chops, tomato with okra; there was cashew wine, made from the fruit of which the Northern Lands know only the seed, which they ignorantly call "nut." And, even, there was coffee, not powdered ick, not grown-in-Brazil-shipped-to-the-United States-roasted-ground-canned-shipped-to-Hidalgo-coffee, but actual local coffee. Here, where coffee grew with no more care than weeds, hardly anyone except the Indians bothered to grow it, and what *they* grew, *they* used.

"Yes," Miss Amelia said, "it can be a very good life here. It is necessary to work, of course, but the work is well-rewarded, oh, not in terms of large sums of money, but in so many other ways. But it's coming to an end. There is just no way that working this good land can bring you all the riches you see in the moving pictures. And that is what they all want, and dream of, all the young people. And there is just no way they are going to get it."

Tom McFee made one of his rare comments. "*I* don't dream of any white Christmas," he said. "I am staying here, where it is always green. I told Malcolm Stuart that."

Limekiller said, "I was just talking to him this morning, myself. But I couldn't understand what he was talking about . . . something about trying to trade with the manatees. . . ."

The Shiloh people, clearly, had no trouble understanding what Stuart had been talking about; they did not even think it was particularly bizarre. "Ah, those poor folks down at Mandee," said Amelia Lebedee; "– now, mind you, I mean *Mandee*, Cape Mandee, I am *not* referring to the people up on Man*a*tee River and the

Lagoons, who are just as civilized as you and I: I mean *Cape Mandee*, which is its correct name, you know –"

"Where the medicine herbs grew?"

"Why, yes, Mr. Limekiller. Where they grew. As I suppose they still do. No one really knows, of course, *what* still grows down at Cape Mandee, though Nature, I suppose, would not change her ways. It was the hurricanes, you see. The War Year hurricanes. Until then, you know, Government had kept a road open, and once a month a police constable would ride down and, well, at least, take a look around. Not that any of the people there would ever bring any of their troubles to the police. They were . . . well, how should I put it? Tom, how would you put it?"

Tom thought a long moment. "Simple. They were always simple."

What he meant by "simple," it developed, was simple-minded.

His aunt did not entirely agree with that. They gave that impression, the Mandee people, she said, but that was only because their ways were so different. "There is a story," she said, slowly, and, it seemed to Jack Limekiller, rather reluctantly, "that a British man-of-war took a Spanish slave-ship. I don't know when this would have been, it was well before we came down and settled here. Well before The War. Our own War, I mean. It was a small Spanish slaver and there weren't many captives in her. As I understand it, between the time that Britain abolished slavery and the dreadful Atlantic slave-trade finally disappeared, if slavers were taken anywhere near Africa, the British would bring the captives either to Saint Helena or Sierra Leone, and liberate them there. But this one was taken fairly near the American coast. I suppose she was heading for Cuba so the British ship brought them *here*. To British Hidalgo. And the people were released down at Cape Mandee, and told they could settle there and no one would 'vex' them, as they say here."

Where the slaves had come from, originally, she did not know, but she thought the tradition was that they had come from somewhere well back in the African interior. Over the course of the many subsequent years, some had trickled into the more settled parts of the old colony. "But some of them just stayed down there," she said. "Keeping up their own ways."

"Too much intermarrying," Tom offered.

"So the Bayfolk say. The Bayfolk, were always, *I* think, rather afraid of them. None of them would ever go there alone. And, after the hurricanes, when the road went out, and the police just couldn't get there, none of the Bayfolk would go there at *all.* By sea, I mean. You must remember, Mr. Limekiller, that in the 1940s this little colony was very much as it was in the 1840s. There were no airplanes. There wasn't one single highway. When I say there used to be a road to Mandee, you mustn't think it was a road such as we've got between Port Cockatoo and Shiloh."

Limekiller, thinking of the dirt road between Port Cockatoo and Shiloh, tried to think what the one between Port Cockatoo and the region behind Cape Mandee must have been like. Evidently a trail, nothing more, down which an occasional man on a mule might make his way, boiling the potato-like fruit of the breadnut tree for his food and feeding his mule the leaves: a trail that had to be "chopped," had to be "cleaned" by machete-work, at least twice a year, to keep the all-consuming bush from closing over it the way the flesh closes over a cut. An occasional trader, an occasional buyer or gatherer of chicle or herbs or hides, an occasional missioner or medical officer, at infrequent intervals would pass along this corridor in the eternal jungle.

And then came a hurricane, smashing flat everything in its path. And the trail vanished. And the trail was never re-cut. British Hidalgo had probably never been high on any list of colonial priorities at the best of times. During the War of 1939-1945, they may have forgotten all about it in London. Many of Hidalgo's able-bodied men were off on distant fronts. An equal number had gone off to cut the remaining forests of the Isle of Britain, to supply anyway a fraction of the wood which was then impossible to import. Nothing could be spared for Mandee and its people; in King Town, Mandee was deemed as distant as King Town was in London. The P.C. never went there again. No missioner ever returned. Neither had a medical officer or nurse. Nor any trader. No one. Except for Malcolm Stuart. . . .

"He did try. Of course, he had his own concerns. During the War he had his war work. Afterwards, he took up a block of land a few miles back from here, and he had his hands full with that. And then, after, oh, I don't remember how many years of stories, stories – there is no television here, you know, and few people have time for books – stories about the Mandee people, well, he decided he had to go have a look, see for himself, you know."

Were the Mandee people really eating raw meat and raw fish? He would bring them matches. Had they actually reverted to the use of stone for tools? He would bring them machetes, axes, knives. And . . . as for the rest of it . . . the rest of the rather awful and certainly very odd stories . . . he would see for himself.

But he had seen nothing. There had been nothing to see. That is, nothing which he could be sure he had seen. Perhaps he had thought that he had seen some few things which he had not cared to mention to Jack, but had spoken of to the Shiloh people.

They, however, were not about to speak of it to Jack.

"Adventure," said Amelia Lebedee, dismissing the matter of Mandee with a sigh. "Nobody wants the adventure of cutting bush to plant yams. They want the adventure of night clubs and large automobiles. They see it in the moving pictures. And you, Mr. Limekiller, what is it that you want? coming, having come, from the land of night clubs and large automobiles. . . ."

The truth was simple. "I wanted the adventure of sailing a boat with white sails through tropic seas," he said. "I saw it in the moving pictures. I never had a night club but I had a large automobile, and I sold it and came down here and bought the boat. And, well, here I am."

They had talked right through the siesta time. Tom McFee was ready, now, to return for the few more planks which the sawmill might – or might not – have managed to produce since the morning. It was time to stand up now and to make thanks and say goodbye. "Yes," said Amelia Lebedee, pensively. "Here we are. Here we all are. We are all here. And some of us are more content being here than others."

Half-past three at the Cupid Club. On Limekiller's table, the usual single bottle of beer. Also, the three chaparitas of rum which he had bought – but they were in a paper bag, lest the sight of them, plus the fact that he could invite no one to drink of them, give rise to talk that he was "mean." Behind the bar, Alfonso Key. In the dark, dark back, slowly sipping a lemonade (all soft drinks were "lemonade" – coke was lemonade, strawberry pop was lemonade, ginger stout was lemonade . . . sometimes, though not often, for reasons inexplicable, there was also lemon-flavored lemonade) – in the dark rear part of the room, resting his perpetually sore eyes, was old Captain Cudgel.

"Well, how you spend the night, Jock?" Alfonso ready for a tale of amour, ready with a quip, a joke.

"Oh, just quietly. Except for the manatees." Limekiller, saying this, had a sudden feeling that he had said all this before, been all this before, was caught on the Moebius strip which life in picturesque Port Cockatoo had already become, caught, caught, never would be released. *Adventure*! Hah!

At this point, however, a slightly different note, a slightly different comment from the old, old man.

"Een Eedalgo," he said, dolefully, "de monatee hahv no leg, mon. Becahs Eedalgo ees a smahl coun-*tree*, ahn every-teeng smahl. Every-teeng *weak*. Now, een Ahfrica, mon, de monatee *does* hahv leg."

Key said, incredulous, but still respectful, "What you tell we, Coptain Cudgel? *What*?" His last word, pronounced in the local manner of using it as a particular indication of skepticism, of criticism, of denial, seemed to have at least three *T*s at the end of it; he repeated: "Wha*ttt*?"

"Yes, mon. Yes sah. Een Ahfrica, de monatee hahv *leg*, mon. Eet be ah poerful beast, een Ahfrica, come up on de *lond*, on."

"Me no di hear *dot* befoah."

"I tell you. *Me* di hear eet befoah. Een Ahfrica," he repeated, doggedly, "de monatee hahv leg, de monatee be ah poerful beast, come up on de *lond*, mon, no lahf, mon —"

"Me no di lahf, sah —"

"— de w'ol' people, dey tell me so, fah true."

Alfonso Key gave his head a single shake, gave a single click of his tongue, gave Jack a single look.

Far down the street, the bell of the Church of Saint Benedict the Moor sounded. Whatever time it was marking had nothing to do with Greenwich Meridian Time or any variation thereof.

The weak, feeble old voice resumed the thread of conversation. "Me grahndy di tell me dot she grahndy di tell *she*. Motta hav foct, eet me grahndy di give me me name, b'y. Cudgel. Ahfrica name. Fah true. Fah true."

A slight sound of surprise broke Limekiller's silence. He said, "Excuse me, Captain. Could it have been 'Cudjoe' . . . maybe?"

For a while he thought that the question had either not been heard or had, perhaps, been resented. Then the old man said, "Eet could be so. Sah, eet might be so. Lahng, lahng time ah-*go*. . . . Me Christian name, Pe-tah. Me w'ol' grahndy she say, 'Pickney: you hahv ah Christian name, Pe-tah. But me give you Ahfrica name, too. Cahdjo. No fah-get, pickney? Time poss, time poss, de people dey ahl cahl me 'Cudgel,' you see, sah. So me fah-get . . . Sah, hoew you know dees teeng, sah?"

Limekiller said that he thought he had read it in a book. The old captain repeated the word, lengthening it in his local speech. "Ah boook, sah. To t'eenk ahv dot. Een ah boook. Me w'own name een ah boook." By and by he departed as silently as always.

In the dusk a white cloth waved behind the thin line of white beach. He took off his shirt and waved back. Then he transferred the groceries into the skiff and, as soon as it was dark and he had lit and securely fixed his lamp, set about rowing ashore. By and by a voice called out, "Mon, vhere de Hell you gveyn? You keep on to de right, you gveyn vine up een *Sponeesh* Hidalgo: mah to de lef, mon: mah to de lef!" And with such assistances, soon enough the skiff softly scraped the beach.

Mr. John Samuel's greeting was, "You bring de rum?" The rum put in his hand, he took up one of the sacks, gestured Limekiller towards the other. "Les go timely, noew," he said. For a moment, in what was left of the dimmest dimlight, Jack thought the man was going to walk straight into an enormous tree: instead, he walked across the enormous roots and behind the tree. Limekiller followed the faint white patch of shirt bobbing in front of him. Sometimes the ground was firm, sometimes it went squilchy, sometimes it was simply running water – shallow, fortunately – sometimes it felt like gravel. The bush noises were still fairly soft. A rustle. He hoped it was only a wish-willy lizard, or a bamboo-chicken – an iguana – and not a yellow-jaw, that snake of which it was said . . . but this was no time to remember scare stories about snakes.

Without warning – although what sort of warning there could have been was a stupid question, anyway – there they were. Gertrude Stein, returning to her old home town after an absence of almost forty years, and finding the old home itself demolished, had observed (with a lot more objectivity than she was usually credited with) that there was no *there*, there. The *there*, here, was simply a clearing . . . with a very small fire, and a *ramada*: four poles holding up a low thatched roof. John Samuel let his sack drop. "Ahnd noew," he said, portentously, "let us broach de rum."

After the chaparita had been not only broached but drained, for the second time that day Limekiller dined ashore. The cooking was done on a raised fire-hearth of clay-and-sticks, and what was cooked was a breadfruit, simply strewn, when done, with sugar; and a gibnut. To say that the gibnut, or paca, is a rodent, is perhaps – though accurate – unfair: it is larger than a rabbit, and it eats well. After that Samuel made black tea and laced it with more rum. After that he gave a vast belch and a vast sigh. "Can you play de bon*joe*?" he next asked.

"Well. . . . I have been known to try. . . ."

The lamp flared and smoked. Samuel adjusted it . . . somewhat . . . He got up and took a bulky object down from a peg on one of the roof-poles. It was a sheet of thick plastic, laced with raw-hide thongs, which he laboriously unknotted. Inside that was a deerskin. And inside that, an ordinary banjo-case, which contained an ordinary, if rather old and worn, banjo.

"Mehk I hear ah sahng . . . ah sahng ahv *you* country."

What song should he make him hear? No particularly Canadian song brought itself to mind. Ah well, he would dip down below the border just a bit. . . . His fingers strummed idly on the strings. The words grew, the tune grew, he lifted up what some (if not very many) had considered a not-bad-baritone, and began to sing and play.

Manatee gal, won't you come out tonight,
Come out tonight, come out tonight?
Oh, Manatee gal won't you come out tonight,
To dance by the light of the –

An enormous hand suddenly covered his own and pressed it down. The tune subsided into a jumble of chords, and an echo, and a silence.

"Mon, mon, you not do me right. I no di say, 'Mehk I hear a sahng ahv *you* country'?" Samuel, on his knees, breathed heavily. His breath was heavy with rum and his voice was heavy with reproof . . . and with a something else for which Limekiller had no immediate name. But, friendly it was not.

Puzzled more than apologetic, Jack said, "Well, it *is* a North American song, anyway. It was an old Erie Canal song. It – Oh. I'll be damned. Only it's supposed to go, '*Buffalo gal, won't you come out tonight,*' And I dunno what made me change it, what difference does it make?"

"Vhat different? Vhat different it mehk? Ah, Christ me King! You lee' buckra b'y, you not know w'ehnnah-teeng?"

It was all too much for Limekiller. The last thing he wanted was anything resembling an argument, here in the deep, dark bush, with an all-but-stranger. Samuel having lifted his heavy hand from the instrument, Limekiller, moved by a sudden spirit, began,

Amazing grace, how sweet the sound,
To save a wretch like me.

With a rough catch of his breath, Samuel muttered, "Yes. Yes. Dot ees good. Go on, b'y. No stop."

I once was halt, but now can walk:
Was blind, but now I see . . .

He sang the beautiful old hymn to the end: and, by that time, if not overpowered by Grace, John Samuel – having evidently broached the second and the third chaparita – was certainly over-powered: and it did not look as though the dinner-guest was going to get any kind of guided tour back to the shore and the skiff. He sighed and he looked around him. A bed rack had roughly been fixed up, and its lashings were covered with a few deer hides and an old Indian blanket. Samuel not responding to any shakings or urgings, Limekiller, with a shrug and a "Well what the Hell," covered him with the blanket as he lay upon the ground. Then, having rolled up the sacks the supplies had come in and propped them under his head, Limekiller disposed himself for slumber on the hides. Some lines were running through his head and he paused a moment to consider what they were. What they were, they were, *From ghoulies and ghosties, long-leggedy feasties, and bugges that go* boomp *in the night, Good Lord, deliver us.* With an almost absolute certainty that this was not the Authorized Version or Text, he heard himself give a grottle and a snore and knew he was fallen asleep.

He awoke to slap heartily at some flies, and the sound perhaps awoke the host, who was heard to mutter and mumble. Limekiller leaned over. "What did you say?"

The lines said, Limekiller learned that he had heard them before. "Eef you tie ah rottlesnake doewn fah me, I veel freeg eet."

"I yield," said Limekiller, "to any man so much hornier than myself. Produce the snake, sir, and I will consider the rest of the matter."

The red eye of the expiring fire winked at him. It was still winking at him when he awoke from a horrid nightmare of screams and thrashings-about in the course of which he had evidently fallen or had thrown himself from the bedrack to the far side. Furthermore, he must have knocked against one of the roof-poles in doing so, because a good deal of the thatch had landed on top of him. He threw it off, and, getting up, began to apologize.

"Sorry if I woke you, Mr. Samuel. I don't know what –" There was no answer, and looking around in the faint light of the fire, he saw no one.

"Mr. Samuel? Mr. *Samuel*? John? Oh, hey, *Johhhn*!? . . ."

No answer. If the man had merely gone out to "ease himself," as the Bayfolk delicately put it, he would have surely been near enough to answer. No one in the colony engaged in strolling in the bush at night for fun. "Son of a bitch," he muttered. He felt for and found his matches, struck one, found the lamp, lit it, looked around.

There was still no sign of John Samuel, but what there were signs of was some sort of horrid violence. Hastily he ran his hands over himself, but, despite his fall, despite part of the roof having fallen on him, he found no trace of blood.

All the blood which lay around, then, must have been – could only have been – John Samuel's blood.

And the screaming and the sounds of something – or some things – heavily thrashing around, they had not been in any dream. They had been the sounds of truth.

And as for what else he saw, as he walked, delicate as Agag, around the perimeter of the clearing, he preferred not to speculate.

There was a shotgun and there were shells. He put the shells into the chambers and he stood up, weapon in his hand, all the rest of the night.

"Now, if it took you perhaps less than an hour to reach the shore, and if you left immediately, how is it that you were so long in arriving at Port?" the District Commissioner asked. He asked politely, but he did ask. He asked a great many questions, for, in addition to his other duties, he was the Examining Magistrate.

"Didn't you observe the wind, D.C.? Ask anyone who was out on the water yesterday. I spent most of the day tacking –"

Corporal Huggin said, softly, from the wheel, "That would be correct, Mr. Blossom."

They were in the police boat, the *George . . .* once, Jack had said to P.C. Ed Huggin, "For George VI, I suppose?" and Ed, toiling over the balky and antique engine, his clear tan skin smudged with grease, had scowled, and said, "More for bloody George III you ask *me*. . . ." At earliest daylight, yesterday, Limekiller, red-eyed and twitching, had briefly cast around in the bush near the camp, decided that, ignorant of bush-lore as he was, having not even a compass, let alone a pair of boots or a snake-bite kit, it would have been insane to attempt any explorations. He found his way along the path, found his skiff still tied up, and had rowed to his boat. Unfavorable winds had destroyed his hope of being of getting back to Port Cockatoo in minimum time: it had been night when he arrived.

The police had listened to his story, had summoned Mr. Florian Blossom, the District Commissioner; all had agreed that "No purpose would be served by attempting anything until next morning." They had taken his story down, word by word, and by hand – if there was an official stenographer anywhere in the country, Limekiller had yet to hear of it – and by longhand, too; and in their own accustomed style and method, too, so that he was officially recorded as having said things such as: *Awakened by loud sounds of distress, I arose and hailed the man known to me as John Samuel. Upon receiving no response,* etcetera.

After Jack had signed the statement, and stood up, thinking to return to his boat, the District Commissioner said, "I believe that they can accommodate you with a bed in the Unmarried Police Constables' Quarters, Mr. Limekiller. Just for the night."

He looked at the official. A slight shiver ran up and down him. "Do you mean that I am a prisoner?"

"Certainly not, Mr. Limekiller. No such thing."

"You know, if I had wanted to, I could have been in Republican waters by now."

Mr. Blossom's politeness never flagged. "We realise it and we take it into consideration, Mr. Limekiller. But if we are all of us here together it will make an early start in the morning more efficacious." Anyway, Jack was able to shower, and Ed Huggin loaned him clean clothes. Of course they had not gotten an early start in the morning. Only fishermen and sandboatmen got early starts. Her Majesty's Government moved at its accustomed pace. In the police launch, besides Limekiller, was P.C. Huggin, D.C. Blossom, a very small and very black and very wiry man called

Harlow the Hunter, Police-Sergeant Ruiz, and white-haired Dr. Rafael, the District Medical Officer.

"I wouldn't have been able to come at all, you know," he said to Limekiller, "except my assistant has returned from his holidays a day earlier Oh, there is so much to see in this colony! Fascinating, fascinating!"

D.C. Blossom smiled. "Doctor Rafael is a famous antiquarian, you know, Mr. Limekiller. It was he who discovered the grave-*stone* of my three or four times great-grandsir and -grandy."

Sounds of surprise and interest – polite on Limekiller's part, gravestones perhaps not being what he would have most wished to think of – genuine on the part of everyone else, ancestral stones not being numerous in British Hidalgo.

"Yes, yes," Dr. Rafael agreed. "Two years ago I was on *my* holidays, and I went out to St. Saviour's Caye . . . well, to what is left of St. Saviour's Caye after the last few hurricanes. You can imagine what is left of the old settlement. Oh, the Caye is dead, it is like a skeleton, bleached and bare!" Limekiller felt he could slightly gladly have tipped the medico over the side and watched the bubbles; but, unaware, on the man went. "– so, difficult though it was making my old map agree with the present outlines, still, I did find the site of the old burial-ground, and I cast about and I prodded with my iron rod, and I felt stone underneath the sand, and I dug!"

More sounds of excited interest. Digging in the sand on the bit of ravished sand and coral where the ancient settlement had been – but was no more – was certainly of more interest than digging for yams on the fertile soil of the mainland. And, even though they already knew that it was not a chest of gold, still, they listened and they murmured *oh* and *ah,* "The letters were still very clear, I had no difficulty reading them. *Sacred to the memory of Ferdinando Rousseau, a native of Guernsey, and of Marianna his Wife, a native of Mandingo, in Africa.* Plus a poem in three stanzas, of which I have deposited a copy in the National Archives, and of course I have a copy myself and a third copy I offered to old Mr. Ferdinand Rousseau in King Town –"

Smiling, Mr. Blossom asked, "And what he tell you, then, Doctor?"

Dr. Rafael's smile was a trifle rueful. "He said, 'Let the dead bury their dead' –" The others all laughed. Mr. Ferdinand Rousseau was evidently known to all of them. "– and he declined to take it.

Well, I was aware that Mr. Blossom's mother was a cousin of Mr. Rousseau's mother —" ("Double-cousin," said Mr. Blossom.)

Said Mr. Blossom, "And the doctor has even been there, too, to that country. I don't mean Guernsey; in Africa, I mean; not true, Doctor?"

Up ahead, where the coast thrust itself out into the blue, blue Bay, Jack thought he saw the three isolated palms which were his landmark. But there was no hurry. He found himself unwilling to hurry anything at all.

Doctor Rafael, in whose voice only the slightest trace of alien accent still lingered, said that after leaving Vienna, he had gone to London, in London he had been offered and had accepted work in a British West African colonial medical service. "I was just a bit surprised that the old grave-stone referred to Mandingo as a country, there is no such country on the maps today, but there are such a people."

"What they like, Doc-tah? What they like, thees people who dey mehk some ahv Mr. Blossom ahn-ces-tah?"

There was another chuckle. This one had slight overtones.

The DMO's round, pink face furrowed in concentration among memories a quarter of a century old. "Why," he said, "they are like elephants. They never forget."

There was a burst of laughter. Mr. Blossom laughed loudest of them all. Twenty-five years earlier he would have asked about Guernsey; today. . . .

Harlow the Hunter, his question answered, gestured towards the shore. A slight swell had come up, the blue was flecked, with bits of white. "W'over dere, suppose to be wan ahv w'ol' Bob Blaine cahmp, in de w'ol' days."

"Filthy fellow," Dr. Rafael said, suddenly, concisely.

"Yes sah," Harlow agreed. "He was ah lewd fellow, fah true, fah true. What he use to say, he use to say, 'Eef you tie ah rottle-snehk doewn fah me, I weel freeg eet. . . .'"

Mr. Blossom leaned forward. "Something the matter, Mr. Limekiller?"

Mr. Limekiller did not at that moment feel like talking. Instead, he lifted his hand and pointed towards the headland with the three isolated palms.

"Cape Mandee, Mr. Limekiller? What about it?"

Jack cleared his throat. "I thought that was farther down the coast . . . according to my chart. . . ."

Ed Huggin snorted. "Chart! Washington chart copies London chart and London chart I think must copy the original chart made by old Captain Cook. *Chart!*" He snorted again.

Mr. Florian Blossom asked, softly, "Do you recognize your landfall, Mr. Limekiller? I suppose it would not be at the Cape itself, which is pure mangrove bog and does not fit the description which you gave us. . . ."

Mr. Limekiller's eyes hugged the coast. Suppose he couldn't *find* the goddamned place? Police and Government wouldn't like that at all. Every ounce of fuel had to be accounted for. Chasing the wild goose was not approved. He might find an extension of his stay refused when next he went applying for it. He might even find himself officially listed as a Proscribed Person, trans.: haul-ass, Jack, and don't try coming back. And he realized that he did not want that at all, at all. The whole coast looked the same to him, all of a sudden. And then, all of a sudden, it didn't . . . somehow. There was something about that solid-seeming mass of bush –

"I think there may be a creek. Right there."

Harlow nodded. "Yes mon. Is a creek. Right dere."

And right there, at the mouth of the creek – in this instance, meaning not a stream, but an inlet – Limekiller recognized the huge tree. And Harlow the Hunter recognized something else. "Dot mark suppose to be where Mr. Limekiller drah up the skiff."

"Best we ahl put boots *on,*" said Sergeant Ruiz, who had said not word until now. They all put boots on. Harlow shouldered an axe. Ruiz and Huggin took up machetes. Dr. Rafael had, besides his medical bag, a bundle of what appeared to be plastic sheets and crocus sacks. "You doesn't mind to cahry ah shovel, Mr. Jock?" Jack decided that he could think of a number of things he had rather carry: but he took the thing. And Mr. Blossom carefully picked up an enormous camera, with tripod. The Governments of His and/or Her Majesties had never been known for throwing money around in these parts; the camera could hardly have dated back to George III but was certainly earlier than the latter part of the reign of George V.

"You must lead us, Mr. Limekiller." The District Commissioner was not grim. He was not smiling. He was grave.

Limekiller nodded. Climbed over the sprawling trunk of the tree. Suddenly remembered that it had been night when he had first come this way, that it had been from the other direction that he had made his way the next morning, hesitated. And then Harlow the Hunter spoke up.

"Eef you pleases, Mistah Blossom. I believes I knows dees pahth bet-tah."

And, at any rate, he knew it well enough to lead them there in less, surely, than Jack Limekiller could have.

Blood was no longer fresh red, but a hundred swarms of flies suddenly rose to show where the blood had been. Doctor Rafael snipped leaves, scooped up soil, deposited his take in containers.

And in regard to other evidence, whatever it was evidence of, for one thing, Mr. Blossom handed the camera over to Police-Corporal Huggin, who set up his measuring tape, first along one deep depression and photographed it; then along another . . . another . . . another . . .

"Mountain-cow," said the District Commissioner. He did not sound utterly persuaded.

Harlow shook his head. "No, Mistah Florian. No sah. No, no."

"Well, if not a tapir: what?"

Harlow shrugged.

Something heavy had been dragged through the bush. And it had been dragged by something heavier . . . something much, much heavier . . . It was horridly hot in the bush, and every kind of "fly" seemed to be ready and waiting for them: sand-fly, bottle fly, doctorfly. They made unavoidable noise, but whenever they stopped, the silence closed in on them. No wild parrot shrieked. No "babboons" rottled or growled. No warree grunted or squealed. Just the waiting silence of the bush. Not friendly. Not hostile. Just indifferent.

And when they came to the little river (afterwards, Jack could not even find it on the maps) and scanned the opposite bank and saw nothing, the District Commissioner said, "Well, Harlow. What you think?"

The wiry little man looked up and around. After a moment he nodded, plunged into the bush. A faint sound, as of someone – or of something? – Then Ed Huggin pointed. Limekiller would never even have noticed that particular tree was there; indeed, he was able to pick it out now only because a small figure was slowly but surely climbing it. The tree was tall, and it leaned at an angle – old enough to have experienced the brute force of a hurricane, strong enough to have survived, though bent.

Harlow called something Jack did not understand, but he followed the others, splashing down the shallows of the river. The river slowly became a swamp. Harlow was suddenly next to them. "Eet not fah," he muttered.

Nor was it.

What there was of it.

An eye in the monstrously swollen head winked at them. Then an insect leisurely crawled out, flapped its horridly-damp wings in the hot and humid air, and sluggishly flew off. There was no wink. There was no eye.

"Mr. Limekiller," said District Commissioner Blossom, "I will now ask you if you identify this body as that of the man known to you as John Samuel."

"It's him. Yes sir."

But was as though the commissioner had been holding his breath and had now released it. "Well, well," he said. "And he was supposed to have gone to Jamaica and died there. I never heard he'd come back. Well, he is dead now, for true."

But little Doctor Rafael shook his snowy head. "He is certainly dead. And he is certainly not John Samuel."

"Why –" Limekiller swallowed bile, pointed. "Look. The eye is missing. John Samuel lost that eye when the tree fell –"

"Ah, yes, young man. John Samuel did. *But not that eye.*"

The bush was not so silent now. Every time the masses and masses of flies were waved away, they rose, buzzing, into the heavy, squalid air. Buzzing, hovered. Buzzing, returned.

"Then who in the Hell –?"

Harlow wiped his face on his sleeve. "Well, sah. I cahn tell you. Lord hahv mercy on heem. Eet ees Bob Blaine."

There was a long outdrawn ahhh from the others. Then Ed Huggin said, "But Bob Blaine had both his eyes."

Harlow stopped, picked a stone from the river bed, with dripping hand threw it in the bush . . . one would have said, at random. With an ugly croak, a buzzard burst up and away. Then Harlow said something, as true – and as dreadful – as it was unarguable. "He not hahv either of them, noew."

By what misadventure and in what place Bob Blaine had lost one eye whilst alive and after decamping from his native land, no one knew: and perhaps it did not matter. He had trusted on "discretion" not to reveal his hideout, there at the site of his old bush-camp. But he had not trusted to it one hundred percent. Suppose that Limekiller were deceitfully or accidentally, to let drop the fact that a man was camping out there. A man with only

one eye. What was the man's name? John Samuel. What? – John
Samuel. . . . Ah. Then John Samuel had not, after all, died in
Jamaica, according to report. Report had been known to be
wrong before. John Samuel alive, then. No big thing. Nobody
then would have been moved to go down there to check up. –
Nobody, now, knew why Bob Blaine had returned. Perhaps he
had made things too hot for himself, down in "Republican waters"
– where hot water could be so very much hotter than back here.
Perhaps some day a report would drift back up, and it might be a
true report or it might be false or it might be a mixture of both.

As for the report, the official, Government one, on the circumstances surrounding the death or Roberto Blaine, a.k.a. Bob
Blaine . . . as for Limekiller's statement and the statements of the
District Commissioner and the District Medical Officer and the
autopsy and the photographs: why, that had all been neatly
transcribed and neatly (and literally) laced with red tape, and for-
warded up the coast to King Town. And as to what happened to it
there –

"What do you think they will do about it, Doctor?"

Rafael's rooms were larger, perhaps, than a bachelor needed.
But they were the official quarters for the DMO, and so the DMO
lived in them. The wide floors gleamed with polish. The spotless
walls showed, here a shield, there a paddle, a harpoon with barbed
head, the carapace of a huge turtle, a few paintings. The symmetry
and conventionality of it all was slightly marred by the bookcases
which were everywhere, against every wall, adjacent to desk and
chairs. And all were full, crammed, overflowing.

Doctor Rafael shrugged. "Perhaps the woodlice will eat the
papers," he said. "Or the roaches, or the *wee-wee*-ants. The mildew.
The damp. Hurricane. . . . This is not a climate which helps preserve the history of men. I work hard to keep my own books and
papers from going that way. But I am not Government, and
Government lacks time and money and personnel, and . . . perhaps,
also. . . . Government has so many, many things pressing upon
it. . . . Perhaps, too, Government lacks interest."

"What were those tracks, Doctor Rafael?"

Doctor Rafael shrugged.

"You do know, don't you?"

Doctor Rafael grimaced.

"Have you seen them, or anything like them, before?"

Doctor Rafael, very slowly, very slowly, nodded.

"Well . . . for God's sake . . . can you even give me a, well, a *hint*? I mean: that was a rather rotten experience for me, you know. And –"

The sunlight, kept at bay outside, broke in through a crack in the jalousies, sun making the scant white hair for an instant ablaze: like the brow of Moses. – Doctor Rafael got up and busied himself with the fresh lime and the sweetened lime juice and the gin and ice. He was rapt in this task, like an ancient apothecary mingling strange unguents and syrups. Then he gave one of the gimlets to his guest and from one he took a long, long pull.

"You see. I have two years to go before my retirement. The pension, well, it is not spectacular, but I have no complaint. I will be able to rest. Not for an hour, or an evening . . . an evening! only on my holidays, once a year, do I even have an evening all my own! – Well. You may imagine how I look forward. And I am not going to risk premature and enforced retirement by presenting Government with an impossible situation. One which wouldn't be its fault, anyway. By insisting on impossible things. By demonstrating –"

He finished his drink. He gave Jack a long, shrewd look.

"So I have nothing more to say . . . about *that*. If they want to believe, up in King Town, that the abominable Bob Blaine was mauled by a crocodile, let them. If they prefer to make it a jaguar or even a tapir, why, that is fine with Robert Rafael, M.D., D.M.O. It might be, probably, the first time in history that anybody anywhere was, killed by a tapir, but that is not my affair. The matter is, so far as I am concerned, so far – in fact – as *you* and I are concerned – over.

"Do you understand?"

Limekiller nodded. At once the older man's manner changed. "I have many, many books, as you can see. Maybe some of them would be of interest to you. Pick any one you like. Pick one at random." So saying, he took a book from his desk and put it in Jack's hands. It was just a book-looking book. It was, in fact, volume II of the Everyman edition of Plutarch's *Lives*. There was a wide card, of the kind on which medical notes or records are sometimes made, and so Jack Limekiller opened the book at that place.

seasons, as the gods sent them, seemed natural to him. The Greeks that inhabited Asia were very much pleased to see the great lords and governors of Persia, with all the pride, cruelty, and

"Well, now, what the Hell," he muttered. The card slipped, he clutched. He glanced at it. He put down vol. II of the *Lives* and he sat back and read the notes on the card.

It is in the nature of things [they began] for men, in a new country and faced with new things, to name them after old, familiar things. Even when resemblance unlikely. Example: *Mountain-cow* for tapir. ('Tapir' from Tupi Indian *tapira*, big beast.) Example: Mawmee-*apple* not apple at all. Ex.: *Sea-cow* for manatee. Early British settlers not entomologists. Quest.: Whence word *manatee*? From Carib? Perhaps. After the British, what other people came to this corner of the world? Ans.: Black people. Calabars, Ashantee, Mantee, Mandingo. Re last two names. Related peoples. Named after totemic animal. *Also*, not likely? *likely* – named unfamiliar animals after familiar (i.e. familiar in Africa) animals. Mantee, Mandee: hippo. Refer legend

Limekiller's mouth fell open. "Oh, my God!" he groaned. In his ear now, he heard the old, old, quavering voice of Captain Cudgel (once Cudjoe): *"Mon, een Ahfrica, de mon-ah-tee hahv leg, I tell you. Een Ahfrica eet be ah poerful beast, come up on de lond, I tell you . . . de w'ol' people, dey tell me so, fah true. . . ."*
He heard the old voice, repeating the old words, no longer even half-understood: but, in some measure, at least half-true.

Refer legend of were-animals, universal. Were-wolf, were-tiger, were-shark, were-dolphin. Quest.: Were-manatee?

"Mon-ah-tee ees hahlf ah mon . . . hahv teats like a womahn. . . . Dere ees wahn mon, mehk mellow weet mon-ah-tee, hahv pickney by mon-ah-tee . . ."
And he heard another voice saying, not only once, saying, *"Mon, eef you tie ah rottlesnake doewn fah me, I veel freeg eet. . . ."*
He thought of the wretched captives in the Spanish slaveship, set free to fend for themselves in a bush by far wilder than the one left behind. Few, to begin with, fewer as time went on; marrying and intermarrying, no new blood, no new thoughts. And, finally, the one road in to them, destroyed. Left alone. Left quite alone. Or . . . almost. . . .
He shuddered.

How desperate for refuge must Blaine have been, to have sought to hide himself anywhere near Cape Mandee –

And what miserable happenstance had brought he himself, Jack Limekiller, to improvise on that old song that dreadful night? – And what had he called up – out of the darkness . . . out of the bush . . . out of the mindless present which was the past and future and the timeless tropical forever? . . .

There was something pressing gently against his finger, something on the other side of the card. He turned it over. A clipping from a magazine had been roughly pasted there.

Valentry has pointed out that, despite a seeming resemblance to such aquatic mammals as seals and walrus, the manatee is actually more closely related anatomically to the elephant.

. . . out of the bush . . . out of the darkness . . . out of the mindless present which was also the past and the timeless tropical forever . . .

"They are like elephants. They never forget."

"Ukh," he said, through clenched teeth. "My God. Uff. Jesus. . . ."

The card was suddenly, swiftly, snatched from his hands. He looked up, still in a state of shock, to see Doctor Rafael tearing it into pieces.

"Doña 'Sana!"

A moment. Then the housekeeper, old, all in white. "Doctór?"

"Burn this."

A moment passed. Just the two of them again. Then Rafael, in a tone which was nothing but kindly, said, "Jack, you are still young and you are still healthy, My advice to you: Go away. Go to a cooler climate. One with cooler ways and cooler memories." The old woman called something from the back of the house. The old man sighed. "It is the summons to supper," he said. "Not only must I eat in haste because I have my clinic in less than half-an-hour, but suddenly-invited guests make Doña 'Sana very nervous. Good night, then, Jack."

Jack had had two gin drinks. He felt that he needed two more. At least two more. Or, if not gin, rum. Beer would not do. He wanted to pull the blanket of booze over him, awfully, awfully quickly. He had this in his mind as though it were a vow as he walked up the front street towards the Cupid Club.

Someone hailed him, someone out of the gathering dusk.

"Jock! Hey, mon, Jock! Hey, b'y! Where you gweyn so fahst? Bide, b'y, bide a bit!"

The voice was familiar. It was that of Harry Hazeed, his principal creditor in King Town. Ah, well. He had had his chance, Limekiller had. He could have gone on down the coast, down into the Republican waters, where the Queen's writ runneth not. Now it was too late.

"Oh, hello, Harry," he said, dully.

Hazeed took him by the hand. Took him by both hands. "Mon, show me where is your boat? She serviceable? She is? Good: Mon, you don't hear de news: Welcome's warehouse take fire and born up! Yes, mon. Ahl de carn in King *Town* born up! No carn ah-tahl: no tortilla, no empinada, no tamale, no carn-*cake*! Oh, mon, how de people going to punish! Soon as I hear de news, I drah me money from de bonk, I buy ahl de crocus sock I can find, I jump on de pocket-*boat* – and here I am, oh, mon, I pray fah you. . . . I pray I fine you!"

Limekiller shook his head. It had been one daze, one shock after another. The only thing clear was that Harry Hazeed didn't seem angry. "You no understond?" Hazeed cried. "Mon! We going take your boat, we going doewn to Nutmeg P'int, we going to buy carn, mon! We going to buy ahl de carn dere is to buy! Nevah mine dat lee' bit money you di owe me, b'y! We going make plenty money, mon! And we going make de cultivators plenty money, too! What you theenk of eet, Jock, me b'y? Eh? Hey? What you theenk?"

Jack put his forefinger in his mouth, held it up. The wind was in the right quarter. The wind would, if it held up, and, somehow, it felt like a wind which would hold up, the wind would carry them straight and clear to Nutmeg Point: the clear, clean wind in the clear and starry night.

Softly, he said – and old Hazeed leaning closer to make the words out, Limekiller said them again, louder, "I think it's great. Just great. I think it's great."

SLEEP WELL
OF NIGHTS

"**A**RE THOSE LAHVLY young ladies with you, then?" the Red
Cross teacher asked.

Limekiller evaded the question by asking another, a
technique at least as old as the Book of Genesis. "Which way did
they go?" he asked.

But it did not work this time. "Bless me if I saw them gow anywhere! They were both just standing on the corner as I went by."

Limekiller gave up not so easily. "Ah, but which corner?"

A blank look. "Why . . . *this* corner."

This corner was the corner of Grand Arawack and Queen
Alexandra Streets in the Town of St. Michael of the Mountains, capital of Mountains District in the Colony of British Hidalgo.
Fretwork galleries dripping with potted plants and water provided
shade as well as free shower baths. These were the first and second
streets laid out and had originally been deer trails; Government
desiring District Commissioner Bartholomew "Bajan" Bainbridge
to supply the lanes with names, he had, with that fund of imagina-
tion which helped build the Empire, called them First and Second
Streets: it was rather a while before anyone in Government next
looked at a map and then decided that numbered streets should run
parallel to each other and not, as in this instance, across each other.
And as the Grand Arawack Hotel was by that time built and as
Alexandra (long-suffering consort of Fat Edward) was by that time
Queen, thus they were renamed and thus had remained.

"St. Michael's" or "Mountains" Town, one might take one's
pick, had once been a caravan city in miniature. The average

person does not think of caravan cities being located in the Americas, and, for that matter, neither does anyone else. Nevertheless, trains of a hundred and fifty mules laden with flour and rum and textiles and tinned foods coming in, and with chicle and chicle and chicle going out, had been common enough to keep anyone from bothering to count them each time the caravans went by. The labor of a thousand men and a thousand mules had been year by year spat out of the mouths of millions of North Americans in the form of chewing gum.

So far as Limekiller knew, Kipling had never been in either Hidalgo, but he might have thought to have been if one ignored biographical fact and judged only by his lines,

Daylong, the diamond weather,
The high, unaltered blue —
The smell of goats and incense
And the mule-bell tinkling through.

Across from the hotel stood the abattoir and the market building. The very early morning noises were a series of bellows, bleats, squeals, and screams which drowned out cock-crow and were succeeded by the rattle and clatter of vulture claws on the red-painted corrugated iron roofs. Then the high voices of women cheapening meat. But all of these had now died away. Beef and pork and mutton (sheep or goat) could be smelled stewing and roasting now and then as the mild currents of the air alternated the odors of food with those of woodsmoke. He even thought he detected incense; there was the church spire nearby.

But there were certainly no young ladies around, lovely or otherwise.

There had been no very lengthy mule trains for a very long time.

There had been no flotillas of tunnel boats at the Town Wharf for a long time, either, their inboard motors drawn as high-up in "tunnels" within the vessels as possible to avoid the sand and gravel and boulders which made river navigation so difficult on the upper reaches of the Ningoon. No mule trains, no tunnel boats, no very great quantities of chicle, and everything which proceeded to and from the colonial capital of King Town and St. Michael's going now by truck along the rutted and eroded Frontier Road. No Bay boat could ever, in any event, have gotten higher up the river than the narrows called Bomwell's Boom; and the *Saccharissa* (Jno. Limekiller, owner and Master and, usually – save for Skippy the Cat – sole crew) was at the moment Hired Out.

She had been chartered to a pair of twosomes from a Lake Winnipeg boat club, down to enjoy the long hours of sunshine. Jack had been glad enough of the money but the charter had left him at somewhat of a loss: *leisure* to him had for so long meant to haul his boat up and clean and caulk and paint her: all things in which boatmen delight. Leisure without the boat was something new. Something else.

To pay his currently few debts had not taken long. He had considered getting Porter Portugal to sew a new suit of sails, but old P.P. was not a slot machine; you could not put the price into P.P.'s gifted hands and expect, after a reasonable (or even an unreasonable) period of time, for the sails to pop out. If Port-Port were stone sober he would not work and if dead drunk he *could* not work. The matter of keeping him supplied with just the right flow of old Hidalgo dark rum to, so to speak, oil the mechanism, was a nice task indeed: many boat owners, National, North American, or otherwise, had started the process with intentions wise and good: but Old Port was a crazy-foxy old Port and all too often had drunk them under the table, downed palm and needle, and vanished with the advance-to-buy-supplies into any one of the several stews which flourished on his trade. ("A debt of honor, me b'y," he would murmur, red-eyed sober, long days later. "Doesn't you gots to worry. I just hahs a touch ahv de ague, but soon as I bet-tah. . . .")

So that was *one* reason why John L. Limekiller had eventually decided to forget the new suit of sails for the time being.

Filial piety had prompted him to send a nice long letter home, but a tendency towards muscle spasms caused by holding a pen had prompted him to reduce the n.l.l. to a picture post card. He saw the women at the post office, one long and one short.

"What's a letter *cost*, to St. Michael's?" the Long was asking. "We *could*, *tele*phone for a reservation," the Short suggested. Jack was about to tell them, unsolicited, how fat the chance was of anybody in St. Michael's having a telephone *or* anything which could be reserved, let alone of understanding what a reservation was – then he took more than a peripheral look at them.

The Long had red hair and was wearing dungarees and a man's shirt. Not common, ordinary, just-plain-red: *cop*per-red. Worn in loops. Her shirt was blue with a faint white stripe. Her eyes were "the color of the sherry which the guests leave in the glass." Or don't, as the case may be. The Short could have had green hair in braids and been covered to her toes in a yashmak for all Jack noticed.

At that moment the clerk had asked him, "What fah you?" – a local, entirely acceptable usage, even commonplace, being higher than "What you want?" and lower than "You does want something?" – and by the time he had sorted out even to his own satisfaction that he wanted postage for a card to Canada and not, say, to send an armadillo by registered mail to Mauritius, and had completed the transaction in haste and looked around, trying to appear casual, they were gone. Clean gone. Where they had been was a bright-eyed little figure in the cleanest rags imaginable, with a sprinkling of white hairs on its brown, nutcracker jaws.

Who even at once declared, "'And now abideth faith, hope, and charity, these three, and the greatest of these is charity,' you would not deny the Apostle Paul, would you, then, sir?"

"Eh? Uh . . . no," said Limekiller. Pretense cast aside, craning and gaping all around: *nothing.*

"Anything to offer me?" demanded the wee and ancient, with logic inexorable.

So there had gone a dime. And then and there had come the decision to visit St. Michael of the Mountains, said to be so different, so picturesque, hard upon the frontier of "Spanish" Hidalgo, and where (he reminded himself) he had after all *never been.*

Sometimes being lonely it bothers the way a tiny pebble in the shoe bothers: enough to stop and *do* something. But if one is very lonely indeed, then it becomes an accustomed thing. Only now did Limekiller bethink himself how lonely he had been. The boat and the Bay and the beastie-cat had been company enough. The average National boatman had a home ashore. The two men and two women even now aboard the *Saccharissa* in jammed-together proximity – they had each other. (And even now, considering another definition of the verb *to have* and the possible permutations of two males and two females made him wiggle like a small boy who has to *go* –). There was always, to be sure, the Dating Game, played to its logical conclusion, for a fee, at any one of the several hotels in King Town, hard upon the sea. But as for any of the ladies accompanying him anywhere on his boat . . .

"*Whattt?* You tink I ahm crazy? *Nut*ting like *dot*!"

Boats were gritty with sand to fill the boggy yards and lanes, smelly with fish. Boats had *no* connotations of romance.

Such brief affairs did something for his prostate gland ("Changing the acid," the English called it), but nothing whatsoever, he now realized, for his loneliness. Nor did conversation in the boatmen's bars, lately largely on the theme of, "New tax law, rum go up to 15¢ a glass, man!"

And so here he was, fifty miles from home, if King Town was "home" – and if the *Saccharissa* was home . . . well, who knew? St. Michael of the Mountains still had some faint air of its days as a port-and-caravan city, but that air was now faint indeed. Here the Bayfolk (Black, White, Colored, and Clear) were outnumbered by Turks and 'Paniar's, and there were hardly any Arawack at all. (There seldom were, anywhere out of the sound and smell of the sea.) There were a lot of old wooden houses, two stories tall, with carved grillwork, lots of flowering plants, lots of hills: perhaps looking up and down the hilly lanes gave the prospects more quaintness and interest, perhaps even beauty, than they might have had, were they as level as the lanes of King Town, Port Cockatoo, Port Caroline, or Lime Walk. And, too, there were the mountains all about, all beautiful. And there was the Ningoon River, flowing round about the town in easy coils, all lovely, too: its name, though Indian in origin, allowing for any number of easy, Spanish-based puns:

"Suppose you drink de wat-tah here, sah, you *cahn-not* stay away!"

"*En otros paises, señor, otros lugares, dicen* mañana. *Pero, por acá, señor, se dice* ningun!"

And so forth.

Limekiller had perambulated every street and lane, had circumambulated town. Like every town and the one sole city in British Hidalgo, St. Michael's had no suburbs. It was clustered thickly, with scarcely even a vacant lot, and where it stopped being the Town of St. Michael of the Mountains, it stopped. Abruptly. *Here* was the Incorporation; *there* were the farms and fields; about a mile outside the circumambient bush began again.

He could scarcely beat every tree, knock on every door. He was too shy to buttonhole people, ask if they had seen a knockout redhead. So he walked. And he looked. And he listened. But he heard no women's voices, speaking with accent from north of the northern border of Mexico. Finally he grew a little less circumspect.

To Mr. John Paul Peterson, Prop., the Emerging Nation Bar and Club:

"Say . . . are there any other North Americans here in town?"

As though Limekiller had pressed a button, Mr. Peterson, who until that moment had been only amiable, scowled an infuriated scowl and burst out, "What the Hell they want come *here* for? You think them people *crazy*? They got richest countries in the world, which they take good care *keep* it that way; so why the Hell they want come *here*? Leave me ask you one question. Turn your head all around. You see them table? You see them booth? How many people you see sitting and drinking at them table and them booth?"

Limekiller's eyes scanned the room. The question was rhetorical. He sighed. "No one," he said, turning back to his glass.

Mr. Peterson smote the bar with his hand. "Exactly!" he cried. "*No one!* You not bloody damn fool, boy. You have good eye in you head. *Why* you see no one? Because no one can afford come here and drink, is why you see no one. People can scarce afford *eat*! Flour cost nine cent! Rice cost fif*teen* cent! Lard cost thirty-*four* cent! Brown sugar at nine cent and white sugar at eleven! D.D. milk twen-ty-one cent! And yet the tax going *up*, boy! The tax going *up*!"

A line stirred in Limekiller's mind. "Yes — and, 'Pretty soon *rum* going to cost fifteen cents,'" he repeated. Then had the feeling that (in that case) something was wrong with the change from his two-shillings piece. And with his having made this quotation.

"What you mean, '*fifteen cent*'?" demanded Mr. Peterson, in a towering rage. Literally, in a towering rage; he had been slumped on his backless chair behind the bar, now stood up to his full height . . . and it was a height, too. "*Whattt*? 'Fif-*teen*-cent?' You think this some damn dirty liquor booth off in the bush, boy? You think you got *swampy*," referring to backwoods distilled goods, "in you glass? What '*fifteen cent*?' No such *thing*. You got pure Governor Morgan in you glass, boy, never cost less than one shilling, and pretty soon going to be thirty cent, boy: thir-ty-*cent*! And for what? For the Queen can powder her nose with the extra five penny, boy?" Et cetera. Et cetera.

Edwin Rodney Augustine Bickerstaff, Royal British Hidalgo Police (sitting bolt-upright in his crisp uniform beneath a half-length photograph of the Queen's Own Majesty):

"Good afternoon, sir. May I help you, sir?"

"Uh . . . yes! I was wondering . . . uh . . . do you know if there are any North Americans in town?"

Police-sergeant Bickerstaff pondered the question, rubbed his long chin. "Any *North* Americans, you say sir?"

Limekiller felt obliged to define his terms. "Any Canadians or people from the States."

Police-sergeant Bickerstaff nodded vigorously. "Ah, now I understand you, sir. Well. That would be a matter for the Immigration Officer, wouldn't you agree, sir?"

"Why . . . I suppose. Is *he* in right now?" This was turning out to be more complex than he had imagined.

"Yes, sir. He *is* in. *Un*officially speaking, he is in. *I* am the police officer charged with the duties of Immigration Officer in the Mountains District, sir,"

"Well –"

"Three to four, sir."

Limekiller blinked. Begged his pardon. The police-sergeant smiled slightly. "Every evening from three to four, sir, pleased to execute the duties of Immigration Officer, sir. At the present time," he glanced at the enormous clock on the wall, with just a touch of implied proof, "I am carrying out my official duties as Customs Officer. *Have you anything to declare?*"

And, *So much for that suggestion,* Limekiller thought, a feeling of having only slightly been saved from having made a fool of himself tangible in the form of something warmer than sunshine round about his face and neck.

The middle-aged woman at the Yohan Yahanoglu General Mdse. Establishment store sold him a small bar of Fry's chocolate, miraculously unmelted. Jack asked, "Is there another hotel in town, besides the Grand?"

A touch of something like hauteur came over the still-handsome face of *Sra.* Yohanoglu. "Best you ahsk wan of the men," she said. And, which one of the men? "*Any men,*" said she.

So. Out into the sun-baked street went lonely Limekiller. Not that lonely at the moment, though, to want to find where the local hookers hung out. Gone too far to turn back. And, besides, turn back to *what?*

The next place along the street which was open was the El Dorado Club and Dancing (its sign, slightly uneven, said).

Someone large and burly thumped in just before he did, leaned heavily on the bar, "How much, *rum?*" he demanded.

The barkeep, a 'Paniard, maybe only one-quarter Indian (most of the Spanish-speaking Hidalgans were more that that), gave a slight yawn at this sudden access of trade. "Still only wan dime," he said. "Lahng as dees borrel lahst. When necessitate we broach nudder borrel, under new tox lah, *iay! Pobrecito! Going be fifteen cent!*"

"*¡En el nombre del* Queen!" proclaimed the other new customer, making the sign of the cross, then gesturing for a glass to be splashed.

Limekiller made the same gesture.

"What you vex weed de Queen, *varón?*" the barkeeper asked, pouring two fingers of "clear" into each glass. "You got new road, meb-be ah beet bum-py, but *new*; you got new wing on hospital, you got new generator for give ahl night, electricity: *whatt?* You teenk you hahv ahl dees, ahn not pay ah new tox? No sotch teeng!"

"*No me hace falta*, 'ahl dees,' " said the other customer. "*Resido en el* bush, where no hahv not-ting like dot."

The barkeep yawned again. "*Reside en el* bush? Why you not live like old-time people? Dey not dreenk rum. Dey not smoke cig-arette. Dey not use lahmp-*ile*. Ahn dey not pay toxes, not dem, no."

"Me no want leev like dot. *Whattt?* You cahl dot 'leev'?" He emptied his glass with a swallow, dismissed any suggestion that Walden Pond and its tax-free amenities might be his for the taking, turned to Limekiller his vast Afro-Indian face. "Filiberto Marín, señor, is de mahn to answer stranger question. Becahs God *love* de stranger, señor, ahn Filiberto Marín love *God*. Everybody knows Filiberto Marín, ahn if anyone want know where he is, I am de mahn." Limekiller, having indeed questions, or at any rate, A Question, Limekiller opened his mouth.

But he was not to get off so easily. There followed a long, *long* conversation, or monologue, on various subjects, of which Filiberto Marín was the principal one. Filiberto Marín had once worked one entire year in the bush and was only home for a total of thirty-two days, a matter (he assured Jack) of public record. Filiberto Marín was born just over the line in Spanish Hidalgo, his mother being a Spanish Woman and his father a British Subject By Birth. Had helped build a canal, or perhaps it was *The* Canal. Had been in Spanish Hidalgo at the time of the next-to-last major revolution, during which he and his sweetheart had absquatulated for a more peaceful realm. Married *in church*! Filiberto Marín and his wife had produced one half a battalion for the British Queen! "Fifteen children – and *puros varónes*! Ahl son, señor! So fahst we have children! Sixty-two year old, and work more tasks one day dan any young man! An I now desires to explain we hunting and fishing to you, becahs you stranger here, so you ignorance not you fahlt, señor."

Limekiller kept his eyes in the mirror, which reflected the passing scene through the open door, and ordered two more low-tax rums; while Filiberto Marín told him how to cast nets with weights to catch mullet in the lagoons, they not having the right mouths to take hooks; how to catch turtle, the *tortuga blanca* and the striped turtle (the latter not being popular locally because it was striped) –

"What difference does the stripe mean, Don Filiberto?"

"¡*Seguro*! Exoctly!!" beamed Don Filiberto, and, never pausing, swept on: how to use raw beef skin to bait lobsters ("Dey cahl him *lobster*, but is really de *langusta*, child of de crayfish."), how to tell the difference in color between saltwater and freshwater ones, how to fix a dory, how to catch tortuga "by dive for him –"

"– You want to know how to cotch croc-o-*dile* by dive for him? Who can tell you? Filiberto Marín will answer dose question," he said, and he shook Limekiller's hand with an awesome shake.

There seemed nothing boastful about the man. Evidently Filiberto Marín *did* know all these things and, out of a pure and disinterested desire to help a stranger, wanted merely to put his extensive knowledge at Jack's disposal. . . .

Of this much, Limekiller was quite clear the next day. He was far from clear, though, as to how he came to get there in the bush where many cheerful dark people were grilling strips of *barbacoa* over glowing coals – mutton it was, with a taste reminiscent of the best old-fashioned bacon, plus . . . well, *mutton.* He did not remember having later gone to bed, let alone to sleep. Nor know the man who came and stood at the foot of his bed, an elderly man with a sharp face which might have been cut out of ivory . . . this man had a long stick . . . a spear? . . . no . . .

Then Limekiller was on his feet. In the moon-speckled darkness he could see very little, certainly not another man. There was no lamp lit. He could hear someone breathing regularly, peacefully, nearby. He could hear water purling, not far off. After a moment, now able to see well enough, he made his way out of the cabin and along a wooden walkway. There was the Ningoon River below. A fine spray of rain began to fall; the river in the moonlight moved like watered silk. *What* had the man said to him? Something about showing him . . . showing him *what?* He could not recall at all. There had really been nothing menacing about the old man.

But neither had there been anything reassuring.

Jack made his way back into the cabin. The walls let the moonlight in, and the fine rain, too. But not so much of either as to prevent his falling asleep again.

Next day, passion — well, that was not exactly the right word — but what was? Infatuation? Scarcely even that. An uncommon interest in, plus a great desire for, an uncommonly comely young woman who also spoke his own language with familiar, or familiar enough, accents — oh, well — Hell! — whatever the *word* was, whatever his own state of mind had been, next morning had given way to something more like common sense. Common sense, then, told him that if the young woman (vaguely he amended this to the young women) had intended to come to St. Michael of the Mountains to stay at a hotel . . . or wherever it was, which they thought might take a reservation . . . had even considered *writing* for the reservation, well, they had not intended to come here at once. In other words: enthusiasm (*that* was the word! . . . damn it . . .) enthusiasm had made him arrive early.

So, since he was already *there*, he might as well relax and enjoy it.

— He was already *where?*

Filiberto Marín plunged his hands into the river and was noisily splashing water onto his soapy face. Jack paused in the act of doing the same thing for himself, waited till his host had become a trifle less audible — *how* the man could snort! — "Don Fili, what is the name of this place?"

Don Fili beamed at him, reached for the towel. "These place?" He waved his broad hand to include the broad river and the broad clearing, with its scattered fields and cabins. "These place, Jock, *se llame* Pahrot Bend. You like reside here? Tell me, just. I build you house." He buried his face in his towel. Jack had no doubt that the man meant exactly what he said, gave another look around to see what was being so openhandedly — and openheartedly — offered him; this time he looked across to the other bank. Great boles of trees: immense! Immense! The eye grew lost and dizzy gazing upward toward the lofty, distant crowns. Suddenly a flock of parrots, yellowheads, flew shrieking round and round; then vanished.

Was it some kind of an omen? *Any* kind of an omen? To live here would not be to live just anywhere. He thought of the piss-soaked bogs which made up too large a part of the slums of King Town, wondered how anybody could live *there* when anybody could live *here*. But *here* was simply too far from the sea, and it was to live upon the sunwarm sea that he had come to this small country, so far from his vast own one. Still . . . might not be such a bad idea . . . well, not to *live* here all the time. But . . . a smaller version of the not-very-large cabins of the hamlet . . . a sort of country home . . . as it were . . . ha-ha . . . well, why not? Something to think about . . . anyway.

"Crahs de river, be one nice spot for build you *cabanita*," said Don Filiberto, reading his mind.

"Mmm . . . what might it cost?" he could not help asking, even though knowing whatever answer he might receive would almost certainly not in the long run prove accurate.

"Cahst?" Filiberto Marín, pulling his shirt over his huge dark torso, considered. Cost, clearly, was not a matter of daily concern. Calculations, muttering from his mouth, living and audible thoughts, struggling to take form: "Cahst . . . May-be, ooohhh, say-*be* torty dollar?"

"Forty dollars?"

Don Filiberto started to shake his head, reconsidered. "I suppose may-*be*. Not take lahng. May-be one hahf day, collect wild cane for make wall, bay *leaf* for make *techo*, roof. An may-be 'nother hahf day for put everything togedder. Cahst? So: twenty dollar. Torty dollar. An ten dollar *rum*! Most eeem-por-tont!" He laughed. Rum! The oil which lubricates the neighbors' labors. A house-raising bee, Hidalgo style.

"And the land itself? The cost of the land?"

But Don Fili was done with figures. "What 'cahst of de lond'? Lond not cahst nah-ting. Lond belahng to Pike Es-tate."

A bell went ding-a-ling in Limekiller's ear. The Pike Estate. The great Pike Estate Case was the *Jarndyce vs. Jarndyce* of British Hidalgo. Half the lawyers in the colony lived off it. Was there a valid will? Were there valid heirs? Had old Pike died intestate? ¿*Quien sabe*? There were barroom barristers would talk your ears off about the First Codicil and the Second Codicil and the Alleged Statement of Intention and the Holograph Document and all the rest of it. Limekiller had heard enough about the Pike Estate Case. He followed after Don Fili up the bank. Ah, but –

"Well, maybe nobody would bother me *now* if I had a cabin built there. But what about when the estate is finally settled?"

Marín waved an arm, as impatiently as his vast good nature would allow. "By dot time, *hijo mio*, what you care? You no hahv Squatter Rights by den? Meb-*be* you *dead* by den!"

Mrs. Don Filiberto, part American Indian, part East Indian, and altogether Amiable and Fat, was already fanning the coals on the raised fire-hearth for breakfast.

Nobody was boating back to town then, although earnest guarantees were offered that "by and by somebody" would *be* boating back, for sure. Limekiller knew such sureties. He knew, too, that he might certainly stay on with the Marín family at Parrot Bend until then – and longer – and be fully welcome. But he had after all come to "Mountains" for something else besides rural hospitality along the Ningoon River (a former Commissioner of Historical Sites and Antiquities had argued that the name came from an Indian word, or words, meaning Region of Bounteous Plenty; local Indians asserted that a more literal and less literary translation would be Big Wet). The fine rain of the night before began to fall again as he walked along, and soon he was soaked.

It did not bother him. By the time he got back into town the sun would have come out and dried him. Nobody bothered with oilskins or mackintoshes on the Bay of Hidalgo, nor did he intend to worry about his lack of them here in the Mountains of Saint Michael Archangel and Prince of Israel.

Along the road (to give it its courtesy title) he saw a beautiful flurry of white birds – were they indeed cattle egrets? living in symbiosis, or commensality, with the cattle? was one, indeed, heavy with egg, "blown over from Africa"? Whatever their name or origin, they did follow the kine around, heads bobbing as they, presumably, ate the insects the heavy cloven hooves stirred up. But what did the *cattle* get out of it? Company?

The rain stopped, sure enough.

It was a beautiful river, with clear water, green and bending banks. He wondered how high the highest flood waters came. A "top gallon flood," they called that. Was there a hint of an old tradition that the highest floods would come as high as the top-gallant sails of a ship? Maybe.

The rain began again. Oh, well.

An oilcloth serving as door of a tiny cabin was hauled aside and an old woman appeared and gazed anxiously at Jack. "Oh, sah, why you wahk around in dis eager rain?" she cried at him. "Best you come in, *bide*, till eet *stop!*"

He laughed. "It doesn't seem all that eager to me, Grandy," he said, "but thank you anyway."

In a little while it had stopped. *See?*

Further on, a small girl under a tree called, "Oh, see what beauty harse, meester!"

Limekiller looked. Several horses were coming from a stable and down the path to the river; they were indeed beautiful, and several men were discussing a sad story of how the malfeasance of a jockey (evidently not present) had lost first place in a recent race for one of them to the famous Tigre Rojo, the Red Tiger, of which even Limekiller, not a racing buff, had heard.

"Bloody b'y just raggedy-ahss about wid him, an so Rojo win by just a nose. Son of a beach!" said one of the men, evidently the trainer of *the* beauty horse, a big bay.

"– otherwise he beat any harse in British Hidalgo!"

"Oh, yes! Oh, yes, Mr. Ruy! – dot he would!"

Ruy, his dark face enflamed by the memory of the loss, grew darker as he watched, cried, "Goddammit, oh Laard Jesus Christ, b'y! Lead him by de *head* till he *in* de wahter, *den* lead him by rope! When you goin to learn? – an watch out for boulder! – you know what one bloody fool mon want me to do? Want me to *run* harse dis marnin – not even just canter, he want *run* him! – No, *no*, b'y, just let him swim about be de best ting for him –

"Dis one harse no common harse – dis one harse foal by *Garobo*, from Mr. Pike *stud!* Just let him swim about, I say!"

The boy in the water continued, perhaps wisely, to say nothing, but another man now said, "Oh, yes. An blow aht de cold aht of he's head, too."

Mr. Ruy grunted, then, surveying the larger scene and the graceful sweep of it, he said, gesturing, "I cotch plenty fish in dis river – catfish, twenty-pound tarpon, too. I got nylon *line*, but three week now, becahs of race, I have no time for cotch fish." And his face, which had gradually smoothed, now grew rough and fierce again. "Bloody dom fool jockey b'y purely raggeddy-*ahss* around wid harse!" he cried. The other men sighed, shook their heads. Jack left them to their sorrow.

Here the river rolled through rolling pasture lands, green, with trees, some living and draped with vines, some dead and gaunt but still beautiful. The river passed a paddock of Brahma cattle like statues of weathered grey stone, beautiful as the trees they took the shade beneath, cattle with ears like leaf-shaped spearheads, with wattles and humps. Then came an even lovelier sight: black cattle in a green field with snow-white birds close by among them. Fat hogs, Barbados sheep, water meadows, sweet soft air.

He could see the higher roofs on the hills of the town, but the road seemed to go nowhere near there. Then along came a man who, despite his clearly having no nylon line, had – equally clearly – ample time to fish, carried his catch on a stick. "De toewn, sir? Straight acrahs de savannah, sir," he gestured, "is de road to toewn." And, giving his own interpretation to the text, *I will not let thee go unless thou bless me*, detained Limekiller with blessings of unsolicited information, mostly dealing with the former grandeur of St. Michael's Town, and concluding, "Yes, sir, in dose days hahv t'ree dahnce *hahll.* Twen-ty bar and club! Torkish Cat'edral w'open every day, sah – *every day!* – ahn . . ." he groped for further evidences of the glorious days of the past, "ahn ah fot fowl, sah, cahst two, t'ree shilling!"

Sic transit gloria mundi.

The room at the hotel was large and bare, and contained a dresser with a clouded mirror, a chair, and a bed with a broad mattress covered in red "brocade"; the sheet, however, would not encompass it. This was standard: the sheet never *would,* except in the highest of high class hotels. And as one went down the scale of classes and the size of the beds diminished so, proportionately, did the sheets: they were *always* too narrow and too short. Curious, the way this was always so. (In the famous, or infamous, Hotel Pelican in King Town, sheets were issued on application only, at an extra charge, for the beds were largely pro forma. The British soldiers of the Right Royal Regiment, who constituted the chief patrons, preferred to ignore the bed and used the *wall,* would you believe it, for their erotic revels. If that was quite the right word.)

There was a large mahogany wardrobe, called a "press" in the best Dickensian tradition, but there were no hangers in it. There was a large bathroom off the hall but no towels and no soap, and the urinal was definitely out of order, for it was tied up with brown paper and string and looked like a twelve-pound turkey ready for the oven.

But all these shortcomings were made up for, by one thing which the Grand Hotel Arawack *did* have: out on the second-story verandah was a wide wooden-slatted swing of antique and heroic mold, the kind one used to see only at Auntie Mary's, deep in the interior of Prince Edward Island or other islands in time. – Did the Hiltons have wide wooden swings on their verandahs? Did the Hiltons have verandahs, for that matter?

Limekiller took his seat with rare pleasure: it was not every damned day that he could enjoy a nostalgia trip whilst at the same time rejoicing in an actual physical trip which was, really, giving him just as much pleasure. For a moment he stayed immobile. (Surely, Great-uncle Leicester was just barely out of sight, reading the Charlottetown newspaper, and damning the Dirty Grits?) Then he gave his long legs a push and was off.

Up! and the mountains displayed their slopes and foothills. *Down!* and the flowery lanes of town came into sight again. And, at the end of the lanes was the open square where stood the flagpole with the Union Jack and the National Ensign flapping in the scented breeze . . . and, also, in sight, and well in sight (Limekiller had chosen well) was the concrete bench in front of which the bus from King Town had to disembogue its passengers. If they came by bus, and come by bus they must (he reasoned), being certainly tourists and not likely to try hitching. Also, the cost of a taxi for fifty miles was out of the reach of anyone but a land speculator. No, by *bus*, and there was where the bus would stop.

"*Let me help you with your bags,*" he heard himself saying, ready to slip shillings into the hands of any boys brash enough to make the same offer.

There was only one fly in the ointment of his pleasure.

Swing as he would and as long as he would, no bus came.

"Bus? *Bus,* sir? *No,* sir. Bus ahlready come orlier today. Goin bock in evening. Come ahgain tomorrow."

With just a taste of bitterness, Limekiller said, "*Mañana.*"

"*¡Ah, Vd, si puede hablar en espanol, señor. Si-señor. Mañana viene el bus, otra vez. – Con el favor de Dios.*" An the creek don't rise, thought Limekiller.

Suddenly he was hungry. There was a restaurant in plain sight, with a bill of fare five feet tall painted on its outer wall: such menus were only there for, so to speak, authenticity. To prove that the place was indeed a restaurant. And not a cinema. Certainly no one would ever be able to order and obtain anything which was *not* painted on them. – Besides, the place was closed.

"Be open tonight, sir," said a passerby, observing him observing.

Jack grunted. "Think they'll *have* that tonight?" he asked, pointing at random to *Rost Muttons* and to *Beef Stakes*.

An emphatic shake of the head. "*No*-sir. Rice and beans."

Somewhere nearby someone was cooking something besides rice and beans. The passerby, noticing the stranger's blunt and sun-burned nose twitch, with truly Christian kindness said, "But Tía Sani be open now."

"Tía Sani?"

"*Yes*-sir. Miss Sanita. Aunt Sue. Directly down de lane."

Tía Sani had no sign, no giant menu. However, Tía Sani was *open*.

Outside, the famous Swift Sunset of the Tropics dallied and dallied. There was no sense of urgency in Hidalgo, be it British or Spanish. There was the throb of the light-plant generator, getting ready for the night. Watchman, what of the night? – what put *that* into his mind? He swung the screen door, went in.

Miss Sani, evidently the trim grey little woman just now look-ing up towards him from her stove, did not have a single item of formica or plastic in her spotless place. Auntie Mary, back in P.E.I., would have approved. She addressed him in slow, sweet Spanish. "How may I serve you, sir?"

"What may I encounter for supper, señora?"

"We have, how do they call it in inglés, meat, milled, and formed together? ah! los mitbols! And also a *caldo* of meat with macaroni and verdants. Of what quality the meat? Of beef, señor."

Of course it was cheap, filling, tasty, and good.

One rum afterwards in a club. There might have been more than one, but just as the thought began to form (like a mitbol), someone approached the jukebox and slipped a coin into its slot – the only part of it not protected by a chickenwire cage against vio-lent displays of dislike for whatever choice someone else might make. The management had been wise. At once, NOISE, slightly tinctured with music, filled the room. Glasses rattled on the bar. Limekiller winced, went out into the soft night.

Suddenly he felt sleepy. Whatever was there tonight would be there tomorrow night. He went back to his room, switched the sheet so that at least his head and torso would have its modest benefits, thumped the lumpy floc pillow until convinced of its being a hopeless task, and stretched out for slumber.

The ivory was tanned with age. The sharp face seemed a touch annoyed. The elder man did not exactly *threaten* Limekiller with his pole or spear, but . . . and why *should* Limekiller get up and go? Go *where*? For *what*? He had paid for his room, hadn't he? He wanted to sleep, didn't he? And he was damned well going to sleep, too. If old what's-his-name would only let him . . . off on soft green clouds he drifted. *Up* the river. *Down* the river. Old man smiled, slightly. And up the soft green mountains. Old man was frowning, now. Old man was —

"Will you get the Hell *out* of here?" Limekiller shouted, bolt upright in bed — poking him with that damned —

The old man was gone. The hotel maid was there. She was poking him with the stick of her broom. The light was on in the hall. He stared, feeling stupid and slow and confused. "Eh — ?"

"You have bad *dream*," the woman said.

No doubt, he thought. Only —

"Uh, thanks. I — uh. Why did you poke me with the broomstick? And not just shake me?"

She snorted. "*Whattt?* You theenk I want *cotch* eet?"

He still stared. She smiled, slightly. *He* smiled, slightly, too. "Are bad dreams contagious, then?" he asked.

She nodded, solemnly, surprised that he should ask.

"Oh. Well, uh, then . . . then how about helping me have some *good* ones?" He took her, gently, by the hand. And, gently, pulled. She pulled her hand away. Gently. Walked towards the open door. Closed it.

Returned.

"Ahl right," she said. "We help each other." And she laughed.

He heard her getting up, in the cool of the early day. And he moved towards her, in body and speech. And fell at once asleep again.

Later, still early, he heard her singing as she swept the hall, with, almost certainly, that same broom. He burst out and cheerfully grabbed at her. Only, it wasn't her. "What you want?" the woman asked. Older, stouter. Looking at him in mild surprise, but with no dislike or disapproval.

"Oh, I, uh, are, ah. Ha-ha. Hmm. Where is the other lady? Here last night? Works here?" He hadn't worded that as tactfully as he might have. But it didn't seem to matter.

"She? She not work here. She come help out for just one night. Becahs my sister, lahst night, she hahv wan lee pickney – gorl *beh*bee. So I go ahn she stay." The pronouns were a bit prolix, but the meaning was clear. "Now she go bock. Becahs truck fah go Macaw Falls di *leave*, señor." And, as she looked at the play of expression on his face, the woman burst into hearty, good-willed laughter. And bounced down the hall, still chuckling, vigorously plying her besom.

Oh, *well.*

And they *had* been *good* dreams, too.

Tía Sani was open. Breakfast: two fried eggs, buttered toast of thick-sliced home-baked bread, beans (mashed), tea with tinned milk, orange juice. Cost: $1.00, National Currency – say, 60¢, 65¢, U.S. or Canadian. On the wall, benignly approving, the Queen, in her gown, her tiara, and her Smile of State; also, the National Premier, in open shirt, eyeglasses, and a much broader smile.

Jack found himself still waiting for the bus. *Despite* the Night Before. See (he told himself), so it *isn't* Just Sex. . . . Also waiting, besides the retired chicle-tappers and superannuated mahogany-cutters, all of them authorized bench-sitters, was a younger and brisker man.

"You are waiting for the bus, I take it," he now said.

"Oh, yes. Yes, I am."

And so was *he.* "I am expecting a repair part for my tractor. Because, beside my shop, I have a farm. You see my shop?" He companionably took Limekiller by the arm, pointed to a pink-washed building with the indispensable red-painted corrugated iron roof (indispensable because the rains rolled off them and into immense wooden cisterns) and overhanging gallery. "Well, I find that I cannot wait any longer, Captain Sneed is watching the shop for me, so I would like to ahsk you one favor. *If* you are here. *If* the bus comes. *Would* you be so kind as to give me a hail?"

Limekiller said, "Of course. Be glad to," suddenly realized that he had, after all, other hopes for *If* The Bus Come; hastily added, "And if not, I will send someone to hail you."

The dark (but not *local*-dark) keen face was split by a warm smile. "Yes, do. – Tony Mikeloglu," he added, giving Jack's hand a hearty, hasty shake; strode away. (Tony Mikeloglu could trust

Captain Sneed not to pop anything under his shirt, not to raid the till, not to get too suddenly and soddenly drunk and smash the glass goods. But, suppose some junior customer were to appear during the owner's absence and, the order being added up and its price announced, pronounce the well-known words, *Ma say, "write eet doewn"* – could he trust Captain Sneed to demand cash and not "write it down?" – no, he could *not.*)

Long Limekiller waited, soft talk floating on around him, of old-time "rounds" of sapodilla trees and tapping them for chicle, talk of "hunting" – that is, of climbing the tallest hills and scouting out for the telltale reddish sheen which mean mahogany – talk of the bush camps and the high-jinks when the seasons were over. But for them, now, all seasons were over, and it was only that: talk. Great-uncle Leicester had talked a lot, too; only *his* had been other trees, elsewhere.

Still, no bus.

Presently he became aware of feeling somewhat ill at ease, he could not say why. He pulled his long fair beard, and scowled.

One of the aged veterans said, softly, "Sir, de mon *hail*ing you."

With an effort, Limekiller focused his eyes. There. There in front of the pink store building. Someone in the street, calling, beckoning.

"De *Tork* hailing you, sir. Best go see what he want."

Tony Mikeloglu wanted to tell him something? Limekiller, with long strides strolled down to see. "I did not wish to allow you to remain standing in the sun, sir. I am afraid I did not ask your name. Mr. Limekiller? – Interesting name. Ah. Yes. My brother-in-law's brother has just telephoned me from King *Town*, Mr. Limekiller. I am afraid that the bus is not coming today. Break*down*?"

Under his breath, Limekiller muttered something coarse and disappointed.

"Pit-ty about the railroad," a deep voice said, from inside the store. "Klondike to Cape Horn. Excellent idea. Vi-sion. But they never built it. Pit-ty."

Limekiller shifted from one foot to another. Half, he would go back to the hotel. Half, he would go somewhere else. (They, she, no one was coming. What did it matter?) *Any*where. *Where?* But the problem was swiftly solved. Once again, and again without offense, the merchant took him by the arm. "Do not stand outside in the sun, sir. Do come *in*side the shop. In the shade. And have something cold to drink." And by this time Jack was already there. "Do you know Captain Sneed?"

Small, khaki-clad, scarlet-faced. Sitting at the counter, which was serving as an unofficial bar. "I suppose you must have often wondered," said Captain Sneed, in a quarterdeck voice, "why the Spaniard didn't settle British Hidalgo when he'd settled everywhere *else* round about?"

"– Well –"

"Didn't know it was *here*, Old Boy! Couldn't have gotten here if he *did*, you see. First of all," he said, drawing on the counter with his finger dipped in the water which had distilled from his glass (Tony now sliding another glass, tinkling with, could it be? – yes, it was! Ice! – over to Jack, who nodded true thanks, sipped) – "First of all, you see, coming from east to west, there's Pharaoh's Reef – quite enough to make them sheer off south in a bit of a damned hurry, don't you see. Then there's the Anne of Denmark Island's Reef, even bigger! And suppose they'd *sail*ed south to avoid Anne of Denmark Island's Reef? Eh? What would they find, will you tell me that?"

"Carpenter's Reef . . . unless it's been moved," said Jack.

Sneed gave a great snort, went on, "*Exactly!* Well, then – now, even if they'd missed Pharaoh's Reef and got pahst it . . . even if they'd missed Anne of Denmark Island's Reef and got pahst it . . . even if they'd missed Carpenter's Reef and got pahst *it* . . . why, then there's that great long *Barrier* Reef, don't you see, one of the biggest in the world. (Of course, Australia's the biggest one. . . .) No. No, Old Boy. Only the British lads knew the way through the Reef, and you may be sure that *they* were not pahssing out the information to the Spaniard, no, ho-ho!"

Well (thought Jack, in the grateful shade of the shop), maybe so. It was an impressive thought, that, of infinite millions of coral polyps laboring and dying and depositing their stony "bones" in order to protect British Hidalgo (and, incidentally, though elsewhere, Australia) from "the Spaniard."

"Well!" Captain Sneed obliterated his watery map with a sweep of his hand. "Mustn't mind *me*, Old Boy. This is my own King Charles's head, if you want to know. It's just the damnable *cheek* of those Spaniards there, *there*, in the Spanish Hidalgo, still claiming this blessed little land of ours as their own, when they had never even set their *foot* upon it!" And he blew out his scarlet face and actually said "Herrumph!" – a word which Jack had often seen but never, till now, actually heard.

And then Tony Mkeloglu, who had evidently gone through all, all of this many, many times before, said, softly, "My brother-in-law's brother had just told me on the telephone from King *Town* –"

"Phantom relay, it has – the telephone, you know – sorry, Tony, forgive me – what does your damned crook of a kinsman tell you from King Town?"

". . . tells me that there is a rumor that the Pike Estate has finally been settled, you know."

Not *again*? *Always* . . . thought Limekiller.

But Captain Sneed said, Don't you believe it! "Oh. What? 'A rumor,' yes, well, you may believe *that*. Always a rumor. Why didn't the damned fellow make a proper will? Eh? For that matter, why don't *you*, Old Christopher?"

There was a sound more like a crackle of cellophane than anything else. Jack turned to look; there in an especially shadowy corner was a man even older, even smaller, than Captain Sneed; and exposed toothless gums as he chuckled.

"Yes, why you do not, Uncle Christopher?" asked Tony.

In the voice of a cricket who has learned to speak English with a strong Turkish accent, Uncle Christopher said that he didn't believe in wills.

"What's going to become of all your damned doubloons, then, when you go pop?" asked Captain Sneed. Uncle Christopher only smirked and shrugged. "Where have you concealed all that damned money which you accumulated all those years you used to peddle bad rum and rusty roast-beef tins round about the bush camps? Who's going to get it all, eh?"

Uncle Christopher went *hickle-hickle*. "I know who going get it," he said. *Sh'sh, sh'sh, sh'sh*. His shoulders, thin as a butterfly's bones, heaved his amusement.

"Yes, but *how* are they going to get it? What? How are you going to take care of that? Once you're dead."

Uncle Christopher, with a concluding crackle, said, "I going do like the Indians do. . . ."

Limekiller hadn't a clue what the old man meant, but evidently Captain Sneed had. "What?" demanded Captain Sneed. "Come now, come now, you don't really *believe* all that, do you? You *do*? You do! Tush. Piffle. The smoke of all those bush camps has addled your brains. Shame on you. Dirty old pagan. Disgusting. Do you call yourself a Christian and a member of a church holding the Apostolic Succession? *Stuff!*"

The amiable wrangle went on. And, losing interest in it,

Limekiller once again became aware of feeling ill at ease. Or . . .
was it . . . could it be? . . . *ill?*

In came a child, a little girl; Limekiller had seen her before. She
was perhaps eight years old. *Where* had he seen her?

"Ah," said Mikeloglu, briskly the merchant again. "Here is me
best customer. She going make me rich, not true, me Bet-ty gyel?
What fah you, *chaparita?*"

White rice and red beans were for her, and some coconut oil in
her own bottle was for her, and some tea and some chile peppers
(not very much of any of these items, though) and the inevitable tin
of milk. (The chief difference between small shops and large shops
in St. Michael's was that the large ones had a much larger selection
of tinned milk.) Tony weighed and poured, wrapped and tied. And
looked at her expectantly.

She untied her handkerchief, knot by knot, and counted out the
money. Dime by dime. Penny by penny. Gave them all a shy smile,
left. "No fahget me when you rich, me Bet-ty gyel," Tony called
after her. "Would you believe, Mr. Limekiller, she is one of the
grand*child*ren of old Mr. Pike?"

"Then why isn't she rich already? Did the others get it all? –
Oh. I forgot. Estate not settled."

Captain Sneed grunted. "Wouldn't help her even if the damned
estate *were* settled. An outside child of an outside child. Couldn't
inherit if the courts ever decide that he died intestate, and of course:
no mention of her in any will . . . if there *is* any will . . ." *An outside
child.* How well Jack knew that phrase by now. Marriage and giving
in marriage was one thing in British Hidalgo; begetting and bearing
of children, quite another thing. No necessary connection. "Do you
have any children?" "Well, I has four children." Afterthought:
"Ahnd t'ree oetside." Commonest thing in the world. Down here.

"What's wrong with you, Old Boy?" asked Captain Sneed. "You
look quite dicky."

"Feel rotten," Limekiller muttered, suddenly aware of feeling
so. "Bones all hurt."

Immediate murmurs of sympathy. And: "*Oh,* my. You weren't
caught in that rain yesterday morning, were you?"

Jack considered. "Yesterday morning in the daytime. And . . .
before . . . in the night time, too – Why?"

Sneed was upset. "'*Why?*' Why, when the rain comes down
like that, from the north, at this time of year, they call it 'a fever
rain'. . . ."

Ah. *That* was what the old woman had called out to him, urging him in out of the drizzle. *Bide*, she'd said. *Not* an "eager" rain – a *fever* rain!

"Some say that the rain makes the sanitary drains overflow. And some say that it raises the mosquitoes. *I* don't know. And some laugh at the old people, for saying that. But *I* don't laugh. . . . You're not laughing, either, are you? Well. What are we going to do for this man, Mik? Doctor *in*, right now?"

But the District Medical Officer was not in right now. It was his day to make the rounds in the bush hamlets in one half of the circuit. On one other day he would visit the other half. And in between, he was in town holding clinics, walking his wards in the hospital there on one of the hills, and attending to his private patients. Uncle Christopher produced from somewhere a weathered bottle of immense pills which he assured them were quinine, shook it and rattled it like some juju gourd as he prepared to pour them out.

But Captain Sneed demurred. "Best save that till we can be sure that it is malaria. Not they use quinine nowadays. Mmm. No chills, no fever? Mmm. Let me see you to your room at the hotel." And he walked Limekiller back, saw him not only into his room but into his bed, called for "some decent sheets and some blankets, what sort of a kip are you running here, Antonoglu?" Antonoglu's mother, a very large woman in a dress as black and voluminous as the tents of Kedar, came waddling in with sighs and groans and applied her own remedy: a string of limes, to be worn around the neck. The maid aspersed the room with holy water.

"I shall go and speak to the pharmacist," Captain Sneed said, briskly. "What – ?" For Limekiller, already feeling not merely rotten but *odd*, had beckoned to him. "Yes?"

Rotten, aching, odd or not, there was something that Limekiller wanted taken care of. "Would you ask anyone to check," he said, carefully. "To check the bus? The bus when it comes in. Two young ladies. One red-haired. When it comes in. Would you check. Ask anyone. Bus. Red-haired. Check. If no breakdown. Beautiful. Would you. Any. Please? Oh."

Captain Sneed and the others exchanged looks.

"Of course, Old Boy. Don't worry about it. All taken care of. Now." He had asked for something. It had not come. "What, not even a thermometer? *What?* Why, what do you *mean*, 'You had one but the children broke it'? *Get another one at once.* Do you wish to lose your license? Never mind. *I* shall get another one at once. *And* speak to the pharmacist. Antonoglu-*khan-um*, the moment he begins to sweat, or his teeth chatter, *send me word.*

"Be back directly," he said, over his shoulder.

But he was not back directly.

Juan Antonoglu was presently called away to take care of some incoming guests from the lumber camps. He repeated Captain Sneed's words to his mother, who, in effect, told him not to tell her how to make yogurt. She was as dutiful as anyone could be, and, after a while, her widower son's children coming home, duty called her to start dinner. She repeated the instructions to the maid, whose name was Purificación. Purificación watched the sick man carefully. Then, his eyes remaining closed, she tiptoed out to look for something certain to be of help for him, namely a small booklet of devotions to the Señor de Esquipulas, whose cultus was very popular in her native republic. But it began to drizzle again: out she rushed to, first, get the clothes off the line and, second, to hang them up in the lower rear hall.

Limekiller was alone.

The mahogany press had been waiting for this. It now assumed its rightful shape, which was that of an elderly gentleman rather expensively dressed in clothes rather old-fashioned in cut, and, carrying a long . . . *something* . . . in one hand, came over to Jack's bed and looked at him most earnestly. Almost reproachfully. Giving him a hand to help him out of bed, in a very few moments he had Limekiller down the stairs and then, somehow, they were out on the river; and then . . . somehow . . . they were *in* the river. No.

Not exactly.

Not at all.

They were *under* the river.

Odd.

Very odd.

A hundred veiled eyes looked at them.

Such a dim light. Not like anything familiar. Wavering. What was that. A crocodile. *I* am getting *out* of *here*, said Limekiller, beginning to sweat profusely. This was the signal for everyone to let Captain Sneed know. But nobody was there. Except Limekiller. And, of course, the old man.

And, of course, the crocodile.

And, it now became clear, *quite* a number of other creatures. All reptilian. Why was he not terrified, instead of being merely alarmed? He was in fact, now that he came to consider it, not even all that alarmed. The creatures were looking at him. But there was somehow nothing terrifying in this. It seemed quite all right for him to be there.

The old man made that quite clear.

Quite clear.

"Is he delirious?" the redhead asked. Not just plain ordinary red. *Copper*-red.

"I don't have enough Spanish to know if saying '*barba amarilla*' means that you're delirious, or not. Are you delirious?" asked the other one. The Short. Brown hair. Plain ordinary Brown.

" '*Barba amarilla*' means 'yellow beard,' " Limekiller explained. Carefully.

"Then you aren't delirious. I guess. – What does 'yellow beard' mean, in this context?"

But he could only shake his head.

"I mean, we can see that you do have a blond beard. Well, blond in *parts*. Is that your nickname? No."

Coppertop said, anxiously, "His pulse seems so *funny*, May!" She was the Long. So here they were. The Long and the Short of it. Them. He gave a sudden snort of laughter.

"An insane cackle if ever I heard one," said the Short. "Hm, *Hmm*. You're *right*, Felix. It *does* seem so funny. Mumping all *around* the place – Oh, hello!"

Old Mrs. Antonoglu was steaming slowly down the lake, all the other vessels bobbing as her wake reached them. *Very* odd. Because it still *was* old Mrs. Antonoglu in her black dress and not really the old Lake Mickinuckee ferry boat. And this wasn't a lake. Or a river. They were all back in his room. And the steam was coming from something in her hand.

Where was the old man with the sharp face? Tan old man. Clear. Things were far from *clear*, but –

"What I bring," the old woman said, slowly and carefully and heavily, just the way in which she walked, "I bring 'im to drink for 'ealth, poor sick! Call the . . . call the . . . country *yerba*," she said, dismissing the missing words.

The red-haired Long said, "Oh, good!"

Spoon by bitter spoonful she fed it to him. Sticks of something. Boiled in water. A lot of it dribbled down his beard. "Felix," what an odd name. She wiped it carefully with kleenex.

"But 'Limekiller' is just as odd," he felt it only fair to point out.

"Yes," said the Short. "You certainly are. How did you know we were coming? We weren't sure, ourselves. *Nor* do we know you. Not that it matters. We are emancipated women. Ride bicycles. But we don't smoke cheroots, and we are *not* going to open an actuarial office with distempered walls, and the nature of Mrs. Warren's profession does not bother us in the least: in fact, we have thought, now and then, of entering it in a subordinate capacity. Probably *won't*, though. Still . . ."

Long giggled. Short said that the fact of her calling her Felix instead of *Felicia* shouldn't be allowed to give any wrong ideas. It was just that *Felicia* always sounded so goddamn silly. They were both talking at once. The sound was very comforting.

The current of the river carried them all off, and then it got so very still.

Quite early next morning.
Limekiller felt fine.

So he got up and got dressed. Someone, probably Purificación, had carefully washed his clothes and dried and ironed them. He hadn't imagined everything: there was the very large cup with the twigs of country *yerba* in it. He went downstairs in the early morning quiet, cocking an ear. Not even a buzzard scrabbled on the iron roof. There on the hall table was the old record book used as a register. On the impulse, he opened it. Disappointment washed over him. *John L. Limekiller, sloop* Saccharissa, *out of King Town.* There were several names after that, all male, all ending in *-oglu*, and all from the various lumber camps round about in the back bush: Wild Hog Eddy, Funny Gal Hat, Garobo Stream. . . .

Garobo.
Struck a faint echo. Too faint to bother with.
But no one named Felix. Or even *Felicia.* Or May.
Shite and onions.
There on the corner was someone.

"Lahvly morning," said someone. "Just come from hospital, seeing about the accident victims. Name is Pauls, George Pauls. Teach the Red Cross clahsses. British. You?"

"Jack Limekiller. Canadian. Have you seen two women, one a redhead?"

The Red Cross teacher *had* seen them, right there on that corner, but knew nothing more helpful than that. So, anyway, *that* hadn't been any delirium or dreams, either, *thank God.* (For how often had he not dreamed of fine friends and comely companions, only to wake and know that they had not been and would never be.)

At Tía Sani's. In came Captain Sneed. "*I say!* Terribly sorry! Shameful of me – I don't know how – Well. There'd been a motor accident, lorry overturned, eight people injured, so we all had to pitch in, there in hospital – Ah, by the *way.* I *did* meet your young ladies, thought you'd imagined them, you know – District Engineer gave them a ride from King Town – I told them about you, went on up to hospital, then there was this damned accident – By the time we had taken care of them, poor chaps, fact is, I am *ashamed* to say, I'd forgotten all about you. – But you look all right, now." He scanned Limekiller closely. "Hm, still, you should see the doctor. I wonder. . . ."

He walked back to the restaurant door, looked up the street, looked down the street. "*Doc-tor!* – Here he comes now."

In came a slender Eurasian man; the District Medical Officer himself. (Things were *always* happening like that in Hidalgo. Sometimes it was, "You should see the Premier. Ah, here he comes now. *Prem-ier!*") The D.M.O. felt Limekiller's pulse, pulled down his lower eyelid, poked at spleen and liver, listened to an account of yesterday. Said, "Evidently you have had a brief though severe fever. Something like the one-day flu. Feeling all right now? Good. Well, eat your usual breakfast, and if you can't hold it down, come see me at my office."

And was gone.

"Where are they now? The young women, I mean."

Captain Sneed said that he was blessed if he knew, adding immediately, "Ah. Here they come now."

Both talking at once, they asked Jack if he felt all right, assured him that he looked well, said that they'd spent the night at Government Guest House (there was one of these in every out-district capital and was best not confused with *Government House,* which existed only in the colonial capital itself: the Royal Governor lived there, and he was not prepared to put up guests below the rank of, well, *Gov*ernor).

"Mr. Boyd arranged it. We met him in King Town. He was coming here anyway," said Felix, looking long and lovely. "He's an engineer. He's . . . how would you describe him, May?"

"He's an engin*eer,*" May said.

Felix's sherry-colored eyes met Limekiller's. "Come and live on by boat with me and we will sail the Spanish Main together and I will tell you all about myself and frequently make love to you," he said at once. Out loud, however, all he could say was, "Uh . . . thanks for wiping my beard last night . . . uh. . . ."

"Don't mention it," she said.

May said, "I want lots and lots of exotic foods for breakfast." She got two fried eggs, buttered toast of thick-sliced, home-baked bread, beans (mashed), tea, orange juice. "There is nothing *like* these exotic foods," she said.

Felix got egg on her chin. Jack took his napkin and wiped. She said that turnabout was fair play. He said that one good turn deserved another. She asked him if he had ever been to Kettle Point Lagoon, said by They to be beautiful. A spirit touched his lips with a glowing coal.

"I am going there today!" he exclaimed. He had never heard of it.

"Oh, good! Then we can all go together!"

Whom did he see as they walked towards the river, but Filiberto Marín. Who greeted him with glad cries, and a wink, evidently intended as compliments on Jack's company. "Don Fili, can you take us to Kettle Point Lagoon?"

Don Fili, who had at once begun to nod, stopped nodding. "Oh, Juanito, only wan mon hahv boat which go to Kettle Point Lagoon, ahn dot is Very Big Bakeman. He get so *vex*, do anybody else try for go dot side, none ahv we odder boatmen adventure do it. But I bring you to him. May-be he go today. *Veremos.*"

Very Big Bakeman, so-called to distinguish him from his cousin, Big Bakeman, was very big indeed. What he might be like when "vex," Limekiller (no squab himself) thought he would pass up knowing.

Bakeman's was the only tunnel boat in sight, probably the only one still in service. His answer was short. "Not before Torsday, becahs maybe not enough wah-teh get me boat ahcross de bar. *Tors*day," he concluded and, yawning, leaned back against the cabin. Monopolists the world over see no reason to prolong conversation with the public.

Felix said something which sounded like, "Oh, spit," but wasn't. Limekiller blinked. *Could* those lovely lips have uttered That Word? If so, he concluded without much difficulty, he would learn to like it. *Love* it. "Don Fili will take us to," he racked his brains,

"—somewhere just as interesting," he wound up with almost no pause. And looked at Don Fili, appealingly.

Filiberto Marín was equal to the occasion. "*Verdad.* In wan leetle while I going up de Right Branch. *Muy linda.* You will have pleasure. I telling Juanito about it, day before yesterday."

Limekiller recalled no such conversation, but he would have corroborated a deal with the devil, rather than let her out of his sight for a long while yet. He nodded knowingly. "Fascinating," he said.

"We'll get that nice lady to pack us a lunch."

Jack had a quick vision of Tía Sani packing them fried eggs, toast, beans, tea, and orange juice. But that nice lady fooled him. Her sandwiches were immense. Her eggs were deviled. She gave them *empenadas* and she gave them "crusts" – pastries with coconut and other sweet fillings – and then, behaving like aunts the whole world over, she ladled soup into a huge jar and capped it and handed it to Limekiller with the caution to hold it like *this* so that it didn't leak. . . . Not having any intention to have his hands thus occupied the whole trip, he lashed it and shimmed it securely in the stern of Marín's boat.

He had barely known that the Ningoon River *had* two branches. Parrot Bend was on the left one, then. The dory, or dugout, in use today was the largest he had seen so far. Captain Sneed at once decided it had room enough for him to come along, too. Jack was not overjoyed at first. The elderly Englishman was *a decent sort.* But he talked, damn it! *How* he talked. Before long, however, Limekiller found he talked to May, which left Felix alone to talk to Jack.

"*John Lutwidge Limekiller,*" she said, having asked to see his inscribed watch. "there's a *name.* Beats Felicia Fox." *He* thought "fox" of all words in the world the most appropriate for her. He didn't say so. "– Why Lutwidge?"

"Lewis Carroll? Charles Lutwidge Dodgson, his real name? Distant cousin. Or so my Aunty Mary used to say."

This impressed her, anyway a little. "And what does Limekiller mean? How do you kill a lime? And *why?*"

"You take a limestone," he said, "and you burn it in a kil*n.* Often pronounced kill. Or, well, you *make* lime, for cement or whitewash or whatever, by burning stuff. Not just limestone. Marble. Oyster shells. Old orange rinds, maybe, I don't know, I've never done it. Family *name,*" he said.

She murmured, "I see. . . ." She wound up her sleeves. He found himself staring, fascinated, at a blue vein in the inside of her arm near the bend. Caught her gaze. Cleared his throat, sought for something subject-changing and ever so interesting and novel to say. "Tell me about yourself," was what he found.

She gave a soft sigh, looked up at the high-borne trees. There was another blue vein, in her *neck*, this time. Woman was one mass of sexy *veins*, damn it! He would simply lean over and he would kiss – "Well, I was an Art Major at Harrison State U. and I said the Hell with it and May is my cousin and she wanted to go someplace, too, and so we're here. . . . Look at the *bridge!*"

They looked at its great shadow, at its reflection, broken by the passing boat into wavering fragments and ripples. The bridge loomed overhead, so high and so impressive in this remote place, one might forget that its rotting road-planks, instead of being replaced, were merely covered with new ones . . . or, at the least, newer ones. "In ten years," they heard Captain Sneed say, "the roadbed will be ten feet tall . . . if it lasts that long."

May: "Be sure and let us know when it's going to fall and we'll come down and watch it. Ffff-*loppp*! – Like San Luis Rey."

"Like *whom*, my dear May?"

The river today was at middle strength: shallow-draft vessels could and still did navigate, but much dry shingle was visible near town. Impressions rushed in swiftly. The day was neither too warm nor too wet, the water so clear that Limekiller was convinced that he could walk across it. Felix lifted her hand, pointed in wordless wonder. There, on a far-outlying branch of a tree over the river was an absolutely monstrous lizard of a beautiful buff color; it could not have been less then five full feet from snout to end of tail, and the buff shaded into orange and into red along the spiky crenelations on the spiny back ridge. He had seen it before. *Had* he seen it before? He *had* seen it before.

"Iguana!" he cried.

Correction was polite but firm. "No, sir, Juanito. Iguana is *embra*, female. Dat wan be *macho*. Male. *Se llama 'garobo.'* . . ."

Something flickered in Limekiller's mind. "¡*Mira*! ¡*Mira*! Dat wan dere, *she* be iguana!" And that one there, smaller than the buff dragon, was of a beautiful blue-green-slate-grey color. "Usual," said Filiberto, "*residen en* de bomboo t'icket, which is why de reason is call in English, 'Bomboo chicken.' . . ."

"You *eat* it?" – Felix.

"Exotic *food*, exotic *food*!" – May.

"*Generalmente*, only de hine leg ahn de tail. But is very good to eat de she of dem when she have egg, because de egg so very nice eating, in May, June; but even noew, de she of dem have red egg, nice and hard. *Muy sabroso.*"

Jack turned and watched till the next bend hid the place from sight. After that he watched for them – he did not know why he watched for them, were they watching for *him*? – and he saw them at regular intervals, always in the topmost branches: immense. Why so high? Did they eat insects? And were there more insect to be taken, way up there? They surely did not eat *birds*? Some said, he now recalled in a vague way, that they ate only leaves; but were the top leaves so much more succulent? Besides, they seemed not to be eating anything at all, not a jaw moved. Questions perhaps not unanswerable, but, certainly, at the moment unanswered. Perhaps they had climbed so high only for the view: absurd.

"Didn't use to *be* so many of them, time was. – Eh, Fil?" asked Captain Sneed. ("Correct, Copitan. Not.") "Only in the pahst five, six years . . . it seems. Don't *know* why. . . ."

But whatever, it made the river even more like a scene in a baroque faëry tale, with dragons, or, at least, dragonets, looking and lurking in the gigant trees.

The bed of the river seemed predominantly rocky, with some stretches of sand. The river ran very sinuously, with banks tending towards the precipitate, and the east bank was generally the higher. "When river get high," explained Don Fili, "she get white, ahn come up to de crutch of dem tree – " he pointed to a fork high up. "It can rise in wan hour. Ahn if she rise in de night, we people cahn loose we boat. Very . . . *peligroso* . . . dangerous – ¡*Jesus María*! Many stick tear loose wid roots ahn ahl, even big stick like dot wan," he pointed to another massy trunk.

Here and there was open land, *limpiado*, "cleaned," they said hereabouts, for "cleared." "*Clear*. . . ." Something flickered in Limekiller's mind as he recollected this. Then it flickered away. There seemed, he realized, feeling odd about it, that quite a lot of flickering was and had been going on his mind. Nothing that would come into focus, though. The scenes of this Right Branch, now: why did they persist in seeming . . . almost . . . familiar? . . . when he had never been here before?

"What did you say just then, Don Fili?" he demanded, abruptly, not even knowing why he asked.

The monumental face half turned. "¿*Que*? What I just say, Juanito? Why . . . I say, too bod I forget bring ahlong my fisga, my pike . . . take some of dem iguana, garobo, cook dem fah you. – Fah *we*," he amended, as one of the women said, *Gik*.

"*We* would say, 'harpoon' ": Captain Sneed, judiciously. "Local term: 'pike.' "

The penny dropped. "Pike! Pike! It was a pike!" cried Limekiller. His body shook, suddenly, briefly. *Not* a lance or a spear. A pike!

They turned to look at him. Abashed, low-voiced, he muttered, "Sorry. Nothing. Something in a dream . . ." Shock was succeeded by embarrassment.

Felix, also low-voiced, asked, "Are you feverish again?" He shook his head. Then he felt her hand take his. His heart bounced. Then – Oh. She was only feeling his pulse. Evidently it felt all right. She started to release the hand. He took hers. She let it stay.

Captain Sneed said, "Speaking of Pike. All this land, all of it, far as the eye can reach, is part of the Estate of the Late Leopold Albert Edward Pike, you know, of fame and story and, for the last five or six years, since he died, of in*term*inable litigation. He made a great deal of money, out of all these precious hardwoods, and he put it all back into land – Did I know him? Of *course* I knew him! That is," he cleared his throat, "as well as *any*one knew him. Odd chap in a multitude of ways. *Damn*ably odd. . . ."

Of course that was not the end of the subject.

"Mr. Pike, he *reetch*. But he no di *trust* bonks. He say, bonks di go *bust*, mon. People say he'm, now-ah-days, bonks ahl *in*sure. Mr. Pike, he di say, Suh-pose *in*sure company di go bust, too? ¿*Ai, como no?* Ahn he di say ah good word. He di say, 'Who shall guard de guards demselves?' "

Some one of the boatmen, who had theretofore said nothing, but silently plied his paddle, now spoke. "Dey say . . . Meester Pike . . . dey say, he *deal.* . . ." And his voice dropped low on this last word. Something went through all the boatmen at that. It was not exactly a shudder. But it was *there*.

Sneed cleared his throat again as though he were going to cry *Stuff!* or *Piffle!* Though what he said was, "Hm, I wouldn't go *that* far. He was pagan enough not to believe in our Devil, let alone try to deal with him. He did, well, he did, you know, study things better left unstudied . . . *my* opinion. Indian legends of a certain sort, things like that. Called it 'the *Old* Wisdom.' . . ."

Limekiller found his tongue. "Was he an Englishman?"

The matter was considered; heads were shaken. "He mosely *Blanco*. He *lee* bit *Indio*. And he hahv some lee bit *Block* generation in he'm too."

Sneed said, "His coloring was what they call in the Islands, *bright*. Light, in other words, you would say. Though color makes no difference here. Never *did*."

Marín added, "What dey cahl Light, here we cahl Clear." He gestured towards shore, said, "Lime*stone*." Much of the bankside was composed of that one same sort of rock, grey-white and in great masses, with many holes and caves: limestone was susceptible to such water-caused decay. In Yucatan the water had corroded deep pits in it, immense deep wells and pools.

"Now, up ahead," said Captain Sneed, "towards the right bank of the river is a sort of cove called Crocodile Pool – No No, ladies, no need for alarm. Just stay in the boat. And almost directly opposite the cove, is what's called the Garobo Church; you'll see why."

Often in the savannahs they saw the white egrets with the orange bills, usually ashore amidst the cattle. Another kind of egret seemed to prefer the sand and gravel bars and the stumps or sawyers in midstream, and these were a distinctive shade of blue mixed with green, though lighter than the blue-green of the iguanas. Something like a blackbird took its perch and uttered a variety of long, sweet notes and calls.

Swallows skimmed and brighter colored birds darted and drank. And like great sentinels in livery, the great buff garobo-dragons peered down from the tall trees and the tall stones. Clouds of lemon-yellow and butter-yellow butterflies floated round the wild star-apples. *Here*, the stones lay in layers, like brickwork; *there*, the layers were warped and buckled, signs – perhaps – of some ancient strain or quake. But mostly, mostly, the stone rose and loomed and hung in bulbous worm-eaten masses. And over them, among them, behind them and between them, the tall cotton trees, the green-leaved cedars, the white-trunked Santa Maria, and the giant wild fig.

"Now, as to how you *catch* the crocodile," Captain Sneed answered an unasked question; "simple: one man stays in the dory and paddles her in a small circle, one or two men hold the *rope* –"

"– rope tie around odder mahn belly," Marín said.

"*Quite* so. And that chap *dives*. Machete in his *teeth*. And he ties up the croc and then he *tugs*. And then they haul them *up*, . . . you see. Simple."

Felix said, "Not *that* simple!"

May said, "Seems simple enough to me. Long as you've got a sound set of teeth."

Limekiller knew what was coming next. He had been here before. That was a mistake about his never having been here before, of course he had been here; never mind, Right Branch, Left Branch; or how else could he know? Down the steepy bluff a branch came falling with a crash of its *Crack!* falling with it; and the monstrous garobo hit the water with a tremendous sound and spray. It went *down* and it did not come up and it did not come *up*.

And then, distant but clear: the echo. And another echo. And – but that was too many echoes. Jack, who had been looking back, now turned. Spray was still flying up, falling down. *Ahead:* one after another the garobo were falling into the river. And then several at once, together. And then –

"Call *that*, 'The Garobo Church,' " said Captain Sneed.

That was an immense wild fig tree, hung out at an impossible angle; later, Limekiller was to learn that it had died of extreme age and of the storm which finally brought half of its roots out of the ground and forward into the water and canted it, thus, between heaven, earth, and river. It was a skeletal and spectral white against the green *green* of the bush. Three separate and distinct ecologies were along that great tangled length of great gaunt tree: at *least* three! – things crept and crawled, leaped and lurched or lay quiescent, grew and decayed, lived and multiplied and died – and the topmost branches belonged to the iguana and the garobo –

– that were now abandoning it, as men might abandon a threatened ship. Crash! Crash! Down they came, simply letting go and falling. *Crash!*

Sound and spray.

"Won't the crocodiles *eat* them?" cried Felix, tightening her hold on Jack's hand.

The boatmen, to whom this was clearly no new thing, all shook their heads, said No.

"Dey goin *wahrn* he'm, *el legarto*, dot we comin. So dot he no come oet. So cahn tehk *care*. *Horita el tiene cuidado*."

"Tush," said Sneed. "Pif-fle. Damned reptiles are simply getting out of our way, *they* don't know that we haven't any pike. Damned old creepy-crawlies. . . ."

Only the sound of their crashings, no other sound now, and Limekiller, saying in a calm flat voice, "Yes, of course," went out of his shirt and trousers and into the river.

He heard the men cry out, the women scream. But for one second only. Then the sounds muffled and died away. He was in the river. He saw a hundred eyes gazing at him. He swam, he felt bottom, he broke surface, he came up on his hands and knees. He did not try to stand. He was under the river. He was someplace else. Some place with a dim, suffused, wavering light. An odd place. A very odd place. With a very bad smell. He was alone. No, he was not. The garobo were all around and about him. The crocodile was very near up ahead of him. Something else was there, and he knew it had crawled there from the surface through a very narrow fissure. And some *thing* else was there. *That!* He had to take it and so he took it, wrenching it loose. It squilched, but it came. The crocodile gazed at him. The garobo moved aside for him. He backed away. He was in the water again. He —

"Into the *boat*, for Christ's sake!" old Sneed was shouting, his red face almost pale. The boatmen were reaching out to him, holding hands to be grasped by him, smacking the waters with their paddles and banging the paddles against the sides of the boat. The women looked like death. He gasped, spat, trod water, held up something —

— then it was in the boat. Then, all grace gone, he was half in and half out of the boat, his skin scraping the hard sides of it, struggling, being pulled and tugged, wet skin slipping. . . .

He was in the boat.

He leaned over the side, and, as they pulled and pressed, fearful of his going back again, he vomited into the waters.

Captain Sneed had never been so angry. "Well, what did you *expect* crocodile's den to smell like?" he demanded. "Attar of roses? Damndest foolishest crack-brainedest thing I ever saw — !"

Felix said, smoothing Jack's wet, wet hair, "*I* think it was *brave!*"

"You know nothing whatsoever about it, my dear child! — No, damn it, don't keep waving that damned old pipkin pot you managed to drag up, you damned Canuck! Seven hours under fire at Jutland, and I never had such an infernal shock, it was reckless, it was heedless, it was thoughtless, it was devil-may-care and a louse for the hangman; what was the *rea*son for it, may I ask? To impress *whom?* Eh? *Me?* These good men? These young women? Why did you *do* it?"

All Limekiller could say was, "I dreamed that I had to."

Captain Sneed looked at him, mouth open. Then he said, almost in a mutter, "Oh, I say, poor old boy, he's still rambling, ill, *look*ed well enough, must have the *fever*. . . ." He was a moment silent. Then he blinked, gaped; almost in a whisper, he asked, "You *dreamed*. . . . Whom did you *see* in your dream?"

Limekiller shrugged. "Don't know who. . . . Oldish man. Sharp face. Tan. Old-fashioned clothes. Looked like a sort of a dandy, you might say."

And Captain Sneed's face, which had gone from scarlet to pink and then to scarlet again, now went muddy. They distinctly heard him swallow. Then he looked at the earthenware jar with its faded umber pattern. Then, his lips parting with a sort of dry smack: ". . . perhaps it *isn*'t stuff and piffle, then. . . ."

Ashore.

Sneed had insisted that the police be present. It was customary in Hidalgo to use the police in many ways not customary in the northern nations: to record business agreements, for instance, in places where there were no lawyers. And to witness. Sergeant Bickerstaff said that he agreed with Sneed. He said, also, that he had seen more than one old Indian jar opened and that when they were not empty they usually contained mud and that when they did not contain *mud* they usually contained "grahss-*seed*, cahrn-*ker*-nel, thing like that. Never find any gold in one, not before *my* eye, no, sirs and ladies – But best you go ahead and open it."

The cover pried off, right-tight to the brim was a mass of dark and odorous substance, pronounced to be wild beeswax.

The last crumble of it evaded the knife, sank down into the small jar, which was evidently not filled but only plugged with it. They turned it upside down and the crumble of unbleached beeswax fell upon the table. And so did something else.

"Plastic," said May. "To think that the ancient Indians had invented plastic. Create a furor in academic circles. Invalidate God knows how many patents."

Sergeant Bickerstaff, unmoved by irony, said, "Best unwrop it, Coptain."

The plastic contained one dead wasp or similar insect, and two slips of paper. On one was written, in a firm old-fashioned hand, the words. *Page 36, Liber 100, Registers of Deeds of Gift, Mountains District.* The other was more complex. It seemed to be a diagram of sorts, and along the top and sides of it the same hand had written several sentences, beginning, *From the great rock behind Crocodile Cove and proceeding five hundred feet due North into the area called Richardson's Mahogany Lines. . . .*

It was signed, *L. A. E. Pike.*

There was a silence. Then Felix said, not exactly jumping up and down, but almost, her loops of coppery hair giving a bounce, "A treasure map! Jack! Oh, *good!*"

So far as he could recall, she had never called him by name before. His heart echoed: *Oh, good!*

Captain Sneed, pondering, seemingly by no means entirely recovered from his several shocks, but recovered enough, said:

"Too late to go poking about in the bush, today. First thing tomorrow, get some men, some machetes, axes, shovels — Eh?"

He turned to Police-sergeant Bickerstaff, who had spoken softly. And now repeated his words, still softly. But firmly. "First thing, sir. First thing supposed to be to notify the District Commissioner. Mister Jefferson Pike."

He was of course correct. As Captain Sneed agreed at once. Limekiller asked, "Any relation to the late Mr. Leopold Pike?" Bickerstaff nodded. "He is a bahstard son of the late Mr. Leopold Pike." The qualifying adjective implied neither insult nor disrespect. He said it as calmly, as mildly, as if he had said step-son. Cousin. Uncle. It was merely a civil answer to a civil question. A point of identification had been raised, been settled.

D.C. Jefferson Pike was taller than his father had been, but the resemblance, once suggested, was evident. If any thoughts of an estate which he could never inherit were in his mind, they were not obvious. "Well, this is something new," was all his initial comment. Then, "I will ask my chief clark. . . . Roberts. Fetch us Liber 100, Register of Deeds of Gift. Oh, and see if they cannot bring some cups of tea for our visitors, please."

The tea was made and half drunk before Roberts, who did not look dilatory, returned, wiping dust and spiderwebs off the large old book. Which was now opened. Pages turned. "Well, well," said the District Commissioner. "This *is* something new!

"Don't know how they came to overlook *this*," he wondered. "The lawyers," he added. " *Who* registered it? Oh. Ahah. I see. Old Mr. Athelny; been dead *several* years. And always kept his own counsel, too. Quite proper. Well." He cleared his throat, began to read:

> I, Leopold Albert Edward Pike, Woodcutter and Timber Merchant, Retired, a resident of the Town of Saint Michael of the Mountains, Mountains District, in the Colony of British Hidalgo, and a British subject by birth . . . do execute this Deed of Gift . . . videlicet one collection of gold and silver coins, not being Coin of the Realm or Legal Tender, as follows, Item, one hundred pieces of eight reales, Item, fifty-five gold Lewises or louis d'or, Item . . .

He read them all, the rich and rolling old names, the gold moidores and gold mohurs, and golden guineas, the silver byzants and all the rest, as calmly as though he were reading off an inventory of office supplies; came finally to:

> and all these and any others which by inadvertancy may not be herein listed which are found in the same place and location I do hereby give and devise to one Elizabeth Mendoza also known as Betty Mendoza a.k.a. Elizabeth Pike a.k.a. Betty Pike, an infant now resident in the aforesaid Mountains District, which Gift I make for good and sufficient reason and of my own mere whim and fancy. . . .

Here the D.C. paused, raised his eyes, looked at Captain Sneed. Who nodded. Said, "His own sound and voice. Yes. How *like* him!"

> . . . and fancy; the aforesaid collection of gold and silver coins being secured in this same District in a place which I do not herein designate or describe other than to say that it be situate on my own freehold lands in this same District. And if anyone attempt to resist or set aside this my Intention, I do herewith and hereafter declare that he, she or they shall not sleep well of nights.

After he had finished, there was a long pause. Then everybody began to talk at once. Then –

Sneed: Well, suppose we shall have to inform the lawyers, but don't see what *they* can do about it. Deed was executed whilst the old fellow was alive and has nothing to *do* with any question of the estate.

D.C. Pike: I quite agree with you. *Un*officially, of course. Officially, all I am to do is to make my report. The child? Why, yes, of course I know her. She is an outside child of my brother Harrison, who died even before the late Mr. Pike died. The late Mr. Pike seemed rather fond of her. The late Mr. Pike did, I believe, always give something to the child's old woman to keep her in clothes and find her food. As we ourselves have sometimes done, as best we could. But of course this will make a difference.

Sneed: As it *should.* As it *should.* He had put you big chaps to school and helped you make your own way in the world, but this was a mere babe. Do you suppose that he *knew* that such an estate was bound to be involved in litigation and that was why he tried to help the child with all this . . . this *treasure* business?

Marín: Mis-tah Pike, he ahlways give ah lahf ahn he say, nobody gweyn molest *he* treasure, *seguro,* no, becahs he di set such watchies roun ah-bote eet as no mahn adventure fi trifle wid day.

May: I can't help feeling that it's someone's cue to say, "*This all seems highly irregular.*"

Roberts, Chief Clerk (softly but firmly): Oh, no, Miss. The Stamp Tax was paid according to regulations, Miss. *Everything seems in regular order, Miss.*

Watchies. A "watchie" was a watchman, sometimes registered as a private constable, thus giving him . . . Jack was not sure exactly what it gave him: except a certain status. But it was obvious that this was not what "the late Mr. Pike" had had in mind.

Finally, the District Commissioner said, "Well, well. Tomorrow is another day. – Richardson's Mahogany Lines! *Who* would have thought to look there? Nobody! It took eighty years after Richardson cut down all the mahogany before it was worthwhile for anybody to go that side again. And . . . how long since the late Mr. Pike cut down the last of the 'new' mahogany? Ten to fifteen years ago. So it would be sixty-five to seventy-five years before any-body would have gone that side again. Even to *look.* Whatever we may find there would not have been stumbled upon before then, we may be sure. Well, Well.

"Sergeant Bickerstaff, please take these gentleman's and ladies' statements. Meanwhile, perhaps we can have some further cups of tea. . . ."

Taking the statement, that action so dearly beloved of police officials wherever the Union Jack flies or has flown, went full smoothly. That is, until the moment (Limekiller later realized it was inevitable, but he had not been waiting for it, then), the moment when Sgt. Bickerstaff looked up, raised his pen, asked, "And what made you go and seek for this Indian jar, sir, which gave the clue to this alleged treasure, Mr. Limekiller? That is, in other words, how did you come to know that it was there?"

Limekiller started to speak. Fell silent beyond possibility of speech. But not Captain Sneed.

"He knew that it was there because Old Pike had dreamed it to him that it was there," said Captain Sneed.

Bickerstaff gave a *deep* nod, raised his pen. Set it down. Lifted it up. Looked at Jack. "This is the case, Mr. Limekiller, sir?"

Jack said, "Yes, it is." He had, so suddenly, realized it to be so.

"Doubt" was not the word for the emotion on the police-sergeant's face. "Perplexity," it was. He looked at his superior, the District Commissioner, but the District Commissioner had nothing to advise. It has been said by scholars that the Byzantine Empire was kept alive by its bureaucracy. Chief Clerk Roberts cleared his throat. In the tones of one dictating a routine turn of phrase, he produced the magic words.

" '*Acting upon information received,*' " he said, " '*I went to the region called Crocodile Cove, accompanied by,*' and so carry on from there, Sergeant Bickerstaff," he said.

In life, if not in literature, there is always anticlimax. By rights – by dramatic right, that is – they should all have gone somewhere and talked it all over. Talked it all out. And so tied up all the loose ends. But in fact there was nowhere for them all to go and do this. The police were finished when the statement was finished. District Officer Pike, who had had a long, hard day, did not suggest further cups of tea. Tía Sani's was closed. The Emerging Nation Bar and Club was closed, and in the other clubs and bars local usage and common custom held that the presence of "ladies" was contra-indicated: so did common sense.

Wherever Captain Sneed lived, Captain Sneed was clearly not about to offer open house. "Exhausted," he said. And looked it. "Come along, ladies, I will walk along with you as far as the Guest House. Limekiller. Tomorrow."

What should Limekiller do? Carry them off to his landing at the Grand Arawack? Hospitality at Government Guest House, that relic of days when visitors, gaunt and sore from mule transport, would arrive at an even smaller St. Michael's, hospitality there was reported to be of a limited nature; but surely it was better than a place where the urinals were tied up in brown paper and string? (– Not that *they'd* use them anyway, the thought occurred.)

May said, "Well, if you get sick again, yell like Hell for us."

Felix said, reaching out her slender hand, whose every freckle he had come to know and love, she said, "*Will you be all right, Jack?*" *Will you be all right, Jack?* Not, mind you, *You'll be all right, Jack.* It was enough. (And if it wasn't, this was not the time and place to say what would be.)

"I'll be all right," he assured her.

But, back on his absurdly sheeted bed, more than slightly fearful of falling asleep at all, the river, the moment he closed his eyes, the river began to unfold before him, mile after beautiful and haunted mile. But this was a fairly familiar effect of fatigue. He had known it to happen with the roads and the wheatfields, in the Prairie Provinces.

It was on awakening to the familiar cockeling chorus of, *I make the sun to rise!* that he realized that he had not dreamed at all.

St. Michael's did not have a single bank; and, what was more – or less – it did not have a single lawyer. Attorneys for the Estate (alerted perhaps by the telephone's phantom relay) arrived early. But they did not arrive early enough . . . early enough to delay the digging. By the time the first lawyeriferous automobile came spinning to a stop before the local courthouse, the expedition was already on its way. The attorney for the Estate requested a delay, the attorneys for the several groups of claimants requested a delay. But the Estate's local agent had already given a consent, and the magistrate declined to set it aside. He did not, however, forbid them to attend.

Also in attendance was one old woman and one small girl. Limekiller thought that both of them looked familiar. And he was right. One was the same old woman who had urged him in out of the "fever rain." The other was the child who had urged him to see "the beauty harse" and had next day made the meager purchases in Mikeloglu's shop . . . whom the merchant had addressed as "Bet-ty me gyel," and urged her (with questionable humor) not to forget him when she was rich.

The crocodile stayed unvexed in his lair beneath the roots of the old Garobo Tree, though, seemingly, half the dragons along the river had dived to alert him.

To walk five hundred feet, *as a start,* is no great feat if one is in reasonable health. To cut and hack and ax and slash one's way through bush whose clearings require to be cleared twice a year if they are not to vanish: this is something else. However, the first five hundred feet proved to be the hardest (and hard enough to eliminate all but the hardiest of the lawyers). At the end of that first line they found their second marker: a lichen-studded rock growing right out of the primal bones of the earth. From there on, the task was easier. Clearly, though "the late Mr. Pike" had not intended it to be impossible, he had intended it to be difficult.

Sneed had discouraged, Marín had discouraged, others had discouraged May and Felix from coming: uselessly. Mere weight of male authority having proven to be obsolescent, Captain Sneed appealed to common sense. "My dear ladies," he pleaded, "can either of you handle a machete? Can either of you use an ax? Can —"

"Can either of us carry food?" was May's counter-question.

"*And* water?" asked Felix. "Both of us can," she said.

"Well, good for both of you," declared Captain Sneed, making an honorable capitulation of the fortress.

May had a question of her own. "Why do we all have to wear *boots*?" she asked, when there are hardly any wet places along here."

"Plenty tommy*goff,* Mees."

"Tommy Goff? Who is *he*?"

"Don't know who *he* was, common enough name, though, among English-speaking people in this part of the Caribbean. Don't know why they named a snake after the chap, either. . . ."

A slight pause. "A . . . snake . . .?"

"And *such* a snake, too! The dreaded fer-de-lance, as they call it in the French islands."

"Uhh . . . *Pois*onous?"

Sneed wiped his sweating head, nodded his Digger-style bush hat. "*Dead*ly poisonous. If it's in full venom, bite can kill a horse. Sometimes *does.* So do be exceedingly cautious. Please."

There was a further word on the subject, from Filiberto Marín. "*En castellano, se llame 'barba amarilla.'* "

This took a moment to sink in. Then one of the North Americans asked, "Doesn't that mean 'yellow beard'?"

"Quite right. In fact, the tommygoff's other name in English is 'yellow jaw.' But the Spanish is, literally, yes, it's yellow *beard.*"

All three North Americans said, as one, "*Oh.*" And looked at each other with a wild surmise.

The noises went on all around them. *Slash* – ! *Hack* – ! And, *Chop! Chop! Chop!* After another moment, May went on, "Well, I must say that seems like quite a collection of watchies that your late Mr. Leopold Pike appointed. Crocodiles. Poison serpents. What else. Oh. Do garobo *bite*?"

"Bite your nose or finger off if you vex him from the front; yes."

May said, thoughtfully, "I'm not sure that I really *like* your late Mr. Leopold Pike –"

Another flash of daytime lightening. Limekiller said, and remembered saying it the day before in the same startled tone, videlicet: "Pike! Pike!" Adding, this time, "*Fer-de-lance . . .!*"

Felix gave him her swift look. Her face said, No, he was not feverish. . . . Next she said, " '*Fer*,' that's French for 'iron,' and . . . Oh. I see. Yes. Jesus. *Fer-de-lance*, lance-iron, or spear-head. Or spear-*point*. Or –"

"Or in other words," May wound up, "*Pike.* . . . You dreamed that, too, small John?"

He swung his ax again, nodded. *Thunk.* "Sort of . . . one way or another." *Thunk.* "He had a, sort of a, pike with him." *Thunk.* "Trying to get his point – ha-ha – across. Did I dream the snake, too? Must have . . . I guess. . . ." *Thunk.*

"No. I do *not like* your late Mr. Leopold Pike."

Sneed declared a break. Took sips of water, slowly, carefully. Wiped his face. Said, "You might have liked Old Pike, though. A hard man in his way. Not without a sense of humor, though. And . . . after all . . . he hasn't hurt our friend John Limekiller . . . has he? Old chap Pike was simply trying to do his best for his dead son's child. May seem an odd way, to us. May *be*. Fact o'the matter: *is*. Why didn't he do it another way? Who's to say. Didn't have too much trust in the law and the law's delays. I'll sum it up. *Pike liked to do things in his own way.* A lot of them were Indian ways. *Old* Indian ways. Used to burn copal gum when he went deer hunting. *Al*ways got his deer. And as for *this* little business, well . . . the old Indians had no probate courts. What's the consequence? How does one guarantee that one's bequest reaches one's intended heir?

"Why . . . one *dreams* it to him! Or, for that matter, *her*. In this case, however, the *her* is a small child. So – "

One of the woodsmen put down his tin cup, and, thinking Sneed had done, said to Limekiller, "Mon, you doesn't holds de ox de same way we does. But you holds eet well. Where you learns dis?"

"Oh . . ." said Limekiller, vaguely, "I've helped cut down a very small part of Canada without benefit of chain saw. In my even younger days." Would he, too, he wondered, in his even older days, would he too ramble on about the trees he had felled? – the deeds he had done?

Probably.

Why not?

A wooden chest would have moldered away. An iron one would have rusted. Perhaps for these reasons the "collection of gold and silver coins, not being Coin of the Realm or Legal Tender," had been lodged in more Indian jars. Larger ones, this time. An examination of one of them showed that the contents were as described. Once again the machetes were put to use; branches, vines, ropes, were cut and trimmed. Litters, or slings, rough but serviceable, were made. Was some collective ethnic unconscious at work here? Had not the Incas, Aztecs, Mayas, ridden in palanquins?

Now for the first time the old woman raised her voice. "Ahl dis fah *you*, Bet-ty," she said, touching the ancient urns. "Bet-tah food. Fah *you*. Bet-tah house. Fah *you*, Bet-tah school. Fah *you*." Her gaze was triumphant. "*Ahl dis fah you!*"

One of the few lawyers who had not dropped out along the long, hard way, had a caveat. "Would the Law of Treasure Trove apply?" he wondered. "In which case, the Crown would own it. Although, to be sure, where there is no attempt at concealment The Crown would allow a finder's fee . . . Mr. Limekiller . . .?"

And if anyone attempt to resist or set aside this my Intention, I do herewith and hereafter declare that he, she, or they shall not sleep well of nights. . . .

Limekiller said, "I'll pass."

And Captain Sneed cried, "Piffle! Tush! Was the Deed of Gift registered, or was it not? Was the Stamp Tax paid, or was it not?"

One of the policemen said, "If you have the Queen's head on your paper, you cahn't go wrong."

"*Nol. con.,*" the lawyer said. And said no more.

* * *

That had been that. The rest were details. (One of the details was found in one of the large jars: another piece of plastic-wrapped paper, on which was written in a now-familiar hand, *He who led you hither, he may now sleep well of nights.*) And in the resolution of these other details the three North Americans had no part. Nor had Marín and friends: back to Parrot Bend they went. Nor had Captain Sneed. "Holiday is over," he said. "If I don't get back to my farm, the wee-wee ants will carry away my fruit. Come and visit, all of you. Whenever you like. Anyone will tell you where it is," he said. And was gone, the brave old Digger bush-hat bobbing away down the lane: wearing an invisible plume.

And the major (and the minor) currents of life in St. Michael of the Mountains went on — as they had gone on for a century without them.

There was the inevitable letdown.

May said, with a yawn, "I need a nice, long rest. And I know just where I'm going to find it. *After* we get back to King Town. I'm going to take a room at that hotel near the National Library."

Felix asked, "Why?"

"*Why?* I'll be like a kid in a candy warehouse. Do you realize that on the second floor of the National Library is the largest collection of nineteenth century English novels which I have ever seen in any one place? EVerything EVer written by EVerybody. Mrs. Edgeworth, Mrs. Trollope, Mrs. Gaskell, Mrs. Oliphant, Mrs. This and Mrs. That."

"Mrs. That. *I* remember *her.* Say, she wasn't bad at all —"

"No, she *wasn't.* Although, personally, I prefer Mrs. This."

Felix and Limekiller found that they were looking at each other. *Speak now,* he told himself. *Aren't you tired of holding your own piece?* "And what are you going to be doing, then?" he asked.

She considered. Said she wasn't sure.

There was a silence.

"Did I tell you about my boat?"

"*No.* You didn't." Her look at him was a steady one. She didn't seem impatient. She seemed to have all the time in the world. "Tell me about your boat," she said.

LIMEKILLER
AT LARGE

NIGHT . . . AND NOT plenilune, either. You can bet your boots. Limekiller has no boots, he has, though, a shovel. Limekiller feels that if he eats another pannikin of rice and beans or of the thin chowder called fish-*tea* that he . . . that he. . . . What he is after, he is after turtle-eggs so significant a source of insult in the rich, *rich* Chinese culture, largely represented in British Hidalgo, by the canny and philoprogenitive merchant Aurelio Aung and about 327 of his descendants. Better be exceedingly careful in talking about turtles to the Aung. More better say as little as possible about eggs at all to any of them. To ask, even to ask. "Don Aurelio, do you think it's going to rain?" would bring conversation to a sudden and deathly-still halt. As for that sole man ever known to have placed his hand on the ancient and naked head of old Aurelio Aung (for what reason, knows only God), death did not exactly come on swift wings, but it is certain that Aurelio Aung III felled him with a kick he had learned before kung fu became well-known in the regions of the dark west and that Aurelio Aung, Jr. had assisted III to propel the man down a flight of steps at the bottoms of which a throng or tong of unnumbered Aung were waiting to and did kick him with many sharp kicks of their sharp-pointed shoes (they being fashionable, and Old Aung had imported them and sold them in considerable numbers) before P.C. Oscar Spencer C. Featherstonehaugh Smith, then on duty, had finished strolling over quite leisurely. It may not have been a capital offense "to kill a Chinaman" in Pecos, Texas, during the incumbency of Judge Roy Bean; but it was quite a serious offense to insult Aurelio Aung in King Town, the ancient and moldering capital – as the man commonly called Bloody Whoop-whoop, a citizen of a Commonwealth Country (*not*, thank God, Canada!) soon found out. For not only was he subsequently refused service at hotels, bars, and brothels, but within no less than eighty-seven hours had been declared an Inadmissible Person ("in that he did disturb the peace of Her Majesty's Realm in British Hidalgo in a state of drunkenness by shouting 'Delete the Queen and all those other damn Dutch delete,' and did assault one Aurelio Aung Senior a loyal subject of her Majesty," etc. etc. for several other charges: of which others he had indeed been guilty but otherwise nothing more than a tolerant smile would have come of them); and was propelled by the pink palms of no less than three police sergeants across the Spanish-speaking border of a neighboring Republic. Which was the end of that. Though the pelicans and the hedgehogs may have picked his bones, and the satyrs danced upon them; serve him right.

For, over the course of many, *many* years, as John Lutwidge (Jack) Limekiller had learned, as follows: the turtle having a shell cannot copulate with other turtles and hence has conjugal union with a snake and is therefore (the turtle) written with the Chinese character meaning *Forgets Filial Piety*; by touching with one's palm the shell of the turtle one can tell if it is going to rain or not (Jack did not learn exactly *how*, and very much forebore to ask): therefore to imply that some one is a turtle or a turtle's eggs is somehow to insinuate several ugly matrimonial skeletons in some one's family closet . . . or sandalwood chest. *Oh* dear.

And as for the flexible yet muscular neck-and-head of the turtle extendable and retractable, references to and comparison with any particular member peculiar to the male anatomy are surely so obvious that only a turtle – But enough. The Aung family was clever. It was cognitive. It was commercial. It would do business in almost anything from galbanum to guppies. But it would not do business with turtles. And it would certainly not do business with turtles' eggs. Indeed as a general thing it would not admit knowing that turtles *had* eggs.

This left the local turtle-egg-hunting field narrowed down to only the Bayfolk, the Black Arawack, the White Creoles, and the Brown Panyars. All of whom admired the Aung family tre*men*-dously.

But did not share their prejudices.

At all.

But Smith-Piggott cared for none of these things.

Augustus Smith-Piggott, Permanent Undersecretary to Government, was a fixture. Legislatures, Governors, Cabinet Ministers, came and went: Smith-Piggott alone remained. His laccolithic face was in itself a monument to Empire; indeed, he was a one-man proverb all in his own right, to wit, "You no say 'No' to Smeet-P*ee*gott!" And on the day when he had decided that the turtles of the deeps (and perhaps even the shallows) might be endangered, the fate of legal hunting of their eggs was sealed.

Suppose that you were a young man, of full age, and although in very good health, felt that you had admired the Canadian snowscape fully as much as Kipling had, and now desired to copy Kipling in another manner, and survey the warmer souths: you, too (provided that your passport was in good order and that you were not on one of those *Wanted for Extradition* information sheets which circulate, sunset or not, throughout what used to be the British Empire. You might also have found yourself considering coconuts in place of maple leaves; Dr. Benjamin Jowett *(My name it is Benjamin Jowett/ Whatever is knowledge I know it/ I'm the Provost of Trinity College/ And what I do not know is not knowledge.)*, in a bit of a snit, had once observed that there were more sun-worshippers than Anglicans in Her Majesty's dominions; and perhaps there still are.

All of which is beside the point at issue or where is it at, the point being (a) that Limekiller was hungry, and (b) that it was Inhibited "to trap, dredge, catch, dig, trench, or otherwise secure the eggs of the great sea-turtle, the lesser-sea-turtle, the green or the hawksbill turtle, or any other turtle. tortoise, hiccatee, or bocatura whatsoever from any point upon or within one league of the seacoast of Her Majesty's Colony of British Hidalgo during such months which may be gazetted for purposes of said Inhibitions and all persons who may contravene such inhibitions shall be given into custody . . . to serve at hard labour at Her Majesty's pleasure for not more than one year and one day, etc." – it being damned well-understood in common-law and chancery that you might, if the Crown wanted it, serve every single day of such sentence for every single egg they caught you with.

Limekiller was *very* hungry?

He was.

Otherwise catch *him* at the wane of the moon with very little light save that supplied by the phosphorescent wash of the waves and the great and glittering stars clad only in shirt and britches (it was his bad shirt, too, for his good one had been just washed and hung drying from some ratlines or something on his boat *Saccharissa*) and with a shovel. Limekiller did indeed appreciate the need for keeping the sea-turtle or whatever was its particular name (Sadie? Lou? Jane?) from being egg-hunted to extinction; he also appreciated that its newly-surfaced hatchlings en route to the Stream of Ocean (just open Homer at random. . . . "Agamemnon shook his great purple cloak and with a great cry [or, loudly breaking wind], spake these winged words, 'Out upon thee, thou caitiff dog, and get thee gone from the camps of the well-greaved Aechaeans [or, pos. the Greeks with swollen legs], ne'er taking breath till thou reach the Stream of Ocean, and take care thou offend not the Turtle-eaters dwelling thereby, whom Apollo and Poseidon delight twice a year to visit. . . .' " *See?*) the newly-hatched and tiny turtles on route from their nests to the water were swooped down upon and eaten by predators innumerable, and he hoped that the dozen or so eggs he might take never would be missed; though perhaps in all this he was Wrong. And if he were asked *why*, nevertheless, he was doing so, he might answer, as did a well-known vegetarian found eating a steak, "I was hungry."

Aurelio Aung *y companía* might extend credit once, he/they might (though less likely) extend credit twice, but after that appeals for credit would only send him/them back to the abacus. Hence see Limekiller, his boat moored up a creek by the mangroves brown, pacing the beach under cover of night. And what would George II have thought about it all?

Neither history nor poetry had been very kind to George III. One poet has perhaps summed it up:

George Third
Ought never to have occurred.
Such a blunder
Makes one wonder.

Deft, no? Eh?

Of George I, we retain dull memories that he, not being able to speak English, thus became the first British Sovereign not to attend cabinet meetings, to the great advantage of Constitutional Government. But of George *II* – well, what *of* George II? The answer must only be: nothing. Nothing much in England, nothing good in Scotland, nothing much good in Ireland, and certainly nothing at all in British Columbia. But in British Hidalgo: a great deal more than nothing: for when it came to the second George's attention that the Spanish Viceroy of Mexico or perhaps Peru (history is a little blurry as to this) was caught out in sketching plans to invade the sea-coast of British Hidalgo (which was, in those days, almost all sea-coast), did not George II declare that, if this were done, "He vould, py Got, pompard der coasts of Shpain!"? This has been forgotten in Britain (it has probably been forgotten in Spain, both nations having had very long and very bad headaches from their respective and very disrespectful empires); it has never been forgotten in British Hidalgo; "the Spaniard" – as he is always called, collectively – having foreborne to make the planned invasion.

To this day, in fact, in Woodcutters Cove, that forgotten last refuge of the White Creoles, there is still a statue of this bristly little monarch. True, it is only half life-size, and the sculptor has pictured him wearing the armor and tunic of a Roman general, with the result that there is a subversive school of thought which maintains stubbornly that it is a statue of Queen Victoria in corset and petticoat. But that is neither here nor there; and, alas, increasingly, that is where one nowadays mostly finds the White Creoles of the Colony, to wit: neither here nor there . . . the principal exception being, of course, Woodcutters Cove. Darker and more vigorous races have in large part taken over, elsewhere. The children of Asia (of both ends and of the middle) run most of the shops. The civil service and police constabulary are mostly Bayfolk (which is to say, mostly Black or Tan). Most of the farming around there is done by Panyars, as the entirely Mestizo population is called. The Black Arawacks, who are culturally Amerindian, do most of the fishing. What then do the White Creoles do? They do what log-cutting is still being done thereabouts. Aniline dyes have swept away the demand for logwood, and the mahogany has long been exhausted. But when baulks of rosewood and spars of pine or Santa Maria, logs of serricoty, or emmory, are cut, it is the White Creoles who cut it. And when not doing that, they sit upon their verandahs, drinking rum and watered lime-juice, and they murmur of Good King George's Golden Days . . . that Good King being, of course, George II.

"'Tired of fish-tea and rice-and-beans'?" Ruddy – for Rudderick – Goforth repeated, as one should repeat, "'Tired of life?'"

"Pretty tired of'm, yes," Limekiller agreed. He sipped from the bottom of his glass. There hadn't been much rum to start with and it had been of low proof: but the lime-tree after all grew in the front yard, and even if one didn't know much else, one knew that lime-juice kept away the dreaded scurvy. There was, this time, a different and a more bitter taste in the glass, but no mystery was involved . . . and neither was Angostura . . . idly he picked up the piece of paper which Ruddy had copied, he said, from an old book, and read once more the careful capitals.

A Sovran Cure for The Small Feaver. Take one small bottle of white Rum called by Ye Spaniard a chaparita and lay therein three twigs of the Yerb Contribo and lett it steep for three Dayes. Drink 1 oz. morning and one ozz Evening for 3 dayes and Ye maye see Ye Feaver abate. Cauton [sic] do not use same Twiggs more than thrice.

It was an *old* "old book." Ruddy asked how "Jock" was feeling. "Jock" shrugged. "I guess the fever's gone down," he said. "It wasn't much of a fever anyway."

Ruddy covered his long chin with his long hand, and took thought. "Well . . . if the fever has gone down . . . and you still hasn't got no appetite –"

"Didn't say that I have no appetite. Said that I have no appetite for fish-tea and rice-and-beans."

Goforth looked upward, as though an information might be lodged on the ridge-pole of his house. From the outside, nothing looked trashier than the thatched roof of a "trash house," at once shaggy and so soon shabby: from the inside, nothing looked more beautiful and more symmetrical: compensation, this was called. John L. Limekiller could not see it, but evidently Rod. Goforth could, and – having found the information – took his hand away from his chin and slowly opened his mouth. Also in the yard were the purple-drooping jacaranda trees. The book said its flowers were blue . . . *blue!* . . . but any fool could see they were purple.

Almost as though determined to exhibit a prime feature of the classical old White Creole accent, R. Goforth said, "Vhat you vants to do is to elewate your wittles." He gave a great nod.

"'Elevate my –'"

"Get you a tin of carn-*beef.* Get you a tin of peas-with-salad-cream."

He almost smacked his lips as he named these imported delicacies, and sounded rather like a physician of the previous century recommending a couple of dozen oysters, some canvasback duck, and a pint of champagne.

His guest sighed. "What I'd like to get me is some back-bacon and a couple of eggs. But when I mentioned *write-it-down* to Domingo Aung," the entire Aung extended family, to which Aurelio was Titular Uncle, maintained the tradition of Spanish-language given-names perhaps dating back to days when kings named Alfonso reigned over Manila as well as Malaga; "to Domingo Aung, he suddenly got very hard of hearing."

R. Goforth signified by a sort of rictus that well he knew the occasional auricular difficulty of Aurelio Aung and Clan. Then, "I tells you vhat," said he. "You vants to picquet the beach at night, and get you a few tortle eggs; bock-bacon, forget about it until you gets rich again."

And he told Jack this, and he told Jack that, and he told Jack a few other things; also he told Jack *this*: "Ond in case they *should* apprehend you, vhich I wery much doubts, as po-licemen doesn't vant to poke around such places at night unless eat ease really big-*time*, but suppose they *should*: here is vhat you remember: stout denial. You does understand that? Neh-wer confess! E-wen if ah dead body lie before you, stout. . . denial! Maybe it fool you, get up and valk avay, maybe somebody help it valk. . . . The Lah of Ewwidence is ah chancy thing. This is a British country – this is not a *Frinch* country – not a *Span*iard country – the police gots to produce ewwidence you are guilty. So –"

"'Stout . . . denial.'"

"*Stout . . . denial.*"

Likely, (Limekiller was thinking, waiting on the log just above highwater mark) likely if his lovely lady, Felix, was hereabouts he would have found something better to do of nights. Also, Felix (*née* Felicia) would have spurred him on to borrow a shotgun and go hunting gibnut, or maybe even armadillo . . . wild-*hog* . . . ante*lope* (very well: it was really a small dear, it *ate* well, didn't it). . . . But Felix and her cousin May were in King Town, getting their residence permits renewed, shopping for piece goods and native arts and crafts, getting books out of the National Library: officially. *Un*officially: also going to parties and to events very generally called *funs.* Maybe he, Jack, did not altogether like this last notion, for who knows whom Felix might *meet*? But he did not own her, nor her gleaming copper-red hair, nor her lovely long body; and he could not control her goings or her doings. So. . . .

Here he was, and what was that, barely he could see it but he *could* see it, its back breaking the surface of the water (not the surf, no, there was no surf to speak of within the reef-protected waters of the Great Bay of Hidalgo: the water) . . . ? Sure enough, as it came nearer and nearer, only a turtle would be homing in to land amid the shallows. The creature seemed to give no heed to possible danger, it hesitated not for a single moment, on it came, in it came, up it came, it dragged its large body up upon the beach and, propelling its bulk across the sands, crawled and crawled and . . . then it stopped. Began to dig. Kept on digging.

He could not only see the sand it was excavating with its hind flippers, he could hear it falling back down; he could also hear . . . and had been hearing . . . faint sounds of music from Woodcutters Cove Town . . . principally the faint sounds of the juke-boxes in the various "liquor booths," not indeed of Creole or Bayfolk music, for those traditions were alas dying: of the record-ed popular music of the United States, of Jamaica. . . . And also, or instead, as the soft wind shifted, as the rock and reggae paused long enough sometimes for the records to be changed, he heard something else, heard a music quite different: it was, must be, could only be, the sound of Mrs. Standish playing her spinnet. It was of course softer than the sounds of the clamorous juke-boxes, but it was also nearer. Almost an axiom: the tropics are not kind to stringed instruments. No, and perhaps the tropics were not particularly kind to Mrs. Standish, either; she was the wife of the Anglican minister, Limekiller had not officially met her, but he had more than once seen her, an aging woman with a loosening face and figure. Mister Standish had a Dedicated countenance and it grew more Dedicated with the passing of time; Mrs. Standish's face merely grew older.

The sand flashed, the sand fell. Why should the sand flash? Was that only the *sand* he was hearing? Did sand clash and ring? He did not want to disturb the great sea-she-turtle, assuming it to be disturbable, but he was moved to arise and to get him, so softly as he could, adown the nighttime sands. The turtle showed no signs of alarm – of, even, awareness: slowly he drew near. Surely . . . surely *not*!

> I walked along the evening sea
> And dreamed a dream which could not be.
> The evening waves, breaking on the shore,
> Said only, Dreamer, dream no more.

Where was that from? Who cared. He stooped. His hands moved in the heap of cast-up sand. His fingers clutched a something, and he drew it out. He drew out a few more. Deliberating himself be calm, he took his shirt off and spread it on the beach a few feet away from the constantly-increasing heaps of sand, and, finding no stone, anchored it first with a chunk of coconut shell. Then he could contain himself no longer; into the wood which fringed the beach he went, crouched, carefully considered the matter of direction, struck a match. Looked. *Was* Charles II indeed King of France as well as of England, Scotland, Ireland? Probably not, probably it was not even an idle boast but merely a habit, a reflex, to describe him as such. *No King of England if not King of France* . . . ? – but that was long before. The mosquitoes, no longer kept even somewhat at bay by the sea-breezes, fiercely sounded their shrill sounds and attacked: let them. He held in his hand, John Lutwidge Limekiller, a coin of twenty-one shillings and minted (presumably) from gold mined in *the great Kingdom of Guinea*; he had little idea – he had *none*! – what the current value of such a coin might be, but he knew that it had to be more than twenty-one shillings – twenty-one pounds would not value it enough!

Money! Money! Here he had had scarcely enough to eat, and now he would be rich! for, although he had as yet no way of knowing how many golden guineas there were . . . let alone where they had come from . . . some foundered ship whose timbers perhaps broken on the reef, yet had (perhaps) managed to get inside that same before sinking altogether and before the officers or crew were able to manage salvaging the gold, or all of it . . . perhaps it was indeed the universally-magic thing, a Buried Treasure! . . . perhaps the loot of some captured galleon or – what difference did it make! – a thousand perhaps! He, John Lutwidge Limekiller, was rich! – comparatively speaking – he was (maybe) *rich*!

Only maybe not.

The she-turtle had had enough of digging, her nest-hole was now deep enough, and began to lay.

Rich? Only maybe not. His fingers told him, after he had crept back to the great chelonian, that there were many coins in the hoard: how might that coast have shifted over the centuries because of storm, erosion, hurricane, and flood . . . and his mind told him something else.

In every grant of freehold stood the words, and he knew them well, for he had, after all had been granted more than one freehold himself, for all that they were for but small acreages; there stood the words, *All Indian Ruins and Mines of Gold and Silver and Precious Stones are the Property of Her Majesty the Queen, Her Heirs or Assignees:* these words were emphatic and clear and admitted of no dispute. Well . . . almost none. Suppose such gold were already mined? Coined? Abandoned? Kicked up on a beach by the hind-flippers of a gravid sea-turtle with no more on her membrane-thing template of a mind than digging a hole in which to plash her scores and scores of opalescent eggs; what? Why, for that matter, was there only *one* turtle here and now? A matter for enquiry; would anyone enquire?

And . . . wasn't there something, somewhere, amidst all the antique and baroque legal terminology about treasure-trove and bonavaconcia, wasn't there something about high-water mark? low-water mark? What should Jack *do*? For certainly he had to *do* something . . . and right now: one could hardly expect the turtle would remain fixed for a landmark whilst he ran loping along the strand to report the matter.

And so he had taken the gold, he had shoveled and sifted, long after the turtle's instinct, located in that reptilian little head protruding between carapace and carapace, had told her that her oviducts might now rest; and off she had waddled, struggled, crawled, dipped into the water, sank into the water, was gone into the water: and, about the sum of two-score and ten coins had he sifted from the sands. He had carefully set them down on his shirt, and, since it was the bad shirt, rent in at least one place and worn thin in others, he had tied the treasure by the sleeves and knotted them and then he had stripped off his trousers and slipped the swag inside of them and closed that outer covering up, then –

Then he hied him down to the mangroves brown where the sea-tide sucked and sawed . . . or something like that . . . very much like that . . . and had heaved it up onto his own boat, videlicet the

Saccharissa, then lying at the mouth of Mangrove Creek, with all her apparel. And, after counting it a few times, say, about forty or fifty times, had stowed it in the cubby; well . . . he had taken the trousers back, first, because really he needed them *now*.

Also he had recollected to bring along a few of the eggs, and he set up the caboose, which, in British Hidalgo had no reference to railroad trains but referred to the little wood-stove set in a sand-box; and he had cooked them at leisure and eaten them with relish, and with salt and with pepper.

They had tasted better than rice and beans.

Eggs.

As for turtle-eggs, very well, *never* mention the matter to anyone Chinese, however defined. As for eggs as something other than victuals (*wittles*, as Rud Goforth called them), as something thick with legendary qualities, there were also the *o*beah eggs. *O*beah eggs came color-coded: a clean white egg meant one thing, a clean brown egg meant another; a speckled egg, whether the birdy sings of them or not, meant worst of all; and then there were eggs still stained with chickenshit and clotted with tufts of down and, sometimes, blood. A chapter in a local grimoire (were there such a thing, and there wasn't) might be written about eggs stained red with anatto and eggs stained red with red mangrove bark . . . and the immense difference (qualitative rather than quantitative) between them.

But . . . why does the egg left at night symbolize death?

Because the egg left at day symbolizes life.

Is why.

He had meant to report it.

But the hours, as hours will, had gone by. The gold still stood (or sat) in the cramped cubby of his boat. And he had not reported it.

Sailing south you see the weird sugarloaf-shaped hills behind Spanish Bight; whereas elsewhere, some hills seem five miles away and are actually twenty-five, these hills seem to be one-and-twenty miles away, but are really only one. One mile away, that is. A curious phenomenon. They rise out of the midst of palm trees which look rather like the giant ferns of earth's past eras; easily one may imagine dinosaurs nibbling on the tops of them. Something similar . . . could one call it confusion . . . delusion . . . afflicted Limekiller. He had forgotten to cross off how many days on his calendar (it advertized *30 Pure Turkish Cigarette 3o / M., Grower and Mfger* rather garishly, and was generally understood to have been also of, if not the growth, then of the manufacture, also, of M.: but that was another story. Indeed.) how many days had he forgotten to cross off? he could not think how many. When had he found the trove of gold coins? had it been last night? the night before last? several nights ago? Limekiller was no longer, and perhaps had never been, from the moment Doubt entered his mind, quite sure. At all sure. And, on the other hand, if he stayed aboard his boat, he would only be driven again to count the coins, and he could see himself becoming a latter-day Silas Marner: this would not do.

If he left the boat, might not someone come aboard of her and peek and peer and probe and. . . . Nobody ever *had.* Before. So he had gone, he told himself, for a Walk. And the possibilities for walking being limited, had found himself going into the hamlet called Woodcutters Cove. A hamlet it might be (might *be*? it *was.*), but it was also what foreigners sometimes called "the provincial capital": not quite. A District was not really a province, being a Canadian Limekiller knew all about provinces, provinces had lieutenant-governors, premiers, legislative assemblies – a District had none of these. It had a District Commissioner, who was an administrative officer, the name of the District was Seville (pronounced by every man, woman, and child in British Hidalgo as *Civil,* just exactly the same as Shakespeare pronounced it, *The King is as civil as an orange,* a pun which had baffled Shakespearean scholars – none of whom had ever lived in British Hidalgo – almost ever since the death of James I and V), and its capital was Woodcutters Cove . . . though there was talk of moving it to Seville Town, where the citrus works were, and the bitter "civil oranges" made into marmalade. But they had been talking about that at least since King Edward had abdicated, not that there was necessarily a connection.

Limekiller passed the old Anglican Church, the Parson's Paddock, the Parsonage, and expected next to pass about a quarter of a mile of trash houses until he came to the shops and the liquor booths, and had begun to wonder at which one of the latter his credit might still be good, not at the Juno Club, not at the New Africa, not at the Bayman's Bogue, maybe at the Little Bit of

Heaven? maybe at the Hidalgo Club? when his wonders were interrupted by his being hailed from the Government Building in the following words, "Mr. Limekiller! May I give you a hail?"

Grammatically, the question was not without fault. And to reply with some such reply as, "What in the hell have you just been *do*ing you dumb son of a bitch?" was socially contra-indicated. The man who from an office window had called to him was Percival FitzEvans Blythe; Percival FitzEvans Blythe was perhaps not very distinguished-looking, he was perhaps not very well set-up, and even perhaps he had not a very intriguing personality; but there was one thing about him which admitted of no *perhaps*: and Limekiller, suddenly a prey to the dismals, was well aware of what this was.

"Good afternoon, District Commissioner," said Limekiller.

"Would you just step inside, Mr. Limekiller," said Mr. P.F.E. Blythe, without a question-mark. And popped his head back in. The Stamp Acts, which had caused so many heart-flutterings and tea-bashings in British North America (old boundaries) had never disturbed a single soul in British Hidalgo, where in proposing a written contract it was proverbial to remark, "If you has the Queen's head on a stamp, and a dollar for earnest, you cahn't go wrong." Limekiller now felt, dimly recollecting Mark Twain's comment that the average man would rather see General Grant in full dress uniform than Lillian Russell naked, felt that he would much, *much* rather pay to see the Queen's head on a thousand stamps than Percival FitzEvans Blythe at a window or anywhere else for free, stepped inside. And whilst doing so he encountered a licensed (so to speak) beggar commonly called Wee-Wee; Wee-Wee seldom encountered Jack without asking for a dime or a shilling or a glass of rum or a plate of rice and *bean*, always with a face the most ingratiating; his face now seemed to say, "I may not be six feet tall and blonde and I may be just getting out of gaol again for being publically intoxicated and Pissing on The Plinth but on the other hand neither have I just been asked by the District Officer if I would step inside." They passed each other in a strange and strong silence.

"You wanted to see me, District Commissioner?"

The District Commissioner curtly gestured towards a chair facing him and, when Limekiller had seated himself, stared at him a moment without words, then asked, "Well, Mr. Limekiller, what about this gold?"

* * *

The shock was immense. Had he not already been suffering from a guilty conscience, the shock would have been even more immense and it was to be feared that he would almost at once have incriminated himself, had he not suddenly remembered Rud Goforth's advice; "What gold?" he asked.

Another silence. Then the D.C. said, "Mr. Limekiller, anyone may bring charges and make accusations," said the D.C. "And anyone may bear witness, true or false. But under our system of British Justice," there was a slight but significant emphasis, *British Justice*, "something more is needed, and that is Evidence. Evidence openly presented in an open court at an open trial," the word *trial* doing more to chill Limekiller's blood than his sole trip to northern Labrador had done. "Mere testimony is not sufficient. We require *evidence*. Ev-i-dence. No evidence? No case." He made a gesture.

Someone else now appeared, namely Police Constable Lucas; more than once P.C. Lucas had helped Jack demolish a chaparita of rum (without the herb Contribo) at a club or booth; there was no trace of any such memory on the P.C.'s face now. "Would you read your notes," said the District Officer. *Would* you step inside. *Would* you read your notes. The District Commissioner was expert in the donning of the velvet glove. But well did John L. Limekiller know what lay inside.

"Acting upon information received," read P.C. Lucas, "I went in the police launch to the place called Mangrove Creek, accompanied by Mr. Stopford the District Surveyor –"

Limekiller was puzzled, for the first time, genuinely. "The, ah, Sur*vey*or?" he interrupted.

The skies did not fall at this interruption. It was explained to him that it was well-known that the mouth of Mangrove Creek had at one time been located just inside the limits of Woodcutters Cove Town. And it was well-known that the effects of Hurricane Henrietta had closed that mouth and opened another . . . which lay outside the Town limits. It was also known that Hurricane Elvia had quite estopped this and opened yet another. But it was not known if this new mouth lay in or out of the limits. "The question of mooring fees," explained the D.C. *Money*.

On coming into sight of the vessel known to them as the boat *Saccharissa* registered as belonging to Mr. John Lutwidge Limekiller, P.C. Lucas and Surveyor Stopford observed two individuals unfamiliar to them moving about on the deck of aforesaid vessel and attempting to hand down an object not immediately identifiable to a third individual in a cayuco; did the two Officials open fire upon them? did they attempt to cut off their retreat? was the Magna Carta written in Volapük?

". . . we then hailed the three individuals," read P.C. Lucas, virtuously, "but they at once made their craft to the opposite bank, and escaped into the bush. We would have pursued them but," here the P.C. raised his eyes to those of his superior, who evaded them in a manner which indicated that he was at that moment passing no judgment as to *should* they have pursued said three individuals into the bush but might raise the matter at a time subsequent; ". . . but upon observing that the object they had dropped was spilling gold coins we thought it best to return with it and them at once and to report the matter to the District Commissioner," and here he closed his notebook and stood with his legs apart.

"You recognize this shirt, Mr. Limekiller?" Limekiller would at that moment have been willing to swear upon a copy of Domesday Boke and/or the British North America Act that he did not even recognize that it *was* a shirt, except that –

– except that it had been mended once by Felix who, not content with sewing up its rents and tears had also sewed onto the right breast the initials *JL* in very large letters: and if there was anyone in the entire District of Seville who had not seen him wearing it, it could only have been Blind Bob who sat in the Market Place, with his sightless eyes rolling, making baskets out of native rushes. Hardly perhaps a case where the principle of Stout Denial seemed in order. "Yes," said Mr. Limekiller.

"We have examined these coins and find them to be golden guineas of the Reigns of Charles II, James II, and William III," said the District Commissioner . . . and indeed one would scarcely have needed to be a member of the Royal Association of Numismatists to have done so . . . with the monarchs' names and titles emphatically emprinted on the coins in neat Latin abbreviations.

"You may know, Mr. Limekiller, that although it is not forbidden to own such coins, their ownership must be registered with the Treasury," Mr. Limekiller took advantage of the pause to say nothing, "in order to establish the question of rightful ownership." Pause. Mr. Limekiller continued to say nothing. "So you see there is more than one question we have to answer," the D.C. began to tick them off on his fingers. "One, are these your gold coins? Two, if they are, then why have they not been registered? Three: if they have not been registered because you have just recently acquired them, then where and when and *how* did you acquire them? We perceive that there seems to be sand mixed among the gold and lying in the shirt which they were wrapped in. Can it be that the coins of gold were just recently dug up somewhere? – say, somewhere on the shore? In such a case we would have to add Question Number Four: was the gold obtained in an illegal manner or fashion?" Jack noted that the possibility that he had obtained the gold whilst illegally taking turtle eggs had not been raised: he himself was not going to raise it. "Question *Five*: is it not so that even if the gold was taken from someone who had himself illegally failed to register it, would that make the taking of it by someone else other than illegal? no – it would NOT! Theft would be and is *theft*! Mind you," said the D.C., "I don't accuse you of theft. Nor do I accuse you of having the gold in your possession – although you don't deny do you, *having* the gold in your possession, do you? – other than legally?"

Limekiller cleared his throat, but with great control refrained from saying, "Ahh." Or even "Umm." He said, "Who says it was in my possession?"

The District Commissioner sat for a second with his mouth open. "Why who? Two of our Government officials . . . no . . . well . . . if the gold was not in your possession, then how did it come to be on your boat?"

"Maybe the same ones who were taking it off, put it on?"

The D.C. brushed away an invisible fly. "Why would they have done *that*?" And Limekiller quickly pointed out that it was not for him to ascertain their motives. "Best that you ask *them* that," he suggested. And the D.C. looked up at the P.C. But P.C. Lucas continued to stand At Ease, saying nothing.

The District Commissioner now looked his invited guest straight between the eyes and said, "Now, Mr. Limekiller, it is not prohibited to own gold coins regardless of are they legal tender or not and the question, 'Are such coins still legal tender or not' is one into which I will not go;" echoes of Churchill's reply to the new secretary telling him not to end a sentence with a preposition: "This is an impertinence up with which I will not put." – "however, we are obliged to ahsk, I will not say demand" (and, *Damned nice of you!* thought Jack) "how you did get these coins, because they are not in shall we say common ownership. So I shall now ahsk you that question."

There was a loonng pause. Then the D.C. said, "Very well." He gestured to P.C. Lucas, who gathered up the shirt and its precious contents, the D.C. meanwhile unlocking the huge and antique safe, which would certainly not cause Mr. Jimmy Valentine or his successors much trouble; but where was *he*? It would certainly baffle anybody in Woodcutters Cove, Seville District: shoved the stuffed shirt in under the shelves of official documents, closed and clicked it shut. "We shall, I trust, see you here at shall we say eight of the morning. Good evening, Mr. Limekiller . . . and I should advise you to think it over."

And think it over Jack did. All night long.

There was nobody for him to think it over aloud with . . . save his former First Mate, Skippy the Cat who had been demoted in favor of Felix. *Did* Skip chant pieces of eight, pieces of eight? Nope: he offered no grounds for belief that because and just because Jack had not been confined in the district gaol for the night that he might not find himself confined there – or in the national one – at some future time. D.C. FitzEvans was a Bayman and hence "cradled on the water," as were they all: he would know the state of the winds without even taking thought, and he would know that the state of the winds would not carry Limekiller on a flight from Colonial waters at this time. Not only not to "Republican waters," not to anywhere well – the winds would indeed carry him now right onto the Muggleton Shoals and there he . . . or his boat . . . might have to wait a very long time indeed before any friendly boats and their crews appeared to help tow . . . push . . . pull . . . shove him off; because right on the mainland circumjacent to the Muggleton Shoals was the cabin of old Sully Simpson, a very *loud* lunatic who notoriously kept open house for Tata Duende, the Spook of the Woods; and nobody darker than lard would come or go within a marine mile of the area.

Therefore, even if he, John Lutwidge Limekiller, was safely out of gaol for the night, such safety could hardly be expected to continue for very long. Maybe they *couldn't* prove that he had the gold illegally (though maybe they *could*). And if not, maybe they couldn't get him for not having registered it. Or maybe the question of, had he been poaching turtle eggs wouldn't be raised (*would* Ruddy Goforth . . . ? not without incriminating himself for Abetting, he wouldn't).

Back and forth his mind raced, with many and many a *But,* a *So,* an *And* all night long. And all the early morning . . . because in British Hidalgo, "eight of the morning" was absolutely not *early!*

– and as, for that matter, *who* were The Individuals who had boarded the *Saccharissa* and attempted to rob her – Limekiller had no idea. The Colony . . . which, being irrevocably on its way to independence . . . would not be a Colony for much longer . . . had been for long out of the way of the world: but the world, with its internal combustion engines, its radios, its vices, and its crimes, was inexorably creeping in. Jack did not wish to think that the robbers were Nationals (the phrase was replacing the old, bad word Colonials), but it seemed unlikely that foreigners would have come up from Republican waters in a cayuco – but it really didn't matter . . . just as it really didn't matter that if he had been content to, in the delicate Hidalgo phrase, "ease himself" near to the boat instead of seeking the privacy of the bush on his way to town then he might have spied the intruders and scared them off. . . .

Once again, as so often, he passed the Parsonage, passed the Parson's Paddock, passed the Anglican Church, and came to the Government Building.

This time Wee-Wee (he was named after the wee-wee ant, which, with its voracious appetite, counterfeits the leaf-eating wee-wee disease) was not on the steps. But that didn't really matter, either.

The District Commissioner wasted neither time nor words. "Now, Mr. Limekiller, what about this gold?"

J.L. recalled yet again Ruddy Goforth's Principle: "'Stout denial,' Regardless and whatever: '*stout . . . denial.*'" For . . . after all . . . what alternative? Even if he didn't get charged with this offense or that offense there was the very good (or very bad) chance of being ordered to leave the country and not come back. And he had, really, grown to love the little land, smaller than Newfoundland, British Hidalgo, the "country that you can put your arms around," even if it was also "the end of the line." Being there, even with its bugs and spooks, was and had for quite a time been better than being in Toronto in the snow-and even if it rained just as much as it rained in Vancouver, well the rain was warmer. And also . . . well . . . never mind. . . .

"What gold?" he asked.

The D.C. looked a moment at him. Then he swiveled his chair around and worked at the dial of the old safe. The official papers laced with their red tape were where they had been. Nothing much else was there. The D.C. scraped his hands along the bottom. Some grains of sand. Some crumbles of dirt. The bad old shirt. Nothing else. *Nothing* else. The D.C. turned around. His mouth worked. Then he said, "Mr. Limekiller. *Where is that gold?*"

Jack felt his lips crack. But all he said was, staunchly, "What gold?"

Another silence. Then, moved by the devil, Limekiller said, "District Commissioner, *I will thank you for that shirt —*"

The District Commissioner took out the shirt, shook it, handed it over. Then he made an emphatic gesture, Limekiller left. He sneaked a look at Police Constable Lucas, but Police Constable Lucas, carefully looking at the wall, did not sneak back. The D.C. was, suddenly, shouting, "I shall call in the C.I.D.! I shall have the safe dusted for fingerprints! I shall discharge every police constable on duty lahst night! I shall take it up to the Colonial Privy Council! I shall take it up to the Law Lords in London! I —" The door closed on him and on what else he should do. Only, of course, he wouldn't. For —

No evidence?

No case!

Because —

British Justice!

The outside world had begun to bring in its rot and corruption. But it had only begun.

Outside . . . well, not outside the District Office Building . . . outside the office of the District Commissioner . . . Limekiller found himself in the familiar-enough out-district police room. These rooms served for many purposes which were not always involved with crime, and, while not always the same, were always similar. This one had of course been whitewashed-but not very recently. It was immaculate. As always. On the wall (invariably), two framed photographs: Her Majesty the Queen, who theoretically *owned* British Hidalgo and might, theoretically, sell it all to a real estate syndicate — but probably wouldn't; that was one of the photographs. The other, just a mite smaller, was of the Honourable Llewellyn Gonzaga MacBride, the Queen's First Minister in British Hidalgo. She was in full regalia. He was wearing a short-sleeved shirt open at the neck, no tie. They both wore smiles.

Overhead the slow fan.

At the dais, no one.

Not now, at any rate.

Behind a table doing extra duty as a desk, a police constable. He and Jack exchanged civil looks.

"Yes, Mr. Limekiller?"

"Am I, well, free to go? Eh?"

The P.C. slightly pursed his lips, slightly raised his eyebrows. It was the studiously non-committal face of a man being asked to guess the value of a sand-sailing-barge. He rose to his feet in a smooth motion. "If you will just make yourself at ease a moment, Mr. Limekiller, I will just go into the. . . ." He did not finish the sentence, but its meaning was obvious. The door of the inner office was opened for a moment, a voice (previously muffled) was heard, loud and clear, demanding to know "Why is there no Canadian High Commissioner in this Colony? – do they think that they can come down here and commit all kinds of tricks, just because they are from a Commonwealth country? I – what? *what*? He is still here? Out, *out*, OUT – get him *out*! I shall –" and the door closed again and the police-constable returned to his desk.

Slightly he shook his head, said, "Jock, you w'only vex de man!" "Only," in Bay talk, an intensive: during a heat wave, it was "only" hot; during a downpour, it was "only" raining.

Jack said, "Eh?"

The police constable was once again studying the sand-barge. Very politely, though, he indicated the door to the outside world. "Mr. Limekiller," he said, "you are now at large."

Limekiller walked down the street. First building in the next block, shaded by a purple-drooping jacaranda tree, was . . . still . . . sun-worshippers or not . . . the Anglican Church, crusted with lichens and moss. Would he go in and give thanks? There was, really, a lot of work he should be doing on his boat before Felix got back. *Whatsoever thy hands find to do, do it with thy might.* Best he got back to his boat and think his pious thoughts there. But the way took him past the Parson's Paddock, where no horse had pastured for many years. And then the way took him past the Parsonage and its late Tropical Gothic verandahs shielding the inner rooms from view. But not from sound. In the Parsonage was, evidently, the

Parson's wife, Mrs. Standish. The climate was, indeed, "not kind" to the spinnet. Perhaps also Mrs. Standish's singing voice was past its prime. But gallantly she played and sang. He could hear her quite clearly. *Believe me, if all those endearing young charms,* sang Mrs. Standish, *which I gaze on so fondly today, were to fleet by tomorrow and fade in my arms,* Mrs. Standish sang. The waters of the Bay of Hidalgo slapped languidly along the shore. What had happened during the night? what had *hap*pened? – *like fairy gifts fading away,* sang Mrs. Standish.

Limekiller got into his skiff.

A FAR
COUNTRIE

AT THAT TIME Jack and Felix were living in Eden, Felix was really Felicia, Love had just been invented, and the Garden was on the sea.

Limekiller gave his sunstained hair a shake, and began to get the sail up. Felix had already finished tying the skiff – he no longer checked to see if she were doing it right – and, jaw set, was giving an extra push down on the pole to which the *Saccharissa* had been, and the skiff now was, tied. *Prob*ably the skiff would still be there when they returned. It would be an extra drag to tow it under sail, and besides, they would not need it where they were going. It had taken them from Cornmeal Wharf to the wide waters of the harbor, but there was a wharf or dock at their destination. Behind, ahead, and all around them, others there, in the mouth of the Belinda (or Old Main) River, which was King Town's Harbor, were doing the same or similar things to their own vessels. Some were going out for conch, some for sand or pipeshank-coral. Some for lobster. And some for fish. Well . . . some mainly for fish, and some for fish as well.

From astern Limekiller heard a voice ask the familiar question, "You no forget de 'drop,' mahn?"

And the answer, in the pearly light of pre-dawn: "Me forget me head, may-be. But no forget me 'drop.'"

The somewhat more than colony of British Hidalgo abuts on the Great Bay of Hidalgo; the main things about the Great Bay of

Hidalgo is that God has put in it fish for the Bayfolk and the Black
Arawack to eat but that God has not put enough fish in it for the
Bayfolk and the Arawack to eat all the fish they want to eat. That is
not to say that they are always hungry, but it is to say that they are
always hungry for fish. A local proverb goes, *If there is not a plantain,
there is a banana*; and there is usually, also, for the Arawack, cassa-
va, and, for the Bayfolk (who are also called Creoles), rice and
beans. Both people will eat meat, *Yea but we will eat flesh*, when they
can get it; except that the Bayfolk will not eat any fowl which has
served an obeah purpose (and if you ask them why not, they say
because it will make a man lose his "nature" and a woman lose her
milk); and the Arawack will never under any circumstances eat goat
meat whether they can get it or not: and you must never, *ever*, ask
them why not.

But best of all and most of all, they both love fish.

It is not only unheard of for any of them deliberately to take to
the water without a "drop" (i.e., a drop-line) to tow behind, it is
inconceivable. They will eat the quash, a sort of lean-tailed raccoon;
they will eat the gibnut, a kind of large and large-eyed rodent; they
will eat the dark mauve meat of the "mountain-cow," or tapir; they
will eat crocodile tail and the 'bocrob" or blue crab and the hind
legs and red eggs of the iguana: but most of all, given any opportunity at all, they will eat fish.

But Limekiller and Felix were not going out for fish.

A brochure printed by what was still graciously named The
Visitors' Bureau contains the lines: *"British Hidalgo's numerous and
picturesque lagoons, colorful coral reefs, sand banks and beaches together
with clear blue skies and tropical vegetation, combine to provide this lovely
little country a scenic beauty which, together with a mild climate and the
friendly welcome of its people, forms the basis of its tourist industry."*

This is, in fact, or, at any rate, very often in fact, a True Relation:
although perhaps *industry* is too strong a word, and despite the
Hotels Encouragement Act, Conrad Hilton somehow lacked the
courage. Still, it *is*, in so many ways, a "lovely little country," that
one can perhaps understand its being coveted by other and rather
larger countries.

Not so many years ago, it is well-known, the Director of
Correspondence in the *Republic* of Hidalgo struck yet another blow
for the liberation of what he and his countrymen still (after three

hundred years) call *Hidalgo Occupado*, or *Hidalgo Ingles*: letters addressed to *Inglaterra*, he ruled, would be no more delivered . . . not, at least, until the Occupied Districts, falsely called "English," were returned to their rightful allegiance, *videlicet*, the *Republic* of Hidalgo. This was front-page news for one full day throughout *Centroamerica y Darien*, with the implication of an isolated England supinely treating for a pax hispanica. (The ruling is, so far as any-one knows, technically still in effect; and the few letters which actually travel between Ciudad Hidalgo and, say, Birhmagnan, Mahcesthre, Liberpül, and Londres – these being, it is also well-known, the only inhabited places in that distant and ice-bound Island, with its odd-*odd* names – are required to disguise their destination under the novel sobriquet of *Gran Bretannia*.) – A blow! Unquestionably a blow. One which could certainly not fail of effect, and of immediate effect at that time.

And yet . . . somehow . . . somehow . . . British Hidalgo, for reasons inexplicable (or, anyway, inexplicable in *Centroamerica y Darien*), failed to become Republican, Roman Catholic, and Mestizo-Ladino; and remained, as long it had been, Autonomously Monarchial, Nominally Protestant, and Predominantly Black. And, also, possessed of a memory like a wind of long fetch: not a single schoolchild cannot tell you how, when Don Diego Bustamente y Bobadilla, Sub-Admiral of the Spanish Main, came crawling down the Crawfish Channel with his armada of three shallow-draft gal-leys, intent on lowering the Union Jack, establishing the Inquisition, and raising both the Spanish Ensign and the tax on nutmeg – the Royal Navy being elsewhere at the time, either fighting the French for Canada or perhaps it was the Swedes for Spitzbergen – the Baymen both Black and White hastily mounted logs on cartwheels, stained them cannon-black with tar, and vigorously rolled up barrels of, presumably, gunpowder (actually: *rum*); and thronged threateningly around with lighted matchrope as they sighted their pseudo-weaponry. . . . Don Diego and his three galleys prudently crawled back.

"And him de same mon who defeat de Torks at Toronto! Ah, but de Sponiard is ah fool, mon! De Sponiard is ah *fool!*"

Limekiller had once earnestly urged that the site of Don Diego's victory over the Turks must have been *Lepanto* –

Strong gongs groaning as the guns boom far,
Don John of Austria is going to the war.

Stiff flags straining in the night-blasts cold,
In the gloom black-purple, in the glint old-gold ... *

— as a Canadian he could hardly do less — but found that the
dates did not fit, and so gave up. *Be that as it may.*

Be that as it may: although the boulevard which sweeps along
the lower foreshore of King Town, then as now the capital of British
Hidalgo, has some time since been renamed "Caribbean Crescent,"
hardly anyone ever calls it anything but *Artillery.* Like *Government,*
it requires no definite article. This road, once the open space of the
"quaker cannon" which had frightened off much the smallest
squadron of the much-cuckolded king; *I disdained to risk the valued
vessels of* el Rey *against so wretched a rabble of heretics and slaves,* reported Don Diego; after a long and preoccupied pause, *Yo el Rey*
rewarded this thoughtfulness with a barrel of amontillated sherry
which had gone bad in the royal cellars — though at least he did not
invite Don Diego to descend and sample on location — this road is
planted with palms and jacarandas and palms and casuarinas and
palms and more palms; it contains Government House and many
fine private residences at one end, and the Chief Minister's House
and many fine private residences at the other; and in between are
such edifices as the National Library and Archives, the United
Banana Boat Company offices, the two leading hotels and the three
leading guest houses (and, since we are on the subject, many fine
private residences): also the Public Park, and the Princess Minnie
Monument. All these buildings are invariably in as fine a state as
paint and labor can keep them in, which is, usually, very fine
indeed. From the sea, then, King Town presents a very fine appearance indeed. There is, however, more to King Town than its foreshore buildings and boulevards, however called and however kept
... much *much* more. And not all of this appears quite so fine at all.
Perhaps this is inevitable. And perhaps not.

A bumboat passed by the *Saccharissa,* carrying fruit for the
South, or Main, Market (the North, or Little, Market was supplied
via Cutlass Creek; it was also one of the three places roundabout

---

* *Lepanto,* G.K. Chesterton

King Town where the smoking of weed was, if not condoned, tolerated). The bumboatman had opened his mouth for a jovial and innocently obscene greeting, but, suddenly seeing Felix, had left his mouth silent but still open; his eyes moved to Limekiller, expressed appreciation and respect; then he plied his paddle again. There were not many beautiful redheads in King Town.

There were not even many ugly ones.

A full score of vessels were silently swooping out onto the Bay on sails catching the early breeze, hulls catching the early tide, the wings of the morning sails and hulls took. A few although an increasing number of them did have auxiliary engines (an "ox," it was called), but no true Bayman would use gas when he had a wind or tide. The *Saccharissa* of course had nothing but her mainsail, her jib, her spare pole, and her paddle . . . actually, her skiff's paddle, but kept aboard when the skiff was not in use. As now. The air was grey and moist and cool, so cool that each of the million mosquitoes had his or her head tucked under its wing, so to speak. The sun was so far just an anticipatory smudge on the horizon, but there was light enough.

The *Saccharissa* was John Lutwidge Limekiller's boat and Felix Anne Fox was John Lutwidge Limekiller's lady: of course the apostrophe-s did not imply the same degree of affiliation in each case and so it would probably be much better to say that the *Saccharissa* was John Lutwidge Limekiller's boat and John Lutwidge Limekiller was Felix Ann Fox's lover. She had been "settling into" the boat; if she had felt even surprise not to say disappointment that it was absolutely no landlubber's conception of a yacht, that it had rough and largely unpainted wooden insides (the hull, of course, had to be regularly painted outside . . . after, of course, having been previously and regularly scraped clean, and caulked), a soggy inner bottom with here and there a small though very real, very alive crab which had come aboard as inadvertent cargo during the vessel's days as a sandboat; if the total absence of brightwork, if the sanitary conveniences were barely sanitary and certainly inconvenient (consisting of a jury-rigged curtain over the doorless cubbyhold behind which – the curtain – there was a can (not a slang "can," a real can, though a very large one) with sometimes sand inside, which went over the side – taking very good care it went with and not against the wind – with the rest of its contents; sloshed with sea-water and replaced for next time – if Felix had or had had any qualms about any or all . . . well, nothing like a complaint had shown.

She had, which was just as important, every bit as, not gone, either, to the other extreme to overpraise. She had accepted. Accepted the rough old boat and all, as simply as she had, simply, accepted him. "I'm just travelling and ravelling," she'd said. "Travel and ravel along with me," he'd said, heart leaping. And she? "Yes." That was all. *All*? Is there a more joyful syllable in the language? In the tongue of men and of angels?

Felix had learned to balance her long legs in the rudely made skiff, shaped almost like a flat-iron, seatless, so that you had to squat to paddle or stand up to pole. She had learned to share with him the simple way of cooking the few simple foods in the sand-filled scrap metal firebox called the caboose; and as for ropes or lines or sails . . . well, well, she had learned. And learned well; never having learned any boating before, she had anyway nothing to unlearn now. All of this, and much more, then, she had learned to do for the boat, and so, in no small way, for him: what had he learned to do for her? he found himself asking now, watching her. There were, of course, all the lovely things which they had learned to do for each other: she/he, he/she. They had of course their problems: but they had been nice problems. And it had certainly been nice the way they had learned to solve them. Together. Mostly they had solved them on their first voyage. He recalled that now. He recalled her voice in his ear. He recalled how much he had rejoiced in that: and how much also he had rejoiced in that the bamboo boom – the spar to which the foot of the mainsail fastened – was hollow, and slightly cracked lengthwise – it still was, of course, and never would he fix it now! – this had anyway not at all impaired its usefulness and the hollow and the crack and the wind had turned it into a sort of aeolian harp, and it had sung for them all the day long its long sweet song for "their watery epithalamion. . . ."

The boom at right angles rode the mast in a wooden yoke; the mast was of local Santa Maria wood, twenty-six years old, and still looked fresh.

The date today was early in December.

Abruptly, Felix asked, "What kind of rope are you using there?"
"What kind of – Why . . . hemp . . . of course. Why do you –"
She broke into his perplexity with, "What? Not nylon?"

A moment more he stared; then his blunt and shaggy face relaxed, and he guffawed. Her seriousness now revealed as merely mock-seriousness, she laughed with him: what a delight her laugh was. And what a more-than-delight, her presence.

A day or two before, on Cornmeal Wharf, a conversation between two Bayfolk wharfside superintendents; the subject: *rope.*

"Nylon rope very modern."

"*Oh* yes. Fah true, fah true."

"Nylon rope *very* modern, nah true?"

"*Oh* yes."

"Hempen rope, *w'old* style, nah true?"

"*Oh* yes. Time of my *great*-gron-fahder, he hahv sailing-*ship* go four time ah year fah Cuba, fah Jamaica: use hempen rope. . . ."

"De Mexicans punishing, so many people buy ny*lon*, not buy hemp. Mexican grow *hemp*, not ny*lon.*"

"Ny*lon* rope lahst much *lahng*-ah."

"*Oh* yes. Eet sleek, some."

"What you say?"

"Ny*lon* rope *very* sleek. Sleep t'rough you hond. Sleep de knots, you know."

"Well, dot ee's true. Ny*lon* rope very sleepery. Muss use cleats."

"Cleats cahst *mon*-ey, mon. Nah true?"

"Fah true, fah true. Ny*lon* rope cahst *mah* dan hemp, mottah ahv fock."

"*Oh* yes. Me no want buy eet."

"*Me* no want buy eet. Sleep de knots, cahn't get greep on eet, requiah *cleats*, cahst too much."

"Fah true, fah true."

"Yes, mon Fah true. . . ."

So much for nylon rope, then, at Cornmeal Wharf. And, for that matter, on the sloop *Saccharissa,* Jno. L. Limekiller, owner and master.

Who sniffed. "Ah, the sweet salt air!"

"A contradiction in terms, surely?"

"'Do I contradict myself? Very well, then, I contradict myself.'"

"Yes, I know. You are vast, you contain multitudes."

He wondered if he should swagger on this; decided that he would not. Instead, he said, "Sweet to me, anyway. – Gallards Point Caye, ho!"

"Gall*i*ards."

"Gal-lards."

"The map –"

"The chart –"

They laughed. They laughed a lot when they were together. She went and got both chart and map. Maps. She looked. She looked triumphant. Then she saluted, pouted. Laughed again. "Both right. Chart says *Gal-lards*, map says Galliards – Oh. Well, *poot*! The big map says *Galliards*, the little map says *Gallants*."

He shrugged. "Can't spell for sour owl stools, some of them down here." She said, Look who was talking. He asked, surprised, What was *wrong* with his spelling. She said, Anyone who would spell Labor Department with a *u* – He said, quickly, defensively, That was the way all British countries spelled it. She asked, with the *u* before the *o*? He thought it best to ignore this cavil, gestured off to starboard. "Can you say what those are?" *Those* being some greenery-brownery blurs. 'I mean, find them on the chart...?"

"I already know. The Duck and Ducklings – *oops*!"

They laughed again, together, at her error. That tiny archipelago was called The Goose and Goslings. By and by they came close enough to observe the shack of the aged light-keeper. No doubt that was the aged light-keeper himself, standing and waving. And . . . what was *that*?

Answering Felix's question, Jack said that *That* was the Union Jack. "Of course the country does have its own flag now, but not all of these old-timers, you know – "

"I can tell that *That*'s the Union Jack, but I mean, *That* – underneath it. Is he surrendering? Or what?"

Jack took a closer squint, but she, on the spy-glass, was already answering her own question. "Oh for goodness sake! That's not a white flag, that's his *shirt*! Just like in a cartoon. . . ."

She looked at him, questioningly.

He grunted. "Means he wants something. Custom says we have to go see what it is. And, ah . . ."

"'Help him out,' yes." She was already picking up the local idiom. Can you help me out for a pint, Sir? ("– of rum," being understood.) Can you help me out, gi' me a borrow of t'ree shilling? Me truck bruck down, could you help me out with a drop to de ga*r*age, mon?

The Goose was of course the biggest, but Captain Barber kept his light on the South Gosling, which long experience had shown was just that much higher as to make a difference in anything short of a hurricane. There was no lighthouse, the old man just lit his lamp and hoisted it on high; *his* lamp, he had to supply it himself, Government from early days having felt that this would make whoever kept the light keep it more carefully. Government however did supply the oil, plus a minuscule stipend on which he was not expected to live. On what *did* he live? Menander said that we live as we may and not as we would; there was fish, was there not? Conch. Turtle. He sent, old Captain Barber, now and then a load of red mangrove bark to King Town for Lemuel the tanner there; a stinking trade, but money has no odor. He had some coconut, too. And, also, once a month, from that ancient bequest called Lady Bucknam's Bounty he had once a month a barrel of biscuit. And a bottle of wine.

In a country where prematurely grey meant grey at sixty, Captain Barber's hair was quite white; but he was straightbacked or all of that. He had, on realizing that Felix, dungaree trousers or not, was a woman, gone back into his lee' house and put on his "next" shirt. Now he gave her a courtly bow and a grave, rather shy smile. "Well, Captain," Jack said, "what's this I heard not long ago in Town: you found the iron chest at last?" For this was, after all, probably the real reason for his isolated existence, and not alone a desire for solitude. *The iron chest.* Every stretch of Caribbean coastline has its own iron chest for which men seek and women yearn, full of gold and silver and precious stones; the stranger does right to be often skeptical, but he would do wrong to be always skeptical, for – every now and then – the iron chest is found . . . and, *some*times, at least, *is* found full of gold and silver and precious stones. Who put it there? Who knows? Who *cares*? Sometimes the breath of Hurikan, the old Arawack god of winds and storms. Sometimes the reefs and shoals. Sometimes enemy cannon-shot. And sometimes, of course, *of course*: Captain Edward England. Major Stede Bonnet. Calico Jack Rackam. Terrible Tom Tew. Horrible Ben Hornigold. Unwomanly Anny Bonny. William Kidd, who "murdered Billy More/And laid him in his gore,/Not many miles from shore,/When he sailed . . ." And maybe even Flint, he of the impeccable taste in rum. Even thinking of this made Jack Limekiller hear in his inner ear the parrot screaming.

Pieces of eight! Pieces of eight!

Heat or no heat, timbers or no timbers, Limekiller shivered.

"Well, sir. Yes, sir. Oi did foind an oiron chist. For true, sir . . . and mistress. But not the righteous one. No. *Emp*-ty. . . ."

"*Oh*," Felix gave a sympathetic and quite sincere sigh.

Barber's smile, which had ebbed, renewed itself. "But Oi niver fret nor poine about that, mistress. Ah no. Where there is a one oiron chist, bound to be a next one." His tone did not exactly drop off, and they waited for him to explain his reasons. But he did not do so: useless, clearly, to dawdle in hopes of details as to which stretches of beach or bog or mangrove bluff he went a-prowling and a-probing with his long iron rod, on which bay or bight or cove or creek his dory glided over of nights – if not with its oarlocks muffled, at least with his grapples not assisted by lamplight –

– and then, perhaps, too, *with* its oarlocks muffled –

"What can we do for you, Captain Barber?" asked Jack, returning with silent sigh entirely into the twentieth century.

The old man gave a deep nod. "Do you suppose, sir . . . sir and mistress . . . that you could help me out with just a bit of sugar for me tea?"

"A cup of sugar?" Felix instantly had on an imaginary gingham apron. "Why of course;" she half-turned to go –

"Oh, *no*, mistress! Not a *cup*. Half a cup will do. Be some other boat, some next one, by and by . . . today, tomorrow . . . when God send . . . whenever. Sailingmen must help the old loightkeeper out: else, may-be: boi and boi: no light. Not *your* task to do it ahl yourself. – Where you bound, mahn?"

South Gosling *was* as near the desert island of the cartoons as anything could be; Jack realizing and relishing the fact – and the sight – was a bit slow in answering. Back came Felix with the sugar, asked, with an air that showed the question had just occurred to her, "Do you say, 'Gallards Caye,' Captain Barber? Or 'Galliards Caye'? Or –"

Limekiller broke in, "Or 'Gallants Caye.' Eh? Which?"

Old Barber nodded slowly. "Galleons Caye, so . . ." Then quite evidently a thought suddenly came to his own mind. He faintly frowned. "What day, today? Not St. Nicholas Day?"

Still rolling over in his mind the sound of "Galleons Caye" and mildly amused by yet another variation on a theme, Jack said, "Beats *me*. Why?" ("*Galleons* Caye?" murmured Felix, half-smiling, half-surprised, herself.)

Aloud (said she): "But I *will* have to ask for the cup back. Because we only have two, and he likes his sweeter than I do."

The abstracted, faintly unhappy look vanished from the old man's face; face a sort of worn and faded map onto which Europe, Africa, India, and Amerindia had blended. He gave once again that antique, courtly bow. "'Sweeter than you . . .'? Why, what could *be* sweeter than you, me choild? Captain Limekiller, sir, you have certainly plucked a beautiful blossom in the garden of love." No bullshit about, perhaps they were just *crew*ing together: in tropical British Hidalgo (and is not one of the Tropics that of old goat-footed Capricorn?), a he and a she of any age above the snotty-nosed and below the entirely senescent never did anything like just *crewing* together: any more than they ever lived together as brother and sister . . . unless of course they happened to *be* brother and sister . . . in which case one could be damned sure that the *he* was involved with someone else's sister and the *she* with someone else's brother.

And why not.

"Why, Captain Barber, how very nice and gallant of you. . . . *Not* Gallants or Galliants Caye, then? You say, 'Galleons Caye'?" Captain B. at the moment was saying nothing. From one pocket he was drawing a pair of specs of gothic mold, and from another a copy of the five-year almanac which, from frequent usage, looked as old if not older. Having searched out the current year, he slowly traced down the days with one finger. Came to a line. Stopped. Read slowly. Slowly looked up. 'Why, yes, oh yes. You see —" He held the almanac up and out. "The 6th of December. St. Nicholas's Day. Can't *go* there today, Oi doubt." And he waited for them to acknowledge the truth of what he said. And waited.

"What, 'can't get there from here'?" – Limekiller. Amused.

"Is there some local superstition against it?" – Felix (original name, *Felicia*; and the hell with it, she'd said). – Felix. Interested.

Also, tactless.

She had used a word which, like treason, like perversion, is never acknowledged to be such by those who practice it. Anything as impolite as a display of annoyance was not likely to be shown by Captain Barber to A Lady. Not even disapprobation. He did allow himself, however, to become exceedingly grave, and, in so doing, wiped the smiles off their own faces most effectively.

"Oi am not superstitious. Oi have been educated at the old Anglican Academy. And Oi recollect quite well what St. Pahl said to the Athenians. The sea does not roise boi superstition. The wind does not drop boi superstition. The rains do not commence in Yucatan the same week they do in Darien. Is the day longer on St. John's Day than on Christmas? Tis, 'tisn't it?"

St. *John*'s Day. Great-uncle Leicester Limekiller, a great Freemason, always let everyone know when St. John's Day was, that day of Masonic festivity, or should one say solemnity? Either. Both. What the hell. . . .

"June 21st? Longest day in the —"

"Just so. Just so. And today is St. Nicholas's Day. And no day to be going to Galleons Caye. Oi tell you. A bod day for it. Maybe you won't even be able to fetch up there at all. Oh, not that Oi say that St. Nicholas has anything to do with it himself Maybe. Patron of sailors, though, hm . . . so . . . *No.*" Captain Barber got a firm Anglican hold of himself. "Oi cannot hold with the vain worship of the Saints. Simply, you do see, this 6th day of December, however it be marked: *not* a good day to go to Galleons Caye. It be the wind, you see."

He reached for the worn old almanac, now so close to obsolescence and desuetude. 'No," said Limekiller. "Frankly, I *don't* see." He held the little booklet out, waited.

The old light-keeper took it back.

"You will," he said.

It was because of Alex Brant.

There were a number of North Americans down there in old British Hidalgo, down there on the boggy barm and brink, the soggy margin, of the Carib Sea: and some were very good people and some were not and most of them were variously in between. This is of course true of most people in most places, Truisms are called them because they tend to be true. And one of these North Americans was Alex Brant, and Limekiller had known him for quite a while. Had they first met in the Pelican Bar? Or in Reuben Swift's boatyard? And if in the Pelican Bar, adjacent and adjunct to the Hotel of the same name, had they been waiting for a drink? Or for a woman? Because they had met, and not just once and again, in both those places. And in others. Someone had summed Alex up as being "slim, muscular, and nervous"; like all summings-up, it left much unsummed. Sometimes he had a moustache or a beard or both. Sometimes he had not. He had formerly lived in another Commonwealth Country, on an island thereof, which he persistently, and, it may be, a trifle bitterly, referred to as "Great Exzema." Had Limekiller himself been asked to sum up his friend, it would have been at greater length, and somewhat as follows:

"Is currently running a small plantation but on occasion acts as a 'White Hunter' or maybe he is *not* now running a plantation but maybe it's chicle time and he is a chicle buyer . . . or buying crown gum, which Wrigley's will not take but will be taken by Third World markets which don't care about any difference but price.

Brant buys tortoise-shell, too. Sponges. When available. Exports orchids. At times. Has a small distillery and when sugar is cheap, makes cheap-cheap rum. Sometimes takes boat charters, or he sometimes may plant rice. – Doesn't ha ha hunt *White*s, hunts *tigers*, not *his* fault that the local jaguar is locally called a tiger, always explains the critter has spots not stripes; still, the very *name*, you know. . . . Well. Tiger hunts as run by Alex Brant in these 1960s are $1,500 for ten days, *kill guaranteed* or money back; if an early kill leaves days unused, will run wild hog hunt if desired, at no extra cost. Sometimes runs boat charter. Lost his ass once in an inter-island cargo schooner and doesn't like to get that tied up (or down) since that time. Will mate with White women or Brown, Black, or Brindle. Smuggling? A wry grimace. Spent seven months in a Spanish-speaking jail once for that; took him seventeen months to recover. Has been All Around, but prefers British Hidalgo because, well, 'it's too poor to be too much corrupted, small enough to put your arms around, just big enough to keep you from getting claustrophobic. Unspoiled? – yes, well – Great Salt Caye is unspoiled, too, but there's nothing there worth spoiling, damnit.'

"Trustworthy? As a friend? Certainly. As a businessman? *Not* necessarily. As company? Always good company."

Alex *Brant.*

The party had been a rather crowded one, but, then, in British Hidalgo, *all* parties were by definition crowded ones. According to the Nationals, a party couldn't *be* too crowded. Of course, not everyone in the Emerging Nation was a National thereof, and so not everyone down there felt accordingly.

"Do you remember, Jack," Alex asked, "that New Year's Eve, we go to that place and she comes out on the verandah as we're coming up the steps and she says to you, 'I'm sorry, but we're quite full up here, and besides, these are *your* guests, not mine,' and with that she turns around and goes back inside again, eh?"

Jack said that he remembered. "She only invited me because I was wearing a necktie and I was only wearing a necktie because I'd been to see the bank manager – didn't help – and I suppose she found *out*."

Felix, sipping her rum-and-Coke, asked, "Who was *she*?"

Alex said, "Lady Bumtrinket."

"*What*?"

"Not her real name," said Jack. Sipping his. "Close, though."

"Cecilie, anyway. Wife of the Commonwealth Corn Commissioner, or something like that. They didn't stay down here long."

"*Pit*-ty!"

The record player was blaring out the latest hit, hot from Jamaica, where they liked it hot, *I Am Not A Qualified Physician, So I Don't Like To Give De Decision.* Some of the guests were dancing while they were drinking and some were drinking while they were dancing. And some were standing around and –

"Can I get you anything from the buffet, Felix?" asked Alex. "It's just loaded with fashionable munchies, and not a local item among them."

"Well –"

"Imported potted meat product and byproduct, white bread sandwich, with the bread crusts carefully cut off, London style? Salad of imported Republic of Nueva Cartagena cabbage with imported Heinz Salad Cream and imported tinned peas? Some imported sweet-and-soggy biscuits? ('Crackers,' *we* call them.)"

Oh Doctor, I Don't Like De Size of Your Needle, shrieked the record-player. Felix said she thought she'd pass over the fashionable munchies for the time being. Someone said that the Chief Minister, the Rt. Hon. Llewellyn Gonzaga McBride, was present. Or had been. Or was going to be.

"*Really?*" Felix. Looking around eagerly.

"Bound to be. *Has* to be." – Alex; "Part of his official duties, laid down in the British Hidalgo Official Duties Act of 1958 as Amended by Orders-in-Council, 1965, '66, and '67: '. . . *and the Chief Minister shall be everywhere at once. . . .*' Fact. That *God* is omnipresent, we take on faith. That the Chief *Min*ister is omnipresent we don't have to take on faith, we can see him for ourselves. – You guys coming out to the Caye tomorrow?"

The party was now at full blast. So was the record player. *He Put It In, He Take It Out; He Put It In, He Take It Out.* The Queen's picture rattled on the wall. The three North Americans gathered close together in order to be able to hear each other shout.

WHICH caye?

GALLARDS Caye.

What's doing THERE?

Party.

What?

A PARTY.

WHOSE party?

Well, really more of a PICnic. *Sort of.*
What?
A JAUNT. *God damn it.*
How come?
Noddy and Neville are going out, too.
Noddy and WHO?
And NEVILLE.
ENGLISH *Neville?*
Oh for Christ sake. NO. NorWEgian Neville.
Norwegian WHO?
Oh for Christ sake. YES: ENGLISH NEVILLE.
Oh. Well –

The plenty-decibels saga of the Doctor and His Needle, for which perhaps "suggestive" was far too feeble a word, came to its hysterical conclusion; while someone was trying to fumble the record over to its flip side in haste, lest, God forbid, there should be two seconds' Silence, Alex managed to say that Neville and Noddy were going out to visit Major Deak, whoever Major Deak was, at Gallards Caye, along with Neville's girlfriend and Noddy's lady (ladies lived-in, girlfriends did not) and large hampers of victuals and Alex Brant and lots to drink and a couple of Nationals and their wives, ladies, and/or etc. and so – Alex suggested – why not Jack and Felix, too?

"We're going in my launch," he wound up.

Felix knew Alex's launch, at least by sight. "Wouldn't it be kind of crowded?" she asked, half-eager and half-doubtful.

"We'll go in our *own* boat. Get an early start." Said Jack.

Someone said, "*Where* is the C.M.?"

Someone said, "In the kitchen, showing how to cut sandwiches in the least wasteful manner possible."

Someone said, "And who is *this* lovely young lady?"

"Felix Limekiller," she said.

"Ah, Mr. *Lime*killer! *Here* you are! You do not mind if I dance with this lovely young lady?"

"No, Sir, I don't. Felix, this is –"

The music began again and in the second or so before it swelled up to shake the walls again Jack heard the words, "Llewellyn Gonzaga Mc –" as the introduction dissolved into the dance: and they were off.

"See what I mean?" – Alex, into Jack's ear. "Everywhere. At one time."

"One does see what you mean."

One did indeed. Did one's car find itself tipped almost on its side in the famous Breakbone Gorge, who was that suddenly appearing with a winch-equipped truck? Who else but the tireless figure of Llewellyn Gonzaga McBride, the Queen's Chief Minister. Did an Indian, overwhelmed by piety and rum at the Feast of the Four Crowned Martyrs, give the well-known signs of adding via his own machete to the number of the martyrdom, who was *that* appearing from nowhere and, addressing *el Indio* in his own language, getting the machete away and tucking it under his own arm as though it had been an umbrella? Llewellyn Gonzaga McBride, the first (and so far the only) Chief Minister of British Hidalgo. Was who. Was who. Instances innumerable; "– and he's probably also, right now," said Alex, "in his office, working on the Budget."

"Something almost theological about it."

Make You Big and Strong, blared the record player.

"Something absolutely theological that this country even exists!" shouted Alex. His lips moved some more, but hearing him was now impossible. They shrugged; then, the two kitchen-women having come out to beam at "the funs," he and Jack swept them up and danced away with them.

And so now it was the next day, and Jack and Felix were out on the waves of the waters of Eden; they had for the time being anyway left the, mangrove bluffs and the coral shoals and shallows behind them and were out in "the blue," in the deep water: deep being hereabouts a relative term. It was already somewhat hot in the sunlight but not boiling hot as it sometimes was. It was for that matter hot in the shade but in no wise uncomfortably hot. There was no longer exactly a wind, but there was a sort of languid breeze, and it blew now and then like a warm pat in the face. On the coast of British Hidalgo there was no surf, the surf beat against the Reef, about ten miles out. But the wind acted upon the water . . . or, now, the breeze did . . . and after each gust . . . and before the next . . . the water would surge slightly against the boat with a small soft slapping sound.

"What's May doing, these last few days," he asked, realizing that he had lately seen nothing of his lady's cousin and (until recently) travelling companion.

"Hmm . . . Well, when did we last see her?"

Felix had a characteristic slight frown which enchanted him. Not near so much, of course, as her smile, or her laugh. Still. It was perhaps more intriguing than either. Because you never knew exactly what it meant. Oh, it never meant wrath, of course. Still . . .

"Oh. Couple of *days* ago. In the New Chinese Grand Grotto."

"'And Restaurant.' Yes . . . Was that the day we had the *chichen cashewseeds*? As the menu said?"

Something large in the water, to port. He glanced. Looked like a great ray-fish, slowly following the sun. "Uh. *No*. It was the day we had the *prypish potato*. As the menu said." Blue sky. Cotton clouds. Hot sun. Dry my white hair. "And she said, 'There is nothing *like* these exotic foods.' Remember?"

"Oh, that's what she *al*ways says."

There was a soft silence. "Reading her way through the National *Li*brary, I suppose. . . . I suppose we *could* have asked her to leave off for a day, and come out with us. . . ."

Cayes blurry to the port distance. Cayes blurry to the starboard distance. Behind, the low, low coast had sunk from sight. Of a sudden, also low, the cracked, hollow boom sang out; a fresh slap of wind, struck his cheek.

But it was not followed by another.

"And I suppose she'd say that she could always go on a picnic, back in the Thousand Islands: but where else could she find the Compleat Planter's Almanac for 1800 through 1818?"

Felix had that slight frown, still, as she turned to face him. Or again. "That *is* what she would say. That's exactly what she'd say. How could *you* know?"

Looking into her eyes, the color of water flowing over mangrove bark, Limekiller opened his mouth. Realized that whatever he was about to say was bound to be the wrong thing to say. And a spirit touched his lips with a glowing coal. And he said something else, instead.

"Reef the mainsail, would you?"

She turned. A moment later, in an entirely different tone of voice, she asked, "One reef enough?"

"Just exactly enough."

And Skippy the Cat, in no wise resentful of his demotion, since Felix's arrival aboard, from first mate to supercargo, at that moment rubbed his off-white pelt against her aft leg. She bent down to pet him and to utter endearments. Next she said, "Do you know,

Skippy, what pleased me so much last night? It was when Captain Jack said, '*our* boat.' Not '*my* boat.' But '*our* boat.'"

In a sudden up-flowing of joy, Captain Jack said, "*Well*, Skip, if you want to know what made *my* night, it was when First Mate Felix introduced herself to Chief Minister McBride as 'Felix Limekiller.'"

Skippy's comment was, "*Must* I put up with all this mush so early in the morning? *Ee*yoo. Blech. – a little more scratching abaft the starboard ear, Biped. *Ahh*. . . . "

And then, for a white, nobody said anything at all, but everybody seemed very well-content.

They had been heading east to begin with (never *mind* about Marley), with a good east wind behind them, and this had gradually dropped . . . so gradually that, being blissful all together there in Eden, they hardly noticed. And, in fact, they were slow to notice when the wind shifted and began blowing right up their noses. The flapping of the dirty old sail brought the change to their attention. The boat was now quite out of sight of the low-lying mainland; talk about the Lowland *Sea* . . . or sing. . . .

But the boat had come in sight of some other point of land.

"There it is," Jack gestured to something small and bright, a house with the sun on it. "Galleons Caye . . . or whatever it's called."

She gave her ruddy hair a shake. "Whatever it's called, we don't seem to be going there. Or anywhere else."

"No. . . . No way to steer, this way. The boat is in irons."

Felix's face wrinkled. "In *what*?"

"'In irons. . . .' Dead-assed still. As you've noticed."

Felix said that she preferred *in irons*. It sounded, she said, much more romantic. "though kind of grim. Though."

He nodded. "It used to be very grim indeed, when this happened in the open sea. Well. Often. However. Time to start tacking."

They hauled the sails in, and, thus close-hauled on the starboard tack, the sloop proceeded to windward at a reasonable pace: they were heading, still, or, rather, again, out from land. But they were not steering toward Galleons Caye. Not yet. Neither were they heading dead away from it; they were away from it at an angle . . . but only at an angle. The jib had been loosed, and, with a "Ready – about," Jack put the tiller over, the boat crossed the wind, the mainsail came over, the jib slithered across, and she pulled it in on the other side by the other sheet: *sheet*, here, not meaning sail, but the line that trimmed it. This being a close-hauled tack, the jib-sail did most of the work. The boat heeled over, then came back a bit, with the sea (seemingly, and perhaps, exactly) rising to meet it.

"*Ugh*," said Felix, wincing at the shock.

"Pounding a bit."

She said she was glad it was only a bit.

"Not exactly a downhill run, is it?"

". . . not exactly . . . I guess. . . ."

After a bit he felt the wind shift; "Ready – *about*," he ordered. He was to say it again. And again. . . .

The small bright building came nearer, after a while. It had never, after the first sighting, been out of sight at all. She asked, "Is it Gallard? Or is it Galliard? – Oh! I don't mean the damned *name*! of the *caye*! – I mean: which is the *dance*? You don't know, either? Well, I just had this picture. In my mind. Of those eighteenth cen-tury buccaneers dancing gaily out there, in the muck." He smiled. She returned the smile, though somewhat more faintly. And, through the many tacks, the building became many times larger; Jack said to himself that he was glad to see it become so, become nearer. But something was odd. Sophia. Something was very odd. Sophia. What? So*phia.* Well, who and what was Sophia? A woman's name, of course. *Of course*! Well, actually a girl's. He had been just a boy. How old? Seventeen, maybe, all legs and nose. *I am in love with Sophia and any minute now I am going to see her and what a won-derful minute that will be,* his thoughts had run, there in the station in Victoria, he having come over on the ferry from Vancouver for to see her and no other reason, she coming down on the train from whatever ossified moss-covered hamlet near the Island's eastern shore where her family had been summering: and then he realized that he was not, after all, feeling wonderful: instantly she appeared and instantly he realized that he was not at all in love with her.

After all.

– Oh, of course; not the same thing. He had never fancied him-self in love with Galleons, Gallards, Galliards Caye: still. . . .

"But I can't *be* pregnant," Felix whispered, suddenly, almost fiercely.

He was less startled by the, to him, utterly unexpected prospect of fatherhood, than by the intensity of her voice.

"Would that be so terrible?" he asked.

"No." She said this less reluctantly than thoughtfully.

"Well, then why –"

"Because I can't *be*. Is why. I've already had my period: you ought to know; you haven't forgotten so soon, have you?"

No, he hadn't forgotten so soon. Yes, he ought to know; remembering his impatience. And all the rest of it. Slowly . . . almost, really, thinking out loud . . . he said, "Though I *have* heard –"

"– so have I," she said, quickly, interrupting him. "But it – I *feel* pregnant, and not in the way it was before."

Warm day. Why should he feel cold? "Have you been –" He stopped. What a question to ask, when she'd never mentioned a child. Or anything about –

"Yes," she said. She said, "Yes," as simply as she might have said it to, "Have you been in Bridgeport?" He said nothing more. Was he waiting for her to say more? If so, he waited in vain. A few staple thoughts ran through his mind. Abortion. Adoption. Miscarriage. The child is at home with her mother, aunt, sister; she was married young; divorced: it was none of his goddamned business.

It *was* none of his goddamned business.

Unless, of course, she were to feel it was. And, of course, she wasn't. Anyway, not right now. And so, right now, he had all the time in the world to think about this possible progeny. And the oddest thing he felt, as he thought about his feeling, was how odd it was that he didn't feel much of anything about it at all. *Was* she, then? Okay. Or: she after all *wasn't*? Also okay.

"Maybe it's just that you're sort of sea-sick . . . all the pounding the boat's been doing . . . all these tacks, these winds – maybe."

She said, "Maybe."

Her voice was flat. She sounded not happy. She sounded not unhappy. She heard, she answered, but she wasn't really there, she was really somewhere else, a million miles away, far away somewhere in her own bloodstream: *So far, he could not call to her.*

So. Still. What. Ah. Of course. The wind. No wind of long fetch, this one. "Ready," he said, ". . . *about* . . ."

And meanwhile, what else was the boat doing? The boat was shipping water, was what else the boat was doing. And had to be pumped. And so he pumped it. The common pump he had learned from the local boatmen how to make, use and repair, and use again.

It was part rubber, part leather, part wood, and had a long straight wooden handle and worked exclusively with an up-and-down motion, like the "plumber's friend," or plunger; it would probably never make the pages of *Yachting Magazine*, but, applied with vigor, it brought the intrusive water in a cold boiling froth up inside its long narrow rectangle of a case and out the spout and over the side. It beat bailing for sure: but though you expel Ocean with a plunge-pump, still, she will always return. Always. Always. Always.

That past winter an unexpected charter out to the Welshman's Cayes had left Limekiller with, all costs paid and reserves set aside for the inevitably lean and rainy days, with fifty dollars more than he had thought to have had: so he thought to buy a pair of binoculars . . . used, of course . . . eyetracks don't wear the lenses out, was his thought . . . at Sitwell's Sports Shop, on "Artillery." (Sitwell was Honorary Vice-Consul for Iceland; "Do you get many Icelanders here?" was Jack's question. Said Sitwell, "I never gits any . . . but it saves me thirty-five dollars a year tax exemption."). However, on his way there he chanced to glance into a tiny optician's shop, and the small sign in the small window caught his eye. William Wilson Setsewayo Smith, it read, *Licentiate of the Worshipful Company of Spectacle-makers, London.* How could he resist a further look? And there, propped in a corner, was a, well, no, it really wasn't a telescope, it was an early nineteenth-century or maybe even late eighteenth-century Spy Glass, bound in only slightly-flaking light brown leather; the pricetag: *seventy-five dollars.* In he went, "Will you take fifty dollars for that?" The worshipful spectacle-maker was just about the same color. "I'll take forty-nine," he said, "and leff us boath have a nog of Governor Morgan Rum with the difference." After setting down his glass with an appreciative sigh, "May ye see rare sights with that," he said. "Best I be gittin bock to work now." There was a slight, a very slight prismatic effect, an effulgence, which was not met in modern optical glasses: but it served him well enough. Besides: sliding the thing in and out: such *fun!*

"See what you make of this," Limekiller said now, handing it over.

All morning long, and into the afternoon, that little yellow house danced in the distance before their eyes . . . advancing . . .

receding . . . yellow . . . what was yellow, what had been yellow, and what had yellow been and stood for? "– *that fellow/ in Austrian yellow*," no, no, certainly not Joyce; "*In the porch of my printing insti-tute/The poor and deserving prostitute/Every night plays catch-as-catch-can/With her tight-breeched British artilleryman –*" How ridiculous; they, Jack and Felix, they weren't exiles, they were travellers. Just travelling and ravelling. – Ah yes. Ah. Yes. Yellow was the color of the old quarantine flag. Flags. Odd thought. Infection. Taint. (And a lot of use that thought was, too.) And, ah, and equally inapplica-ble, the yellow passport of Imperial Russia for the exclusive use of prostitutes: not for foreign travel, no, a sort of ID: "internal passport." Bad joke, if so intended. *This imperial government has fall-en* (old Prince Lvov, first premier of the Provisional Government which took its place) *because history has not known of a government more cruel and more corrupt. . . .* But history was to get to know. *A?* Plenty.) Yella Isabella. Wouldn't change her undies till Ghent was relieved; Ghent held put for *how* long? Was it Ghent? Was it Gal-lards, Galliards, Galleons, or – Isabella not of Spain but of Austria, *there* we go *again. . . .*

The little yellow house danced and blurred. Must be Major Deak's house. Whoever Major Deak was. Had the house been quite finished? Wasn't part of a framework of a second story visible there? Just a few timbers. Something odd and yet familiar about it . . . *them*. . . . Also, somehow: not nice. Some shapes, some angles, somehow not sympatico . . . or whatever the hell. Heat haze. Heat fever? Wasn't *that* hot. The spy glass was *old. . . .*

"Oh, Jack, I don't like it," she said, low-voiced. So. Felix felt it too. Whatever the "it" of it was, this time. Or perhaps it was the other way round. Perhaps not part of a framework of a house-yet-to-be, but of a house-which-once-was. Maybe the last remnants of an upper story . . . either unfinished or torn off in some hurricane or bayama or other wind of, *really*, long fetch. Maybe it was after all the *wind* like the squalid *sirocco*, the wretch *mistral*, or *fehm*, which was bothering Felix, like the *khamsin* which blew for fifty dreadful days, they say that under the old Ottoman Turkish law anyone who killed a spouse would be acquitted if the *khamsin* had been blowing for even a month. . . . But: here: now: no: only a matter of hours . . . or, not so long as that, surely the wind had been a far-better feeling wind, until . . . well, long minutes . . . so: *no.*

So, then, what?

Not every building in this country (not so much forgotten by the rest of the world as to it unknown), not every one afflicted by hurricanes, tempest-torn, had been rebuilt, even ashore. Limekiller passed one such each day in King Town, squashed almost into a parallelogram, but still inhabited. Others. Plenty of others. So no big sweat that old Major Deak (and why "*old*"? He could be a major and yet young, na true?) had not gotten around to — Flaps of wallpaper flapped and dangled and flew about in the breeze, the hot, dry, cold, sticky breeze. *Suddenly*: no breeze *here*, though. *Was*. But not *now*. Over *there*. . . .

*Wall*paper? Out on the *Cayes*? Not very damned likely . . . curtains, *yes*, rags of curtains — part of a window frame with parts of the curtains still dangling —

"I bet that's Alex," she said, very suddenly. He held the glass. He squinted. Maybe those were, yes of course those were. People. But — "You've got better eyes than I, I guess. *I* can't make out Alex."

"Oh," she said, easily, "neither can I. Make him *out*. But the one on the end, I mean, somehow he just *seems* like Alex."

Their eyes met. Instantly he knew that if he said a single word about Alex, she would say at least a single word about May. And wouldn't that be silly? What a day this had turned out to be.

Water flowing over mangrove bark. . . .

The traps we dig for ourselves.

"It looks," she said, as though judiciously, and as though judiciously changing the subject, "it looks as there must be another house on that caye, with the second story sort of ruined, you know what I mean? And from this *dis*tance, at a certain *ang*le, it's sort of as though the top of that one is sort of superimposed onto the other one. The yellow one. If you see what I mean. . . ."

"I do see. Yes."

But later, once they'd gone ashore, and thought to ask, they were told, no such thing. Nothing like that. One caye. One house.

The caye. Mangrove bluffs. Shallows. Looking down, in some places, so clear, almost one could lean over and touch the negrohead coral, and the garfish. The insufferable wind. When there was wind. And yet, now, smoke coiling from cigarettes and scarcely rising. *Much* wind, coming out . . . but now, here at last, the air was dull above the mangrove bluff and reclaimed land, the sky was now slate-colored; even, half-turning, the color of the sea had changed, too.

"It seems somehow *dead* here," she murmured, low-voiced, as they put ashore. It did. Haunted. Oppressive.

But now there was little time for such thought.

They were no longer alone.

Loud good cheer.

"What *took* you so long?"

"Had to make many tacks."

"Thought you'd *never* get here! Well! Have a drink!"

"Why didn't you come in the *launch*?" (Limekiller to himself: Because it's Alex Brant's launch. Is why. And was shocked to find he'd thought so.)

"*Glad* to see you! Glad to *see* you!"

"Here's a bottle of beer for each of you, then" – this was Neville (*Eng*lish Neville. There was not, really, any Norwegian Neville) producing the beer with an air of innocent sinfulness possible only to someone raised by a Baptist grandparent. Neville had a thin blond body and a thin blond beard.

"Felix! Gyel! Me wait-wait-wait fah you! Fret-fret-fret, may-*be* you hahv frock nice-ah dan mine! And what I see? Nutting like dot! Dun-gah-*ree*! What! Nicholine?" – This was Adah, Noddy's lady. Nicholine was Neville's girlfriend. Nicholine's comment, couched in the form of a proverb, and said, in a low-quick mutter, was "Piggy play dead fih cotch corby live." Nicholine was short and squat, and Nicholine was jealous. Adah threw back her head, laughed her friend's comment into the air, and so, away: then she passed her hands over her lime-green-nylon-covered hips. Winked at Felix. At Jack. They did not wink at each other. Alex strolled up, casual and easy. "Come on over to the house and meet the official host. Well, we *are* paying him for the use of the place for the day. But he *is* our host. Adds class. – Some of us were worried, you being so long getting here. I told them, no sweat. Not to worry." A smile for Felix.

Noddy said, "Yes, come along. You've got quite a lot of good drinking to catch up on." Noddy was portly and ginger-moustached and learned and cheerful . . . except when you were trying to crash his party. Which was not now. There were others who had come strolling out to meet them, to help with the tying up. To bring drinks. Just In Case. The Honourable Somerset Summerville,

Secretary to Government, and a not-bad-poet in his own right and on his own time, was there. So was his wife. ("Yes," the Honourable was now and then heard to say, "I was the typical Colored Colonial student in London, and so, typically, I married my landlady's daughter . . . well . . . actually . . . *grand*daughter . . . !" And, actually, he had; the Dowager Lady Blenkinson did not of course let lodgings: she owned the whole *street.* And the next one. And the next one. "– and, as my wife already was an Honourable, why, I had no choice but to become one, too!" His wife showed neither amusement nor annoyance; she was wearing khakies, and was the authority on the orchids of the Hidalgo Littoral.). Also present was Ethelred Edwards, a master adzeman at Nahum's boatyard, and *his* wife – he and the Hon. Mrs. Summerville were the only wives at the party (or picnic) . . . or, at any rate, the only women who had been "married in church" to the men with whom they were currently affiliated. British Hidalgo was strong on being married in church. Divorce, however, was something else altogether. It was difficult. It was expensive. And it was, finally, irrelevant.

It was unlikely that people from classes as diverse as Nicholine and Adah, the Summervilles, and the Edwardses would ever, in King Town, be at the same social gizmadoo. But foreigners, somehow, or, anyway certainly some of them, were outside the peripheries of caste. And could act as a catalyst. Or whatever.

They walked to the yellow house along a sort of boardwalk. "What do you think of the looks of the land?" asked Alex. Both Jack and Felix said, almost together, that it "looked funny." Brant nodded. "Just step on it," he suggested. "After they cut down the mangrove, they burned it off, and – well, just step on it. Go ahead. Won't bite you." Somewhat gingerly, the newcomers did. The signs of the burning-off were still visible, and it felt soggy beneath their feet. It, in fact, quivered. The effect was somewhat unsettling; Jack and Felix were glad to step back onto the boards.

"It will dry out, eventually . . . and then, to help it out, they'll fill it with sand and with pipeshank. Those vertical planks you see will be helping it drain. It *was* dryer, once, the men have found signs that people had lived here before . . . old nails . . . old pieces of timber . . . old bones . . ." he rolled his eyes toward Felix, Felix shuddered, Alex laughed. "Old turtle bones. Rare and protected now, when I'm not catching them . . . they used to be common as fish."

Rare? increasingly so. Expensive . . . accordingly. Protected? somewhat. Alex . . . somehow . . . was never caught catching them in legally protected areas, so it followed . . . didn't it? that he had caught them in legally *un*protected areas. And sold them . . . when he sold them . . . at great prices to such places as that stately old guest house the Queen Adelaide, and to the Empire Hotel and the Tropicalia Inn. Felix, perhaps uncomfortable about the turtles, asked if there were any interesting mammals. ". . . on Gallans or Galliard or whatever its name?"

The caye, whatever its name, probably had no mammals at all except perhaps for bats which perhaps ate the silver-pale hog-plum or the pale yellow governor-plum. But it hospitted the pelican, locally called the stork, which, bill empty, it did resemble. The insect-like hummingbird was there, though not in great numbers, for there were not many nectar-yielding flowering plants on that sombre islet. Plovers and sandpipers sometimes strolled the small stretch of strand and sand, and the shrieking gull and the tern were sometimes there . . . and the carrion-buzzard ("the corby") furtively patrolled the place with its ugly croak and its filthy feathers. The dead air weighed them all down.

The newcomers rounded the angle of the boardwalk, the yellow house stood there on stilts before them, one story in all, and, from that first glance, one which led you in through the open door and came to a quick conclusion: one room in all.

Someone was coming toward them, walking very slowly. Said the Honourable Somerset, "And here is our host." Jack felt something like instant recognition upon seeing Major Deak, and yet he knew he'd never seen him before . . . he seemed actually a giant tortoise walking upright, – the convex back, the waving fipperlike arms and hands, the head out-thrust from the loose collar at almost a right angle, the face here wrinkled and there divided into platelets, the absence of head or facial hair. The eyes lacked alike the clearness of youth and the milkiness of age; the eyes (Limekiller concluded) the eyes looked *sick*. He heard, in his inner ear, his own voice saying, You're wrong. And, a second later, realized that he'd been replying to something not addressed to himself . . . something murmured back there a moment ago between Edwards and his wife.

De Major looking ageable.

Yes, mon, ahnd aging fahst.

But it was not age. The cayes were commonly considered to be of a healthier air than that of King Town; often Limekiller, comparing the fresh winds out on the islets to the soggy smells of the badly drained capital, had agreed. But clearly the air here was doing Major Deak no good . . . and, if today's dead-sullen calm and . . . the phrase rose up in his mind and silently burst like a bubble of gas . . . and *bad vibes* . . . were typical . . . he did not finish the thought. He was being introduced, he had to speak.

"How are you, sir?"

And Major Deak, alas, proceded to *tell* him ". . . thought I was choking, strangling . . . doctor finds no evidence of asthma or emphysema . . . *can't* go elsewhere to live," he said, slowly moving his head from side to side, as though Limekiller had urged him to move on. ". . . all my savings here . . . planned to add a few rooms . . . receive a few people, retired people . . . paying guests . . . labor troubles . . . can't seem to catch my breath for long . . . thought that in a place with underemployment there'd be no problem hiring workpeople, but . . . nothing seems to get *done* . . . eating up my capital . . . pension a trifle . . . say that from today on for a *month* nobody will do a job of work . . . would have retired in the Golconda Colony but the fanatics have gained control there. . . ."

There was one word which, Jack thought, described the man's state. *Misery.*

Upstairs, surprisingly, the air was by far less dead. It was not only to discourage Critturs that this house, like so many in the country, was built on stilts: the chief purpose was to catch the wind. And it caught it. But the wind did not stay caught. And someone else was upstairs, as though waiting for them. Stickney Forster.

Stickney Forster was a Member of the Bar, and by now the only actively practicing White member. Those who liked him said, "Ah very clever mahn, he went to the Oxford College, you know." Those who did not like him said that if he had ever been to Oxford it was only to use the toilet. "That Limey bahstard," they called him. Although on this occasion he was not in his black robe and white tie and wig, Jack recognized him at once, had long been quietly amused by his having once said, "I have placed in my will that on my tombstone it should read, *Father of the Illegitimate Children's Sustentation Act*, being the shortest Act in the Law Code. Do you know it? It reads in its entirely, *The Illegitimate Children's Sustentation Act shall follow in every detail the provisions of the Legitimate Children's Sustentation Act.* Caused a few grumbles, I can tell you, fat lot I care, but it makes sure that no 'outside' child is going to go raggedy-arsed while his half-sibs are fully-clothed just because their parents were 'married in church.' " *Married in church* and *An outside child*, Jack knew the words well, as they often appeared in casual conversation in British Hidalgo; B.H. being, he had often thought, the one country he knew of in which absolute adherence to the old-time religion went hand in hand with absolute heterosexual freedom. (There was as yet nothing like a "Gay Rights" Movement in British Hidalgo; very very rarely was the matter even mentioned, and then usually in a very tight-lipped line in the official *Gazette*: Sixteen months in gaol for having committed the crime against nature.)

However. . . .

Outside child. . . .

Married in church. . . .

These phrases now restored to the top-level of his mind, Jack now began to think about them and about their implications; and, whilst somebody's record-player shrieked loud good times and loud bad music, think of them he did. He lacked the languorous tropical attitude toward carnal congress and parturition and the sustentation of children: and so, he was sure, did Felix. There was no likelihood that she would cut cane in the field till her time arrived and then retire behind a clump of trees, easily to give birth to the offspring of their love. There was no likelihood that Jack would simply give her what he chanced to have in his pockets and inform her that if rations grew scarce his great-aunt in Ladysmith Street would always have an extra plantain or an extra banana. And, although *Grandy* was always willing and indeed more than willing to take in the tot, Felix did not have a *Grandy* in the Colony, and neither did Jack, and in the colder climates hearts were at least in this respect less warm. Which left what? The choice. Abortion? And, if not . . . marriage.

In short, he was perhaps now being obliged to ask himself if he would rather slay the baby in her belly or at long last Settle Down and bend his sunburned neck beneath the yoke. "Shandy*gaff?* Shandy*gaff?*" this was Noddy asking, and, taking some murmur or motion for Yes, he stuck a glass in Jack's hand and simultaneously and deftly, poured out half a bottle of Coca-Cola and half a bottle of Tennant's Milk Stout (imported, and well worth the importation). Jack quaffed deeply. "Noddy, thank you," he said. "Usually I don't care for fantods in my drink, but this one is just great." Noddy made a brief mock-bow, murmured something about Native Arts and Crafts, mimed that he would pour another, shook his head briefly at Jack's No; was off. Mr. J.L.L. asked, "Hey, Felix, do you want," her eyes turned away the exact second that they met his, and she rose from the rough bench and moved off. A prey once again to the Dismals, Jack said, "a drink," in a low, helpless voice. Knew as well as he knew anything that if he did not follow after her he would later be furiously accused of neglect; that if he did follow after her, she would turn on him like a cornered wildcat, with a forced-out, "Don't *follow* me!" Why, with all the Hazards of the World, did people feel the need to devise new ones? The heavy air produced no answer. Jack decided he would pay his respects to the nominal host, a matter at which she would perhaps decide she need not resent; and, the second he saw her, call out an invitation to be introduced to the man. It would not be correct to say that he failed to meet Deak's eye, or that he listened with half an ear; but his attention was not altogether with it.

Just at the moment, however, Major Deak was talking to the two Honourables and Jack did not care to horn in. He was too well-bred for one thing, and for another he knew not but that the major as principal local landlord might not still exercise medieval powers – say, "the *alcalde* jurisdiction" or pervoynter in uccage and flemage, say, and order him to be staked out on the foreshore at Sandy Caye until two tides should have flowed and ebbed – and anyway a voice in his ear murmured, "Jock" and he turned to fight.

"It's not *Jock*, it's – ah, Stickney!" They shook hands, Limekiller explaining that he didn't wish to be *Jock* to anyone who wanted to trot out a sporranful of old Scotchman jokes, but, "and what brings you here? didn't know you were a party-goer . . . ?"

"Came to see Judge Deak, Major Deak, that is, my older brother knew him well when John Deak was a judge in Golconda Colony and Richard was the Assistant Colonial Secretary. They both went back into the Army during the War, John became a major and Richard became dead; awfully pretty woman, that, you ugly young troll, ah youth! ah woe, the fleeting hours!" Very deftly did Stickney Forster give Jack all the information needed, and then turn the conversation so as to leave no room for feeling a formal need to express regret on the long ago death of someone he had never till now heard of, which expression could be nothing but hypocrisy, or, as Dr. Johnson called it, cant (Sir, clear your mind of cant!). "Deftly," yes. Part of being a gentleman, and having nothing to do with money, position, and a command of the pickle forks. Jack envied.

Major Deak moved off and the Honourable Mrs. Whatsis stopped rummaging in her shoulder-bag or was it a knapsack, it

looked roomy enough and durable enough to pack a waree or a
wild bush hog in, assuming it to have been cleaned and quartered
and cut up into chops, chines, and hams. The Black Arawack were
very fond of the cheaper cuts of pig, referring to their favorite cuts
as *pigtaili* and *pigsnoutu*. But neither they nor those were present.
"Don't know what I'm looking for," she murmured. 'Yes, I *do*. But
it's not in *here*. Somerset!" she adjured her husband, who looked up
with a yes-my-dear expression on his lean and naturally tan face. "I
think perhaps you ought to tell these people what you were telling
me about the *caye* . . . you do recall, don't you? the night after Sir
Joshua prorogued the Assembly and we discovered that Mrs.
Hodkins had stolen the cheese again. The caye, Somerset!" and,
leaving her Honourable husband neither time nor chance to reply,
swept on. "She's a good housekeeper, a fine cook, and an absolutely splendid laundress, my sister Alice once compared her to Queen
Elizabeth's Silk Woman, of course one understands the *first*
Elizabeth, I do think that was *so* squalid of the King of Spain to have
kept a spy in the Virgin Queen's laundry to see if she were still
capable of having children. But she does '*tote*' as the Americans say.
Somerset?"

Limekiller, slightly dazed, nevertheless understood that it was
not the first Elizabeth who had chosen to make off with the cheese.
The Honourable Mrs. did not often speak at length, socially, but
when she did, she *spoke*.

The Honourable Minister to Government carefully put his glass
down. He gave a glance over his shoulder. "Where is Major – Ah.
Down there. I am not quite sure that I wish him to hear this. Of
course he must be told eventually. Well. What I said to my wife is
this. This present attempt to develop this caye is not the first, you
know. No, it is not. The United National Investment Association –
what? Oh, yes, one of the Harrisite groups, remarkable man,
Aurelius Harris, pity that those remarkably large hands were so
remarkably sticky – mm, yes, the UNIA had bought this caye from
the Crown, cash down, and planned to build an hotel here; my
uncle George was one of the board of directors, a remarkable
farseeing man, foresaw the tourist possibilities of such a place, and
it was he who told my father about what they found. I was just a
youngster at the time, but naturally I was all ears. The story seems
to have quite faded away, but *I* well remember it, yes. . . ."

Jack, either still dazed or dazed again, trying hard to make the
connection between Queen Elizabeth I and Aurelius Harris, of

whom he had barely heard; Limekiller wondered if the Honourable Lady had learned discursiveness from the Honourable Minister, or if it had been the other way around, or if a mutual tendency had first attracted them to each other. *Be that as it may. . . .*

Time: the late Nineteen Twenties. *Scene*: Galliards or whatever name Caye. *Cast of Characters*: A band of men, Nationals, delving and digging with shovels and spades and buckets in the mud and muck of the quaking soil, in the partially dried and partially drying soil, in the wet and mucky and boggy soil, had come across some heavy timbers. What kind? Some said, teak. Yes: *teak.* Despite a total absence of elephants, teak did grow in the hospitable soil of what was once called His Majesty's Settlement of Woodcutters on the Bay of Hidalgo. Hard to cut, teak? Damnably hard to cut, teak. But that didn't mean that they didn't cut it. Teak. Others said that the timbers were mahogany. Would mahogany have been brought over from the mainland to a "pure mangrove bluff," as these cayes were called? Surely not to make furniture? No. Surely not to build a boat, for example? Nothing surely about it. For building purposes the wood of choice hereabouts had always been pine, the tropical hardwood pine. In fact, it was so choice, that one could not always obtain it. Jack well recalled a local builder of rowboats and skiffs telling him that he had gone looking for boat wood, and, "Wanted *pine*, you know, mahn: cou'n't git it. Had to take mahogany," a sad shake of the head. And, for that matter, he well knew that when Lemuel Cracovius the dentist had built a second house along the Spanish River he had built it out of mahogany, that being at the time cheaper than pine, European market had been depressed; had built the entire cottage out of mahogany, Lemuel: and then he had painted it green. *Protective coloration, John*, his only explanation.

"Well, it's well known that wood kept under water or anyway well wet," said the Honourable, making gestures to his Lady Wife, who delved into her dittybag and came out with a pipe and a pouch of tobacco and proceeded to fill the pipe as her lord talked on; "will keep very much better than wood which is seasoned dry. So it was no surprise that the timbers gave every evidence of being very old . . . the axe-marks and adze-marks had not been made by any modern tools, they saw that at once. Thank you, my dear." He put the filled pipe between his teeth while she struck a large wooden "Swede's match," as they were locally called (on the Prairies they were called – farmer matches"; merely proves that there were a lot of Swedes farming on the Prairies; nothing new about that) and a

puff of smoke from a pipe tobacco which had never been cured or
blended by the Indians (whose slash-and-burn farmings were indus-
triously ruining the slopes of the Mayan Mountains) filled the room
with its delicious scent.

And they had puzzled over the timbers, their shapes and
purpose, and in a few moments realized what they were. Puff. Puff.
Puff.

And the warm wind seemed to echo: puff. . . puff . . . puff . . .

"And what were they?" Felix could not wait, needs must ask.

"Don't know if you've ever wondered, puff," the Honourable
Minister said, "what the right name of this caye *is*, puff, puff."

"*Never* gave it a thought," she said, mendaciously. "Gal something, isn't it?"

How those lovely lips could lie! – Jack's admiring thought.

The clouds of Three Grommets Cut Shag, or was it Lord
Tweedweevil's Prime Shaved Plug, filled the room. "'Gal something,' just so. Galliards, Gallards, Gallants, Galleons, Gal-this and
Gal-that. Eh? What, Mr. Brant? 'Gal Cut and Run?' Ah, but that is
on the Old Belinda River. Well, not to make a very long matter of
it, puff' puff; the timbers fitted very neatly into an old engine of
execution, that is to say, a gibbet, or in other words, a –"

And Jack and Felix in one gust of breath cried out, "*Gallows!*"

The matter of *why* the Gal had Cut and Run, fascinating though
it probably was, and for that matter *who* the Gal was, must needs
wait another occasion, as Sheherazade doubtless told the sultan as
he sipped his cup of cawwa tinged with ambergrise through his
musky-scented moustache. Uncle George realized at once that this
was *Gallows* Caye and that the timbers were those of *the* gallows,
and nought else. They thought of burning them, but they were too
damp. So they just reburied them again until they could think of
something else, because naturally they didn't wish the story to get
out ("Naturally!") or the workmen would have downed tools at
once. And no one would have stopped at the hotel. And in fact the
work on the building scheme alas went no further because the
Slump, the Depression, you know, simply destroyed the foreign
mahogany market and eventually the caye was sold for half the
purchase price to Merchant Henricus Deak who didn't really want
it and did nothing with it whatsoever, and after he died I believe it
was the Grasshopper Bank in London paid the taxes for oh

donkey's years. Then came forth from over the seas Major John Deak, formerly Judge Deak: nephew, isn't he?"

"Cousin," said Stickney Forster. Briefly.

Briefly. And everyone had time to think thoughts. Puff . . . puff . . . puff . . . – How long did or had the gallows tree remained there? "Too long by far. Timber's always been cheap here . . . too cheap, you know . . . and it was even cheaper back then. No reason to dismantle the damned engine," he used the word in an archaic meaning without hesitation but not without emphasis; "and bring the baulks and beams back, bring them anywhere for that matter – there was after all another gallows in King Town – so here it stayed, tainting the very sky, as you might say, till down they fell. Did any-one topple them? I doubt it. Probably tumbled down in some strong wind, a wind of long fetch . . . not one of hurricane strength, else the pieces would've been flung afar. . . ."

The few pieces of exotic furniture, a painting showing a jungle scene, similar to but not the same as the local "bush," brassware and other foreign finery, scarcely filled or disguised the bareness of the room; and through the open doors on each side the breeze blew fitfully but without interruption for very long. Sounds of gaiety accompanied at times by the tunes from Alex Brant's gramophone, snatches of loud amused conversation, came to them in fits and snatches; from time to time the drone of Deak's monologue into the ears of, by the murmur of an occasional comment, good-natured Neville. Felix asked, "But what do you mean, 'another gallows in King Town'? If there was one there, why did they have another one here?"

Ah, said the Honourable (with a wave of the by now puffed-out pipe), ah, *that* was another story. "My uncle George became inter-ested in the matter and he copied an account of it out of some annal or archive and I made a copy of his copy and I placed it in that book, the yellow one there on the shelf between the Bible and the Dictionary, which I lent to Major Deak with the intention that he should read it as a sort of preparation of the, well, ha ha, no, not for the Gospel; you know Eusebius, do you –" "*Somerset!*" "Mmm, yes, my dear; preparation for knowing the background of the – but I suppose he hasn't read it, eh?"

"He hasn't read it." – Stickney Forster. Still brief.

"Mm. Well, I thought the book might anyway interest him, like most men I assume that if a book interests *me*, it must interest *others*, and –"

Jack knew exactly what the man meant, and, knowing that the man spent very long hours trying to prepare such arid items as *A BILL to ascertain that the SEWERS and DRAINS of the Municipality of KING TOWN, as set forth in Sanitary Act 3317, Schedule B, Article 6C of the 18th April, 1959, be hereby AMENDED, as follows;* so that the National Assembly might prevent being up to its nostrils in SLUDGE: whereas the Members of the Assembly would much, much rather have been adopting resolutions condemning the Repressive Regime of Zambazunga — or, better yet, voting to adjourn early to see the Middle Schools cricket game; Jack, knowing this, felt a burst of sympathy for the Honourable Minister for Government's rambling away on other subjects. "What book is *that*, Sir?" he asked.

"It is a copy of the Planter's Annual for 1810."

It was absolutely astonishing how all at once Jack's eyes and Felix's eyes were locked into each other's gaze; and in hers he read with alas all too absolute certainty the charge that by knowing that May was fascinated by that series of historical volumes he was somehow convicted of being privy to some passion between May and himself — a passion of which he knew himself utterly innocent. He had never given May any more than a cousinly kiss; May was sweet in her own dry, acerbic way; her face was a plate of pudding with just enough nose to hold her eye-glasses up, and her blouse concealed no more curves than would hospit a pair of doorknobs; all this was beside the point, the point being that (a) he had perhaps gat Felix with child when she would probably rather not be gat, and (b) at a time when he had a felonious intuition of May's preferred taste in historical reading matter. Surely Queen Elizabeth, the *High and Mighty Prince, Elizabeth,* daughter of Henry VIII, "that vile monster," as Who? had called him, would have sent any man to The Tower on just such a charge. And Felicia Ann Fox, the sole true love of John Lutwidge Limekiller's life and perhaps the bearer of his baby beneath her beating heart was now staring at him with a blazing gaze which seemed to accuse him of every crime and conceivable offense from masturbation to simony: and defying him to have any expression upon his face or even to drop his eyes.

"If it weren't for the breeze I couldn't tolerate being out here," said the Honourable Mrs.; "*and I don't much like the breeze.*"

• • •

Now was heard from a different quarter a puffing and a huffing which was neither the offending breeze nor the Honourable's pipe. Major Deak was slowly lifting his large tortoise's body up the shallow steps from the sand-filled yard to the house, with nice Neville at one elbow. ". . . and horrid dreams," the Major was saying, between gasps. "Thought I was choking or strangling . . . but doctor finds no sign of asthma or emphysema . . . can't *live* here," he sank into the chair which Jack vacated, "and can't live else-where." He paid no attention as Felix, who had taken the yellow book from its shelf, proceeded to drop it, fumbled picking it off the floor, quite twisting herself around, got it at last, replaced it. "For Christ's sake pour me a drink, Stickney. . . ."

Limekiller, glad to be free of that freezing gaze, bent over the bottles. "Whiskey, Major?" he asked, solicitously. "Water? Soda?" There was no ice.

For the first time Deak gave him the benefit of his attention. "Whiskey?" he demanded. "*Whiskey*? Before the sunset gun? *Ce*rtainly not. Gin and tonic, Stickney." Limekiller, fairly crushed, yielded his place at the bar.

Squatting peacefully in the shade as she smoked her pipe, a middle-aged Arawack woman had given Jack a brief nod; he supposed she was the housekeeper. The floor here must have certainly been swept, for the Arawack were notoriously vigorous sweepers; but sand had been tracked inside, and the breeze, that same breeze which had been so reluctant to waft the *Saccharissa* along with any speed at all, now blew the sand in little swirls and eddies. "I'd thought to retire here," Major Deak, perhaps none the better for his deep sip of Mother's Ruin (and perhaps none the worse: he did not, somehow, have the look of a drinkard), contin-ued his plaint. "Thought to put up a house and several cottages, take in a few congenial paying guests. The only solid place on the caye is under this house, this half-built house. Got to *pave* the rest of the place, in effect, clear off the mangrove, which I can't even sell, market for tanbark is sated, not to say cloyed; clear off the mangrove, box in the bog and fill it with sand like a kiddies' sand box . . . half the time when we've dumped I don't know how many boatloads of sand, I find that the plot *was*n't boxed in at all, and the sand just slips away. 'Cottages'? Can't even seem to get this house finished, let alone cottages. Can't hire proper workmen, they don't want to work out on the caye, don't want to stay overnight, they come late and leave early, collect their wages and are gone till they're spent, demand advances, don't return to earn them back, steal tools," the drone went on. Limekiller had little doubt that there was much to complain. Bayfolk would work hard, would work very hard indeed . . . but they much preferred to work their hard work in King *Town*, the ancient capital which was London, Paris, Rome, and Jerusalem to them. Away from King Town and its incessant cheerful noise, away from the dram-shops with their convivial ten-cent glasses of low-proof local rum and local water, away from the chance to lime the passing women and girls, away from the contin-uous opportunity to break the monotony of labor with a purchase from passing vendors of fried conch-flitter or a handful of peanuts or a cluster of fibrous pocono-boy nuts; away from all this and from the very bumboats gliding along the Foreshore or the canals, the Bayman tended to wilt and to lose interest. All this was nothing new to Jack. Nor did Deak seem at all the type to toil alongside his workmen and cheer them up with a jest or a quip.

And he certainly did not look as though a jest or a quip would cheer him up. At all. And as for his very evident bad health, Jack, in the words

of the song, was not a qualified physician and did not want to give the decision. Perhaps the man had picked up one of the multitude of little-known bugs which added to the White Man's Burden . . . or for that matter, the Black and Brown. Whoever. Or, if a psychosomatic illness, well, a perforated ulcer, for example, caused by worry, was a hole in the stomach just as much as a hole in the stomach *not* caused by worry. Or, putting it another way, three and three equals six and so does four plus two equals six and so five and —

"*Oh, I works fih Whitemon fih* mon*ey*," sang someone in the cheerful yard, "*ahn I geeves eet to my* hon*ey*," and at once Nora or was it Gwendolyn or Eva, cried out in a cheerful shriek, "You naw geeve eet to *me!*" Much laughter. The singer shouted "What I *does* geeve you, gyel? Eef you no like eet, senn eet bock!" Much, *much* laughter.

"Did *you* have much trouble getting here today?" was Jack's question to Stickney Forster.

"No. None. We've a good little engine in the boat. One of yours, you know, Johnson."

Perhaps not every boat motor in the waters of "the Colony" was a Johnson-Evinrude, but *Johnson*, in Hidalgo-English — or anyway, in Baytalk — was *the* word for an outboard engine. "Ah, you came by motorboat," said Jack, nodding.

"Yes. You not? No, I see not. I well remember, on my old boat, sometimes trying to avoid this caye, yet it keeps coming back into sight. And sometimes, try as one will, it seems that one can hardly get here at all: the winds require one to tack back and forth. Well, on certain days. And the old people, *de w'old people*," he slipped into Baytalk, not at all in mockery but as though to reinforce his own statement; "*they* used to say, those days are the anniversaries of hangings." Having said this, in a tone slightly that of saying something in confidence, Stickney Forster seemed rather resentful at having said it. He gave a covert look at Major ("Judge") Deak. Who had not seemed to hear it, was studying his gin. It was, after all, *his* gin; was he perhaps recollecting the sign over the cellar in Hogarth's Gin Lane engraving . . . *Drunk for a penny. . . . Dead drunk for two pence. . . . Clean Straw for nothing . . .* ? George IV brand gin cost a deal more than a penny.

But someone else had heard it. Felix removed her water-over-mangrove-bark-dark gaze from Limekiller's eyes (but what have I *done*? he cried in his heart; she did not seem to have heard it), and turned to – almost *on* – Stickney Forster. "You still hang people here, then?" she asked.

Stickney Forster seemed, suddenly, or once again, a very model of a model English gentleman. With no trace of the old colonial or modern North American tones which had overlaid his accent previously, he said, "Yes . . . I'm afraid we do . . . you know. . . ."

"Yes . . . I'm afraid I do know. But isn't that a very terrible thing to do?"

As an attorney, either for the Crown or in private practice, he was usually capable of speaking crisply and succinctly. Now? Not. "Hm, well, still, hm, you know, I don't know," he said, brushing back the tip of his auburn moustache with the tip of his auburn finger, and sounding almost as if he had determined to burlesque himself. "I don't know, you know. About that. Not so sure. About that. You know."

"No," said Felix, suddenly as calm as the eye of a hurricane. "I *don't* know. Explain it to me."

Stickney concentrated. Cleared his throat. "*Well.* You are from The States, I take it." "You may." "Well, you see. Now you must be familiar with at least one large city in The States. Hmm. Ah, Chicago. You've been in Chicago?" Felix had been in Chicago. "Well. There you are."

"I am *where*?"

Clearly she was going to give him no help at all. He made a long, slow motion with his long, slow hand, tawny from the tropic sun. Made up his mind to make his point. "Well. In which place do you feel safer? At night, I mean?"

Felix was hostile. But, whether poor or not, she was honest. "Here," she said.

He nodded. "Exactly so. And do you know why? Because of Murderers. Beg pardon. But you do let them get away with murder there. Perhaps what you call 'a good lawyer' gets them off. If not, what then? Found guilty? Appeal. Appeal*s*. Chap wears the courts out, often. Evidence grows stale. New trial? Witnesses have died. Or grown forgetful. Or reluctant. Chap often walks away free. *Or.* Guilty? *No* new trial? 'Life imprisonment'? Out on the streets in six years. Perhaps does it *again.*

"You see. . . .

"Here . . . no.

"*Evi*dence. *Tes*timony. *Guilty. Sen*tenced. Three Weeks *late*r: *Dead,* you know. Result? *Very* few murders." He paused a moment, said, "You *see. . . .*"

Felix, it was clear, *did* see. But still didn't like what she saw. After a moment she murmured, "A twelve-year-old boy for stealing a pearl-handled penknife?"

"Ahh —" Stickney's groan was deep in his throat. "*Ter*rible. I quite agree. *Two hundred years ago.* Time when George Washington owned slaves. When *free Negroes* owned slaves. . . ."

There was silence. Limekiller stared at the flaccid sea. Then Major Deak's sick eyes drooped. Blinked. Opened wider. "Freshen your drinks?" he asked. "Freshen mine, Stickney, a good chap."

More George IV gin (and less tonic) added to his glass, Deak, who had listened absolutely silently to Stickney Forster, now said, with the by now familiar breath-breaks and gasps and sighs, "During my years as District Judge I had to pass sentence of death on between I suppose oh twenty to thirty men. Only one woman." A voice not his: "*Ohhh*?" A gasp. His. Then, "Mmm. First she killed her baby because child didn't look like her husband. Then killed her husband. Too." A gulp of air.

Outside, someone shouted, "Dahnce, everybody? Dahnce? *Dahnce!*"

The joviality note at once rose high. So did the music. Someone's familiar voice sang out, "*Oh baby, oh, baby; O Baby: Oh!*" Jack wondered if it were Alex Brant . . . and by Felix's quick glance out the door, wondered if she were not wondering, too; her glance returned, met his, blazed. Suddenly he thought of National Senator Weston's remark (at which he had then laughed), "Frahnkly, me dear Jahk, my trouble is that my wife understonds me!"

Felix asked, "And *was* she hanged?"

An inhaustion of gin. Of air. "Of course."

Silence. Felix asked, in a strained voice, "I don't suppose you took into account her state of *mind* –?"

"*Oh* yes."

The glass of gin and its minuscule dose of quinine went up . . . and up . . . came down . . . came down. Shimmering. Very slight tinge of blue?

"– and the Hell she must have been in –"

"Yes." The thrust-out, hairless, tortoise-head nodded, twice. "First off, she had taken her great knife to be sharpened. Secondly, she had dug up her jewelry *and* her husband's savings and placed it all in her travelling trunk. Then killed them both. And left. Found her waiting for the train, ticket in her hand. Premedi*ta*tion. Flight to avoid prosecution. Jury found her *guilty*. My duty was to pronounce *sen*tence."

"Which you did." Eyes smoldering into Jack's as if he himself had donned the Black Cap over the wig. *Aft*er accurately guessing her cousin's taste in reading matter. *Well,* he eyeballed to her, *May's taste in books is one hell of a lot better than your friend Alex Brant's taste in music –*

"Which," choke, gasp, "I did."

Silence. Even, for some reason, the music. The eyeball semaphore informed him what be could *do* with his opinion.

"*Stifling weather* all this past week," said Major/Judge Deak. "Can't *breathe.* Doctor says *no* trace of asthma," bad sounds in chest; "*or* of emphysema." He made Stickney Forster a signal to recharge his glass. Judge Deak's expenses were exceeding his income. *But he drank the best gin.*

Somewhat suddenly several of the sitters-in-the-room were gone downstairs, and, as though in a game of Musical Chairs/Going to Jerusalem, several of the dancers-in-the-yard were come upstairs. "Are there rather a lot of sea-turtles around here?" asked English Neville. Deak said he'd seen a few. "Ah, there must have been more than a few in the days of yore," Neville reckoned; "we found you jolly well wouldn't believe how many ghastly old turtle-bones just dug up recently and thrown over there in the bog. *Burnt,* I shouldn't wonder –"

"Kept them in a crawl," the Honourable said.

Noddy: "In a *what?*"

"A cor-*ral,* in North America. Africa? K-r-a-a-l. We say '*crawl.*'"

"Well, I daresay they *do.* Never heard of a turtle *trot,* eh? Haw haw!"

"*Who* kept them in the crawl?"

"Pair of cut-throats, who –"

"Cut-throats? Here on Galleon's Caye?"

Jack had not remembered seeing the National improbably named Pony-Boy here before, but here he was: bottle of rum in one hand, bottle of ginger stout (temperance beverage) in the other: And feeling no pain. "Planty of cut-t'roats here on Galliard's Caye in de w'old days," he said, clearly pleased to contribute to the general enlightenment. "Live for *mont's* on tortle-meat! Galliard, he was ahn Ehnglishmahn, me grahd*fahd*er knew he'm . . . well . . . me *great* grahdfahder." Immediately, regardless of the shades of antiquity, for Stephenson the explorer had remarked, back in those very days, that "all the Baymen are boatmen, and cradled on the water," Pony-Boy said, "Jock, as your boat hasn't got no ox –"

Noddy: "No *what?*"

"– no ox, no oxilliary engine, just sail; as you hasn't got none, Jock, meh-be best you be starting bock. Else you gwayne be oet on de wah-tah ahl night."

What response Limekiller might have given to this unsolicitate advice, with its implication that he was a mere suckling-child where these things were concerned, might or might not soon have been known. But Felix very civilly and very swiftly made her farewells and was gone down the stairs. Leaving Guess Who to follow after. Hastily. Lest she be off, and leave him up to his huckle-bones in the bog. Doomed to live on broiled turtle-meat, and the leavings and drippings of the shandygaff. And the gin.

The need to set the sails and sheets and tackle-in-general to rights relieved either of them from the need to say anything. Certainly a damned good thing. The fading sun would probably serve them well enough until the light tended by Old Captain Barber was visible, and after that sank more-or-less behind them, the lights of King Town would be visible. And even if a mist were to come up (not an impossible thing at this season of the waning year) so that they couldn't see the nation's only city: well, they could damned well *smell* it: the drains of the capital (scarcely above sea-level) were notorious, let the Honourable draft how many Sanitary Ordinances as he would.

By and by, what between steering, pumping, and scanning the horizon, Jack was aware that his temper had gone down to nearly normal. And he looked around to see what Felix was doing. She was being mighty quiet. This was the first real quarrel that they had had, and he hoped that she was not making any plans to scuttle the boat; lo! she was crouching very near to him, and she was shining the flashlight. Was she planning to −? Shucks. The water was so shallow he could almost walk ashore. She wasn't as tall as he was? Very well. He would carry her on his shoulders; vague thoughts of Saint Christopher. . . .

What was she *doing*?

She was reading a sheet of paper.

He leaned over. It was a, it was a . . . well, it was something typed.

Hoping that being the first to speak would not result in a pudding or a cheese or something attached to his nose, he said, "What's *that*?"

"It fell out of the book . . . back there."

"And you just *took* it?" Whoa, there, Limekiller!

She shifted, shrugged, and swiftly shook her shoulders, as if trying to cast off a touch which he had not applied. "Well, he *said* it was a *copy*. So he can easily make another one, and besides Iwanted to finish it without seeming nosy; why are *you* being so judgmental?"

Iniquity, transgression, and sin. Judge not, that ye −

Limekiller had learned enough to know that he still had much to learn, and so, silently complimenting himself on his wisdom, thought to drop the matter. Only to learn some more, to wit, that when someone wants an argument, really *wants* it, nothing and nobody is going to prevent it. There is then no Right Way to Handle It. So they had It. Not "Had it Out," just had it. And he felt miserable. How could love turn to this? And then by and by she opened the paper again and they both read it and read it together.

Linzer and Quashee. About that time, one Linzer or Linzen, a Native of Austria and Quashee a Natuve of Guinea, made a Devilish plot to blow up the Poweder Magazine which would worke great loss of Life both Black and White and in the Confusion they rightly expected to follow, it had been their Plot to steal the Gold in the Publick Treasury, which they had reckoned to have opened with a small Blast of Powder simultaneous with the greater and thence they would head for Spanish Waters not doubting but to receive a Welcome after they'd dishonestly profess the Papish Religion. But one or the other attempting to inviegle a Woman of Colour along of them, she having the fear of God before her eyes, divulged the Scheme. Linzer and Quashee were taken tried and sentenced to be hanged. HOWEVER it having come about that the Chapalin's Wife Mris. Manningtone being at that Time in a delicate Condition and their being no point in the Settlement, scarcely, which was not overlooked from the Chamber in which twas expected she would be confined, Governour Endderby a most humane and merciful Man, gave orders that contrary to the usual prackticke, Sentence of Execution was not to be carried out in the Settlement but ye Gallowes was erected on Tanbarke Caye as twas then known, on 6th Decem being St. Nicholas Daye. Quashee expressed a degree of Contritione but Linzene with many Oaths and blusterings declared that 'by G—' he was glad of the Excursion 'Yea he had eat many a great green tortle on said Caye and had rather be hanged there where the Sea Winds blew than in any stinking Settlement and regretted Nothing.' Sentence was carried out and that Part of Tanbarke Caye (the red-brown Mangrave being used for the Purpose of preparing Hydes) has since ben known as Galleowes Point.

Two pennys in the Pund a Bounty on Torbinado Sugar

"Couldn't spell worth a fiddle-head fern," he began, hoping that the Black Dog might be sent firmly from their midst by a diagonal change in subject. But it was not to be. Her look was no friendly one. It was still the slightly sidewise gaze of an accountant who wishes to make clear that although he has yet to lodge an Information with the police he *has* by jove become fully aware of the attempt to queer the books; "You *are* sailing under a curse aren't you?" – and what, demanded the Look, had he done which deserved it? he must have done *some*thing to deserve it, said the Look; sacked a cathedral, or what? and *what* did he plan to do to *un*deserve it? malignantly involving *her*, said the Look –

"What do you mean? *What* curse? Why just *me*?"

Protests of innocence would get him nowhere, said the Look. "It's just one weird thing after another with you, isn't it? Was one of your ancestors a hanging judge, too?" And she cited and related to him other of his odd adventures which he had . . . with some hesitation . . . related and cited to her, events explicable only by accepting the fantastic and the metaphysical. Events which had happened *here* within the compass of this so small yet so astonishing nation: the size of Wales? larger than the Atlantic Province of Prince Edward's Island, where so many Limekillers were buried within sight and sound and scent and touch of the circumambient sea. – But he would accept no guilt on his own broad shoulders. "That's the kind of *country* it is. When you're in a country that's still partly in the last century –"

"'the *last* century'! Jesus –"

"– or the century before *that*, well, that's what it's *like* here. Nobody travels to Harvard or McGill in a dugout and nobody's car in Ohio ever gets hit by a tapir, but here, *here*, that's what it's *like*. Here. In North America," he used it in the Canadian sense of *The United States and Canada*, "in North America you've got smog –"

"I haven't got smog!" – and so they were at it again. Having it again. "And oh my God that's what those 'curtains' were! Those 'bundles of *rags*' and that 'window frame' as I thought they were! It was a gallows and it was those bodies hanging on it until they rotted and fell down! Oh Christ pity women," she moaned.

And there in the dying day, with the curls of white foam, the *perilous seas of faerie lands forlorn*, and the emerging stars, and a line of fading light to the west above the Mayan Mountains, he was astonished and vexed and perplexed and pleased and all the rest of it: *was* he to be a father? *Good*! "– but I thought you said you'd decided you weren't pregnant."

And she: "Oh I don't mean *me*. I don't mean *me*. I mean that poor woman in the old paper. That chaplain's wife. Life within her, life inside of her, because that damn dumbell dominus vobiscum man of hers couldn't get it together to pull out in time, life inside of her and then from any window she could look out of, all she could see was *death*. A child hanging inside of her from a cord, and anywhere she *looked*, what were they getting ready to do, why hang some other woman's child by cords. Ropes, lines," she gestured to those on the boat; "goddamn you all, goddamn it all, all of it –"

A new noise out of the sea, a hum and a buzz, and new lights out of the sea: Noddy's motor-cruiser, or Alex's, and the faint sounds of music and laughter; she lifted the flashlight and waved it and shouted; he made to seize it more in astonishment than anything else, shouted *What was she doing?* and she made to strike him with it and then she just as suddenly flung it down and ran a few steps and leaned against the side; he could hear her heavy breathing. She was sorry, she was not sorry, she wept, she did not weep.

The new noises and new lights faded and were merged into the sea again. A new star rose up from the sea, wavered an instant, then it swung slightly to and fro. Then it was still and hung steady in the firmament. Captain Barber's light. Limekiller adjusted his perceptions. Nodded. Swung the helm just a bit to port.

Having adjusted the inadvertancies of the boat, he thought, he still thought, still he thought he might, readjust the inadvertancies of their lives . . . their life. . . . In a low and calm voice, he said, "Well, we don't like it, but we don't have to like it, that the wind almost didn't take us there. It's the anniversary of some grim event, but it's also the anniversary of St. Nicholas Day, and he *is* the patron saint of sailors. So the wind wasn't very willing, but it took us there, and now it's more willing and it's taking us back." Another and a farther and a fainter star skimmed over the sea further out: another of the motor-craft bringing the guests back to port: Alex Brant? Stickney Porster? and who else? Didn't matter. He saw that she saw it. "And, anyway, now we've got the name cleared up. We don't *like* the name? Not Gallants, not Galliards, not Galleon's. So it's *Gallows* Caye. At least now we know. Now we know, eh. Maybe that ghastly tree *does* fill the air there with its . . . whatever they are. Whatever it is. Vibrations? 'Vibes'? Emanations?" He did not say, but he thought, and he thought that she thought so too: affecting the very winds to drop, to slow, and to delay, one's arrival. The winds had no power over the power boats? So be it. The twentieth century moved on, moved on; dissipating what once had been projected: the infinite reluctancy of those ancient criminals and their prayers not to get quickly to their destination. For St. Nicholas *was* the bringer and giver of gifts. It was grotesque, was it, to recall that St. Nicholas became Santa Claus? Life was often grotesque. And death, too.

Small wonder the large severalty of names: any variation of the basic one. Galleon Caye. Gallon Caye. Galliards. . . . Gallants. . . .

Had he not even heard *Callous* Caye? . . . for stealing a puncheon of rum, *to be hanged by the neck until dead* . . . for striking his superior officer, *to be hanged by the neck until dead* . . . for selling plated silver as sterling . . . for breaking and entering . . . for arson . . . *to be hanged by the neck until dead.* . . . They must, it would seem, have felt incalculably sure of themselves to pass and carry out such sentences for such crimes. And yet it seemed they felt what Anthony a Wood called a *Great Reluctancy* to name the plot of bog and sog where the carrying-out took place, and call it by its rightful, awful name. To call it by its dirty name.

Callous indeed.

But not that callous.

The wind blew better, coming in. But . . . somehow . . . the cracked boom no longer sang to them.

Felix (from "Felicia," happiness), Felix didn't speak. That is, she didn't speak words. But a tiny figure moved from who knows where, from the cubby-hole, probably; and uttered a tiny voice. Skippy. The little cat. And she picked it up, and she crooned a sound to it as she cuddled it and bent her head over it. And he realized that it had originally been *his* cat and comrade alone, that it had shared its master and captain with her; that she could not fail to recall these things herself. Skippy had been a part of him longer than she had. And she held it. And she sang a small wordless song to it.

Off to starboard in the very last light he saw a waterspout, rather like a sketchy impression of a brontosaur with a long twisty neck coming out of the water. Two things were essential to create a spout: for one, you had to have the funnel-shaped vortex of wind; and for another, you had to have the ever-yielding ocean, drowner of men. Neither one could do it alone. Was this a metaphor for his own life down here? Seemingly so calm, his own persona, sometimes calm to the point of indolence, was there nevertheless something latent within him which roused up the elements and elementals of this seemingly placid little nation, itself apparently calm to the point of indolence: so that when the two of them came together, heaven and earth and fire and water were torn apart and reassembled to form shapes unheard of? The, whatever it was, call it the national collective unconscious, may have lain inert until he came upon the scene: a national undersoul awaiting his own catalytic presence? An ambience composed of history, the jungle, the ocean and the night: long subdued . . . and long awaiting. . . . . Was that it? Could that be true? that the explanation? Of course, as an explanation, it was incredible.

But what credible explanation was *there?*

The seemingly sweet and placid pre-Columbian Indians, touring the antique waters of the not-yet Spanish Main in their long dugout canoes with their long cane bows: arriving on these coral strands to sack and burn, enslave the children and the women, and then eat the men in their great victorious cannibal feasts (cannibal, carribal, caribee, Caribbean) . . . then the Spanish swineherds, pious killers of Moors, suddenly becoming overseas conquistadores and viceroys, destroyers of enemy . . . the French fishermen converted into buccaneers . . . the English merchant adventurers and woodcutters transformed to pirates and warriors. . . . Black folk caught and enslaved by other Black folk and sold like codfish in the African markets to strange White folk who carried them over the seas to till the soil and clear the forests. Red men enslaved by Red men, White men enslaved by White men and sent over the wild wastes of seas for the crimes of having supported King Charles or King Monmouth. Cannibal fires, galleons plundered and burned, stinking sullied slaveships each one leaving at least one burning village behind; and the forge fires which heated the shackles. . . . Colonial wars and slave rebellions, Indians massacring Black folk and White, Whites and Blacks massacring Indians; American spilling American blood because of dynastic wars initiated in Europe. And then the fearful rites of Hurican, Quetzalcoatl, and Setebos, overlaid with Old World witchcraft and with ju-ju and óbeah, and wax mommets thrust through with thorns, and the voodoo dolls, and the unclean spirits conjured up and given forms and escaped into the woods, there lying latent until –

– until there came down from the oft-times frozen North the very quick corpus of one John Lutwidge Limekiller, from the wild lands of hungry Wendigo: and the Beothuck and Micmac and Huron, torturing their own captives until themselves dead of musket-balls and brandy rum and small-pox –

Was it that he carried with him a pressure like an aura which none might see but which nevertheless and at once and from time to time in its times and seasons swooped down, turning and twisting and sucking up the sea of superstition to form some (so to speak) waterspout, capable nonetheless of killing and of laying waste? Did he, had he, not alone once, but again and again, turned the latent lewdness of ancient times into psychopomps and psychodramas to be played out again and again in the present?

Was he, although as unwilling as any hunchback with his immovable hunch, a wizard with his own immovable wizardry?

Did he, like some old Italian "thrower of evil eye," cast infection by his very glance?

It was a fearful summing-up for him to make, and while making it, and speaking it, he stared intently at Felix: and intently she stared back. And, when at the ending of his summation he stumbled into excuses, "I can't help it, I can't help any of it, I just –"

"I know," she said, 'you 'just work here.' Isn't that what the hangman says? No wonder your friends the Nationals prefer hempen rope; *tend to your helm*," she flung at him, fiercely, as he moved toward her. "*Typhoid Mary couldn't help it, either*!" a breath she took; then: "*Sorcerer*!" and "*Sorcerer*!"

The sails luffed, *crack! crack!* The bow-wave curled around the prow, shedding phosphorescence as a plow sheds loam. "If I *am* a sorcerer," he said, slowly (slowly! for this was quite a new conception) – and Felix: "*If*" – scornful, almost: if the woman with child can be almost pregnant. "If I *am* a sorcerer," he repeated, now white-hot with emotion, "*then you are my familiar*!"

It hit her, he saw on her stricken face the apprehension that it just might be true. Then she turned away.

Winds of good fetch or not, it was hours before they came into port into that small port and ancient haven there on the barm and marge of the Carib Sea: *For the world is wondrous large – Seven Seas from marge to marge –* Lights reflected and shimmered. Music sounded, not the music of any classic instruments, *indeed (It is sweet to dance to music, when love and life are fair./ To dance to lutes, to dance to flutes, is delicate and rare./ But it is not sweet, with nimble feet, to dance upon the air . . .*); the instruments were raw and the music raucous; the Holiday season had begun, and from St. Nicholas Day on the 6th of December to the Day of Epiphany on January 6th, Holiday would hold sway in a Saturday night that was one month long. To and fro, to and fro, the people: they did not, indeed, talk of Michelangelo, their talk was of the New Year's new linoleum and of the Christmas turkey and the Christmas ham: of the presence of these traditional favors. Or of their absence. And of the chaparitas and the pint and, if one were especially fortunate, of the quarts and the "galleon" jugs of festive, festive rum. The vendors were setting out the fresh cabbages and the boxes of fresh apples, be sure most of them were ruddy and sweet-scented and (Limekiller knew) Canadian. The shops had set out the currants and the scented glazed citron rinds both alike from the Isles of Greece, and the raisins and the nutmeats from manywhere and the brandy and the cashew wine: to start the making and the baking of many and many a holiday fruitcake. Peppery cowfoot *soup* was cooking odorously in cauldrons. Millions of mosquitoes whined and hummed, but the Nationals, dismissing these as mere *flies*, danced around as though there was nothing in the warm night air anything like a vexation or a bother.

And those who had none of these material things (save the *flies*) and not even any hopes of them? What joy had they of the season? They had the inalienable joys of watching and mingling with those who did have, they would baste their scant bread in the rich smoke of the others' cook-fires. And would pay with the sounds of their inextinguishable laughter, like the ringing of many rich coins. And they had the infinite joys of song. St. Nicholas did not leave them with nought.

Jack and Felix took down the sail. The sails. The mainsail and the jib. Coasted a ways. Then put over to where their pole, *their* pole, still hospitted *their* skiff. Indeed, she said it: *There's our pole and skiff.* . . .

A spirit touched his lips with a glowing coal. Enough of Oscar and of Rudyard and Tom. "*Rowing in Eden./ Ah, the sea!/ That I might moor myself/ In thee.*" She whirled around (Felix), her face demanding immediate knowledge of Who? "Emily Dickinson," said he. Added, "Critics assure us that of course she had *no* idea — virginal *Emily?* — that it might be a metaphor of —"

She said, very, very rapidly, "Believe that, you'll believe anything;" said it with emphasis . . . and without emotion . . . whirled around and jumped onto the stone coping of Corn Meal Wharf. And was off into the throng. A moment he thought of striding after her, did not. A moment he thought of shouting . . . something. Did not. Watched and observed that she was not heading toward the Swinging Bridge over the Old Belinda River which bisected King Town, and therefore not toward any of the large hotels with their wicked bars; he observed that she almost at once flitted into Spyglass Alley. And was gone. For a scant fraction of a second he thought she might be making for the Spy Glass itself: a liquor booth, but respectable enough that *ah 'oman* might enter without total loss of respect or reputation: but almost at once he knew better.

"Tidings of gret jye, Coptain," a soft, soft voice wished him. He looked down and saw it was the half-hydrocephalic little cripple called, God knows why, Baron Benjamin. (Nicknames in British Hidalgo were a subject on which a thesis might be written: easy enough to say why a certain gaunt, pale missioner was called *Holy Ghost* and why a certain rough-skinned merchant was known as *Mawmee Opple* . . . but why was a certain clerk called "Mr. Mottram" to his face but otherwise referred to as *Noncy-hahv-ah-behby-in-de-high grahs*s? go know . . .) "I am begging for my charity," said Baron Benjamin. Limekiller reached into his pocket and found there a coin of two shillings, a fifty cent piece, still here if nowhere else called a *florin*; gave it to him, and, with a gesture, said, "Keep [meaning, guard] the boat;" and was off. Never so bad a boy or even so brazen a thief would risk the little Baron's displeasure: "Me no want heem to give me ah *bull*-eye, mahn!"

Spy Glass Alley was not very long, and its end was quite ended by a great wooden barn of a building, the property of an ancient endowment and popularly called The Hall. Over its wide-open doors was a weathered sign reading, Society for the Promotion of Christian Evangelism, in large letters. Under this, in only slightly smaller ones: Make ye a joyful noise unto the Lord. To one side on a blackboard was chalked in colored chalk, St. Nich Day Dance *Join the Funs*. Limekiller heard the joyful noise, thought he might as well join: anyway, this was where Felix must have gone. It was as good a *where* to go as any, and better than many.

Also about to enter were a man and a woman. Jack politely stepped aside; it was Neville. And Nicholine. Their faces, which had been fairly appropriate for Making a Joyful Noise, drew formally downcast as they recognized him. "Bad show, eh?" said Neville.

"Poor mahn," said Nicholine.

"Who? What? eh?"

"Major Deak, you know."

"What do you mean?" Was Neville going to mention the sad decay, the rapidly increasing *ageable* quality, the illness, the –?

"Ah, you've not heard." Nicholine's face grew rather cheerful at being arm-in-arm with a bearer of sad tidings. Neville took a deep breath. "Well, he'd said goodbye to Stickney Forster and me and Nicky, and as we were leaving, you know, we saw him start up the steps, and we turned away to stow our gear, you know, in the boat. And we heard him give this ghastly cry. And down he fell! We dashed up directly, but it was clear that he was quite dead."

Jack at once said, "Heart attack."

Neville pulled his nose. It was a long and very English-looking nose. "Don't know about *that*, old boy. Praps. Been no *au*topsy. Yet. Broke his *neck*. Hmm. *Quite* obvious, angle which . . . yes. *Dead*.

"You know. . . ."

And, laying their hands upon him, they passed on into The Hall with him.

Who was *in* there? Felix, of course. And Alex Brant. Dancing . . . don't you know. Jack didn't mind this anymore than he would have minded an ice-pick up his sphincter. Alex was his *friend*. Wasn't he. And anyway Felix didn't look as though she were terribly intensely enjoying it. Although neither did she look as though it *hurt*. Why shouldn't she be dancing with, well, anybody? No reason at all. Though of course Alex was not anybody. He was a lecherous, treacherous son of a bitch. He was probably, among men, his, John Lutwidge Limekiller's, best friend. Who immediately recalled Clair Hoffman's definition, worthy of Ambrose Bierce, of *Cuckold*, as *Someone whose best friend has it in for him*. Immediately after that at once noted and noticed the really impressive number of really charming women, ivory to ebony, who clearly did not equate the Promotion of Christian Evangelism with the wearing of a chastity belt: way they looked at him. Why *not*? He was certainly lookable, wasn't he. What said Solomon the King? *Rejoice, young man, in the days of thy youth, ere the evil days draw nigh*. Was what. At that moment the music stopped. And as he began to look around with more precision, a voice which well he knew in British Hidalgo, and who did not? was heard speaking in a not unpleasantly penetrating tone.

Someone who was supposed to be everywhere at once (but had not been, Jack now realized, at Gallows Caye . . . and no wonder that for almost two hundred years folk had been somehow reluctant to call it by its necessary but nasty name; had called it' by any other name sounding enough like it to identify it): "Ah, Mr. Jack Limekiller and where is your lovely lady, ah *there* you are me dear Mrs. Felix, hello me dear Alex! I can only stop a moment as I am due at a Convocation of the Grand Lodge of the Wise Men of Wales of which I am Titular Grand Wise Man –"

"Yes, Chief Minister."

"Yes, Chief Minister."

The familiar night tumult of the port city was all around, increased by the place and the occasion, but the Honourable Llewellyn Gonzaga McBride's voice, though not particularly loud, was a voice which carried well (and, Gad! it better!). "– but I have just come down from Benbow Bight, where I was being hospitted by the White Creoles at Woodcutters' Cove, and there I heard for the first time what I am sure must be an old folk song, Mr. Thomas Hardy cites it in one of his stories and I am sure you will be interested to hear it –" Jack was not sure he shared that surety, but the Queen's Chief Minister in British Hidalgo had already raised his voice (somewhere in between tenor and baritone, and if musicologists had no term for it, so much the worse for them) in song: one listened.

> *Oh me trade it is a qveer vun,*
> *Simple sailors all,*
> *Me trade it is a soight to see!*
> *For me customers Oi toi*
> *And Oi svings 'em up on hoigh,*
> *And Oi vafts 'em to a far countrie-ee-ee!*
> *And Oi vafts 'em to a far coun-trie!*

The Black Bayfolk paused and laughed and called out to hear their clear tan leader singing in perfect imitation of the archaic accent of the White Creoles; called for more, *More*! but L. G. McBride, saying something about "a rather grim and grisly humor, eh?" with a wave of his hand and a smile passed on. Alex Brant also smiled at Limekiller, his rather thin, cool smile was neither friendly nor defiant, but seemed ready to be either. Limekiller looked at Felix and Felix looked at him. *Her* look . . . and it was a long, long look . . . was really neither grim nor grisly, neither defiant nor friendly; what was it then? he had never seen it nor anything like it until just these few hours: once again: it contained emphasis but emphasis of *what?* It was not familiar, this look, but he felt that he was going to have to become familiar with seeing it again. And perhaps again and again.

For, without having been swung up on high he had indeed been wafted to a far countrie, a very, very far countrie indeed. He had yet to learn exactly where it was.

But wherever it was, it was very far from Eden.

AFTERWORDS

Avram Davidson's Limekiller stories are rooted in his travels in British Honduras in 1965-1966 and an extended period of residency in 1968. After the first visit, Davidson wrote a travel memoir that charts his itinerary in B. H. just before independence. Unpublished during his lifetime, *Dragons in the Trees* is colorful, rich in detail and filled with unusual characters and events. There are descriptions of Belize City and its leisurely pace of life; St. George's Caye, devastated by a hurricane, with ruined burial grounds still visible; a visit to a vacation house at Gallows Point; accounts of Mennonite communities; the last traces of a settlement established by former Confederates; and boom time among the chicleros and mahogany cutters in Cayo, where "They call the Lebanese 'Turks.'" Readers of the Limekiller stories will recognize many of these locales.[1] "Along the Lower Moho (The Iguana Church)" is one of the most memorable portions of *Dragons in the Trees* and offers some insights into how Davidson's fiction grew out of actual experience. This extract was published with two others in the special Avram Davidson issue of *The New York Review of Science Fiction*, June 2000.

– Henry Wessells

[1] In an earlier article I have discussed specific correspondences ("'A place that you can put your arms around': Avram Davidson's Jack Limekiller stories." *Foundation* 69, Spring 1997).

ALONG THE LOWER MOHO (THE IGUANA CHURCH)

THE DRAGON DUET I
BY AVRAM DAVIDSON

THE LOWER MOHO is far different from the Upper Belize's Eastern Branch, in which I so delighted when at Cayo; the latter, with its rushing current, visible bed of rock or of gravel, narrow and granite-bony banks, and its cataracts, is like muscular and sinewy arms. The full flow of the Moho, current languid and slow, banks low and wide, bottom invisible but seeming to hint of mud, lush and lavish, is reminiscent of soft thighs and armpits. Often it is so wide and smooth as to resemble a lake, – I observed, bemused and entranced, a snow-white egret skimming slow and low across the surface, his reflection like a double-goer companying with him beneath the mirror surface.

The first sign of human settlement was a barking dog. Then a thatched hut. And an Indian-dark Ladino boy who stared dully at us, not returning any of the greetings waved from our boat . . . totally different from the bright, alert, cheerful Mayan children of San Antonio. Then downstream came a very long motor-dory (remember, again, *dory* here always means dug-out) – perhaps a *pin* – containing eight people of all sizes: six Caribs and two Mestizos; the long boat towing a smaller one alongside. Hails were exchanged. Next from the bank a bulky Carib lady with a multi-colored broadbrim straw hat atop her red kerchief lowered her machete and waved. The tree line became broken, here was a corn-patch, here were bananas, and then came a house and groves.

"There is Bul's place. He wants to sell. Do you want to buy?"

"How much for how much?"

"Ten acres cleared and planted. He ask $300."

"What does it cost to clear land here?"

Our commodore reflected. "For high bush . . . $20 an acre. For low bush . . . a little bit less."

It seemed, then, to me, that "Bul" was in effect selling land for $10 an acre. Later I learned that things were not at all that simple. I gazed at the tangled shores, and asked about iguana – after all, the purpose of our voyage. "What shall I bring you back?" I'd asked. "Bring me back an iguana," she'd said. And so here we all were. Before, I had seen the dragons in the trees; now I was to see them considerably closer up.

"No fear, there are plenty of iguana here. The next place belongs to the Spanish people who are good hunters of them. You will see."

One of the boatmen looked at me. "You like bamboo chicken in the country you belong to?"

"Sir?"

"Bamboo chicken. Iguana and garobo . . . They not have them? Too bad. Taste *veh*-ry good. Just like chicken." He smacked his lips.

"*Not* to eat . . . I don't want them to eat . . . alive, alive-O," I insisted.

He nodded. "We put them in box, put in leaves, she live six weeks. You feast she in your country." After some vigorous, if confused interchange, it was established that (a) the iguanas could live six weeks just on the "leaves" put into their box; it was not meant that they would drop dead after only six weeks; and (b) it was not my intention to export them as victualry, ceremonial or otherwise. "He want keep for pet," the boatmen said. And they gazed at each other and at me and at the river and the shores, with a blandness and toleration for foreign foibles which was mighty fine to see.

And so at length and at last to our first stop, the "Spanish people", who were cunning and canny at hunting the dragon-minor. Now I perceived the utility of a muddy bank: they cut the motor and let the boat go, slide up, soft and easy, easy as can be . . . Higher up stood a newmade dory, upside down on blocks: easy, then, to understand why in some other country (I forget just where) dugouts are called "skins": this one, of tawny-ruddy Santa Maria wood, looked indeed as though it had been fashioned from a skin of fine pale leather. This was the Martinez plantation; these, however, were Mestizo Martinezes, and hence no kin to the Carib Martinezes of Stann Creek. Also present were the Sanchez family people – they and those we passed in the big dory had been visiting here – and each family agreed to contribute one hunter for our little expedition.

Tomás Martinez was perhaps nineteen, taller than his hunt-partner (though not tall by northern standards) and broader, too, with a very fine Mestizo face, and a very light Mestizo coloring. Santiago Sanchez was perhaps sixteen and small and slender; his tilted nose, full lips, and darker skin perhaps hinted pleasantly of a Creole or Carib grandparent.

The house, thatched roof and pole sides, was actually two houses in some intricately connected fashion. Handsome black and white ducks abounded, of a sort I had never seen before ("What are these birds called? Have they a special name?" "Yes – they are called 'ducks' – d-u-c-k-s.") and at the top of the steps a board blockade (in San Antonio it was a board blockade) served to keep the livestock out and the toddlers in. The forest pressed very nigh the little houses. Inside it was narrow and on the dark side, walls as usual covered with magazine and newspaper pages; I wondered what the settlers made of such pictures, here on the remote and incredibly quiet backwaters of the world.

"Many visitors here for the velorio, eh?" Mr. Zuniga asked. "Plenty rum?" A comely, middle-aged señora smiled faintly and shook her head. There was no sign of any excesses. A table stood near the wall, converted into an altar with a baldachin-canopy adorned with colored paper barber-stripes. An enamel dish of copper coins, candles, and a curious black-and-white photograph of a religious nature involving (but not seeming to be confined to) a crucifix, completed my rapid glimpse of the scene, and something was said of "Los Señores de Esquipula" – or so I understood it – but soon we were out of the house again and into the dories again. The whole thing was very Latin-American, Catholic, child-bright, and pagan.

I noted that each young hunter had a barbed harpoon with thin greenish nylon line (ubiquitous in B. H.) attached, intricately. Mr. Faustino Z. caught my glance and conveyed my alarm: We didn't want to kill our dragons, we wanted them to live. The boys nodded. They spoke English well enough, but exclusively Spanish among themselves.

It was hopeless for me to estimate how far upstream we were, but later I learned that "Bul" (the place taking its name from the man) was approximately six miles from the sea; I'd guess that Casa or Quinta Ramirez was a few miles above Bul; and after that we proceeded perhaps another mile, foam-flecks floating on "the buxom flood" – and then they cut the motor and glided towards an enormous, colossal, gigantic monster of a giant wild fig tree, white and slick. It must have been at least a century old. Two of its immense branches hung far out over the stream. It had vines twisting all over it, and I do verily believe that its *vines* had vines! Clumps of grass flourished on it as it loomed up from the feathery green thickets of wild bamboo thorns, and on it, too, were all sorts of parasites and saprophytes; and likely enough (remembering the Anecdotes of Joseph Roberteau R-o-b-e-r-t-e-a-u) there were tortugas and crocodiles in cavernous hollows under its roots. It was an absolute Eighth Wonder of a tree, it was a whole ecology all to itself.

As we approached, the great gargoyles carven into the tree came alive, enormous garobos lifted their heads and commenced to dive off it into the water. The younger hunter, Santiago, took his harpoon and went ashore to climb the tree: he had to approach it from behind as the water side was too sheer and smooth. And all the while the Iguana Exodus continued – I expected Tomás to produce something like a huge butterfly net and catch them as they come down – *scrabble! fall! PLOP!* SPLASH! SPLASH! SPLASH! – but, no. Instead, he buttoned his shirt firmly over his thick, sturdy chest and said, "Put me under that limb over there" – the dory was paddled thither – several of the limbs trailed into the river, where they had collected enough debris to harbor minnows and insects and water weeds: enough to constitute a sort of sub-ecology –

To my perfect astonishment, he seized hold of the thin lower branches and, saying, "No other way up this tree," proceeded to pull . . . haul . . . grip . . . and shinny himself from limb to limb . . . up and up . . . holding his harpoon with his *toes*, mind you – his *toes*! Mr. Zuniga grinned at me. "Tar-san," he said. And indeed it was – the most Tarzan-like thing I have ever seen, in the movies or out. Up and then in, on hands and feet along one of the chief-most limbs, Tomás proceeded slowly from the left; meanwhile, holding onto the thick vines and the branches which partially obscured him from us beneath, Santiago moved in from the right. And all the while, the iguanal Descent From Olympus continued, showering us time and again, till one would think they must surely all have dived off by now – but both small green girls and (in effect) great grim old men might still be seen glaring and crawling and be heard scrabbling and clattering . . .

. . . Tomás struck – hurled his barbed harpoon – an archaic, primitive, and beautiful gesture, one which I had never expected to see in my life: alas, it failed of effect, a twig deflected it, staff and barb and line alike fell like stones into the water. And did not rise again.

This surprised me, rather. I was more greatly surprised, though, when I realized that the line was not devised ever to be used (as I had thought) as a snare – picturing something like the pole-and-loop the Mongols used to take wild ponies on the run . . . I was a bit disturbed on seeing that the staff was to be used as harpoon alone – and now my surprise as the whole apparatus sank like a stone, for, surely, the weight of the iron barb could not have been sufficient; perhaps some troll, or, likelier an irate garobo, is holding it under? – Curious, unlike systems in often use elsewhere, there was no device attached anywhere which floated to show the location of the sunken staff (and it's called just that, "the staff") –

Santiago did not strike as yet (and that's what *it* is called, too, "to strike"), and Tomás called to us that he saw a mountain cow drinking of the river, upstream. Off we paddled, not particularly quietly, and, not surprisingly, the tapir wasn't there when *we* were; though the signs of its having been there were evident . . . underbrush broken by its heavy body, soft muddy bank enprinted by its heavy feet. Indeed, the slots and slides of tapir are evident all along the river: I looked back and, just for a few seconds, before grass and tree and bush intervened, saw the odd black form on the side of the hill . . . too big for a pig, too low for a cow, making its way in a gait between a trot and a lumber; it looked *wrong*, somehow – didn't look dangerous, just *wrong* – "There ought not to be such an animal," was my instant half-thought; seen broadside, in broad day, I felt no more than that about it; but had I for the first time "seen" it out of the corner of an eye and no hint as to what it was, I might well have wound up in the tip top of the great fig tree before I had stopped making *ik-ik-ik* noises: Mountain cow, go away from my door.

Meanwhile, back at "the Iguana Church" (for such, I later learned from a knowledgeable and pretty Papal Volunteer, was the local name for the Monster Tree), Santiago had been stalking a monster garobo: no sooner had we glided up, he struck – and pierced – the dragonet; the barb entered and held in the skin beneath the spiny crest, the staff came loose, as was intended, and followed, clattering and slithering, held fast by the line, as the great garobo carried it after him into the underbrush . . . We shouted, pointed, Santiago saw the staff, seized it, hauled it in slowly and steadily by the line with one hand as, machete in the other, he chopped away at the concealing vegetation –

– and all this *on the tree*! for, as I have said, grass and shrub and thicket had all taken root and flourished on the great canting trunk and limbs –

Tomás came to his assistance. What a thrashing there was in the tree! And so at length down came Dragon, by a line tied around his lengthy tail, was firmly grasped by Chocho and Ranq'el, the Carib boatmen, one hand at the nape of the neck and one at the back abaft the hind legs. He *was* a monster, at least five feet long from the slate-blue/grey-mottled snout and wattled chin to the tip of his tapering orange-brown tail, and dull near-black stripes vertically along his body . . . whence the name of *tiger iguana*, and rather seldom seen in the United States . . . He was, it seemed to me, of a somewhat duller color than the bright buff dragons of the East Branch of the Belize – but, fo' true, I never saw one of these last up close. And his spines (whose perceptible limpness at the moment made visible the basic meaning of "crestfallen") lacked the red tips of the Cayo dragons.

The manner of his being rendered harmless was curious. "Pull the claw through the hole where you strike," advised Mr. Faustino Z., who knew whereof he spoke. The barb only penetrated the skin just below the spinal crest and only went in a short distance, – through this orifice (which F.Z. assured me would soon heal: "We put some mud or ash on it; cure him good.") one claw of each fore-limb was passed, after the limbs had been drawn up behind and above. The hind legs were similarly fastened by making a slight incision in the spare skin of one of them and passing the claw of another through it. He was now, if not totally immobilized, at least semi-totally so, being able only to slither a wee bit on his belly. "Touch his back if you like –" "I don't like–" "– but don't go near his head. He can almost mangle off a man's finger if he get it in his mouth. Now," he said, turning to the Nature Boys, "*buscamos una embrita* – Let's look for a little female."

I demurred, suggesting that one was, after all, enough . . . that I didn't intend to *ranch* the beasts, after all. But Mr. Z. merely smiled. "No, no, must have another. Can't leave poor brute alone – no one to talk to? – no one to scratch his back? No, no . . ." he shook his head reproachfully, and added, "Altogether against the Natural Law." He, too, I perceived, had been well-educated by the Jesuits.

Going upstream a bit, close to the north bank, I observed the covert of the bamboo thickets to be *alive* with dragon . . . no wonder Mr. Chocho (or Mr. Ranq'el) called it "bamboo chicken"! Santiago stood in the prow with his lance poised: a young Tashtego. Often his fingers tightened, his muscles tensed. Then he relaxed, murmuring, "*Es macho . . . macho . . . tambien . . .*" We seemed to see nothing but males. Had they sent the females to the rear? Were *all* the ladies in hiding? Shame, if so . . . since they are all members of the Lucy Stone League. Or is it that the larger size and greater strength of the males stands less in need of protective coloration? Or do the females need it most now because they are with egg? Perhaps when the eggs are laid, when the dry time comes, when the rivers droop and the grass grows sere, perhaps then the garobo would be as near-invisible as the iguana now.

Meanwhile, Mr. Chocho has been thinking things over for himself. "Next garobo you see, *Viejo*," he says, companionably to young Sanchez; "you can strike for me. We feast him tonight at the velorio . . . Yes, yes . . ." The idea clearly pleases him, he comes to a visible and audible decision; and, with exactly the same firm tone of an Englishman ordering a brace of grouse from his poulterer, "*Put me up two . . .*" So first one garobo is "struck" for the festal pot, then another. As these are not destined to live long, Santiago is under less need to be particular about his aim –Tomás, too, who takes the harpoon for the second strike (we had grappled for the sunken staff, in the river beneath The Tree, unsuccessfully: but Tomás knows just where it fell, and I have no doubt will recover it later, in his own good time). A big garobo is lanced next, the dory grounds, Santiago leaps ashore and reels him in, chopping away bush, but being careful not to chop line as well. Big – but not as big as mine. The barb has sunken deep behind the coin-shaped mark above the wattles. Santiago saws at the barb with his machete, and I wince – probably needlessly, for, although the brute receives the treatment with a good deal of sullenness, he doesn't so much as hiss.

And, finally, after a second festal bamboo chicken is secured, a fine green iguana, perhaps a third of her *promessi sposo's* bulk, is taken. "*En la pierna!*" cries the boy, pleased at having not pierced the trunk. "Good!" Mr. F.Z. declares. "Now they have someone to talk to, each of them." But Mr. Chocho's attitude is perhaps a shade less philanthropic, "She have red egg in her," he says, and he eyes her hungrily.

The catch or prey is trussed as described before, and we slip downstream, dropping off Tomás first, then Santiago; their fee for a good two hours of incredible dexterity being so low I am ashamed to record it here. Down the broad river once again. "There is Bul," says Mr. Zuniga. "You want to see Bul?" I say, so let me see Bul. The dory noses up the crumbly bank and I hop gingerly ashore . . . intrigued, frankly, at the prospect of getting ten acres of cleared land planted in fruit trees and improved with a several-roomed thatched house, for $300. As a bargain, it's hard to beat. "Oranges ready to reap," says my guide, waving his hand. "Oranges here, banana and plantains there. Cassava: make good bread, good eating by self. Over there, [alligator] pears. This one tree is star-apple." Or was it rose-apple? Anyway, no resemblance to lichee at all: pulpy fruit, custardy, with limp seeds: odd, but not bad at all.

I allowed myself to fall into neo-colonial reveries and dreams . . . Devise ways to net and snare iguana and garobo, more saving both of their lives and of the time involved: ship them to the U.S. for sale . . . Use Bul Farm as a focal point, hire Indians to grow rice and pay them in milpa land-use. With profits, hire them further to clear bush from surrounding Crown lands available on location ticket. Grow coffee, hire Indian woman to roast and pound and package in bark "bags" such as they make for other uses: drive Nescafé from its pre-emptive position . . .

Float good building stone down from San Antonio along Mafredi Creek to Black Creek and thence along the Moho, using barges fabricated of rafts and empty gasoline-drums (Drums Along The Moho): make sound foundations and two-storey walls thereof, with beams and maybe roof of Santa Maria wood, and panels of cedar – adopt local use of partitions of pole and palm to allow internal circulation of air . . . Furniture of mahogany, of course, – locally so cheap that it's often left to rot. Maya girl. Creole girl. East Indian girl. Spanish, Carib girls. Each with own small but sufficient plantation. Knocked-up and barefooted. Cattle gotten cheap and one by one, grazing in the rice paddy-lands after the harvest of grain. Patriarch. Marry grandchildren/cousins to each other, create new not-totally-dusky race. Populate Toledo with my seed . . .

A mosquito bites me. And another. And another. I ignore them, observing the incredibly attractive carpet of the plant called "Bleeding Heart," leaves like green valentines bearing upon them as though press-printed a similar design in purple-red. "Well," says F.Z., pointing. I see the well, an unwalled pit in the dirt, and, beyond, the close-lapping river. I ask, "Isn't this rather low along the water?" He assures me it is not. "Even in flood, never come up past here," he explains, his gesture including most of the visible environs. To him, floods are mere inevitabilities of no great matter, and mosquitoes obviously do not exist at all. How thick they are! *Slap. Slap. Slapslapslap!*

— The bubble bursts, the dream subsides into the Moho with a gentle plop. So perish all plans in the Toledo, put into practice or not. Gently, very gently . . . not necessarily with hurricanes . . . not even firmly: but invariably and inevitably and seemingly without exception, the Toledo defeats every plan larger than a plantain patch. How long will it be before the bush takes over the rice-fields as it has taken over the old Confederate-planted sugar-fields? — tall trees now growing within the old stone walls the unreconstructable Rebels slowly built at Seven Hills, shouldering slowly aside the vasty flywheels, red with rust. Who knew this land first and best? The Mayans. And they abandoned it for a thousand years! Land which defeated even the humble and patient and toiling Mayas, how long before you would defeat *me*? — my rafts sunken, my dories stove, my crops washed away, my house blown in, my women fled into Belize or the bush — Well, it wouldn't take that long. One year of mosquitoes and no fresh books to read would do it.

"How sick and gaunt poor Llewelyn-Rhys looks," I had commented in Punta Gorda. "Known him for years," was the reply. "He looks *much better* now than he used to — !"

I lead the way down the crumbling bank to the boat. The day had been mostly overcast and cool, now the sun came out and I donned my dark lenses. Mr. Faustino Zuniga dripped water on the dark dragon heads to cool them. Slowly the forest receded, the mangrove swamps resumed. "Is there *no* high land around here?" I enquired. He nodded. "Inland . . . or upstream . . ." A gesture of a dark hand leftwards, where the mangroves parted to reveal another stretch of water. "That is called Amado Creek . . . it goes up to Crique Antonio: very high lands there." And he told me of this tributary, and of that, and for further fading moment dream and dream-house glimmer faintly in the fading sun. Maybe I will return, I thought . . . some day . . . and trace each stream to its source and find Arcadia.

Only maybe not.

DRAGONS IN SAN FRANCISCO - A SEQUEL

THE DRAGON DUET II
A MEMOIR BY GRANIA DAVIDSON DAVIS

"What shall I bring you back?" I'd asked.
"Bring me back an iguana," she'd said.

Thus spoke Avram Davidson in "The Iguana Church", an excerpt from his unpublished travel account *Dragons in the Trees*.

I HAVE A confession to make. I am She who asked for the iguana. I didn't really expect to *get* an iguana. Anyway I was thinking of the little green ones from the pet store, not big wild Tiger Iguanas.

It was the mid-1960s. Avram was traveling in British Honduras (now Belize), and young Ethan and I were living in a Victorian flat in Bernal Heights in San Francisco, where I was writing and teaching. One day we got a notice to pick up a package from an obscure location, I'll spare you the details. The sender was Avram in B. H., so off we went to fetch the package. It was made of rough wood, about the shape of a big guitar case. It didn't rattle. Something inside scrabbled. Something alive.

The paperwork said *Iguanas.* Nowadays we'd probably be cited for a wildlife violation, but back then I was still thinking maybe a nice little pet for Ethan. Fortunately we had the sense to open the box in the bathtub.

Out from a tangle of leaves leaped two angry wild beasts; the great black and yellow striped he-Tiger, who filled most of the bathtub, and the smaller gray-striped she-Tiger, who flicked her tongue, rose up on all her claws, and bared her teeth at us like a miniature angry dinosaur.

An unexpected surprise. We threw some ripe bananas in the bathtub, prayed they wouldn't scramble out, and tried to figure out what to do next. Next was that little Ethan was now afraid to use the bathroom, so we had to go to a neighbor's.

Some fine fannish friends helped us get a very large mesh cage, the kind used to transport big dogs. We propped the cage over the bathtub with some fruit inside, and eventually lured the dragons in. Resourceful are us. We put the cage next to a heater, and plied the dragons with fruit. They huddled near the heat and glared at us. Clearly this relationship wasn't going to work.

Another friend gave us the phone number of a herpetologist at the Aquarium in Golden Gate Park, which happens to have a well-designed iguana exhibit. We phoned. Yes, they would take the dragons! We took the cage to the Aquarium, and they all exclaimed that this was about the biggest and finest he-Tiger ever seen in these parts.

Avram Davidson, mighty hunter and protector of endangered wildlife.

We went to visit the dragons at the Aquarium sometimes, and they seemed quite relaxed, perched on big branches. At least they didn't glare at us anymore. Eventually we lost track of which were our dragons, and which were other acquisitions. I don't know the lifespan of Tiger Iguanas, but drop by the Aquarium next time you visit San Francisco. Maybe they are still there.

Later we traveled down to British Honduras, by train through Mexico and the Yucatan, so Ethan and Avram could be nearby. I got to see the Moho River for myself.

Ethan and I lived in a tiny cottage, with no electricity or running water, on a long palm-fringed sandbar called Gales Point, surrounded by a large lagoon. We drank rainwater collected in barrels. In our front yard was a giant mango tree twined with white orchids. Our neighbors were a matriarchal Afro-Creole family; Miz Jane Garnet and her daughters, and their boyfriends and children. Jane's consort was a silent one-legged man, who had amputated his own leg with a machete after a snakebite in the bush. Miz Jane adopted us. I brought her cloth and sugar and rum from Belize City, and she gave us fruit and fish and bush-food. Miz Jane was famous for her armadillo in Spanish sauce.

Nearby was the shabby hut of Brother John, the nearly blind old bushdoctor. Brother John made drums out of rusted tin cans and deer-hide (he gave me one that I still treasure). At night, Brother John played his drums hypnotically, and chanted Afro-Creole invocations to the healing saints and African spirits. Avram visited Gales Point to listen to Brother John's lore.

To reach the Moho River, we had to take the twice-weekly mail-boat through the mangrove swamps to Belize City, an all-day trip. Then the big ramshackle packet-boat down the Caribbean coast, to the southern town of Punta Gorda, an overnight journey. The comforts on board were minimal. A roach filled "cabin" to stow your gear; bring your own bananas.

In the darkness before dawn, the packet boat gave a sudden lurch – and stopped. Were we sinking? No, but we were stranded on a reef, and had to wait for the tide to come up to depart. There we sat, with the boat sort of tilting to one side, watching an astonishing red sunrise. Then villagers from the town of Placencia appeared in dories, with bunches of sweet ripe bananas for the passengers, and ropes to pull the stranded boat off the reef. The boat was made of old peeling wood, which looked like it could splinter at the least pressure. But when the tide came up, they gently teased the groaning packet boat off the reef, and down we sailed to Punta Gorda Town, just a day or so late.

In remote PG town, in the south between the Guatemalan and Honduran borders, we were met by Avram's friends, the Zuniga family, who were Caribs or Garifuna, an Afro-Indian blend. They had helped Avram buy a sort of homestead title to a property called Moho Bul, and they were looking after the land. We were there to see it, swathed in mosquito netting like Katherine Hepburn in *African Queen*.

Yet another boat trip, this time a motorized dory, along the Caribbean coast to the mouth of the Moho River. Then up a lazy river, through endless shades of green, to Moho Bul. It was beautiful. Ten acres cleared and planted with mangos and alligator pear (avocado) and citrus and all the wonderful tropical fruits, and rice. Forty more acres of bush with stands of old growth mahogany trees. A mud and thatch hut, and even a dory tied to a little dock. Moho Bul had everything. It also had mosquitoes. Many mosquitoes. The British were doing some mosquito abatement in the settled areas, but not at Moho Bul.

It was too late to sail to the Iguana Church, so I never saw it, alas. We swam in the warm green Moho River (later we heard rumors of alligators) and feasted on mangos and other ripe fruit. Then it was time to sail back to Punta Gorda Town. By the time we reached the Caribbean, the sun had set. That night there was a phosphorescent sea, and the water glittered and sparkled like a thousand galaxies.

Later, Avram left British Honduras to write his immortal *Limekiller* stories. B.H. became the independent nation of Belize, famed for its Mayan ruins, beautiful barrier reef, and ecotourism. The elder Zunigas died, and the family dispersed. Nobody took care of Moho Bul, and it reverted to bush. The old growth mahogany trees were poached, and the Tiger Iguanas were hunted to near extinction (except perhaps for one pair of senior citizen Dragon-Tigers, comfortably retired in the San Francisco Aquarium).

Recent reports have brought better news. A Mayan family now lives at Moho Bul, with some help from an aid group. They are keeping the planted area cleared, and keeping their culture alive. Now there are fruit trees again at Moho Bul, and a thatched hut, and a dory tied up to the little dock. Mayan children, and turkeys poke around in the dirt. I suppose the mosquitoes are still there too. It's a timeless place. Drop by and see it yourself, next time you're down that way.

AFTERWORD

BY ETHAN DAVIDSON

I WAS VERY young when I lived with my father, Avram Davidson, in British Honduras. My main memory is of being attacked by an angry chicken. But I also remember him taking me up the Moho river to look at the plantation of Moho Bul, with its fruit trees and its one room house, which had a roof made of coconut thatch, and a dirt floor.

After Avram left British Honduras in the 60's, he continued to send money to a local family to maintain Moho Bul. In 1977, he sent me down to what was, by then, Belize to see how it was doing.

As there is no transportation from Punta Gorda to the property, I hired the services of an Englishman who lived next door to Moho Bul.

He took me up to his home in his boat, a dugout canoe with a motor. Traveling up the Moho river, I saw what Avram had described, the trees full of iguanas in many different colors, some green, some red, some grey.

He cooked and served dinner. The menu was rather limited. Seven-up, rum, and iguana. It really did taste like chicken.

We drank, and he told me about his life. He ran a small hunting lodge for British soldiers stationed in Punta Gorda. What do you suppose they hunted? Iguanas.

He was not alone. On market day, Mayans would come into town with dugout canoes full of live iguanas, their mouths sewn shut. As for the Garifuna (an ethnic group made of Africans and Indians who had intermarried), they enjoyed digging for buried iguana eggs in the sandy beaches.

The next day, he took me to Moho Bul. Swatting away mosquitoes, I saw the sad truth. The place had not been maintained. It was in ruins. The house had fallen down. Some of the fruit trees had survived, but only because fruit gatherers had cleared bush from around them so that they could take the fruit.

I contacted Avram and explained the situation. He sent me some money, which I gave to the Englishman, with the understanding that he would hire some Mayans to clear the bush around the surrounding trees. And this he did.

In 1993, shortly before Avram died, I returned to Belize again to look in on the land. I settled the taxes, and visited Punta Gorda. But the Englishman was not there. He had had an argument with a local policeman, and had been shot.

So I hired a Garifuna man to take me to Moho Bul. There, I was once again in for a surprise. The land was clear, because there was a small Mayan village there. Apparently, after the Mayans had cleared the land, the Englishman had told them they could stay, and they did.

I didn't really object to the Mayans living at Moho Bul, they were putting it to better use than I ever would. But there was one thing that did make me sad. During the whole boat trip, I did not see one dragon in the trees.

¡LIMEKILLER!

First Edition

2003

¡Limekiller! by Avram Davidson, edited by Grania Davis and Henry Wessells, was published by Old Earth Books, Post Office Box 19951, Baltimore, Maryland, 21211-0951. Two thousand copies have been printed by Thomson-Shore, Inc.. The typeset is Berthold Baskerville, Newsel, and Lithos Black, printed on 60# Glatfeltner Supple Opaque Recycled Natural. The binding cloth is Pearl Linen. Design and typesetting by Garcia Publishing Services, Woodstock, Illinois.